# More Than Sorrow

## Books by Vicki Delany

Constable Molly Smith Series
*In the Shadow of the Glacier*
*Valley of the Lost*
*Winter of Secrets*
*Negative Image*
*Among the Departed*

The Klondike Mystery Series
*Gold Digger*
*Gold Fever*

Other Novels
*Scare the Light Away*
*Burden of Memory*
*More Than Sorrow*

# More Than Sorrow

## A Mystery

## Vicki Delany

Poisoned Pen Press

Copyright © 2012 by Vicki Delany

First Edition 2012

10 9 8 7 6 5 4 3 2 1

Library of Congress Catalog Card Number: 2012936475

ISBN: 9781590589854      Hardcover
      9781590589878      Trade Paperback

Poisoned Pen Press
6962 E. First Ave., Ste. 103
Scottsdale, AZ 85251
www.poisonedpenpress.com
info@poisonedpenpress.com

Printed in the United States of America

*For Alex, Julia, and Caroline.*

# Acknowledgments

No novel is truly an independent effort, and I am grateful to my friends who gave so generously of their time and talents to help make this a better story. Violette Malan, D.J. McIntosh, R.J. Harlick, Donna Carrick, Madeleine Harris-Callway, Joan Boswell, superb writers all, provided critical eyes and made great suggestions. County author and storyteller Janet Kellough corrected my numerous historical errors. Those which remain are strictly mine.

Vicki Emlaw of Vicki's Veggies showed me around her small-scale vegetable farm and talked to me about growing food and running a farm. Vicki grows what has to be the world's greatest tomatoes (www.vickisveggies.com). Thanks also to Cheryl Freedman for directing me to medical information on brain damage, and to Karl Wu for providing details.

The book Lily cherishes is *Afghanistan: Hidden Treasures from the National Museum, Kabul,* edited by Fredrik Hiebert and Pierre Cambon, published by the National Geographic Society, 2008.

*More Than Sorrow* is set in Prince Edward County, Ontario, which is a real place, inhabited by real people. None of them, however, appear in this book.

# Chapter One

They tell me it was an IED hidden in a truck full of goats going to market, pulled off to the side of the road with an apparent flat tire.

But of that I have no memory.

I rubbed small pebbles between my fingers. The sun burned hot on the scarf on my head and dust was thick in my mouth. A goat cried out—no, not a goat. A chicken. Not crying in fear or pain but clucking with hungry impatience.

I opened my eyes and studied the objects in my hand. Not stones, but chickenfeed. On my head was a Toronto Blue Jays baseball cap, not a scarf, and the land around me was lush and green and fertile, not brown and destroyed.

The bird stared at me. Tiny black eyes in front of a tiny brain. Only a chicken. A white rock hen pecking for worms and bugs in a patch of weeds and overgrown grasses in a farmyard in Prince Edward County, Ontario.

Memory flooded back, and I knew where I was, and I threw a handful of grain onto the ground. Chickens rushed to feed.

My sister was watching me, frozen in the act of crossing the yard, her face pinched with worry. "Okay, Hannah?"

"Okay."

"Good," she said. "After you've finished that, collect the eggs, will you? I want to make a cake this afternoon for Lily's birthday."

"Will do." I put on what I hoped was a convincing smile. Joanne gave me a long look before she continued down the path toward the greenhouse.

I let out a sigh and tossed the rest of the grain onto the ground. Eager chickens came running from all directions. Pressure was building behind my right eye and I hurried to get out of the glare of the rising sun into the dark, cool henhouse.

I don't care for chickens. Noisy, vicious, stupid beasts. I tried to get them out of the coop before venturing in to raid the nests. A pair of heavy yellow work gloves was kept on a nail by the door, and I slipped them on to offer my hands some protection in case one of the birds had remained behind to defend her eggs. They didn't want me stealing their offspring out from underneath them and used their sharp beaks to fight me off.

Isn't that what mothers do? Protect their children?

The coop was dark and quiet, all the residents outside enjoying the spring sunshine. I collected ten large brown eggs and laid them gently into a wicker basket. The heavy smell of ammonia and straw both fresh and molding that permeated the hen house did nothing for my oncoming headache.

We were raised in the city, Joanne and I. In a proper modern bungalow in a neat well laid-out suburb on a street lined with Norway maples and houses exactly the same as ours. Why my sister took so eagerly and happily to the life of a small-scale farmer is a mystery to me.

Perhaps not a total mystery. I came out of the chicken coop, egg basket over my arm, in time to see my brother-in-law Jake Stewart climbing into his truck, ready to deliver the first of the spring produce to local restaurants. He lifted a well-muscled arm in a lazy greeting but didn't give me a smile. I waved in return.

I put the eggs on the kitchen counter and dropped into a chair. Pain lurked behind my right eye, a black spot, evil and threatening and ever-present. Sunlight streamed through the French doors leading to the deck, and the old farmhouse was beginning to heat up. I closed my eyes, knowing I had to get upstairs and lie down while I could.

"Would you like me to fetch your pills, Aunt Hannah?" said a soft voice behind me.

"Thank you, dear, but no. I've had enough for now."

"They don't help much, do they?"

"I'm sorry to say they don't. But this will pass, and I'll be fine soon."

"I'm glad," she said. I felt a cool hand on my arm and smelled toothpaste and hay. Lily was ten years old, and today was her birthday. She was a bright, cheerful, happy girl who absolutely adored her aunt Hannah. The feeling was mutual. With great effort, I lifted my hand and touched hers.

*What if,* I thought...

A stab of pain interrupted the thought, and my hand dropped to the table. "Can you pull the blinds, sweetie?" I said. "The light's too strong."

The chain rattled, and the blinds clattered as they slid along their track. Even though my eyes were closed, I knew when the sun was gone.

The light of the sun had become my enemy.

Sunlight had been strong in my eyes when it happened. We'd been driving west, the setting sun a brilliant, round yellow ball hovering above naked tan hills. I was adjusting my sunglasses, trying to cut the glare when a light so bright it seared my eyes followed instantly by a wave of sound overwhelmed me. I remember wondering if the sun had exploded, but that might have only been later, when I woke to the glare of pure white hospital lights.

Afghanistan. Where the sun always shone in a sky of brilliant blue and the hills were bare and the streets dusty tracks and behind every scrubby bush or mud hut death might lurk.

I called my headaches Omar because they were so like the scowling, black-bearded, filthy-gowned, malicious mullah who'd treated me with unmitigated contempt that last day in Afghanistan. I stood in front of the bathroom mirror sometimes, peering into my own face, looking for him, trying to see him hiding behind my eyes, willing him to come out and fight me, face to face. Don't get me wrong: I know he's not there, not in spirit nor in body. I doubt he's spared me a thought since our convoy rattled down the track heading out of his village. It's just that it makes me feel better, sometimes, to think I have an enemy I might actually be able to fight. To defeat.

"Can I help you upstairs, Aunt Hannah?" Lily normally had a loud voice, full of fun and enthusiasm and always madly excited about something. Around me, she whispered. They all did. They kept the radio and TV low and my sister hushed her children if they got too noisy. As children should.

Everyone walked as if crossing a road covered in egg shells.

"That would be nice." I leaned on the girl as I struggled to my feet. I opened my left eye, just a crack, and looked into her face. Pretty and concerned. Immediately after breakfast she'd gone out to tend to her beloved horses, and hay was caught in the back of her blond braid, and a streak of mud crossed her left cheek. She was all knees and elbows, bony chest, long thin legs, arms like sticks, luscious black lashes, and a perpetually laughing mouth. I thought she was incredibly beautiful.

"Be sure your mom wakes me up in time for the birthday dinner," I said. "I wouldn't want to miss that. What are we having anyway?" In my sister's family, as in ours, the birthday child chose the celebratory meal.

"Hamburgers. Dad's going to do them on the barbeque. Then cake. I've asked for chocolate."

"Ummm. My favorite."

"Grandma and Grandpa are coming."

"That's nice."

We made our way up the stairs, one careful tread at a time. Lily pushed open the door to my room and led me in. I lay on the soft bed and sighed. Lily glided slippers off my feet and pulled up the duvet. "Comfy?" she asked.

"Comfy," I replied.

I heard her tiptoe away and then the sound of her running down the stairs, taking the last three in one leap. All fell quiet.

The windows were closed, the curtains drawn. They hadn't been opened in all the time I'd been in residence.

The back door, the one off the farm office, slammed and I almost smiled to myself. No matter how she might try, it was impossible for a ten-year-old to stay quiet for long.

And that's the way it should be. I thought of girls I'd seen in Afghanistan. No older than Lily, but already squelched by life, living in constant terror of attracting attention, anyone's attention.

There's something about an old house, a way you can tell when it's empty. The walls seem almost to relax, and settle deeper into the foundations as they do so, taking a brief break until doors fly open and people flood back inside.

This house was old. Parts of it dated from the early 1800s. It had been expanded over the years, modernized many times. But the old bones remained, strong and resilient.

I lay back into the pillows and let my mind drift. The pain retreated. It was not defeated. It would never be defeated, but was merely regrouping its forces prior to a renewed attack.

# Chapter Two

The birthday dinner was a huge success. It was early May and warm enough to sit outside on the big wooden deck running off the kitchen. Jake flipped hamburgers on the barbeque, and Joanne made a salad with the first of the delicate baby greens from the gardens. It was a lovely evening, and my head felt almost normal. I fancied that Omar couldn't bear to be in the presence of a happy laughing family. Particularly not when the birthday child was a beautiful young girl with tangled hair, a big laugh, and long tanned bare legs.

Jake's parents, Marlene and Ralph, had joined us for dinner. They lived not far away, close to the town of Wellington, where they ran an industrial chicken operation. Ralph rarely said much but smiled at his son and grandchildren with warm affection. Marlene, as scrawny as a barn cat and about as tough, didn't approve of organic farming. She lectured Jake at length about the better yields he'd get using chemical fertilizer and decried the extra effort that went into heirloom vegetables. Jake focused on his meal and said, "We like to do it our way, Mom," and Joanne bit her tongue. I glanced at my sister. It was costing her, I thought, to keep quiet and not defend her farm, her husband, their choices. Her shoulders and her lips were set in tight lines and a small vein throbbed in her neck. Marlene changed course abruptly and asked Jake if he'd had time to look through any more of the boxes.

"It's spring, Mom," he said. "Spring on a farm. You know what that means. No time to do anything but turn soil, plant seeds, and try to get ahead of the weeds."

"Yes," she agreed. "Life on a farm's hard work. For most of us, anyway."

Suspecting she'd aimed that comment at me, I got up to help Joanne clear the dishes and prepare dessert.

Inside the kitchen, Joanne rubbed at the side of her neck and gave me a rueful grin. "Sorry about that."

"Not a problem. What boxes is she talking about?"

"In the attic. When we bought the house it came with just about every bit of stuff accumulated since it had been built. Marlene's trying to encourage Jake to take an interest in his family legacy. He is interested; he just doesn't have the time."

"What family legacy? You guys bought the house, you didn't inherit it."

"This house was built by Jake's great-great-many-times-grandparents on his father's side. Generations of Stewarts lived here until around 1945, when they sold it and moved into town. Something about one son being killed in the war and the surviving one not interested so no one was left to run the farm. Marlene's family were farmers, and when she and Ralph married, he helped work their farm. When her parents retired, Ralph and Marlene took it over. You can take the farm family off the land, but you can't always take the farm land…whatever. I guess you can take the farm land away. Anyhow, that's a long way of telling you why Jake grew up on a farm, but not this one. Marlene might be dismissive of our farm—she thinks Jake should be working out at their place, but she sure was excited when we bought it. Marlene's own ancestors came over from the Ukraine in the twentieth century, so she's somehow gotten it into her head that the Stewarts were an important family, rather than just common-or-garden settlers like all the rest. Now, she needs to prove it to everyone else. "

I smiled. "Isn't everyone looking for an exiled aristocrat or the bastard son of the King of England in their family tree?"

"People around here are proud of being Loyalist descendants. The property's a fraction of the couple of hundred acres it was originally, but we have the old house. The original grant covered the land right down to the lake front. When the road went in, that strip of land was expropriated. Which is a good thing. We never would have been able to afford this place if it had lake frontage." While she talked, her voice low, Joanne arranged colorful candles on the homemade cake and piled a tray with plates and forks. "Get the door, will you?" We went back outside.

Lily blew out the ten candles on her cake with one breath, while Jake held his hand over his son's mouth because Charlie had made threatening puffing gestures while the candles were being lit. Lily stuck her tongue out at her brother, and then she opened her presents while her mother sliced and served cake, and her grandmother babbled to no one about some precious silver tea pot someone had found in *their* attic.

I'd bought Lily a pashmina, a genuine Afghan one, pale gray and so fine the entire thing would slip through a wedding ring. It was somewhere in my parents' house, still in the boxes of possessions which had been packed up and sent after me. Instead of the pashmina, I'd given her a twenty-dollar bill. She was saving to buy an iPhone.

For a brief moment silence stretched across the deck and across the farm while everyone ate birthday cake. Even Marlene stopped talking for a while. Only the top of the orange sun was visible above the poplar trees that marked the boundary of the fields. The line between inertia and contentment is very fine, but I settled back into my chair and thought that perhaps, just this once, I was content.

"Have some cake, Aunt Hannah," Lily said. "It's really good."

I've never been overweight, but like most women I've always worried that I was. I'd lost thirty pounds in the last three months, and not a thing I owned fit me. I'd also lost a great deal of muscle in my arms and legs and knew I needed to put some weight back on and get some exercise. Joanne had suggested that Jake drive me to the swimming pool at the rec center in Picton in the mornings, but it seemed like far too much bother. I used to run half-marathons. These days a walk to the mailbox at the top of the driveway was an effort. I had an appointment with the neurologist in Toronto later in the week and he'd bug me about the importance of exercise and a good diet. I'd nod and agree and come home deciding to go to the pool the next day.

And never quite get around to it.

There were times when I wanted to get better, when there was nothing I wanted more. But those times were quickly superseded by periods of pure inertia. And, if I were to be honest with myself—self-pity.

I'd barely managed to eat a quarter of my burger and a few leaves of lettuce and had passed on the potato salad. The chocolate cake, covered in a shiny layer of thick ganache, a ball of vanilla ice cream melting alongside, looked highly unappealing. Lily was watching me, "Go on," she said, "Try some."

And so I did. I lifted my fork and broke off a tiny piece of cake, scooped up some of the icing and then ice cream. I put it all into my mouth. It was good.

But I only had one bite.

They were always watching me, my family. My sister and her daughter most of all, but occasionally I could see Jake poised to run for me if I stumbled, and even Charlie, as self-absorbed as only a seven-year-old boy can be, was quick to apologize if he made a loud noise or did anything that startled me.

It was nice to know they cared. It could have been annoying. In that as in many other things these days, I couldn't summon up enough energy to mind.

As soon as she'd finished eating, Marlene pushed her chair back and announced that hard-working farm families need to get to bed early. She gave Lily a hug and a loud smack on the cheek, tousled Charlie's hair, thanked Joanne for the meal, kissed her son, and marched down the steps. Ralph followed after saying his own goodbyes.

I helped Joanne carry in the dishes, while Jake took the kids to the paddock to gather the horses and settle them into the barn for the night.

"Lily's going to be a fabulous young woman," I said to my sister.

"I can only hope so. As soon as Mary Beth's daughter turned thirteen she became a screeching harridan. Poor Mary Beth figured the girl had been replaced by an alien look-alike."

"I seem to remember something like a screeching harridan in my own house," I said with a laugh.

"Oh, god. Don't remind me. Do you think my past sins will come back to haunt me? Do you remember when I went to Dad's office on take-your-child-to-work day in full goth regalia?"

"Yup. Good old Dad. Didn't blink an eye when you marched into the kitchen and announced that you were ready to go."

"And you, goodie two-shoes, looking all prim and proper to go to the hospital with Mom."

I stuck my tongue out in the same way Lily had to Charlie, and Joanne grinned. "Brat."

"Hamster-brain," I replied.

We laughed together.

Then I said, "I don't think your mother-in-law likes me very much."

"Don't take it personally. I don't know why, but that's just the way she is. I sometimes think she spends her life accumulating points. One for her, minus one for everyone else. Except for Jake. He can do no wrong. Well, other than marrying me and getting into organic farming, that is."

We finished cleaning up in companionable silence. Outside, the sun had disappeared and slashes of pink and gray decorated the sky.

My sister and her husband farm ten acres of organic vegetables. Marlene may disdain small-scale organic farming, but despite growing corn and wheat and canola and raising factory-farm chickens they barely eke out a living. Seeing that agriculture's changing and the traditional way of life disappearing, Jake knew if he were to stay on the land he'd have to learn new ways of doing things. He went to the University of Guelph to get a degree in agriculture. There he met Joanne, studying biology.

It was a match, my mother always said with a hearty, approving laugh, made in manure.

Jake and Joanne were lucky to find a good piece of land for sale at an affordable price that they could farm. Land that came with an old barn and even older house. That was the only luck they needed. They worked hard to establish not only the farm, but the business. Can't do much with ten acres of vegetables if you don't have a market.

They've made quite a name for themselves, and their business, J&J Farms, provides the family with an adequate, if not lavish, income. I never would have figured my younger sister, the rebel, for a farmer. Unless it was growing marijuana. But I guess a small-scale, organic farmer has to be something of a rebel.

I snuck a peek at her. She was wiping down the countertops. Her round face glowed with health; the muscles in her arms and legs were strong. Her hair was long and uncut and wayward strands fell out of her casual ponytail. She was dressed in khaki shorts and a matching, but faded, shirt.

We've never been close. Too different, I suppose. But since my…injury, she's watched over me like a mother hen.

"I'm going out to the root cellar," she said. "Cheryl Foster's coming by later for a bag of carrots. We're almost out, and I'll be glad to get rid of them. I have about twenty pounds left. Can you finish up here?"

"I'll come with you. Give you a hand."

She eyed me carefully. "The ramp's steep and it's dark down there."

"Dark is good. I'm fine. Let me help you. Please."

She looked dubious. But I was fine. Omar had temporarily departed. As always he lurked in the back of my right eye where he'd taken up what looked to be permanent residence. A black, malignant dot.

I gave Joanne a smile. I did want to be helpful, when I could. I'd been here for a month, and I was beginning to sense that Jake was wondering how much longer he'd have me on his hands.

"Okay. Might as well show you the cellar." She put down the tea towel and headed for the back door. "You'll need good boots." She pulled on the mud-encrusted Wellingtons she wore around the farm. I'd been provided with a similar pair on my arrival. They were too big for me, but I hadn't needed to go far in them.

The root cellar was beneath the old building close to the road that served as a small shop. Most of the farm's produce is sold to restaurants, community share agriculture holders, or at Saturday market in Kingston, but Joanne kept the store to serve tourists and passers-by. Introducing city people to fresh, local produce, organic or not, getting them hooked on real food and real flavor, she believed, was the key to the farm's profitability. Being spring, not much was for sale yet. Eggs, some early baby greens, jars of soup Joanne and her helpers had put up in the fall. By late summer the shop would be crammed almost to the rafters with an abundance of fresh vegetables. The building was made out of roughly-hewn logs, gray with age, gaps in the mortar. It was about the size of the master bedroom in my condo in Toronto.

"Can you believe a family of five lived there," Joanne said as we crossed the patch of grass and weeds they called a lawn.

"In the shop? It was once a house?"

"Yup. The first settlers here were United Empire Loyalists, refugees from the American Revolution. The British government gave them land and enough supplies to get them started. That old building was built in 1784. They would have lived in tents the first few months while they cleared a patch of land to get the farm started and used the wood to build the house. All the rest," Joanne waved her arm, encompassing the big house, the driveway, the outbuildings, the neat, orderly fields, "came later. Much later."

"Imagine living there. With a family."

"I think they had a maid as well."

"No matter how low you are in this life, there's always someone worse off than you."

"I bet they were glad to have it," she said. "Everything they
owned, except the clothes on their backs, would have been left
behind in the States."

I shuddered. Joanne was right. I'd seen refugees, lots of them,
in my time. They'd be nothing but thrilled if they'd been given
a house like this one. With virgin land to farm. Hardship, yes.
But safety above all.

"How do you know about them? The original settlers?"

"They were Jake's ancestors, and stories get passed down.
Jake's always been interested in his history, and he liked to come
here when he was a kid and poke around. When he was growing
up the land was falling into disuse. The farm people moved away
and sold to city folks who used it as a summer home. Sometimes
he'd find a piece of rusty old metal from a horse's bridle, a broken
wagon wheel maybe, buried in the weeds. He found a belt buckle
once. He still has that. He was over the moon when he learned
that the property was up for sale." She smiled at the memory.

"Must be interesting," I said, "to know something about
your ancestors." Our family history went all the way back to
my grandparents. Who'd come from England at the end of the
Second World War and never talked about it. Not that I'd ever
asked. I didn't even know the maiden name of either of my
grandmothers.

Joanne ducked through a small hole in a jumble of overgrown
bushes. A steep wooden ramp laid over a packed-mud floor led
down to the entrance to the cellar. "Watch your footing," she
said. "Stay in the middle of the boards. It can be treacherous."

I followed her, placing my feet with care. The old wood
creaked and swayed.

"Wait there while I get the light. We had electricity put in
to run the fridge in the shop."

The sun had disappeared behind the trees lining the property.
A soft night breeze had risen, and shadows filled the entrance
to the root cellar. The wooden ramp wobbled beneath my feet,

and my sister made a dark outline ahead of me. The acrid scent of damp earth, stored vegetables, and burrowing earthworms filled the air.

The door opened with the protesting creak of old wood and rusty hinges.

A wave of foul air poured out of the cellar, and I staggered backwards. "What on earth?" I covered my mouth and nose with my hand, but that did nothing to cut the stench. A gush of icy wind reached cold probing fingers beneath my sweater and scraped slowly down my spine. The black spot behind my eyes throbbed and grew. But for once it brought no pain.

"My god, Joanne," I said. "Something's gone bad. Have you stored meat down here?"

"Of course not. It always smells like this. It's the moisture in the dirt walls and floor."

A blaze of harsh white light burst forth. I screamed and clutched my head. Nothing happened. There was no sudden pain, and Omar was still.

"Gosh, I'm sorry, Hannah. I forgot to warn you that I was about to turn on the light. Do you want it off?"

"No. It's okay." I lowered my hands. The smell, of death and decay and rot, was gone, leaving only traces of damp earth and last season's vegetables. The cold wind had died as quickly as it began and air coming out of the root cellar was merely cool.

I ducked my head and carefully followed my sister inside. The roof, packed mud reinforced with round logs that had once been whole tree trunks, was only about five feet high, and the floor was dirt. Piled rubble formed the walls. The room was largely empty. A bunch of brown bags containing carrots and potatoes were stacked against the back wall. The shelves lining the room held a few lonely jars of pickles, jam, and soup. Joanne swiped at a large cobweb hanging from the ceiling. A long-legged, fat-bellied spider dashed for cover.

She picked up one of the bags with a soft grunt and balanced it in her arms. "Got it. Let's go. You first. I'll get the light."

I scarcely heard her. A one-hundred-watt bulb hung from the ceiling. It should have been enough to illuminate the entire small room, but the shadows in the corners were long and deep and very black. Nothing moved.

"Hannah?"

"Sorry, I'm thinking of the people who built this place."

"There are some old documents and things in the attic, if you'd like to look through them. Jake was thrilled when we got possession of the house and found that over the years no one had bothered to throw out several generations' worth of letters. I was downstairs, unpacking, pregnant with Charlie, trying to keep Lily out of everything, and Jake disappeared for hours. His mother would like to take everything to her house, but Jake told her the items need to be properly inventoried first. Since we arrived, no one's had the time to do much about it, although Jake's made a start."

I was vaguely aware of my sister's voice as I walked out of the root cellar, my back bent to avoid the low ceiling. She switched off the light and we were plunged into darkness.

Tendrils of icy cold air wrapped around my ankles as the door shut behind Joanne. Did I hear a moan carried on the wind?

# Chapter Three

Monday morning a crowd had gathered in the farm office at the rear of the house. The seasonal employees had arrived. Two ruddy-cheeked young women and one man. The girls were university students, interested in learning about farming. Joanne had told me, with something approaching wonder in her voice, that young people were going into farming these days, not fleeing for jobs in cities like their parents and grandparents had done. And, as it was entirely possible that these young people hadn't been raised on a farm as were past farm generations, they had to come to places like hers to learn practical agriculture.

The man was older, in his mid-thirties perhaps. He'd been in the army, his letter of application had said, but that life wasn't for him, and he wanted to settle down and grow things.

As the summer went on, Joanne would supplement these three with WWOOFERS: willing workers on organic farms. People who travelled the world working on small farms in exchange for room and board. Jake had bought an old camping trailer at auction and placed it behind the greenhouse. The WWOOFERS would live there for the duration of their stay. The two university girls, introduced to me as Liz and Allison, had taken rooms in town, and the man's family had a summer place in Wellington near the lake. His name was Connor and he looked ex-army, all right. He wore a white T-shirt that stretched across a six-pack, and his arms were thick with muscle. He was good looking with prominent cheekbones, rough stubble on a hard jaw, and shaggy black hair, a mass of curls.

He turned his smile on me, teeth white against the tanned face. "I'm Connor. Farmer-wanna-be." He held out his right hand and I took it. It felt warm and comfortable.

"I'm Joanne's sister, Hannah."

"Pleased to meet you, Hannah."

He held my hand slightly longer than necessary, then let go with a twinkle in his eye and turned his attention back to Joanne, who was telling the group about the farm.

I hadn't slept last night. Omar had visited me, which was rare in the dark and quiet. I took an extra pain pill, which helped only minimally, and lay awake thinking of the root cellar beneath the shop that had once been a refugee family's house.

My doctors had thought a stay on a farm would be good for me. Out in the country where I could enjoy fresh air and peace and quiet away from the bright lights.

The farm was located on a peninsula that jutted out into Lake Ontario in the center of the island that is Prince Edward County, Ontario. Halfway between Toronto and Ottawa, the County, as it's known to everyone, is a place all its own. The 401, Canada's busiest highway, speeds past to the north ferrying people and goods between the cities, and a surprising number of people don't even know there's a big island in Lake Ontario. Nothing stays undiscovered for long, and city people, the comfortably retired or those fleeing high property prices, are moving in bringing with them expensive housing developments and cheap vacation complexes. The Lake Ontario beaches are as good as beaches anywhere and still not overcrowded, although the population of the County quadruples in the summer months.

But what makes the County attractive for people like my sister and her husband is the farming. This is agricultural land, mostly, rich and fertile with a moderate, by Canadian standards, climate. The locavore movement, eating locally and eating fresh and pesticide-free, has been a god-send for farmers here. Restaurants in the cities and shoppers at Saturday farm markets can't get enough of J&J Farms' organic heirloom produce, the soups, sauces, and baking Joanne makes from it, eggs from the chickens I dislike so intently. Largely propelled by local agriculture, there are restaurants in the County as good, maybe better, than in Toronto. Celebrity chefs are living and cooking and farming here. They even make wine, and vineyards and small-scale wineries are popping up all over.

It's a nice place to live, Prince Edward County, but if I was up to doing anything about it, it would be back to the big city for me. Too quiet here, particularly at night, too dark. A forty-five-minute drive to the mall, one solitary theater screen in town, no public transit, no coffee shops or restaurants within walking distance.

Joanne took Allison, Liz, and Connor outside to show them around and introduce them to their duties. Today, I heard her say as they left, they'd be getting the tomato fields ready to receive seedlings which had been started in the greenhouse. I walked through the kitchen, opened the sliding doors leading onto the deck, went outside, and leaned on the railing. Joanne had brought her huge collection of terra-cotta pots out of storage, but hadn't planted the annuals yet. It was still two weeks away from the May 24th weekend, when everyone rushes to the garden center and in a flurry of hopeful expectation puts in their fragile plants. She was hurrying the season a mite bringing the tomato seedlings out, but the forecast was for above-normal temperatures.

I took a deep breath and consciously tried to be aware of my environment. That was supposedly good for me. I could smell the air. Trees coming to life, manure from the horse barn, freshly-turned earth. Perhaps even a trace of freshwater from the lake on the other side of the road.

No exhaust, no neighbor's trash left out too long in the heat, no neighbor burning steaks on his gas barbeque. No neighbor at all, by city standards. There were houses down the road, other farms, some newer homes. But you couldn't see or hear them.

I reminded myself that all this peace and tranquility meant there was no stroll to the corner for a latte and muffin and a relaxing hour spent with the newspaper. No film festivals. No drinking too much at a bar and not worrying about it because home was only a stagger away.

It would be nice, I thought, to set out a cushion, relax, catch some sun. But the sun was my enemy, and so I went back inside.

I found a magazine and settled down in the living room. I've always been a voracious reader, inordinately fond of classic Victorian novels, but since my injury I can scarcely concentrate on more than a sentence or two. Sometimes the words don't make sense, even in books I've read and loved many times before. It's incredibly frustrating, and can bring me to a rage of hurling the book across the room. The brain works in mysterious ways, they always tell me. I can read handwriting as well as I ever did. Just not print. Give it time, my doctor says, as he says about everything. However, there's nothing else I can do, and not a heck of a lot of books are written in script, so these days I pretty much just flip through magazines, looking at the pictures. I tried audio books and sometimes listened to a book in bed, when I had trouble sleeping, but found my mind wandering so much I missed a good deal of what was happening.

I felt mildly guilty at not helping out around the house or farm, but the one time I'd tried operating the rototiller my head hurt so badly, I'd collapsed. Jake carried me into the house and I spent the rest of the day in bed. Now, my duties were limited to feeding chickens, collecting eggs, and tidying up the kitchen.

I woke with a start when the front door slammed shut. "Mom!" Lily yelled. "He's here again."

She came into the living room and saw me, blinking away sleep in the tattered wingback chair that was such a comfortable place to relax and look at magazine pictures or listen to books. "Sorry." Her voice dropped to a whisper. "Were you asleep, Aunt Hannah?"

"No," I said, "Just resting my eyes."

"Where's Mom?"

"I don't know. I haven't been outside for a while. Why are you home so early?"

"It's not early. The bus dropped us off. Regular time."

I'd slept all day. No doubt while the busy household crept around me trying not to make any noise. These old houses did have thick walls. I ran a quick check on my head. No sign of Omar. I struggled to get out of the depths of the chair, and Lily ran over to give me a hand.

"Who's here?" I asked.

"Huh?"

"You said someone's here?"

"That dog from next door. His name's Buddy and he's really old and he wanders down the road sometimes. Mom thinks he can't remember how to get back home. It must be awful to get that old, don't you think?"

I thought of my grandmother, ninety-one last birthday, with her lawn bowling and championship bridge and Caribbean cruises. I could only hope I'd inherited her genes. These days she was more active than I.

"He's sitting on the front step," Lily said. "I'll take him home. It's not far. Tell Mom where I've gone, will you."

"Why don't I come along? I could use the exercise."

She gave me a dubious look. My doctors had told me I needed to walk regularly, keep myself mobile. It seemed like too much trouble. "I'll be fine. And if I'm not, you have your cell phone, don't you? We can call for help if we need it."

"It doesn't always get a signal further up the road."

"Leave your mom a note on the kitchen table. In case she comes looking for me…I mean for you."

"I guess that's okay," Lily said. "I'm getting an apple and some cheese. Want anything?"

"No, thanks. Do we need a leash or anything for this dog?"

"He'll follow me."

I went to the enclosed back porch that had been stuck onto the east side of the house off the office and searched for my hiking shoes in the mad jumble of a farming family's outdoor footwear. I was sitting on the bench tying the last of the laces when Lily joined me, munching on a wrinkled red apple, and slipped into her running shoes.

We walked around the house and there on the front step sat the saddest-looking dog I'd seen since I'd last been in the Middle East. It was a border collie, black and white, with wet and rheumy eyes, half of its right ear missing, and a muzzle completely gray.

He lifted his one and a half ears and struggled to his feet when he caught sight of Lily. The stubby tail wagged.

"There's a good boy," she said, giving him a scratch on the top of his head. Digging into her pocket she pulled out a hunk of yellow cheese, wrapped in a paper towel. Breaking off a piece she held it toward the dog. It instantly disappeared.

*Not so senile after all,* I thought.

"You shouldn't feed him, Lily, if you don't want him coming around."

"I feel sorry for him," she said. "Poor old thing. I hope when I'm old and decrepit someone will give me some cheese."

"Did you leave that note for your mom?"

"Yes."

"Let's go then."

Lily led the way, the dog following eagerly although slowly. Something was wrong with one of his hips, and he walked with a twisted gait. We turned right at the top of the driveway and headed west. We could hear waves lapping on the rocky shore of the lake and catch glimpses of sun-sparkled blue water through patches of old trees and thick undergrowth. The road was lined with stately oaks and maples, buds bulging with new leaves like a woman heavy with child. The high branches reached toward each other creating a tunnel through which we and the road meandered. Dappled green light fell at our feet. Through gaps in the trees I could see across the fields and recognized the shape of my sister behind the wheel of the tractor. Most of the ground was brown and empty, but in the distance Liz and Allison were moving through the soft pale green and dark red foliage of the lettuce beds.

Lily chatted about goings on at school and how she couldn't wait for classes to be finished and all the horseback riding she and her friend Ashley were going to do over the summer. Oh, to be ten years old again with the endless summer vacation stretching out ahead. The dog trotted along behind us, encouraged by pieces of cheese. The occasional farm vehicle drove past, the driver lifting a finger in greeting, otherwise it was perfectly quiet. To the east, about two kilometers up, the road came to dead end and so we didn't get a lot of traffic. A soft wind stirred the nascent leaves.

We walked for no more than five minutes before coming to a driveway. The dog ran ahead up the gravel track.

"Can he find his way home from here?" I asked.

"Better make sure. We'll walk him up to the house."

"Have you thought about getting a dog yourself?"

"Yes," she said with a snap in her voice. "But stupid Charlie's allergic to dogs, so we can't have one."

"There are non-allergenic dogs, I've heard. Bred specifically for families that can't have a regular dog." I snapped my mouth shut, realizing I'd probably said too much. If Joanne and Jake had said no dogs, they wouldn't be happy at me making kindly suggestions.

"Dad says," Lily huffed, "we have chickens and horses and barn cats and that's enough animals for one family. The cats aren't pets, and you can't play ball with chickens, and the horses are great, but they can't come into the house and sleep in my bed, now can they? I'd like a dog."

Obviously this aging Border Collie was Lily's puppy-substitute. I could only hope it didn't get hit by a car one day trotting down the road in search of scratches and cheese.

The driveway was a long one, the house not visible from the road. We climbed a small rise and through the bare trees caught a glimpse of the sparkling blue waters of Lake Ontario stretching out toward the horizon. Eventually the house came in sight. It was much newer than Joanne and Jake's farmhouse, built in the sixties or seventies, with brown vinyl siding and a double attached garage. The garage doors were closed and no cars were in the driveway. Neat flowerbeds, empty, lined the front walk. The wide expanse of lawn had recently been cut. Iron urns overflowing with purple and yellow pansies stood on either side of the front door.

"Doesn't look like anyone's home."

"Hila's always here."

*Hila?*

We didn't need to knock. As we reached the door, it swung open on silent hinges. A face peered out and I sucked in a breath and Omar roared to life. I felt heat and fire. I heard men yelling and women screaming and children crying. I knew hatred, fear, and bloodlust.

I cried out. No one heard me. My legs wanted to move, to flee, to run for my life. But they did not respond.

"Hi, Hila," I heard Lily say from far, far away. "Look who's been out exploring."

Lily's young voice broke through the images in my head. I dug the fingernails of my right hand into the palm of my left. I took a deep breath and tried to remind myself where I was. I fixed my eyes on the pansies until all I could see was their cheerful color.

"Naughty dog," the woman said. "Thank you, Lily, for bringing him home." Her English was nearly perfect, the accent light, her voice soft and low. Her hand rested on the doorframe. Her skin was the color of milky coffee and she had wide dark eyes framed by thick lashes. She wore a black tunic over long black trousers. A black scarf, shot with blue thread as bright as lake water, was wrapped around her head, the ends tossed over her shoulders.

"This is my aunt Hannah," Lily said, very politely. "She's staying with us for a while."

I was standing slightly to one side and I don't think the woman had seen me. Her head moved in surprise. Swiftly, her lashes dropped across her eyes. She hunched her shoulders so the scarf fell over her face. She pulled her hand into her long sleeve.

I struggled to find my voice although my head was wrapped in a cloud of agony. Usually the pain took time to build, slowly and threateningly, like a thunderstorm gathering on the horizon, giving me time to run for cover—and the bottle of pills. This time it had come on me full bore, all at once. Omar reached his long fingers down the nerves and stroked pain back to life. My world began to narrow as the dark veil moved in from the edges of my vision.

"*Salaam Assalam o alykum.*" I struggled to say the greeting in Pashto.

A ghost of a smile touched the edges of the woman's mouth although she still did not look at me. She dipped her head. Lily gave the dog a hearty pat on its rump and pushed it toward the house. It walked inside on arthritic hips without giving us another glance.

"Bye," Lily said, as if from the bottom of a rain barrel.

The woman began to close the door.

I wanted to say something. To ask her where she was from, what her village or city was. Ask her what she was doing here, in the countryside of Prince Edward County, Ontario.

By the time I had recovered what little remained of my wits, the dog was inside, the door shut.

The left side of the woman's face, below the expressive brown eyes and above the full red lips, had been a mass of pink scar tissue stretching into her hairline. Her left hand little more than a lump of flesh, twisted, ravaged, three of the fingers nothing but rounded stubs.

I sucked in a breath.

Lily took my hand. "I'll call Mom to come and get us."

"No, I'm fine. That is, I can walk home. Don't disturb your mom."

And so we made our way up the driveway to the road lined with maples and oaks and down the sun-dappled, dusty road back to the farm. I kept my eyes focused on the ground in front of my feet and leaned heavily on my niece, her hand firm on my arm, the sun warm on my back.

By the time we got home, the pain was almost gone. It had been brought on by shock. The suddenness of seeing an Afghan woman, her horrible face, her tortured hand, her downcast eyes.

I said nothing to Lily or Joanne about what I'd seen in my mind's eye. I would not be telling the neurologist either.

My head trauma brought me pain and the occasional loss of balance and forgetfulness and confusion. I'd never thought it affected my mind. Never before had I had a vision.

It hadn't been like a memory or flash of scenes from a movie seen and then forgotten. It was as if I had been there. At that moment.

An explosion. A car on fire. Guns going off. Men firing rifles and cheering the flames on. Women weeping in horror. Children screaming, calling for their mothers.

# Chapter Four

Hila Popalzai stood behind the curtains and watched the woman and child walk away. They'd come down the driveway with firm steps, smiling in the sun, laughing at a joke, Buddy trailing behind the girl he adored.

They went back with hesitant steps, the girl with her hand on the woman's arm, the woman stumbling as if she couldn't see the ground beneath her feet.

She was in pain, that woman. Pain that never left her, although she might have a moment's relief to laugh with a young girl at the antics of an old dog. She spoke at least two words of Pashto, so unusual in Canada. She must have been to Afghanistan at some time.

Pain. She would have earned her pain in Afghanistan. A country of pain.

Hila studied her own hand, where the thumb and first finger held back the edge of the curtains. The other fingers good for nothing at all.

When she looked up again, the woman and girl were disappearing around the bend in the driveway. The girl, Lily, came by several days a week, leading Buddy home. They'd never said much. Hila scarcely knew what to say to a young girl whose hair swung behind her and whose eyes looked straight into your face. In the winter, she'd worn a heavy jacket, long pants, high boots, gloves. Now that spring was here, she'd discarded all of that and dressed in shorts that showed her bare legs and shirts that revealed her arms and the bones at the top of her thin chest. She was all knees and elbows and collarbones, but she would fill out soon enough.

And even then she would continue to wear clothes in which she could run free.

Hila had seen pictures, of course, back in Afghanistan. Pictures of Western cities and Western people. She'd known how they dressed. But still it had been an enormous shock when the plane landed in Toronto, and she walked into the concourse to be met by Maude Harrison dressed in jeans and a snug sweater underneath her coat. Then the drive through the city! The things she saw.

The first time Mrs. Harrison had suggested Hila take Buddy for a walk, she'd been shocked.

Walk! Outside! Alone!

She'd taken him as far as the bend in the driveway before scurrying back to the house. The next day she'd gone a bit further, and then a bit further after that. She avoided the roads, preferring to walk through the woods that edged the back yard. When snow covered the ground, big loud machines called snowmobiles carved trails through the trees and across the farmers' fields and she could walk for a long time without encountering anyone else.

There, in the snow-covered Canadian woods, she found peace.

She heard the car before she saw it. The Harrisons home from their grocery shopping trip to Picton. She let the curtain drop and forced her ravaged face into a welcoming smile.

# Chapter Five

Joanne was in the kitchen when we got home, stirring onions and garlic in the heavy cast-iron frying pan on the front burner. The sound of the TV came from the family room; screeching voices and canned laughter as fake as the people laughing. Steam rose from a large pot of water on the back of the stove. "Spaghetti for dinner tonight," my sister said to our footsteps. She looked up and read my face. "Oh, dear, Hannah, not again."

"I'll be okay. It's passing. I had a shock." Lily lowered me into a chair. "Why on earth didn't you tell me there's an Afghan woman living next door?"

"There is?" Joanne looked at her daughter. Lily was opening the fridge and getting out the pitcher of apple juice.

"I didn't know she was from Afghanistan," Lily said. "I figured somewhere in South Asia, like the people who own the dollar store in town."

"I'd heard something about an exchange student being at the Harrisons. I didn't give it any more thought. I'm sorry, Hannah."

"Don't apologize. It doesn't matter." But it did. Of course it did.

Lily poured herself a drink. "Her name's Hila."

"How long is she staying there?"

Lily shrugged. She lifted her school backpack off the table. "Don't know. Mrs. Harrison invites me in sometimes for juice and cookies. To thank me for bringing Buddy home, she says.

Hila doesn't talk much, but I like her. She's nice." Lily shifted her pack and looked at the floor.

"What?" Joanne asked.

"Nothing."

"Is there something else about this Hila? Something bothering you?"

"No, Mom. You said it was okay for me to go into their house when I took Buddy home." She shifted her feet again, lifted her head, and stared into her mother's face.

She was lying, but I didn't think it mattered much. It wasn't my place to interfere. I said nothing.

"How old is she?" Joanne asked.

"It's…uh…kinda hard to tell," Lily said.

"What do you mean by that?"

"Did she say?" I swallowed, "what happened to her face and hand?"

"No. I figured a car accident or something. I'm not going to come out and ask, am I?"

"I guess not."

"What's the matter with her face?" Joanne asked.

"She has a scar. Really bad. And she's missing three fingers." Lily hoisted her backpack with a heavy sigh. "Math test tomorrow."

"Then you'd better head upstairs and study. I'll call when dinner's ready. Tell Charlie to turn off the TV."

"Like he's gonna listen to me."

"Tell him if he doesn't listen to you, he'll be listening to me. And he won't like what he hears."

Joanne turned her attention back to the frying pan. "Not very neighborly of me, is it? I never heard anything more about the student, so thought she'd gone home. Come to think of it, if she's from Afghanistan she's unlikely to be an exchange student, right?"

"Do you talk to your neighbors much?"

"The Harrisons? Just about never. They're an older couple, moved in two years or so ago. I went over to introduce myself.

They were friendly enough but didn't return the gesture. I've invited them to farm things, like the seedling sale or the harvest party. She sometimes comes, but never her husband. She's fairly active in the community, volunteers at the hospital, that sort of thing, but he's somewhat reclusive. I tried telling them to keep that dog locked up. It's as old as Methuselah, as deaf as the kitchen table. Shouldn't be wandering the roads the way it does. Mr. Harrison politely told me to mind my own business."

"You know Lily feeds the dog, right?"

"I suspected as much. She'd love to have a dog, but…" Joanne reached for a package of ground beef. "It's not like I need someone else to look after." She whirled around. "I didn't mean… You're welcome here as long as you…"

"I know."

"Did it bother you? Seeing the woman?"

"Reminded me of things I'd prefer not to remember, that's all."

Joanne added beef to the sizzling frying pan. The scent of onions and garlic filled the kitchen. The TV had been switched off, and we could hear Lily crossing the floor above our heads. Outside, a group of finches, chests brilliant yellow in their spring mating plumage, circled around the feeders, jostling for space, pecking at tiny black seeds.

A loud knock sounded on the office door and a deep voice called, "Anyone home?"

"In the kitchen," Joanne shouted.

Connor's white T-shirt was streaked with dirt, as was his face. He wore a ball cap advertising a tractor company, and his curls were damp with sweat. "Just wanted to say bye."

"How was your day?" Joanne asked. "Still think you want to be a farmer?"

"I might reconsider. " His voice was light, teasing. "Darned hard work."

"It is that," Joanne said.

"Well, I'm off. See you all tomorrow."

"Good night."

He glanced at me, gave me a soft smile and a nod, and left.

I felt color rising in my face, nonplused and uncomfortable at the man's attention. Without thinking I touched my head. My long red hair was gone, shaved off by the doctors so they could cut into my skull. The scars, the outward scars, were healing. My hair was growing back although more stubble still than hair.

I'm a foreign correspondent for one of the major Canadian newspapers. Perhaps I should say I used to be a foreign correspondent. They told me my job'll be waiting for me when I'm ready to come back, but I don't know if I'll be able, or willing, to visit the world's hot spots again.

It's been three months since…the incident. One month since I came to live with my sister. The future stretches before me, a road map with all the lines blanked out.

Sometimes I can't muster up the strength to care.

If it's been in the headlines in the past ten years, chances are I've been there. Last year, in another spring, I was assigned to Afghanistan. I'd been arguing for some time to be given that posting.

*Be careful what you wish for,* isn't that what they say?

I hadn't been in Afghanistan for long when I met a photographer with a British paper. His name was Simon Bradshaw and he, like me, was at the top of his profession. Maybe it was fear, the cloud of fear that lay over everyone every time we ventured outside the wire, or the adrenaline from being in a war zone, surrounded by heavily armed troops. Maybe even the emotion, the constant exposure to destroyed homes, destroyed families, destroyed lives.

Destroyed country.

Simon and I became lovers the day we met. Over the year we went our separate ways most of the time, different assignments, different armies to report on. Simon was interested in following soldiers in the field, me more in the political process, such as it is, in that sad country, and what the failure of government meant to the poor and the dispossessed. To the skittish women wrapped in their blue shrouds.

I'd been so focused on the job I hadn't realized I was pregnant. When I finally did, it was getting close to time to make a decision. I didn't think I wanted to marry Simon, and I doubted he wanted to marry me. We were fond of each other. We probably loved each other in our own selfish ways. Settle down and raise a child together?

Unlikely.

I had a lot of thinking to do. If I did have a baby it would probably mean giving up the job. The foreign part of it at any rate. I'd stay on at the paper, working political stories out of Ottawa. Or take an assignment someplace nice and safe. Washington, maybe, or London.

To my surprise I'd been starting to find the idea appealing. Of being a mother, of living in my own home again.

Of being safe.

I didn't tell Simon. I wasn't going to keep it secret. If he wanted a part in the child's life, I'd be happy to have him involved. He was a bit old-fashioned, sometimes, and I wondered if he'd think he had to marry me.

Would that be so bad?

It all became a moot point, soon enough.

I remember leaving the base in Kandahar. We visited a few villages. Simon took pictures of wide-eyed, dirty children, scowling men, women in their hateful burkas. I was accompanied by a female interpreter and spent some time chatting to the women, out of sight of male soldiers and tribesmen. Listening to them, you'd believe their lives were absolutely peachy-keen now that the Canadians and the Brits and the Americans were here. I wished I could speak to them without the stern-faced interpreter.

In the last village we visited, the mullah, a young man with a long black beard and angry black eyes, refused to let me so much as get out of the truck. He exchanged angry words with the interpreter, much shouting and gesturing and puffing up of chests. I couldn't tell what he was saying, but the message was loud and clear. The foreign whore wasn't welcome in his village talking to his women.

We were all whores to the likes of him, Western women who dressed conservatively but were not fully covered and went where and when we liked, whether a man approved or not.

His name, my interpreter told me, was Omar.

We headed back to Kandahar and the safety behind the wire. The vehicles in front kicked up dirt, and the setting sun threw beams of pink and red and pale gray between the particles of dust, and the land was soft and beautiful.

I remember nothing more until I woke between crisp sheets, staring at a bright white light and a plump, smiling, middle-aged face. "Welcome back, Hannah," she'd said.

I was in Germany, in the big military hospital where I'd been for two weeks. An IED had gone off as our convoy passed. Simon and three soldiers had been killed. Two other soldiers slightly injured.

Other than numerous cuts and bruises my only injuries had been internal: a skull fracture and damage to my brain when it rattled around inside my head under the force of the explosion. I'd been put into an induced coma while they repaired the fracture and tried to release the pressure of clotting blood.

I'd lost the baby.

My parents were staying in a hotel nearby and were overjoyed to see me awake. My mom's a family physician. She spent a lot of time conferring with my doctors. I asked them not to tell my family about the miscarriage. I also chose not to tell them about Simon.

# Chapter Six

"Hannah's interested in the story of the settlers," Joanne said at dinner.

Truth be told, I wasn't. A bunch of men in pointed hats waving muskets or walking behind plows, women in bonnets and big skirts cooking over open fires had no appeal for me. My interests lay in what was happening in the world today. I could drum up some attention to history when I wanted to understand the background of whatever story I was covering, but there my curiously ended.

However, to be polite, I nodded.

"That's great," Jake said.

"I hadn't realized until yesterday that Hannah didn't know this property was settled by your ancestors. Imagine, nothing but virgin forest when they arrived."

"What's a virgin?" Charlie asked though a mouthful of meat sauce.

Lily laughed, and her mother threw her a look.

"It means unspoiled," I said. Trees that had never been cut. Forests full of deer and waters teeming with fish. Indians moving silently across the land, bows at the ready. Clearing this land with nothing but an axe and a horse pulling a homemade plow.

"After supper why don't you show her some of the things in the attic, Jake," Joanne continued, smiling brightly. "I bet she'd like to look though the papers."

Jake chewed and thought. "I suppose that would be okay," he said at last. "We've been lucky my family's papers are so well preserved."

"Ow!" Lily said.

Joanne said, "Charlie if you kick your sister again it'll be no dessert for you."

I could guess why Joanne wanted me to show some interest in the history of the house. Jake had welcomed me into their home when I first arrived. But the welcome was fading, rapidly, as he began to worry that I'd never leave. She was hoping to find something Jake and I had in common.

If it would make my sister happy, the least I could do would be to look at some moldy old letters.

We'd barely finished dessert before Joanne got up from the table and said, "I'll do the dishes tonight. Jake, why don't you show Hannah how to get to the attic."

I hadn't even known there was an attic. The second floor hallway turned at Jake and Joanne's bedroom and climbed a few steps onto a small, dark landing. From there a steep set of stairs led up. Jake flicked on the light, but it did little to illuminate the enclosed space.

"Mind your footing," he said, "some of these boards need replacing."

We climbed and reached a door. An old door with wide planks and a round knob and a small, painted-over, keyhole. My own bedroom door also had an ancient keyhole. I'd never wondered before why anyone would lock the doors *inside* their house.

"Surely they didn't lock anyone in there?"

Jake smiled. "This was an important house when it was built, one of the biggest and best around. They likely had a couple of maids. Got to keep safe from servants' inquisitive eyes or wandering hands. Mind your head, the ceiling's low."

He led the way, and I followed.

The room was large and dark. I couldn't stand straight in the middle of the room, and the ceiling pitched so sharply it was only about two feet high where it met the walls. Two small, dusty dormer windows let in a thin stream of light. "The attic doesn't run the length of the house," Jake said. "It would have been part of the original house, which has been added onto several times over the years."

A table, wood cracked with age and damp, held a lamp. Jake reached out and switched it on. It didn't help much, but I didn't mind the gloom. The room was cluttered with camping equipment, water-damaged furniture, several sets of skis and poles, snowshoes, cardboard boxes, and modern plastic storage tubs. A baby's crib and a rocking chair with a broken runner.

Dust rose into the air and spiders ran for safety. Several boxes, mostly empty, of poisonous mouse feed lined the walls.

Three large wooden tea chests stood in the middle of the room. An overstuffed chair, fabric faded into an anemic beige with what might once have been pink roses, sat beside them. Jake waved. "The documents are in there. Letters, farm accounts. Some of them go back a long way. You'll take care of them, won't you, Hannah?"

"Of course I will."

"See that you do," he said, a bit more sharply than was polite. "These papers are important to us."

"Thanks for showing me. Perhaps tomorrow I'll have a look."

"My family sold the farm in 1945. Any papers from later than that are not ours."

"Okay."

Jake looked at me. I tried to smile back. "If you find anything...interesting...let me know."

"What do you mean by interesting? Scandal? Children born on the wrong side of the blanket?" I kept my voice light.

"It's always been rumored in the family that, well, that there are lost jewels."

I laughed.

"Stories. Just stories. Probably nothing more than a child's toy ring that fell through the floorboards and someone wanted to make it sound impressive. Still, it would be nice to find something...valuable."

I didn't express my thoughts on the chances of that happening. More likely if there had been anything of value it had been sold when times were hard. "You haven't read everything?"

"I had a quick look, dug down to the bottom to check for damp or mold, but haven't had the opportunity to read much except what's on the top. Some of the handwriting is out and out indecipherable. You might have more luck than me. It's… uh…almost all writing, not typing."

Jake gestured toward the door and I went out first. He switched off the light and followed.

# Chapter Seven

Tuesday I had an appointment with the neurologist in Toronto. I'm not allowed to drive, and although my mother would be meeting me when I got off the train, Joanne doesn't want me travelling alone, so she arranged for a friend to accompany me. The friend, a plump cheerful woman by the name of Nancy, would go shopping in Toronto and meet me when it was time to get back on the train.

The nearest train station is in Belleville, a small city located smack dab on the 401. Nancy drove us into town. The train was running late, and we sat on uncomfortable chairs to wait. They could use the Belleville train station to film a movie set in Germany during the war. I always half-expect crew-cut, square-faced, heavy-jawed men dressed in gray uniforms and high black boots to walk through saying, "Papers, please." The lighting is bad, the building old and drafty. It's overcrowded with impatient passengers and people waiting for loved ones to get off the next train. Waiting. Waiting. There are two vending machines against the wall. One for pop, one for chocolate bars and chips. No other choice.

No locavores served here.

Nancy and I opened our books. Like everyone else, we waited.

We weren't too late getting into Union Station in Toronto, and my mom was waving at me when we walked into the concourse. Nancy went off in search of a dress to wear to her cousin's wedding.

Mom kissed me on the cheek before studying me intently. "How are you doing, dear?"

I decided to answer as if she'd asked about the trip into the city, not generally. "Great."

"I doubt that." She took my arm and hustled me off to the subway entrance.

When Joanne and I grew up and left the nest, Mom and Dad sold the house in the suburban enclave of Oakville and bought a condo in the heart of Toronto. They, like me, appreciate being near coffee shops and restaurants, stores and theaters, the ballet and the opera. I wondered sometimes if Joanne was a changeling, so different were her tastes from those of the rest of our family.

Although, I reflected as we squeezed ourselves onto the subway car, if I had to travel like this regularly I also might come to prefer the open spaces of a farm in Prince Edward County. A sullen teenage boy with tinny music leaking out of the white buds stuffed in his ears pretended not to notice he was blocking access to the only free seat. Mom kicked his legs aside so I could sit down. All around me were vacant faces, heads nodding to unheard sounds behind ear buds or staring at the free newspaper and turning pages without reading them. Students mostly, intent on course notes or books or their variety of smart phones. The odd businesspeople with shiny briefcases and their own smart phones. The subway car was clean enough, although old and worn, but it smelled of urine and body odor, unwashed clothes, too much heavy perfume, all of it tinged with testosterone and pheromones.

"Our stop's next," Mom said. I got to my feet, knocked the boy's legs aside, and clambered into the aisle as my mother grabbed my arm to keep me from falling. We joined the packed crowd, herded like non-grass-fed cattle, out of the subway car and up the escalator to the exit.

"I have some excellent news," Doctor Singh said with a bright smile.

"I can go back to work? Go home? Drive?"

We'd been through the routine, the examination, the tests, the questions, and were now sitting in his office, where I was dressed once again. My mom was in the other chair, and Doctor Singh usually spoke more to her than he did to me. I didn't mind. It was all gobbledygook anyway.

The good doctor's face fell. I knew full well that any excellent news he had to give me wouldn't be excellent at all, just a feeble attempt to make me think I was making some progress. "I've been told of a neurologist who's living in Picton," he said. "I believe that's close to your sister's place?"

That did get my attention. The trip into Toronto was long and tiring, and I knew that Omar would be, if not accompanying me on the train going back, waiting for me at the farm. "Are you sure? I wouldn't have thought there'd be much need for a brain doc out there in the boonies."

"Doctor Mansour's working as an emergency room physician these days," Singh said. "But she used to be one of the top neurosurgeons in the country and has extensive experience with TBI."

TBI: Traumatic Brain Injury. That was me.

"An older woman?" said my mother dubiously. No doubt thinking, as I did, that if she was treating kids who'd fallen out of trees, car accident victims, and people who waited to go to the doctor until a cold turned into pneumonia, she wasn't likely to be a top neurosurgeon any longer.

"I don't know her personally, but she was recommended to me as a good choice for you, Hannah. I've spoken to her on the phone. She's interested in your case and will be expecting your call." Dr. Singh scribbled on a pad of paper and handed it to my mother. I grabbed it. "I can use a phone, you know."

Mom and Doctor Singh exchanged glances. I tucked the slip of paper into my bag.

# Chapter Eight

Unaccustomed to much use, the springs in the overstuffed attic chair creaked under my weight. I picked up a huge old book with blue binding, settled it onto my lap, and opened it carefully. A column for words, another for figures and one for dates. The farm accounts, presumably. The first date was April 22, 1877. It meant nothing to me, but I enjoyed turning the stiff pages, crackling with age. The type of ink changed as the pages turned and the handwriting changed as the years passed. Some of it was totally incomprehensible, some barely readable, and some in elegant script. An entry for what looked like the purchase of a blk hse: I wondered if this was shorthand or if the writer wasn't literate. In all the pages, the words were crammed close together, a time when paper was precious and books expensive. The last entry was from 1924.

I put the accounts book aside and took up a bundle of letters I'd found near the top of one of the boxes. After the family had retired, I'd lain in bed listening to the dark, and found myself thinking about the people who'd first lived here, what life had been like down on the farm so long ago. I thought it dark out here, in the countryside, but lights were left on over the barn and greenhouse all night, and a nightlight was in the bathroom and another outside the master bedroom in case one of the kids had to get up. Every now and again headlights swept the blinds as a car passed. There were flashlights in all the bedrooms, plugged into the wall, a red light indicating its location in case the electricity went out, which it was known to do on occasion. A set of heavy iron candlesticks sat on a table at the top of the stairs, lighter in the drawer.

What must it have been like in the days before electricity, when the flickering light of candles was extinguished at bedtime?

It could be dark in Afghanistan, in the countryside, but even there lights shone from villages, and cities cast a haze on the horizon, and cars travelled the roads.

On impulse I got up, found dressing-gown and slippers, grabbed the flashlight, and made my way in the blue glow of the nightlight to the attic stairs. I placed one hand on the bannister, flicked on the flashlight, and slowly, carefully ascended. I was not afraid of the dark, nothing had ever come out of the dark to bother me. My fingers found the door, and I was inside the attic room. The shadows in the corners were very deep. In the walls something rustled. I turned on the tabletop light and switched off my flashlight. The light wasn't strong, which was good. It was enough to read by, so I'd opened the top of the first box, pulled out a heavy ledger and settled into the chair.

The air in the room was fusty; full of dust, full of memory. A trace of lavender lingered, a sachet placed long ago to keep drawers fresh. The scent of rotting paper, damp in the roof, slightest trace of death and decay. A dead mouse in the walls? Rain pounded against the roof.

Finished with the accounts book, I went back to the boxes and found a pile of envelopes, tied with a faded red ribbon. I took them out, untied the ribbon and to my delight found that I could read and understand the words on the paper.

I read about babies born and old folks dying, about the harvest being brought in and the crops failing. I read with half a mind, as I wondered what our descendants would discover about us. Precious little of any value. The letter I had in my hands was written in 1912. It came from Demorestville, about a half-hour drive from where I was sitting. The main piece of news seemed to be that the writer had bought a green coat. She wasn't sure if green was her best color, but it was on sale and much less expensive than the black one with the lovely collar which she much preferred. So she bought the green. The letter writer added that it would be nice if 'you' discovered the treasure and we could all buy fur coats. Ha. Ha.

We didn't write letters to Demorestville these days. If we had something to say we phoned. We didn't even write letters to the other side of the world—we Skyped or Facebooked or Tweeted or texted. One hundred and forty characters and we were done. The purchase of a green coat, chosen because of price not desire, was not something we'd be likely to think significant enough to tell anyone about.

I read more letters. Lives lived. Lives full of pain and death. The death of a precious daughter in infancy, a son crushed beneath a wagon, crops failing, valuable animals falling ill.

Sorrow, always sorrow.

I pulled myself up short. I was projecting onto these people. These letters were also about the price of bread and a visit from Aunt Martha.

Life was more than sorrow.

It had to be more than sorrow.

I ran my fingers across the papers, yellow and cracked with age. Dust mites rose into the air. They danced in front of my nose, and I sneezed. I sneezed again.

In the end, did it matter? Sorrow, joy. All ended in dust.

Simon.

Our unknown baby.

Dust.

Unknown unloved unwanted.

Unmourned. No, not entirely unmourned. There was a place in my heart, rarely visited, never discussed, where Simon and the child that might have been lived on.

I sat in the dark, the old letters on my lap, and felt the tears flow.

Then I tied the letters back up, put them away, and took myself back to bed.

◇◇◇

Friday morning, I returned to the root cellar.

Jake woke with a sore throat and a mild temperature and Joanne ordered him to stay in bed. Which meant she'd have to do the deliveries this morning.

Before heading out to the greenhouse to start packing up the boxes, she asked me to get Lily and Charlie up, fed, and ready for school. Feeling quite important at being given the responsibility of cooking breakfast, I offered the kids sausages and eggs rather than the usual schoolday fare of granola and yogurt or cold cereal.

"Great," Charlie said.

"Do you have enough time, Aunt Hannah?" Lily looked dubious.

I pulled out the big frying pan and tossed in frozen sausages. "Sure."

I didn't have enough time and the kids ran for the bus clutching their barely-cooked sausages quickly wrapped in slices of bread. Oh, well. Plenty of scrambled eggs to take upstairs to Jake.

The phone rang. I picked it up, stirring eggs.

"Hey." It was Joanne, calling from her cell. "I've just remembered I need some of the fingerling potatoes for a special order. I guess Jake forgot to get them ready last night. They're in the root cellar. Have Connor or the girls arrived yet?"

"No. I'll get the potatoes for you."

"Yeah, okay. Thanks. I need them right away." She hung up. She sounded frazzled, not at all like the usual calm, Earth-mother Joanne.

I turned off the stove and went to put on my boots.

It had rained heavily throughout the night. Mud squelched beneath my feet and rainwater dripped from the trees onto my head and shoulders. Joanne had let the chickens out and a couple ran up to see if I had anything interesting to eat.

I pushed aside a branch and headed down the ramp. I opened the door and stepped inside. I hadn't thought to bring a flashlight, but as I stood in the blackness I realized Joanne knew exactly where the light was. I didn't.

The bulb hung from the ceiling in the center of the room and was turned on by pulling at a dangling string. Outside it was overcast, and the dim light that seeped in didn't help much. I stepped forward slowly, placing each foot with care. I reached up and swung my arm around, trying to locate the string.

A wave of bad air washed over me. The scent of rotting meat I'd smelled the last time I'd been in here. Ice swirled around my feet and my bare fingers turned numb with cold. Omar began to move.

"You really shouldn't come down here by yourself, you know."

I swung around, heart pounding. The dim light was enough to see that no one had followed me. The shadows in the corners were very dark. Could someone be hiding there?

"It's not safe." It was a man talking. The voice was deep, raspy. A smoker's voice, full of confidence and authority and, perhaps, a hint of lazy aggression.

"Who's there?" My own voice wobbled as I edged for the door.

"Safe?" A woman replied. "Safer than up above? Safer than in the sun and the fresh air?" I heard fabric rustle. I smelled the heavy scent of woodsmoke. Her voice quivered slightly. Trying, I thought, to stay strong. "Is any place safe?"

I felt Omar behind my eyes. But he brought no pain.

Slowly I became accustomed to the light. A shadow broke away from the darker shadows behind.

For some reason I did not run.

"Come upstairs," the man said. "The child is needing you."

"The child," she replied. "Ah, yes. The child."

"Hannah! Hannah!"

As though surfacing after a deep dive, I heard my sister's voice. My head felt like a balloon, flying high and free at the end of an exceedingly long string. It was a nice feeling. After months of constant pain or the threat of pain, to be without sensation was absolutely delightful.

The cold wind had gone, taking the foul smell with it.

The only voice I could hear was my very panicked sister.

"I'm here," I called. "Is something the matter?"

The wooden plank creaked and Joanne's head popped into the doorway. "Is something the matter? Of course something's the matter. Where the heck have you been?"

"You asked me to get the potatoes. I'm getting the potatoes."

"Hannah," she said. "That was ages ago."

"Sorry. I couldn't find the light switch."

I felt her hand on my arm. She drew me toward her and led me outside. Above, the sky was thick with clouds.

Her eyes examined my face.

"What?"

"I'm sorry I sent you in there."

"Not a problem. I'm fine. Just couldn't find the light switch for a minute there." I was fine. Omar was gone. I felt light-headed but I knew where I was. Strange daydream, though.

"Hannah. I got busy with the orders. I forgot about the potatoes until I had the truck packed."

I looked around the yard. Connor's car was parked beside the chicken coop. I hadn't heard it arrive.

"When did you go in there?"

"Soon as you asked me to. Joanne, what are you making such a fuss about?"

"I phoned you over an hour ago."

# Chapter Nine

I'd never before fallen asleep while standing up. I didn't know humans could even do that.

But then again I was doing a lot of things I'd never done before these past three months.

My sister marched me into the kitchen and almost forced me into a chair. When she plugged the kettle in, I said, "Don't you have deliveries to do?"

"You need a cup of tea. Then I'm calling Mom."

"No."

She turned to look at me. "You disappeared for an hour, Hannah. You don't know where you were or what you were doing."

"I was napping."

"You were not napping. Not in that root cellar, for heaven's sake. And even if it was a nice comfy warm place for a little snooze, you weren't lying down. You've no dirt on your clothes."

"I was napping standing up." I knew how ridiculous that sounded. "Daydreaming maybe. I read some of those old letters last night. I guess I was still thinking about them. Wondering what it was like here in the old days. Don't call Mom." Joanne's eyes opened wide. Even I was surprised at the steel in my voice. "I don't want her rushing down here to make a fuss."

The kettle began to boil, and Joanne poured hot water over a tea bag in a sturdy white and red mug. Without another word she added a hefty spoonful of sugar and a splash of milk. She put the mug in front of me.

I kept my eyes on her as I lifted it to my lips. The steam was warm and fragrant on my face.

"Okay," she said. "I won't tell Mom if you don't want me to. But you have to make an appointment to see that new doctor in Picton."

"How do you know about her?"

"Mom told me, of course. She phoned Tuesday afternoon, right after she put you on the train."

*Put me on the train.* As if I were a parcel that had to be delivered from Point A to Point B. When I'd been seven and Joanne five, we'd been sent to visit our grandparents in Florida for March break. Mom handed us to the airline attendants, who put us on the plane, with big signs around our necks saying UM. Unaccompanied Minors. Did they still do that, I wondered? I didn't remember having seen any UMs for a long time. Maybe in this day and age they didn't want the kids to stand out.

"Hannah!" Joanne said. "Are you even listening to me?"

My brief moment of defiance passed. "Yes," I said, "I'll call the doctor."

"This morning."

"This morning."

"Tomorrow's Saturday, so she probably won't see you. Make an appointment for Monday. Jake should be fine by Monday, and he can take you. Speaking of which, I'm really late. You want to come for the drive?"

I cradled my tea. The warmth spread through my hands. I hadn't realized how cold they'd been. "No thanks."

"Finish that tea, make that phone call, and then go and lie down," Joanne ordered.

"Yes, sir." I saluted.

The porch door opened and footsteps sounded on the floorboards. Jake's mother came in. She had not bothered to knock. She looked from Joanne to me and back again. "Must be nice. To have time to sit around and enjoy a cup of tea on a working day."

"What do you want?" Joanne said.

Marlene blinked at the unnatural rudeness. "I called earlier and Jake answered. He's sick. I thought I'd pop over and make sure he's all right." She held up a shopping bag. "I brought some of my chicken soup. Nothing better for what ails you than a mother's chicken soup."

"Whatever. I have deliveries to make. Hannah, do what I said." Joanne didn't smile as she headed out the door.

Marlene smirked. She emptied her plastic container into a pot and put it on the stove. "Nothing to do today, Hannah? It must be difficult for you, being so…useless."

"I'm managing, thanks," I replied.

"Not much longer before you're well enough to go back to work, I hope." She stirred soup and smiled at me. She had a nose like the beak of a hawk. "A farm family has a lot of responsibilities. Hard work, not much money coming in until the crops are ready. But we believe in the value of hard work and in paying our way. That's what built our country, isn't it? Hard work. Not charity."

"Excuse me," I said. "I need to go and lie down on my fainting couch. I feel a headache coming on."

I took my mug to the French doors. Connor crossed the yard, pushing a wheelbarrow full of tomato seedlings. His arms were brown and muscular in a sleeveless T-shirt. A single chicken bobbed along beside him, no doubt wondering if something tasty would fall out of the plants. Marlene rummaged in the cupboards for a bowl, poured hot soup, and took it upstairs. It did smell nice: rich broth, chicken, and vegetables

The grass in my sister's scruffy weed-filled lawn was turning green in the soft rain, and it seemed as though overnight the maple in the yard had burst into full leaf.

New life, all around me.

I rubbed my hand across my empty belly. I'd not told either Joanne or Mom that I'd been pregnant. Dr. Singh knew, from the hospital records, but he wouldn't breach confidentiality and tell Mom.

Simon. Aside than the other night in the attic, I'd scarcely given a thought to Simon since waking up in the hospital. It was all too much sometimes. Omar lurking at the back of my mind, the pain, the lethargy, the confusion. My sister and mother, so much wanting me to get better and become my old self again.

Simon had parents and a big pack of brothers and sisters. They lived somewhere in the south of England. Surrey perhaps. Simon had spoken with a cut-glass accent, indicating generations of good breeding. He didn't talk about his family. I didn't talk about mine. We were lovers, that was all. Not partners. We went our separate ways and got together once in a while for sex. We'd had a nice break in Dubai just before…. We'd never talked about taking the other to meet our family or see our real lives. Our lives away from the job and the battle-zones.

His paper would be able to put me in touch with his family. I'd write to them. Tell them I knew him. Maybe share some stories that put him in a good light.

A drop of moisture landed on my hand. Then another. I realized I was crying.

Crying for what I had lost. For what I had never known I had.

I put the cup of tea down. I walked through the kitchen and the office to the porch, where I put on my walking shoes. I headed out the door, up the long driveway and then west down the road. Rain fell in a light drizzle and mixed with my tears. My feet moved steadily, but I was in no hurry. Mist drifted off the roadway and through the trees. The view of the lake was hidden by foliage and cloud.

I approached the house. The door opened and Hila stood there. Her scarf was again black but this time shot with red thread, not blue. Her ravaged face studied me openly, and she made no effort to hide the burned and crippled hand. She stretched out her arms as I approached. I fell into them and felt the soft black cloth envelop me. Words I did not understand whispered in my ear.

And we cried.

Together.

# Chapter Ten

Tea is the beverage of grief.

I had dimly been aware I was being led into the house. There were three of us: Hila and me, strangers weeping in a way that we hadn't been able to with those who loved us, and another woman. I felt a soft wool sweater around my shoulders, heard kind words spoken in a Canadian accent. Doors opened. A man called to a dog. A deep leather couch enveloped me.

Tea was placed on the table beside me.

When I finally wiped my eyes, I could see that I was in a sun room. Three walls of sparkling glass looked out over a well-maintained lawn and the fresh spring woods behind. Bird feeders were placed at the edge of the tree line and chickadees, blue jays, and sparrows darted to and fro.

Hila was seated beside me.

"Sugar or lemon?" a woman's voice said.

She was in late middle age, thick gray hair stuffed into a messy bundle at the top of her head. Her large brown eyes were calm and her long fingers cradled a delicate tea cup. Royal Doulton, I thought.

"Sugar. I…I'm very sorry. Don't quite know what came over me."

"I do." She handed me the cup. "Grief, pain, sorrow beyond endurance. But we do endure, do we not?"

"What else can we do?"

"Precisely." She poured tea for Hila and added three hefty spoons of sugar.

Hila had to lean awkwardly to take the cup in her good right hand. The woman did not attempt to help her.

"I assume you're Ms. Manning's sister. The one wounded in Afghanistan?"

"You know about me?"

"The whole county knows about you. You can thank your sister and her husband for keeping the vultures of the press from your door. Oh, dear. Did I make a *faux pas?* You're with the press yourself, if memory serves."

"Yes. But not of the vulture kind. I'm Hannah."

"I'm Maude Harrison and this is Hila Popalzai. Hila is our guest."

"Pleased to meet you, Hannah," Hila said, very formally.

I laughed. It had been a strange meeting indeed. Hila smiled at me. Only one side of her mouth turned up, but I could read the warmth in her dark eyes.

We sipped our tea. I told them I'd had a head injury that was almost fully healed. They nodded politely and didn't say they knew I was lying. They did not tell me what had brought Hila to Canada or how she had been scarred. I did not ask. Maude chatted about herself. She and her husband were retired civil servants. She talked about their various postings, Africa and the Middle East mostly. As she talked I looked around the room. The bookcase that filled one wall was full of beautiful African wood and stone carvings. Long women with graceful swooping lines, single heads, jumbles of limbs and heads. The rug under the coffee table was closely woven in shades of red and cream— Afghan probably—and the chest displaying a collection of pots and figurines was intricately carved.

Her husband's last posting, she said, had been in Kabul. She herself had never been to that country, as spouses and families were not allowed to accompany their partners to Afghanistan. "Everyone tells me it's very beautiful."

"It is. The mountains, the sky." I did not add the dust the dirt the destruction the desolation the poverty the legions of wounded and maimed.

Hila nodded. "There is a color to the sunset I will miss always."

In my mind's eye I saw the last Afghan sunset. The deep yellow and orange followed by the brilliant white flash. People screamed and men yelled. Flames licked the vehicle in front of ours and soldiers shouted panicked orders.

I blinked and realized that Maude was crouched on the floor, gathering shards of Royal Dolton off the lovely Afghan carpet.

Hila cradled my hand in her good one.

"I am so sorry," I said. "I've broken your beautiful cup."

"It's just a cup." Maude placed the pieces on the table. "Easily replaceable."

"She has many such tea cups," Hila said, releasing my hand. She gave me her soft twisted smile. The edge of her scarf fell back across her face.

Perhaps, but Royal Doulton wasn't exactly cheap. I felt a flush of shame. Who was I to react so badly to mention of the beauty of Afghanistan? Hila's tragedy was far greater. It was written all over her. On her face and her hand. That she was here, in the wilds of Prince Edward County, living with a retired couple of civil servants, meant she had no family.

For Afghanis family is everything.

We three women looked up at the sound of a door opening and the excited click of long nails on the wooden floor. Buddy ran into the room, as fast as his arthritic legs and twisted hip would allow. He headed straight for Maude, his long wet tongue lolling out the side of his mouth. She leapt to her feet before he could plant his muddy paws into her lap. "Look at you," Maude laughed. The dog was filthy, covered in mud from the top of his half-chewed ear to the tips of his toes. "Were you swimming?"

"Something like that." A man stood in the doorway to the sun room. He was dressed in a raincoat and stocking feet. He had a bushy gray beard, and wet salt and pepper hair curled around his collar. His eyes were large and blue, nestled in deep folds of permanently tanned skin. "There's a puddle in the woods so wide and deep ducks are landing on it." He smiled at me and held out his hand. "The famed Hannah Manning, I presume. Grant Harrison."

I accepted the handshake without getting to my feet. "Not quite so famed."

"But you are. I followed your reports from Afghanistan with much interest. Another time, I'll tell you everything you got wrong. I was sorry to hear about the attack on you."

I appreciated his candor. Most people said nothing about the IED explosion, and if they did they covered it in euphemism.

He glanced at his wife. The look full of a question.

"Will you get that dog rubbed down," Maude said, "before we have to fumigate the house. I suspect he was rolling in something other than mud."

Now that she mentioned it, a particularly acrid odor hung over Buddy.

Maude gave the dog a shove with her toe, and Grant slapped his thigh. "Come on, old boy. Let's clean you up. Might even be able to find a treat in the kitchen."

The dog ran off and the man followed. After giving his wife another meaningful look.

"More tea?" Maude asked.

"Do you have the time?" My watch had not been returned to me. Whether broken and tossed out or stolen, I did not know.

She checked. "Twelve forty-five. Lunch time. Will you join us, Hannah? I'll put some sandwiches together."

"No. Thank you. My sister'll be back from making her deliveries and wondering where I am." My parents had given me a cell phone as soon as I was released from hospital. So I could keep in touch, they said.

So they, and Joanne, could keep track of me, I knew.

I didn't mind. They cared. Today, however, I didn't have the phone with me.

"You can call the house from here," Maude said.

I got to my feet. "Thank you, but no. Another time, perhaps."

Hila also rose. She slipped her good hand into mine. Like most Westerners, I'm highly uncomfortable holding hands with anyone not a romantic interest. Strange how we confide personal intimacies that would shock most other peoples, yet we can't bear to so much as touch hands. Hila's small brown hand felt comfortable in mine.

We walked through the house to the front door. I hadn't noticed anything when I came in, wrapped in my own grief and sorrow. It was a standard modern bungalow, nothing special, but the rooms were full of art collected in the couple's travels. More Middle-Eastern rugs and cabinets, more African carvings. Some tiny, perfectly carved stone figures, some lumps of rock from which vague human or animal shapes were visible. The walls were covered with woven wall-hangings and paintings of baobab trees and the African veldt. Everything was mixed together: a charcoal sketch of a wide-lipped, white-eyed black man next to a pastel of a middle-eastern bazaar; an ebony statue of a cluster of faces on a small table of intricately carved wood. Yet it all fit together. A home full of memories of a well-travelled, much enjoyed life.

I left without seeing Grant or Buddy again.

◇◇◇

I walked home in the rain, slowly, enjoying the moisture on my face.

Joanne was almost frantic when I came in.

"Where have you been?" she shouted as I sat on the bench and pulled off my muddy boots.

"Out for a walk."

"It's raining."

"So. I can walk in the rain. I stopped in at the Harrisons' for tea."

"You didn't take your phone."

"I forgot."

She threw up her hands. "I have a sick husband, and a farm to run, and employees to supervise, and customers to supply. I can't be running after you as well."

"I'm not asking you to."

"Someone has to."

"If it's such a hardship, I can go back to the city, you know." After the tea and kindness, and tears and sympathy at the Harrison home, I was suddenly angry. Even as I was saying the words I knew I was in the wrong. Joanne worried about me because she cared. My mom, my dad, even my doctors. They did care.

But I was tired of being fussed over. "I'll pack my things and be out of here by dinner time. Call me a cab. No, never mind. That would be too much of an inconvenience. I'll call the cab myself."

All the fight left Joanne like air escaping from a popped balloon. "Don't be silly. I don't want you to leave."

I, however, wasn't ready to back down. It was a switch from our childhood roles, when my little sister would huff and puff and I'd run around in circles trying to make everything all right. "I'm going to Toronto. I'll check into a hotel and see about getting the tenants out of my condo early. I'm sick and tired of this place anyway. You can only watch so much damned grass growing before going insane." I marched into the living room, my head high.

Where I tripped over a plastic police car Charlie had abandoned. My head was so darned high, I didn't see it in time. I fell forward with a cry. Joanne was too far behind me to grab me, and I landed hard. Pain shot through my right wrist, up my arm and into my head. Waking up Omar, who'd been blessedly absent all day. The black cloud began to move behind my eyes. I lay on the floor, face down. The wide-plank cedar floor, over a hundred years old, restored to its original glory, felt cool on my face.

I cried.

My sister dropped to her knees beside me. "I'm sorry. I'm sorry. I don't want you to leave. Are you hurt?"

Heavy footsteps pounded down the stairs. Jake crossed the room and knelt beside me. I felt his strong hands on my arms, checking for damage.

I rolled over. Jake and Joanne were looking down at me, eyes wide with worry. "Perhaps I should go and rest for a bit." I said. "I feel a headache coming on."

Jake lifted me to my feet. My wrist throbbed, but I was able to move it, and nothing seemed to be broken. Now awake, Omar was moving in. I imagined him rubbing his hands together in glee.

Joanne kicked the police car across the floor. "That boy," she said, "I'll give him a piece of my mind."

I leaned against Jake and he led me upstairs. Joanne followed, murmuring sweet words of love and encouragement. When we got to my room, Jake left us. Joanne helped me pull off my T-shirt and jeans and slipped my nightgown over my shoulders. I climbed into bed while she went to the bathroom for a glass of water. She fed me my pills. She fluffed my pillow as I swallowed them. "When's your doctor's appointment? I'll make sure Jake's free to take you."

"Sorry. I didn't call. I will later."

"I'll do it. You rest." She kissed my cheek and left me alone.

I didn't sleep. Even through the haze of the pills, I know when Omar's there, banging on my defenses, trying to break his way through. Jake and Joanne were in the kitchen, trying to keep their voices low, talking, arguing. About me, no doubt.

I heard the door slam. She'd gone outside. The house was quiet. Perhaps Jake had gone with her.

It was still raining, the light dim in my room. I liked this room. It suited me, suited my life at the moment. The rest of the house had been modernized, the children's rooms, the master bedroom, the main floor bathroom. Not this room. Perhaps because it wasn't used often and the time of a farm family to spend on decorating is brief. The wallpaper had been red once, but no longer. It had faded to a muddy brown, the exact color of dried blood, except behind the bedhead, protected from all light, where the color was as brilliant as might be found on the walls of a Victorian bordello. I knew that from the time my slipper got kicked under the bed and I was forced to crawl beneath in search.

The window frames were deep, two feet perhaps. They could have been used as window seats, but no one had laid down pretty, soft cushions. Against the wall opposite the bed was the remnant of a fireplace. Now exposed shelves containing a few unmemorable ornaments and generic, purchased photographs in cheap frames. The ceiling slanted sharply, no higher than three feet at the edges, and the modern overhead fan was so low the furniture had been arranged so no one need pass underneath it and risk cracking their skull.

The carpet was thin and beige, stained muddy brown in several places with what I did not bother to think about. The baseboards, cream paint badly chipped, were at least six inches high. The door to the room was old, the wooden planks cracked with age, not at all disguised by a fresh coat of white paint. So old that a keyhole, the kind for a heavy key that might jangle on a chain attached to its fellows, was set into the door. As in the door to the attic room, the keyhole had been painted over. I wondered at the sort of people who locked their bedroom doors. Fear of the servants, as Jake had said?

Before the first war, anyone who had a farmhouse with a second story, a parlor, more than one bedroom, and several fireplaces was likely to be prosperous enough to employ servants. Always someone lower on the social scale. And, until industry came to this area bringing good jobs and good wages, they would have needed work.

Any work.

Hadn't Joanne said that even the first family here, the ones living in a one-room settler's shack, had a maid?

I slipped out of bed and padded across the floor to the window. I'd never opened the blinds. Had never looked out. I pulled the blinds up now. My room was at the front of the house, in the eastern corner, looking across the driveway to the shop. I could see the roof of the old building, the beginning of the earthen path that led to the root cellar beneath. From this angle, I couldn't see the wooden ramp into the cellar, or the door.

But I knew it was there.

Fog filled the yard. As I watched, the mist grew and the trappings of the farm began to recede. The chickens pecking about in the grass and weeds blurred into vague white and orange shapes. The big maple and oak trees faded. A car came down the road. It made no sound and its wheels did not seem to turn: it glided on the mist. I could not see anyone driving.

Wisps of fog curled around the base of the shop. Fog crossed the driveway and the lawn and reached the sides of the house. It drifted in front of my window. I reached out my hand. I placed my palm against hard cold glass.

I turned and walked out of my room. Down the stairs and out the front door. The wet grass was cold on my bare feet; the fog chilled me through my cotton nightgown. Chickens scattered at my approach. They weren't white, but rusty red and black. A wagon came down the road, pulled by a horse. Mud splashed its flanks, and then it, and the road, was gone. The neat fields disappeared; nothing but tree stumps lay between the house and the cloud-wrapped lake. The forest was thick and dark and old.

I slid between the bushes at the top of the ramp. No foul stench assaulted me. I walked down the ramp. I opened the door. I did not bother trying to turn on the light.

Fabric rustled, and I smelled tobacco and woodsmoke and unwashed clothes.

"Your duty here is to the children," the man's voice said.

"I do not need you to lecture me on duty," the woman replied. "I have lost everything because of duty." She moved, and light that came from I know not where lit up her face. She was pale with a mass of black hair tied high on her head. Her neck was long and her eyes flashed green fire.

◇◇◇

### April 19, 1786

The last of the potatoes. A month, at least, until the first of the vegetables would be ready for harvesting. She sighed and shifted sand, fingers digging for the tubers, disappointed at how few potatoes remained. She put them into the folds of her apron, cradled them to her chest and walked in a half-crouch to the door. The candle stub on the shelf flickered in the stale, confined air. She let out a gentle breath, and the flame was extinguished. She stepped into the welcome spring air.

Maggie had come to pride herself on her streak of practical common sense. But something about the root cellar…Something that caused the hairs on the back of her neck and on her arms to tingle and rise. She tried to imagine Hamish and how he'd laugh at her fears and tease them away. She closed her eyes at the memory, and knew she was being foolish to fear the dark damp earth.

When she opened her eyes, he was watching her.

"Don't stand around daydreaming. There's work to be done, you know."

"I am well aware of that, Nathanial. Thank you."

He bit back a retort. "Maria isn't well. She's gone to lie down. Make her a cup of tea, will you?"

She kept her face impassive, although she could have spat on the ground, the way she'd seen soldiers do. Maria was strong. She controlled people, her husband, her children, by pretending to be frail and ill. She tried to control Maggie as well, but she knew full well Maggie saw right through her.

She clambered up the packed earth ramp. He was standing at the top and made no move to get out of her way. He reached out and touched her arm. Weighted down by her place in this life as well as potatoes, she didn't swat his hand away. As she slid past him, his hand brushed against her breast. She shuddered but kept her face impassive.

Her face burned as his laughter followed her into the house.

He had little to laugh about these days. None of them did. Like boys throwing rocks at a lame old dog, some people thought themselves strong, preying on the weak.

The youngest child, Emily, sat under the table, playing with her doll. "Can I have some bread?" she asked, bobbing the toy up and down as if it were the straw person who was hungry.

"In a minute."

"Maggie," a voice whined from the single bedroom at the back of the house. "Come here."

She put the potatoes on the table, wiped her hands on her apron, and answered the summons. Maria was sitting up in the narrow bed. She waved a hand when Maggie entered, the lace and satin of the sleeves of her nightgown falling back to reveal pure white arms. They had fled with nothing more than the clothes on their backs and what meager treasures they could carry. But somehow Maria Macgregor had managed to keep her nightgowns and fancy dresses and shoes and hats.

Not that she had anyplace in Fifth Town to wear such dresses. She kept her fine things only to run her fingers through as candle-light flicked in the long winter nights and tell her daughter that one day they'd regain their place in society. Maggie doubted the family had ever had much of a place in society to lose, and she suspected Maria had either stolen the nice clothes or discovered them abandoned. The dresses were too long and too big around the waist. They'd all lost weight, but no one lost height.

She wore the nightgowns to impress Maggie. She certainly wasn't trying to impress her husband. With only a blanket for a door, Maggie knew more than she wanted of what went on— precious little—in the master's bed.

"I have one of my headaches," Maria said, languidly. "Tea, please, Maggie."

Maggie said nothing. She'd stoked the fire to make breakfast and the kettle was still hot. Tea was a misnomer. The tea, real tea, they'd brought with them had been finished long ago. Now they drank leaves of dandelions or the root of willows steeped in hot water. She peered into the tea tin. Not even much of that left. Maria could wait. Maggie cut a thin slice off a heel of last week's bread and added a bit of dripping. "Come out now, and sit in a chair like a lady."

Emily slid out from under the table. She propped her doll against the small pile of potatoes and pretended to share the food.

Maggie gave the girl a smile, and made tea.

The family kept up the pretense that they were caring for their widowed relative out of Christian charity. In reality, Maggie wasn't much more to them than a servant. A slave, in fact if not in law, because she received no wages and had no place else to go.

She cooked and cleaned, managed the household, farmed the vegetable patch, minded the children, and cared for the lady of the house when she was pretending to be unwell. The only duty Maggie hadn't yet been expected to perform was to service the master's needs.

That day, she had no doubt, would come.

What she would do then, she had no idea.

Maria had birthed ten children, yet she wasn't much past thirty. Two had died in infancy, one of the scarlet fever when he was four years old, two more as war ravaged the countryside and the family starved in their ostracism, one on the long journey north, and then dear, sweet Lucy, only last month. Three children, out of ten, remained. Emily, who liked bread and dripping and loved the straw doll Maggie had made her, and the two boys, Jacob and Caleb, who should have been in school but, aside from the fact that there was no school, were needed to work the hundred acres of wilderness they called a farm.

Maggie didn't often let herself think about all she had lost. Certainly not during the day when there were chores to be done and people watching. She tried not to snap at useless, whining Maria who seemed to think she was the only person who had suffered.

Maggie had had a husband once. Tall, handsome Hamish Macgregor, always laughing, always finding something in life to smile about. Maggie and Hamish had a child. Flora, who looked exactly like her father with black hair and flashing black eyes and long, long lashes and a full red mouth.

"Don't cry, Maggie," Emily said, and Maggie felt a sticky hand resting against her arm. "I don't want any more."

Maggie blinked away tears. She held out her arms, and Emily slipped into them. Nothing but a worn dress and a layer of skin protected the girl's fragile bones. Emily had almost died over the seemingly endless winter they'd spent in Lachine, waiting, just waiting for the ice to melt and the rivers to open. While Nathanial bristled at his reduced station in life, and Maria wept in despair, Maggie nursed the child without pause to bring her through the fever that wracked the tiny body. She'd been unable to save Lucy, and now cherished Emily all the more.

"Soon the plants will be growing, and we'll have plenty to eat," Maggie said, making the effort to sound cheerful. "Won't that be lovely?"

Emily nodded.

It was spring now. The hens would start laying again, the first of the crops would be in, and the rivers were opening so supplies would be coming from Cataraqui and Montreal.

"Why don't you take your mother's tea to her," Maggie said, embarrassed to have let her tears flow. "I'm sure she'd like to see you looking so pretty this morning."

The little girl shrugged, not much caring, and Maggie handed her the cup.

◇◇◇

**June 15, 1786**

Maggie stood in the yard at the entrance to the root cellar, more mud than vegetation, and watched Nathanial Macgregor and his sons struggle to move a fallen branch of a massive tree. He didn't talk to her or to Marie about work on the farm, but Maggie knew they'd cleared far less ground than they'd hoped. First the plow had broken, and then Caleb had sliced his leg open with an axe. The boy might have lost the leg had not it been that the midwife had seen such injuries before and she instructed Maggie on how to care for the wound. Caleb was recovering and the cut was healing well, the skin around it pink and healthy, but he had lost a great deal of working time.

Maggie would never, in her worst nightmares, have imagined her life would turn out like this.

Her father owned one of the best farms in the Mohawk Valley. Tenants rented land from him and servants moved silently through the big white house with the stately Greek columns, wide verandah, and sweeping front drive. Maggie's mother was known far and wide for the quality of her roses and the excellence of her cook. Maggie had three older brothers. Two would study to become lawyers and one would take over management of the farm. Maggie's parents had come to America as newlyweds, and with a substantial dose of luck, as well as her father's small inheritance, they'd done extremely well.

Their only daughter had been raised to be a lady. Maggie could play the piano, although poorly, and paint in watercolors, highly amateurish. She was well read, spoke French, was an excellent horsewoman, and could embroider with the tiniest of stitches. She could distinguish one type of English china from another and was able to identify pests and diseases that preyed upon roses.

There had been little doubt that Margaret Reid would marry Hamish Macgregor, son of their closest landowning neighbor. Fortunately Hamish and Maggie had been great friends in their childhood and friendship turned to love as they grew. Their wedding had been the most lavish, and best attended, that had been seen in the Valley for many years.

The day before the wedding, Hamish, immaculately dressed in brown breeches, white stockings, gray coat, and spotless white cravat, had called upon Maggie and Mrs. Reid. Despite his formal attire and manner, joy radiated from him. Maggie was nineteen years old, Hamish twenty. She smiled at him, careful not to appear too eager in the presence of her mother, and thought that such happiness would be hers forever.

"I have a gift for you, my love," he said. He dipped his head and presented her with a small silver box. "This belonged to my mother. Father told me it would be for my bride." Both of Hamish's parents were dead, his mother when he was very small, his father only last year, shortly after the announcement of their engagement. The elder Mr. Macgregor had not remarried after the death of his wife, and Hamish had no brothers or sisters. He was delighted, he'd told her, to be part of her family.

Maggie glanced at her mother. Mrs. Reid nodded, and Maggie accepted the box. She opened it with trembling fingers.

A pair of earrings was nestled into a mound of cotton. Mrs. Reid, peeking over Maggie's shoulder, gasped. The jewels absorbed light from the wax candles in the chandelier and threw it back in a cascade of color. Each earring consisted of three sections, with a single diamond mounted in the base and clusters of smaller diamonds set in silver forming the extensions. Another large diamond was placed in the center of the third, and largest, unit. The silver was decorated with intricate scrolls and flourishes. Mrs. Reid almost snatched the box from Maggie's hand. She lifted one earring up and held it to the light. The three parts swayed sensuously. At the bottom it was at least an inch wide, perhaps three inches long.

"A fine gift," Mrs. Reid said, reluctantly replacing the earring in its box, "to begin a fine match."

Later, alone in her room on the night before her wedding, Maggie counted the stones. Twenty-one diamonds graced each earring.

Maggie and Hamish honeymooned in Charleston, where she had relatives, and she looked forward to nothing but a life of happiness and prosperity. Now, in the rough patch of land they'd carved out of the wilderness, owning nothing but meager supplies provided by the government, she looked back on those sultry summer days as the last genuine happiness she would ever know. The month passed in a blur of dinners and dances and grand balls. Clouds were gathering, although she did not see them: Hamish would leave Maggie with the women and join the men to smoke and talk politics. Always politics.

For the world was intruding on their perfect lives as men sat on the porch smoking and threw out words such as liberty and tyranny and loyalty.

Her husband would come to her bed with a set to his mouth and a darkness behind his eyes. She would turn her face to him with a welcoming smile, and the scowl would flee when he set his eyes upon her.

◇◇◇

A shriek. Another. I blinked. My entire body shuddered, but from cold not fear. I was leaning against the door of the root cellar and the chill damp leaked through my thin cotton nightgown. I looked down: my bare feet were covered with mud.

What on earth did I think I was doing? Sleepwalking? I'd never walked in my sleep before. I glanced around. Outside, the sun had come out, burning off the thick fog. Enough light reached down here so I could see that an electric bulb—plump, round, and white—was suspended from the ceiling. A long string dangled from it.

No need for candlelight, then.

*Of course not.*

The yells I'd heard were of laughter and pretend fear. Lily's voice I recognized, another girl with her. I crept up the ramp and half-crouched in the shadows. The girls were running in circles, around the row of tall poplars that lined the driveway. They had their arms outstretched as if they were airplanes, swooping and ducking. Lily's friend tripped, rolled over, and bounced back up, howling with laughter. They disappeared around the side of the house, heading for the horse paddock.

I made my way to the house and crept upstairs to my room, seeing no one, feeling like a goddamned fool.

What next? Would they have to guard me like an Alzheimer's patient to keep me from wandering off? A GPS anklet perhaps? The very idea frightened me to my core.

# Chapter Eleven

Monday morning I had an appointment with the new doctor. Her name was Rebecca Mansour, and she was nothing like I'd expected. Instead of an old biddy, tired of endless rounds of golf and volunteering at the library in her retirement, looking to do something to get out of the house, she was around my age, late thirties, and rather attractive with sharp cheekbones in a bony face, dark hair cropped short, and large brown eyes. Her nose was prominent and her skin the color of warm honey. She looked to be of Middle Eastern descent, but her accent was pure Ontario. She didn't have an office to speak of, just a remodeled broom closet off the emergency room of the hospital. While I sat in the uncomfortable metal chair she consulted her computer screen and jotted notes on a yellow legal pad. "The headaches aren't getting any better," she said. It was not a question, and I answered, "No," before remembering that I was telling everyone how much better I was feeling.

I hastened to add. "Sometimes they're better."

"Sometimes."

"Yes."

I'd been told that most of the brain damage I'd suffered as a result of the explosion was to the occipital lobe, located at the back of the head. One of the consequences, along with the narrowing of vision and trouble reading that I experienced, was hallucinations. I hadn't experienced any hallucinations. Not until recently.

Was that all it was? Hallucinations caused by my physical injuries? Had reading old letters up in the attic inspired my poor damaged brain to think I was seeing those people?

The woman in the root cellar, in a long brown dress with a ragged and dusty hem.

The root cellar wasn't a spooky place, just dark and dirty and damp and the ceiling was too low. It wasn't really even all that old. I'd spent a lot of time in the Middle East: nothing in North America could be considered to be old compared to the ancient civilizations. The smell perhaps, that rot which it seemed only I could detect, was setting off something in my damaged head.

I felt a bit better thinking that I wasn't going totally nuts.

But not enough to confide in this doctor.

Every doctor I'd consulted had told me, with a shake of the head as if it were a professional failing, that the working of the brain was a mysterious thing.

Doctor Mansour studied my face. I imagined she was checking to see if Omar watched her from behind my eyes. I shoved aside thoughts of the root cellar, in case she could read my mind, and examined my hands in my lap.

"You don't have to pretend," she said. "The brain is a fragile, mysterious thing. Yours has had an enormous shock."

To my surprise, and some degree of horror, I felt tears welling up behind my eyes. "Am I always going to be like this? Afraid of the sun? Afraid to run or to jump? Afraid that my nephew is going to leap out from behind a chair and yell boo?" Afraid of images of people that are not there? Of wandering off in the night?

"Are those the things that set off the headaches?"

"Almost anything can set them off. Shock or surprise most of all, I guess. Bright light in particular. "

"What makes them go away?"

"Quiet. Dark. No, that's wrong, not dark. He, I mean it, comes on in the night. Not often, but sometimes. I find the woods peaceful. Now that the leaves are coming in and the forest is full of shade." And the damp darkness of the root cellar.

She ran her eyes over my body. "You've lost a lot of weight since the attack. At a guess, I'd say you've lost a lot of muscle mass as well. Do you get any exercise?"

I considered lying. But her penetrating eyes were back on my face. "Not much."

"You need to. I'm sure Doctor Singh told you that."

I shrugged.

"There's a pool at the rec center. I swim there most mornings. Why don't you give it a try?"

I shook my head.

"You're living out in the country, that's good. There are studies showing that the more exposure to nature, trees in particular, one has, the quicker the recovery."

"Is that true?"

She nodded, "Fascinating research. Simply looking at a tree through a window apparently does a person good. Your sister's farm is near the lake, isn't it? Lots of opportunity for walking. You said you like the woods, and the beaches aren't crowded at this time of year."

"Sometimes," I said, feeling the words in my mouth, "it all just seems like too much trouble."

"Lethargy isn't uncommon with severe brain trauma. The brain is afraid of another shock, so it wants to shut down and heal. But that's not good for the mind, is it?"

"No."

"What do you want, Hannah?"

I was surprised at the question. No doctor had ever asked me before what I wanted. Didn't they all just assume that I wanted to get better?

I didn't answer.

She made a steeple out of her fingers and leaned back in her chair. Out in the hallway a child began to cry and a woman made soothing noises. Feet walked rapidly past. The siren of an ambulance got louder as it approached. No doctor had ever waited for me to speak. They were always in such a rush to get onto the next patient.

"I want my life back," I said at last. "I want to get back to work. I want to care about what happens in the world. I want to care about something." I scrambled in my bag for a tissue. I blew my nose.

"That's good. You'd be surprised at the number of people I've seen who simply decide to give up. It's *hard* to heal. Your life isn't going to come back to you on a platter, Hannah. Not without help. I can help you. I can adjust your medication. I can send you for tests so we can see how the physical healing process is advancing. But I can't give you much more than that. If you want to get better, you have to do the hard work yourself."

"How?"

"Start by going to the pool. Play around in the shallow end if that's what you want. Swim one length and then get out."

"I'm not allowed to drive, as you well know. My sister and her husband are busy this time of year. I can't ask them to take me into town."

"Good excuse. But not good enough. You're not destitute, I suspect. There's no public transit in the county, but there are taxis. No matter, swimming was just a suggestion. What about going for a walk?"

"I could do that."

"Good. I'd like to see you once a week. Let's say every Monday morning at ten."

"I don't know if my brother-in-law can drive me that often."

"Don't bother then," she snapped. "I have patients in Emerg who could use my time. It's not me who can't work. It's not me with the headaches. It's not me who doesn't want to fork out ten bucks for a taxi to the hospital."

"There's nothing you can do," I shouted. "I've been poked and prodded and analyzed and examined and drugged and MRIed and CAT-scanned. And he's still there, always there."

"I don't recall doing any of those things to you today. I merely suggested you enjoy a bit of time walking in the woods or at the beach." She got to her feet and came around the desk. She opened the door, and the sounds of a busy hospital came rushing in. "I've had patients who've struggled for years, decades, to overcome TBI. And they have, eventually. It's been three months since your injury, Hannah. Don't give up. Now, I have seriously ill people to see. I'll be here next week. Monday at ten. If you want to come."

It wasn't until I was looking out the window of Jake's truck heading into town that I realized I'd said, "He is always there." Not it or the pain. Hopefully, Doctor Mansour didn't notice the slip. Otherwise, she'd be sending me to a psychiatrist.

Main Street, Picton, is Main Street Canada as it used to be. Small shops, a drug store, a post office, a handful of restaurants, an artist co-op, a gas station, a coffee shop at each end. Even a busy independent bookstore. On this spring morning, the locals were out in force, shopping, taking a break from work, preparing for the tourist hordes that would descend the minute school got out. The library's located next to the restored Regent Theater and is a beautiful building in itself, with a stone façade and a small patch of lawn, a bed of flowers, and benches and tables out front.

Jake dropped me at the library steps and went to find parking. He had business in the restaurants in town, and we'd arranged to meet when he was finished. I liked Jake, and I'd always thought he liked me. But over the few weeks coolness was settling in, and I knew he was thinking I'd overstayed my welcome. Egged on, I was sure, by his mother.

I didn't really care much about the history of this area, but I thought it might help me win points with Jake if I showed an interest things he was interested in.

Not as if I had anything better to do.

I climbed the steps into the library. It was the first time I'd been in public, alone, since…I feared everyone in the place would look up and gasp at the sight of me. Instead they focused their attention on computers or book stacks. A woman behind the counter gave me a welcoming smile as I popped an audio book into the return bin. She said nothing, and I glanced around. It wasn't a big library, but it looked cozy.

"Hi," I said. "I'm looking for some information on the first settlement of the area."

"You've come to the right place," she said. "Follow me."

We went through glass doors into a room at the back. Four people were sitting around a card table, playing bridge. They shifted their chairs aside to clear us a bit of room. "This is our local history and genealogy section," the librarian said. "We have plenty of information on the earliest settlers, the Loyalists. Are you wanting anything in particular?"

"An introduction, perhaps. I'm...uh, I'm new to the area."

"Welcome," she said.

"Welcome," the bridge players chorused, without looking up from their hands. "Pass," the solitary male said with a heavy sigh.

"Three spades."

"Three spades!"

The librarian pulled two books off the shelf. "These would be a good start. Why don't you come up to the desk and I'll make out a library card for you." I didn't like to tell her I needed books with lots of pictures.

"I'm only visiting," I said. "I have my sister's card. Is that okay?"

"Of course."

I passed over Joanne's library card. The librarian's eyebrows might have lifted into her hairline as she read the name, but she said nothing.

"There you go, Ms. Manning." She handed me a slip of paper and my books. "Hope you find what you need."

I turned at the bottom of the stairs to see the librarian bustling across the room to the bridge players. I had no doubt what news she had to impart.

Jake sat on a bench outside, face tilted toward the sun. He glanced at the books I carried as we walked to the truck. "History?"

"I thought this might help me place some of the things I'm learning from the letters in your old boxes," I said, clambering into the truck and fastening my seat belt. I flicked through the books. Small font and not many pictures. "Joanne said the shop was built by the original settlers."

"My father family's been here since 1784." Picton's a small town and we were soon driving through the countryside. "The British government evacuated everyone who'd stayed loyal during the American Revolution and gave them land in Canada. They even freed slaves who'd worked or fought for the British and gave them passage out. The Loyalists got good land and lots of it. Land of their own, enough to make a living. The authorities helped the first couple of years with seeds and supplies and equipment to get the settlers established. Then they were on their own. They had a hard time of it in the early years. Few of them were farmers, and they found themselves in the wilderness with nothing much in the way of farming implements or tools. But over the years they did well, most of them. Marysburgh, were we live, was called Fifth Town at first."

I thought about places I'd been and what happened when newcomers arrived en mass. "Were the people living here okay with that?"

Jake laughed. It was the old Jake, the one I'd always liked. "No one here to object. Not even many Indians. You know the Tyendenga Reserve on the mainland? The Mohawks? Even it's a Loyalist settlement. The Iroquois fought for the British and lost their land when the Americans won. Ontario, what they called Upper Canada back then, was barely settled. The French were in Quebec, and the English and some French in the Maritimes, but no one inhabited Ontario except for trappers and fur traders and scattered groups of Natives. It was Loyalists, refugees from the States, who opened up Ontario."

"I didn't know that," I said. *Refugees. Always refugees.*

"See that flag?" Jake pointed as we drove past a lovely old house. It was painted a pale blue and had a wide wraparound porch and steep roof. A woman was in the yard, bent over a mountain of dead foliage and brown leaves. The flag that flapped in the stiff breeze looked like the Union Jack. But something was not quite right.

"I've seen a few flags like that around. They're missing one of the stripes." I hadn't even bothered to ask why. *And I thought I could still be a reporter?*

"That's the Loyalist flag. The Union Jack as it was then. Some of the old families like to fly it. Some of the tourist places, too." I remembered the sign on the highway as you came into Picton: A Proud Loyalist Town.

"I have some books," he said. "You can borrow them when you leave."

And that was the end of that conversation.

It had been a tiring excursion. When we got home, I took my library books to the wingback chair in the living room and studied the maps and pictures of the history of Prince Edward County.

◇◇◇

Joanne and Jake and the workers came in at noon. I'd decided the least I could do to help out around the farm was to get their lunch. I tossed baby greens with home-made oil and vinegar dressing, made up a stack of ham and cheese sandwiches, and reheated potato and squash soup Joanne had put up in the fall. We gathered around the kitchen table—big enough to seat twelve. The workers dug in with enthusiasm while I picked at a bit of lettuce. I thought of my visit yesterday to Doctor Mansour, chastising me for failing to help myself to get well. What did she know? She was a real bossy boots, I'd decided. But weren't all doctors, brain doctors for sure?

I nibbled on the edges of a sandwich.

Joanne talked about tomatoes, heirloom tomatoes, and the new breeds she wanted to try this year. Next weekend, she said, would be seedling sale day. Hundreds of people would be coming to the farm, most of them, one hoped, to buy tomato plants. As they ate she assigned Liz, Allison, and Connor their tasks. Tables had to be set up in and out of the greenhouse, plants laid out, labels and prices prepared, planting and growing instructions photocopied. All while the regular work of the farm went on.

Liz had brought a carrot cake she'd made and passed slices around. I accepted a sliver and ate half of it. My sister gave me an approving smile.

I really did feel like a five-year-old sometimes.

*Did I want to get well?* the doctor had asked.

I'd thought it a silly question at the time. But sometimes it *was* nice to be like a kid again. No worries, no responsibilities. An adult looking out to make sure you ate your vegetables.

I got up to clear the table, and Connor leapt to his feet. "I'll give you a hand," he said.

He loaded the dishwasher while the others filed back out to the greenhouse and fields.

"Thanks," I said, "But you shouldn't be helping me, in the house. Joanne's not paying you to do housework."

"Consider it a freebie." He studied his watch. "Hum, I'll tack on an extra two minutes and forty-three seconds at the end of the day to make up for it."

I laughed and began putting sandwich ingredients away. "Do you like it? Here, on the farm? Think it's what you want to do with your life?"

He shut the dishwasher door and leaned against it. He crossed his arms over his chest and studied me. A tattoo curled around his right bicep and disappeared into the sleeve of his T-shirt. "Early days yet. But so far, yeah. I travelled a bit, with the army. Saw some things. Things I didn't like. Saw a world I don't like. Some of the same places you've been, I hear." He shrugged and looked away. "I'm ready to settle down. Start a family maybe. And a farm like this one seems a pretty good place to do that." He laughed with embarrassment. "Assuming I can find a woman who'd actually want to settle down with me." He looked at his watch again. It was a good one, with numerous dials and knobs and all the bells and whistles. "Wow, now I owe your sister three minutes and fifty-one seconds. Better get back at it."

He left the kitchen quickly, crossed through the office and out the porch door. I went to the French doors and a minute later he came into sight, heading for the tomato fields.

It was a lovely day. The tulips were in full bloom, scatterings of yellow and pink across the lawn, their faces open to the sun.

Spring is a wonderful thing. One day the grass is brown and the trees are bare. The next, it's as though a paint brush dipped in green has been wiped across the lawns and fields and full-grown leaves tacked onto the maples. A baby tucked into its cradle in the evening, heading for high school the next morning.

I decided to venture out for a walk. Not go far, just get some air. Like the bossy doctor had suggested. I thought of Hila, who no doubt spent all of her time in the house.

I popped my cell phone into my sweater pocket and went to put on my hiking boots.

◇◇◇

The weather warmed and the sun lingered long after dinnertime and spring turned into summer. I continued to see Doctor Mansour on Monday mornings. Jake declared that his schedule wouldn't accommodate waiting around for me and so, as the good doctor suggested, I took taxis. Omar continued to visit me when I least expected him. I didn't venture back up to the attic to look through the boxes because, really, reading old letters is a heck of a lot of work. I looked through the library books that I'd borrowed, and Lily helped me out by reading to me when I had difficulty. Connor fell into the habit of helping with the dishes after lunch and checking off the time he was spending in the kitchen. He said nothing more about his service in the army, and I never told him about my experiences in war zones.

The root cellar was nothing but a dirty root cellar beneath a creaky old building. I had no more visions and decided that I'd been simply dreaming and had blown it all up out of proportion.

It became my custom to stroll down the road after Connor and I had done the lunch dishes and visit Hila Popalzai. Most days we would go for a walk in the woods behind the Harrisons' property. We talked about very little.

She confided nothing about her family or her life in Afghanistan or what had brought her here, and I did not ask nor did I talk about my own time in her country. The bond of shared experiences was there, and we both knew it. It gave me, and I hope her, strength. We had no need to discuss it.

Instead, she told me she was studying online toward the continuation of her degree in mathematics. As someone who has trouble balancing my expenses sheet, I couldn't imagine what a BSc in math would entail.

We have the impression, sometimes, that Muslim women are uneducated. Illiterate. Their minds shrouded as much as their bodies. In the course of my travels I'd met plenty of women who could put my education—a BA in Journalism from Carleton—to shame. Hila confessed that in her spare time she was trying to improve her French and German.

Only once did she say anything approaching intimacy.

"Are you free, Hannah?" The question came out of nowhere, after I'd told her that my mom had phoned the previous night. She and Dad had been to the opera—Carmen—and said that on the way home the streets were packed with people sitting on restaurant patios. The Regent Theater in Picton sometimes showed opera live via satellite from the Met, and I thought perhaps classical music in a dark setting might be a good way to start getting Hila out into the community.

"Free? I don't know. I was free before I came here. I guess I'm still free. I can leave if I want, any time. Is that what you mean?"

"I don't know," she replied "What does it mean, to be free?"

I thought for a while, listening to the debris on the forest floor crunch beneath our feet. "For a woman, perhaps all freedom means is to be safe. To know that you can live your life without fearing someone's going to belt you across the mouth with no warning or take everything you own and leave you and your children to starve. And that if they do so, the law's there to make sure it doesn't happen again. Is that enough?"

"I think it might be."

We walked on. Then she said, "You are so strong."

"I *was* strong. At least I thought I was. Once."

"You will be strong again, Hannah."

On the weekends Lily would come with us and she'd run ahead with Buddy, falling over logs, splashing through puddles, frightening squirrels and birds. Perhaps it was the glories of a Canadian spring, new life all around me; perhaps it was Hila's sturdy quiet company; perhaps it was Lily's boundless enthusiasm. But after the initial shock I'd had upon seeing Hila for the first time, Omar stayed away whenever I was with her.

Unfortunately he didn't leave for good and he'd be waiting in the morning when the sun streamed through the kitchen windows or in the evening when I was tired and my guard was down.

# Chapter Twelve

I never arranged to go walking with Hila. That was unnecessary. Other than into Belleville to the mosque on Fridays, she never went out. If I dropped by and she wanted to walk, then we would. If she was deep in her studies, she'd tell me so and I'd go back to the farm. If Maude was home, she'd make us tea and lay out cookies and we'd sit in the sun room, watching the birds at the feeders. I rarely saw Grant Harrison, but when I did he always smiled politely, although distantly, and inquired after my health without much interest.

It was early July and the fields and forests were green and lush in the summer sun. Joanne and Jake and their workers were hard at it, seven days a week, planting, harvesting, weeding, thinning. It became my responsibility to look after the shop. I checked that produce was in stock and kept an eye on the money box. Perhaps I'm too world-weary, but I was genuinely shocked that Joanne ran the shop on an honor system. A tin box sat on the table, under the chalk board listing prices, and customers dropped their money in. Not only that, but the box was unlocked so they could help themselves to change.

My sister told me she made more money that way. People whose arithmetic skills weren't the best were afraid of making a mistake, so they often overpaid, just to be sure. Or they put in a big bill and didn't bother taking out coins as change. I only half-believed her and was always surprised when I checked the box and found it stuffed with cash.

Perhaps it was the long quiet walks with Hila, perhaps the soft spring rains, perhaps being near trees as Doctor Mansour had suggested, perhaps just the passage of time, but I hadn't had a headache for a couple of days, and I was beginning to hope Omar was leaving me.

It rained on Thursday. Joanne was happy to see it; the plants needed the water. I fixed sandwiches for lunch and as usual talk around the table was all about tomatoes and lettuce and poultry. Joanne had bought fifty baby chicks and they were growing happily in a corner of the equipment shed. Jake had made something he called a chicken tractor, that would take the birds around the farm. Let them enjoy the sunshine and fresh air and pick at weeds and insects to their hearts' content and then they could be moved, en masse, every couple of days, to fertilize another patch of ground. In season they'd provide eggs for the shop, and come fall some of them would give up their lives to keep the family fed over the winter.

"Like so many simple ideas," Jake said, "this one was almost lost in the rush to mass-scale, factory farming."

Connor spread out his big hands. "That's why I'm glad I'm here. To learn this sort of stuff from you guys."

I brought out slices of cake left over from the previous night's dinner, and Joanne assigned the afternoon tasks. Liz was to weed the tomato fields, Allison to plant carrots, and Connor to work the rows of peas which were germinating under landscape fabric at the back of the property. He groaned and said he'd rather babysit the chicks and everyone laughed.

The workers trooped back outside, farm work certainly doesn't stop because of a bit of rain, and as usual Connor and I did up the dishes.

When we finished, he went back to work and I headed for the shop to see what needed replenishing.

As I splashed my way across the yard, with an escort of two chickens, a shiny black SUV pulled into the parking area. A couple got out, city people by the look of their immaculate perfectly-ironed clothes. I caught myself smiling. Since when did I come to regard city people as outsiders?

I helped them buy eggs and lettuce, popped their money into the cash box, and headed back to the house.

Other than the occasional pass-by with the mower, Jake and Joanne's yard isn't looked after. The lawn's as much dandelions and crab grass as grass and once the annuals are planted, weeds are allowed to have their wicked way with them. Vegetation, whether weeds or grass, is thin where family, farmworkers, customers, visitors to the seedling day or harvest party march across the lawn. Masses of orange tiger lilies grew wild in the ditch, as they did at the side of roads all over the county, and tall hollyhocks bursting with pink and red flowers were clustered around the mail box. I was thinking that the shop needed more eggs and wasn't watching where I was going. As I rounded the back, passing the entrance to the root cellar beneath, my foot hit a patch of mud. Before I knew what was happening, I was down, sliding toward the door. My head struck a rock half-buried in the soil.

◇◇◇

**September 12, 1775**

Mr. and Mrs. Hamish Macgregor returned from Charleston to the Mohawk Valley in September, and it became impossible for Maggie to ignore the talk. War was in the air. Revolution.

Such nonsense. Men's nonsense.

She had a household to set up, a staff to assemble. Hostess duties and wifely duties to perform. Which she did with great joy and considerable competence.

She was in the library, writing a letter to the youngest of her brothers. She chatted about the delights of married life—not quite all of the delights!—and news of the family in South Carolina, and all of the wonderful things she and Hamish had done there. She was closing the letter with a few words about the weather when she became aware she was not alone. She turned to see Hamish standing in the doorway. He held a scrap of paper in his hand and was watching her with a look of sadness she rarely saw on his handsome face.

She lifted a hand to the lace at her collar. "Dearest? Is something the matter?"

He crossed the room in quick, angry strides. "A note from George Burkart. He had another visit from the *gentlemen* of the so-called Committee of Public Safety," Hamish's mouth turned up in a sneer, "*Suggesting* that he and the rest of the men in his family sign their blasted American Association."

Maggie signed her letter with a flourish of an "M." "Would they prefer not to?"

"Yes, my sweet. They would prefer not to. As would I. The Association binds its signatories to promise not to trade with Britain or buy British goods."

"If they don't want to sign it, then they shouldn't," she said, quite sensibly. She folded the letter.

"George says he has decided he will have to sign. The *suggestions* are getting stronger. I'm hearing the same thing from other men in the valley. These men calling themselves Patriots are refusing to frequent the shops or otherwise do any business with those of us who are not prepared to renounce the loyalty we have sworn to our King."

Maggie lifted her shoulders. There was a bad streak on the window, most visible in the lovely morning light that was streaming in. Hadn't Mrs. O'Malley, the housekeeper, said something about the maid leaving?

"There's been talk of *making* reluctant men sign." Hamish paced back and forth across the carpet.

Maggie had no interest in politics, but she did care about Hamish. "Jane left yesterday," she said.

"Who?"

"Jane. Or was it Joan? The small dark-haired maid."

He threw up his hands, "I don't care how you run your household, Maggie. Get another maid."

"Something about her father refusing to let her work here any longer," Maggie said.

"Oh. I see." He approached her chair and smiled down at her. He reached out a hand and touched a tendril of hair that had escaped from her bonnet.

"I'm going to New York," he said. "I'll be several days, a week maybe."

"But we just got home! I am so wanting to have a dinner party soon. My first as a married woman at my own table."

"Your party will have to wait. A lot of things," he stroked the lock of hair, "will have to wait."

### May 25 1776

Even Maggie had been unable to ignore the talk of war and revolution that filled the towns and the countryside that winter.

She lost another maid and could see that work on the farm was falling far behind. The crops were late to be planted and eventually Hamish himself was spending hours behind the plough. Most of the men had left. The young and strong ones, he told her, some to join the Continental Army, some to join haphazard assortments of makeshift militia loyal to the King. He had returned from New York as the leaves turned scarlet and yellow and orange, his handsome face dark and troubled, to spend most of the winter reading and writing letters and touring the countryside.

He had no sympathy for the rebels, thought that if they just sat across the table like Englishmen should, they could work out their differences with King and Parliament. But he didn't want to fight for the King either. His maternal grandfather had been with the Bonnie Prince at Culloden. Where he'd died, his wife and children evicted from their land. Hamish didn't talk much to his wife, to Maggie, and she didn't ask. Politics weren't women's business.

It was too late to insist upon being neutral. A man, Hamish explained, was expected to stand for one side or the other. If you weren't for one side, they'd assume you were for the other.

He told her, one morning over breakfast while outside the snow fell heavy onto the dark fields, that he wanted simply to do the right thing. And, he had decided, the right thing was not to take sides. To hope that men of reason could come to a reasonable arrangement. Matters of taxation should never be allowed to result in open war.

Maggie thought that an eminently sensible idea. But, it appeared, not many others did. She and Hamish became increasingly isolated, as their neighbors declined her invitations and women turned their heads if they happened to pass on the streets or in the shops of Schenectady.

Letters began to arrive from Maggie's parents. Mother was worried about her, begging Maggie to visit. Hamish did not read the letters aloud he received from her father, but his face grew dark.

"Your father," he said, tossing one such missive into the fire, "has been infected with this disease the foolish call liberty. I call it treason and warmongering. He is ordering me to appear in front of him and accompany him to a meeting of his committee to explain why I have not joined them. I doubt that even if I did agree I would get much explaining in. Until I do so, it would appear I am no longer welcome in his home. Which is of no consequence because I do not wish to be there. But it will make it most uncomfortable for you to visit."

She gave him a smile. "This is my home, here, with you, and the only place I want to be."

By May of 1776, Maggie was joyously, delightfully, radiantly pregnant. The birth would be in November, and she was confident that the troubles would be over and she'd be able to restaff the house and get everything ready for the arrival of their baby. Hamish was overjoyed and some of the darkness that had lain behind his eyes all winter began to lift.

She was embroidering patterns of roses onto baby blankets when the front door slammed. Hamish came into her parlor, followed by one of the older men, one of the few still working on the farm. She got to her feet at the look on her husband's face. He had been in the barn, seeing to a horse about to foal for the first time, and his boots were thick with mud and straw. The man with him did not even bother to remove his cap.

Maggie lifted her hands to her mouth. "What…" she began.

"Old Robbie Hendricks has been tarred and feathered and run out of town."

"Why?"

"Why? For no reason, that's why! He's an old man who scarcely knows his own name any more. He was stopped in town by a gang of drunken militiamen who demanded he declare his allegiance. 'Patriot or traitor?' they asked. He replied 'Traitor?' as a question. He'd forgotten the meaning of the word. Well, that was enough for them. They set on him, tarred and feathered him and rode him out of town on a rail."

"A misunderstanding, I'm sure," she said.

"Do you not know what tarring can do to a man, Margaret?"

He hadn't called her by her proper name since their wedding. She shook her head.

"This happened a week ago. Robbie's dead. The hot tar burned him, badly, and the burns were not healing well. But it was the rail that did him in. It emasculated him."

Maggie blinked, not understanding at first. Then all the blood drained from her face and she collapsed. Fortunately her chair was behind her knees; Hamish scarcely noticed her distress. "There is no law now, no justice. No one will be held to account for the death of Robbie. It's tyranny by the mob, as the Loyalists have long feared.

"Ben here will take you to your parents. Pack a few things quickly. I've made up my mind, Maggie, and I'm sorry to have had to do it. But if they're forcing us to take sides, then I will not side with a mob of hooligans. I've been in touch with Sir John Johnson and am leaving, now, to join The King's Royal Regiment of New York."

"Hamish! You can't be serious."

He dropped to his knees in front of her. He took both of her hands in hers and looked into her eyes for a very long time. "I've waited too long, Maggie. I thought it would settle down, but the course has been set and it will be a fight to the finish. No civilization can be built on treason and lawlessness. These Patriots don't know what they're doing. You," his eyes dropped to her stomach, "and our child will be safer at your parents." He pressed her hands to his lips and then rose to his feet in one swift liquid movement. "It will all be over soon, and I'll be back. Get ready now, quickly."

With a few long strides he was gone and all the sunlight fled the room.

◇◇◇

## July 11, 1776

Maggie's father was a member of the Colonial Assembly. A constant stream of men passed through their house, and all the talk was about raising an army to fight the forces of the English King. The Americans, Maggie's mother explained, had declared their independence from Britain and they would have to fight to keep it. "There is no more King," she explained. "All men are now equal."

"Women too?"

"Don't be foolish."

"Mr. Hudack owns some Negro slaves. Will they be free now?"

"Don't ask such questions. This is men's business. Nothing to do with us. Go and change your dress. Mrs. O'Reilly and her daughters are coming for tea. What Eunice is going to do with that third daughter of hers, I have no idea. They certainly don't have enough money to make up for the fact that she looks like a particularly stupid horse."

Maggie had not told her parents Hamish had joined a Royal regiment. She'd muttered something about troubles on the farm and meetings in New York and his suggestion that she take the opportunity to rest at the home of her parents.

Maggie's mother hadn't much cared why Hamish was gone from home; she was simply delighted by the opportunity to fuss over her daughter and to assemble clothes and other goods for the arrival of her first grandchild. Her father had puffed on his pipe, ran his eyes over Maggie's face, and said, "Better he be gone then," and left his wife and daughter to women's business. Two of Maggie's brothers had joined the Continental Army.

That evening they were entertaining guests at dinner, three gentlemen travelling to a meeting of the Committee of Safety. Although she was five months into her pregnancy, it was not yet showing, and so Maggie was allowed to join the company for dinner. She listened to the men talk—not one of them had said a word to her since the initial greetings—pushed the overdone roast beef around on her plate and said, "Hamish says we have a duty of loyalty to our King."

One of the visitors, a fat man with a giant red ball for a nose, who'd earlier tried very hard to peer down her décolletage, snorted. "We have no duty to a tyrant three thousand miles away. We are free men."

"Hamish says people are getting far too overwrought. He says a matter of taxation can be settled between right-thinking men without resorting to war."

The second of the visitors, a tall thin man with a hooked nose and pale blue eyes, turned to Maggie's father. His voice was very low. "You allow support of tyranny in your home, sir?"

"I most certainly do not. The lass doesn't know what she's saying."

"Hamish says that once men begin to use words such as tyranny and liberty they lose all meaning, and men of sense no longer communicate with one another."

A chair crashed to the floor. The fat man was on his feet. His eyes bulged and a trail of brown gravy tricked out of one corner of his mouth. "Who is this Hamish, who dares to presume he can lecture free men on the meaning of words?"

Maggie's father gave her mother a jerk of his head. She rose to her feet with considerably more grace than had her guest. Her fingers were entwined in the length of pearls around her neck. "My daughter is overtired," she said. "I beg your forgiveness, sirs. It's her...condition."

The men paled at the word.

"Come dear. You need to rest. Gentlemen, please continue with your dinner."

Maggie remained in her seat, not quite sure why her mother would have been so shockingly unmannered as to mention that a lady was expecting. "Hamish says..."

Father's fist hit the table. Wine sloshed in glasses. "Hamish is mistaken. We will excuse him on the grounds that he is not here to express himself, and no doubt you, foolish girl, have mistaken his words. Leave us."

Maggie felt Richard, the butler, behind her, trying to move her chair to help her rise. She gathered her skirts and stood up. Her father looked as if he might have a heart attack any moment. The visitors glared at her in something approaching pure rage.

And Maggie had been very, very frightened.

◇◇◇

July 12, 1776

The morning following the disastrous dinner, Father summoned Maggie to his study.

She had rarely been in there. As children they were called to Father's sanctum only if punishment was to be dealt out. As Maggie had been a quiet, obedient child, she had never been marched before Father's desk to hold her hand outstretched awaiting a thrashing. It was a man's room, with leather chairs, wooden furniture polished to a high shine, a large fireplace, and paintings of hunting scenes on the walls. It smelled of tobacco and men's sweat.

She stood in front of his desk, hands clasped over her stomach, while he read a long letter. Rain beat against the windows and the branches of the trees swayed in the wind.

He dipped the end of his pen into the ink well and scratched out his signature at the bottom of the page. He carefully placed the pen in its holder before looking up. The corner of his left eye twitched. "You can no longer remain in the house of a tory. I will arrange to have your belongings fetched and brought here. You will have no further contact with Macgregor. There will be no traitors in my family. If we're lucky the scoundrel will be hanged for the traitor he is. Otherwise, in time we will be able to dissolve the marriage and find you a new husband and a father for your child."

He picked up the next letter on the pile. "Good day, Margaret."

"No," she said.

"I beg your pardon?"

"Hamish is my husband. We are one in the eyes of God. He is the father of my child. Of your grandchild."

"He is a tory traitor."

Rebel or tory, she didn't care one whit for either side. What did women care about who ruled or who made the laws or imposed the taxes? Life went on, regardless. All she knew was that she loved Hamish Macgregor beyond all reason.

"He is the man I love, to whom I have promised my life."

Father put down the letter. "If a man can betray his country-men, then his promises mean nothing."

"They mean everything to me, Father. If you cannot, will not, understand, then I fear I will have to take my leave and return to my own home."

"So be it, then."

She walked out of the room, her head high, her stomach churning. Behind her, a pen scratched against paper.

Mother was waiting outside. Maggie closed the door softly behind her. They looked at each other for a very long time but did not reach out. Maggie's mother would side with her husband in all that he commanded, as was natural.

Maggie gathered her skirts in her hand and started walking up the stairs. "Send Helga to my room immediately. I will be ready for the carriage in one hour."

"Margaret."

"Yes, Mother?"

"I wish it did not have to be this way."

"As do I, Mother."

The carriage was waiting in front of the house when Maggie descended. Helga had hastily packed the things Maggie had brought with her. One of the farm hands loaded her trunk into the carriage. There was a box beside it. A big wooden tea chest. Maggie lifted the lid and peeked in. Piles of baby clothes, blankets, and soft toys.

Mother did not come out to say good-bye, but Maggie thought she might have seen the corner of a curtain in the parlor lift.

She never saw her parents again.

◇◇◇

**November 15, 1776**

It was mid-November, and the baby was long overdue, when the first pangs struck Maggie. There were not many servants left, the young ones had gone to the war, joining one side or the other, and some of the older men came to her twisting their caps in their hands and not looking into her eyes, to tell her they'd been threatened with arrest—or worse—if they continued working a tory's land.

Several of the local men had left with Hamish to join the British forces, tenants as well as landowners. No one took their families with them; everyone believed the women and children would be safer if they remained in the countryside away from the fighting.

The group of women whose husbands had gone with the Royal Regiment provided some support to each other, and so Maggie didn't feel that she was entirely alone as the crops rotted in the fields and winter's chill crept down from Canada.

On a cold, rainy night, Maggie woke to a stab of pain. At last, the baby was coming. She called for the housekeeper and sent her out into the wet night to fetch Mrs. Allen, the midwife. Mrs. Allen had two grandsons in the Continental Army, one son was a clerk to no less a figure than Benjamin Franklin, her husband was an important man in the Committee of Public Safety, and she herself had been one of the most vociferous of the Patriots from the first whisper of rebellion. She had attended the birth of hundreds of babies, most of whom had lived, many of whom had not. She knew being born was a dangerous business, and never was it the fault of the child the leanings of their parents. She provided Maggie with the best care of which she was capable over the long lonely months. She never discussed her family's activities, nor did she question Maggie about Hamish.

Mrs. Allen came immediately and helped Maggie to safely, easily for a first-born, deliver herself of a big, strong, lusty girl.

Maggie cradled the baby in her arms and leaned back against the pillows in joyous exhaustion. The maid cleared away the bowl of bloody water and stained towels, a smile on her face for the first time in months.

Mrs. Allen dried her hands on a clean towel. She stood beside Maggie and they were silent for a moment, staring in awe at the screaming infant. She had a mass of thick black hair, pale skin, and long thin fingers.

"A new American. A free woman," Mrs. Allen said. Then she began briskly issuing instructions for the further care of both mother and baby and slipped out into the morning to return to her own family.

Maggie slept.

When she awoke, the baby had been tightly swaddled and laid into a wicker basket placed beside her mother's bed. Long lashes lay against her cheek and she slept. Maggie reached out one hand, and stroked the infant's back. "Flora," she whispered.

Maggie and Hamish had decided to name their child after Hamish's mother who had died when he was young. "Soon," she whispered to Flora, "soon."

◇◇◇

### July 12, 1779

Flora touched a slice of bread to her doll's mouth. She lifted a tiny china cup decorated with pink and blue roses and gave the doll a sip of tea. She dabbed the doll's bright red lips with a napkin.

Sunlight streamed in the parlor windows and lit up the little girl's black hair, tied back with a red velvet ribbon. The two women watched her play, rare smiles touching the edges of their mouths.

"You should think about leaving, my dear," Mrs. Dietrich said, finishing the last of her own tea. "We're going. You and Flora must come with us."

"Why?"

"We dare not stay here any longer. Loyalist property is being confiscated, people turned out of their homes. Women and children left with nothing but the clothes they wear. I heard from Rudy. He says we must leave now. While we still can." Rudy Dietrich had been one of Hamish's tenants. It would have been almost unbelievable only a few years ago, that Maggie would invite his wife to take tea in the parlor. He had left shortly before Hamish, gone to Niagara to join Butler's Rangers. The Rangers, Maggie knew, were a fast-moving, irregular force, moving through hundreds of miles of American wilderness, raiding Rebels and rescuing captured British or Loyalist troops.

"You heard from Rudy?"

"Last night. A knock at the kitchen door in the early hours. One of the Rangers, telling me to gather what families I can and prepare to leave. He will return tonight."

She spoke openly, only because the housekeeper had gone out. No one could be trusted in these dark days.

"Tonight?"

She nodded.

"But that gives you no time to prepare. How will you pack in one day?"

"My dear, we will not be packing. We are to take what we can carry. That is all."

Maggie sat back in her chair and thought. She hadn't heard from Hamish in a year. She had sent word to him of Flora's birth with a family leaving for Niagara. A few months later, a letter had arrived, expressing his joy at the news. A few other letters followed, short, hastily written, expressing the hope that she and the child were well and they would soon be together.

For the past year—not a word.

Which meant nothing, she reminded herself, as she did constantly. Everything was in flux, so many people on the move.

"I don't know where my husband is," she said at last. "How can I leave and not be here when he comes for us?"

"He may not be able to," Mrs. Dietrich said. "Come with us, Maggie."

"Thank you," Maggie said, very formally. "I don't believe it is necessary for Flora and me to leave at this time."

"As you wish, my dear."

◇◇◇

### December 14, 1779

Maggie had not heard from her own parents since her last visit to their home, so long ago Flora hadn't even been born. She'd written several times in the first year, but had never received a reply. Whether her letters did not get to their destination or her father had forbidden her mother from replying, she did not know. She hoped it was the former, yet suspected it was the latter.

Darkness was falling. Mrs. MacDonald lit one of the last of the tallow candles, threw one of the last pieces of good firewood onto the fire, and stirred the watery soup that would be Maggie and Flora's dinner, prior to heading off to her own cold lonely home. They had been discussing the state of the larder and pantry. Barely the beginning of winter and supplies were perilously low. Some of the shopkeepers would still do business with Mrs. MacDonald, as long as she pretended she wasn't buying for her tory mistress, but Maggie was running out of money and of things for Mrs. MacDonald to sell in exchange for food, candles, cloth, and other necessities. There were no men left, no one to bring firewood or to care for the farm animals. Which scarcely mattered as there were no farm animals left either. The cows and chickens had gone long ago, snatched straight from the coop or barn, and last month the one remaining horse, too decrepit to pull a plow or a wagon, was gone in the morning. Taken for horsemeat, almost certainly.

Hamish had left her with money and a fully supplied larder, telling her he'd return in a few months when all this was over.

He had not believed he'd be gone for so long. No one had.

Mrs. MacDonald was a childless widow; otherwise she would probably have left long since also.

The two women started at a rap at the door. They exchanged glances. Flora moved from the corner of the kitchen where she'd been feeding her doll supper and gripped her mother's skirts. They never received visitors. Little Flora scarcely knew anyone at all. Most of the Loyalist families had left with Mrs. Dietrich, and those few who remained were too nervous to venture outside.

*Hamish?*

Maggie twisted her hands together and nodded to Mrs. MacDonald.

It was not Hamish, nor anyone she knew. A man, not much taller than five feet, with rummy eyes sunken into dirt-encrusted cheeks and scarcely a tooth in his mouth. His clothes were home-spun, travel-stained, and well worn. His coat a moth-chewed horse blanket wrapped around his shoulders. Paper, cheap paper of the sort political tracts were printed on, spilled from the holes in his boots. He held out a parcel, wrapped in brown paper, tied with string. His hands were filthy and he was missing two fingers on the right.

Mrs. MacDonald took the offering.

The man did not wear a hat. He touched a finger to his forehead and turned without a word.

"Wait," Maggie cried. "Who are you? Who sent you? Won't you come in and warm yourself? Mrs. MacDonald, quickly, put the kettle on."

He spoke over his shoulder. His accent was New York and surprisingly well educated. "I cannot spare the time, Madam. Consider this a favor for a lady I knew a long time ago. Good day and God bless."

He left and the year's first flakes of snow swirled around him.

Mrs. MacDonald put the parcel on the table, and she and Maggie studied it. There was no writing on the wrapping. Flora stretched onto her toes to get a good look.

"Thank you, Mrs. MacDonald," Maggie said. "It's almost dark, you'd best be off home."

Reluctantly, Mrs. MacDonald took her leave.

Maggie untied the string with shaking fingers, while Flora climbed onto a chair to watch. Maggie expected it to be from Hamish, but it was not.

A shawl, soft pure wool. Two small sweaters in cheerful yellow and cream. Candles, wonderful wax candles of the type the shops no longer stocked, not the cheap, smoky tallow ones the kitchen girl made. When she still had a kitchen girl. A bundle of coins wrapped in a lace-trimmed handkerchief embroidered with Maggie's mother's monogram. A wooden box, inlaid with sea shells. Inside was a pearl necklace, an emerald brooch, and two gold rings, one of which was set with crystals.

Maggie touched the strand of pearls. Flora reached out and took a ring. "Pretty," she said. She slipped it on her own finger and admired it.

The last time Maggie had seen those pearls had been at dinner, the night before she left her parents' home. Her mother had brought no jewelry to her marriage; she did not come from the sort of family that could afford jewelry. Maggie's father had been so proud to be able to buy lovely things for his wife.

The money and jewels were not sent to Maggie for her inheritance. Her mother had wanted her to have them so she and Flora would not starve.

She searched the wrappings, shook out the shawl and sweaters, but she could find no note or message.

"Give me that, precious," Maggie said to Flora. "It's too big for your finger. I'll put it away someplace safe."

"Okay," the girl said. "I'm hungry."

"We'll have our dinner in a minute." Flora was so thin. Too thin.

Maggie climbed the stairs with a heavy heart. It had been easy for her, and her mother, to insist that politics was not women's business. Something men discussed after dinner over port and cigars once the ladies had withdrawn, or when gathering around the paddock to discuss the price of a brood mare or prize bull.

But war took food from women's mouths all the same, and drove mothers and daughters so far apart that a mother dare not even send her daughter greetings or inquire after the health of a grandchild.

She put the coins and jewels into the small box where she kept the diamond earrings Hamish had given her on the eve of their wedding. She had worn them in Charleston, to balls and parties, and to dinner at her parent's home.

But not since. She held them up and the stones sparkled in what dim winter light came through the window. She said a prayer for Hamish, as always, and tucked the earrings away. If the choice came between watching Flora die for want of food or medicine, Maggie would sell the earrings. But for nothing less.

# Chapter Thirteen

"Help. Help."

I was drowning. I tried to swim to the surface. Water was in my eyes. I struck out, heading for shore. I hit something. "Ouch," it said. "Aunt Hannah, wake up."

"Call your mom," a voice said from a great distance.

I took a breath and felt muddy water in my mouth. I struggled to rise.

"Lie still. Help's coming."

"I'm okay." I rolled over. A woman knelt beside me. Lily was punching buttons on her cell phone while her eyes, wide with fear, stared at me.

"I'm okay," I repeated. "Help me up."

"Aunt Hannah's hurt," Lily said into the phone. "You'd better come."

"No. I'm fine." I quickly checked myself out. My head, surprisingly enough, *was* fine. My right wrist hurt when I flexed it but that seemed to be all the damage. I struggled to stand. After initially trying to push me back down, the woman relented and gave me her arm. Between them, she and Lily hoisted me to my feet. I swayed and Lily gripped me tighter. I gave her a weak grin. "See. Perfectly fine. I tripped, that's all."

The rain had stopped and the sun had come out. Some of the smaller puddles were dry already. *That was quick*, I thought.

"I'm Rachel. Rachel McIntyre, from down the road," the woman said.

"Hi. I'm Hannah, Joanne's sister."

"So I guessed."

Now that school was out for the summer, Lily and Charlie spent weekdays at adventure camp. Jake drove Charlie to the younger kids' camp in the morning, and Joanne and her friend Rachel, who had a daughter Lily's age, took turns driving the girls. A young girl was peering out the window of a rusty van, watching us.

I opened my mouth to ask why they were home so early, but instead said, "What time is it?"

Rachel checked her watch. "Four-thirty."

I sucked in a breath. I'd gone to the shop immediately after lunch. That would have been just after one. I'd been here, lying on the ground, for more than three hours. I must have slipped in a patch of mud and lain here at the door to the root cellar. Thick bushes, rarely trimmed, crowded the back of the shop, and I would have been invisible to anyone out in the fields or stopping at the store.

My vision began to clear and I could see Joanne, tearing across the fields on the bike she used to get around. She was pedaling flat out, her braid flapping behind her.

"I'm okay," I said as she threw the bike to the ground. "I slipped and fell. That's all."

"She was unconscious," Rachel said.

"Momentarily stunned. Really, I'm fine."

My sister studied me. She stared into my eyes looking for pain. "Yeah," she said at last. "You look okay. You'd better go inside and sit down. Lily, go with her."

At that moment a blue car pulled into the driveway. Joanne groaned, "Not now, of all times." Jake's mother, Marlene, got out and marched straight toward our little group. "What's going on? What's the matter?" she demanded.

"Aunt Hannah's been hurt," Lily said. "She fell into the mud and was unconscious."

"I was not unconscious," I said, but no one seemed to believe me.

Marlene tutted her disapproval. "Some people aren't cut out for farm life. Too bad when it grinds other people's work to a halt though."

"That's not the half of it," Joanne said. "First Liz phoned in sick this morning and then Connor cut his hand and had to go to the hospital for stitches."

"Is it bad?" I asked.

"Nothing too serious. It's his left hand so he was able to drive himself. He said he'd be okay, but I don't want to chance it getting infected with working in the dirt and all."

Marlene couldn't criticize a hard-working farm hand for getting hurt on the job, so she changed the subject. "I thought I'd bring out the first batch of my raspberry muffins. I know how much Jake likes them. I'll put them in the kitchen, shall I? Then I have to be heading straight back. Work never stops on the farm."

She remained firmly in place.

"Thanks for your help," I said to Rachel.

"Sorry I panicked. You sure looked unconscious there."

I gave her what I hoped was a friendly smile and allowed Lily to lead me into the house as Marlene followed. Lily shifted her backpack and told me today they'd had a visit from a First Nations woman who told them stories. "She was real old."

In the kitchen, Marlene began arranging muffins onto a platter. She offered one to Lily, who accepted quickly. "You be sure and tell your dad I made these specially for him with the first of the raspberries."

"I will, Grandma."

Marlene looked down her hawk's nose at me. "You seem to have recovered quickly."

"I wasn't unconscious."

"No. I'm sure you weren't. No reason to get the whole family in an uproar, was there?" Clearly I was not to be given the honor of tasting the first batch of raspberry muffins.

"No time to be standing around," Marlene said to me. "I'm off home."

She gave Lily a kiss and left the kitchen. As she crossed the office, the porch door opened. Marlene didn't bother to drop her voice. I heard the word malingering and something about "in our day, if we weren't sick we were expected to put in a day's work or go hungry."

"Thanks for the baking," Joanne said.

When my sister came into the kitchen, I was sitting at the table watching Lily polish off her muffin.

"Do you want me to call the doctor?"

"No. Really, I'm fine. I tripped over something and fell, that's all. In fact, I'm quite pleased it didn't bring a headache on." That, at least, was the truth. "Does your mother-in-law regularly pop around uninvited in the middle of the day?"

Joanne sighed. "Lily, go upstairs and change. The horses need a brushing and Dad tells me you didn't do a very good job of cleaning the stalls yesterday."

"Yes, I did," Lily replied, heading out the door. "Black Beauty just poops a lot."

Joanne laughed, but then a cloud settled over her face. "Marlene? She doesn't often drop by like that. She needs an excuse. She can be imaginative about excuses."

"Are you sure Connor's cut wasn't too bad?"

"No. I mean, yes. I'm sure. When are you supposed to go back and see her again?"

"See who?"

"The doctor."

I shrugged. "When I think I need to." I hadn't been to see Doctor Mansour for a couple of weeks. There didn't seem to be much point, and I did think I was getting better.

"You may not have a headache right now, but you need to take it easy for a while. I'll take care of dinner."

"Sure."

Lily ran back into the kitchen, dressed in old jeans and a black T-shirt.

"I'll help you with the horses," I said.

"That wasn't what I meant by taking it easy," Joanne said.

"Great!" Lily said.

The family owned two horses, Black Beauty who was, well, black, and Tigger, a younger and smaller gray one. They were in the paddock next to the barn, tails constantly moving, muscles twitching. As soon as they saw us approaching, both animals meandered slowly over to the fence and waited. Beauty tossed her head, and Tigger scratched his hip against the wood.

"Here," Lily said, "you can feed them." She handed me a couple of carrots. Tigger moved suddenly and his big teeth lunged for them. I jumped back, and Lily smiled. "He's always hungry. Beauty has much better manners, don't you, old girl?" She held a carrot out and the black horse closed its lips over it while Tigger tried to get in on the action. I offered Tigger my carrots and he swung his head around and grabbed the offering as if it were the last carrot on earth. As soon as he'd finished, before I could even enjoy a pat, he wandered away to search for something more interesting.

"You're welcome," I shouted after him.

Beauty remained with Lily. She reached up to stroke the horse's soft nose and ran her thin, long-fingered hands across the powerful neck. Beauty stretched her head out and nuzzled Lily's arm. The girl laughed, and the horse gave a whinny like a puff of air on the summer's breeze, leaned forward, and lowered her head. Lily whispered and cooed and stroked. Beauty stamped her front feet but she did not move. The girl laid her forehead against the horse's long nose. And they stood there, together, not speaking but communicating.

I had never seen anything so beautiful.

◇◇◇

We were sitting down to dinner, pasta with shrimp and fresh peas, and Charlie was telling the family about how he'd almost scored a goal at soccer today when we heard a knock on the front door.

Jake and Joanne exchanged looks, and he got up to answer.

He was back in a moment, leading Grant Harrison.

Joanne rose to her feet, "Grant, is something the matter?"

"Probably not. Sorry to bother you at dinner. I'm looking for Hila. I was hoping she might be here."

"No," Joanne said. "She's never been in our home. Although she's always welcome. Hannah?"

"Sorry, Grant. I haven't seen her."

"What time did you finish your walk?" he asked me.

"We didn't go for a walk today."

His eyes opened in surprise. "I'm sorry. I thought you went with her every day."

"Not every day."

"What did you do this afternoon, then?" Joanne asked. "Before you had that fall?"

"Nothing in particular," I said, very quickly. I stood up. "Are you saying Hila's missing?"

"Maude and I lunched with friends in town, and then we did some shopping. Hila wasn't home when we got back. We assumed you and she had gone for your regular walk. Her hiking shoes are gone. It wasn't long ago when Maude realized it was getting late. She worries, you know. We thought Hila might have come here for tea. I'm sure it's nothing. No doubt she lost track of the time. Sorry to bother you."

I glanced at the clock on the stove. Six-thirty. Hila and I were always back from our walks before four.

"I'll help you look," Jake said.

"I don't know where *to* look. She doesn't have any friends. Other than you, Hannah. She never goes anywhere, and there isn't anyplace she can go. Certainly not on foot."

"Is Buddy with her?" Lily asked.

Grant shook his head. "No. The dog's at home."

"I'm sure she's simply taken a wrong path," Joanne said. "It's easy enough to get lost in the woods, isn't it? Does she have a cell phone?"

Grant shook his head. "Didn't seem any point in getting her one. As I said, she has no one to call."

"Jake'll check our property," Joanne said. "She might have…" my sister looked at me "…tripped and fallen. I'll phone the houses on the road, ask if anyone's seen her."

"I'd appreciate that," Grant said. "We don't know the neighbors." He pulled a slip of paper out of his pocket. "Here's our number."

"We'll call if we find anything," Jake said, accepting the card.

He walked Grant Harrison to the door. He didn't come back into the kitchen, but went through the office to the porch for his boots.

"Finish your dinner, kids," Joanne said. "I have a few phone calls to make and then we'll have dessert."

"Is Hila okay?" Lily asked. "She should have taken Buddy with her. Buddy wouldn't get lost."

"I'm sure she's perfectly fine. Mr. Harrison's worrying about nothing. It's such a nice evening, I bet Hila decided she'd like a lovely long walk, that's all."

I stayed at the kitchen table while the kids finished their dinner. Joanne made her phone calls and came back, giving me a quick shake of her head. She served up ice cream and tiny perfect strawberries and told Charlie and Lily they could take their dessert to watch TV for half an hour. She and I sat at the table, drinking tea. Jake was soon back, saying, "Not a sign of her, but I found that rooster of yours and brought him back. He's lucky it was me found him and not a fox or a coyote."

# Chapter Fourteen

I didn't sleep much that night. Omar was back, as strong as ever. I lay in the dark and listened to the sleeping house and hoped Hila had found her way home. Grant had not called again, but there was a distance to him and perhaps it wouldn't have occurred to him that it would be polite to let us know she was safe.

When the first soft light touched the edges of the blinds, I rolled out of bed and made my way downstairs in my nightgown. I made tea and was hugging the mug between my hands when Jake came in. He was dressed, but his hair was tousled and he was rubbing sleep out of his eyes. He gave me a look and said, "No breakfast?"

"What?"

"You can't even make the coffee? Never mind. I'll get it started. We've got a busy day ahead of us. Tomorrow's Saturday, market day, and we have a lot to do to get ready. You could help out now and again, you know, Hannah. Like make breakfast."

Stung by the criticism, I said, "I'm sorry. I didn't sleep last night. I don't like coffee when I'm not feeling well."

"Some of us do." He got out the frying pan and went to the fridge for eggs and bread. His movements were quick and sharp, and I could tell he was angry.

"Looks like it's going to be a nice day," I said, trying to sound friendly.

He grunted in reply and cracked eggs into a bowl.

Footsteps sounded upstairs and water rushed down the pipes.
It was Joanne's turn to drive to camp, and she said she'd take
Charlie this morning as well. She hustled the children outside as
soon as they finished eating. I remained at the kitchen table with
my now-cold cup of tea. The headache had settled into a dull
throb and it would be gone soon. I glanced at the clock. Seven-
thirty. Too early to phone the Harrisons for an update on Hila.

By the time I had my shower, dressed, and headed out to
collect the eggs, Joanne's car was back in the driveway. I heard
voices in the greenhouse and headed over, thinking I might
volunteer to pack the boxes for market.

"…my sister," Joanne said as I approached.

I stopped walking.

"I know that," Jake said, "But how long do you plan to look
after her?"

"As long as she needs."

"Needs. She'll *need* looking after forever. She swans around
in her nightgown doing nothing but lifting a cold compress to
her forehead, and you and Lily treat her like she's a Victorian
maiden having the vapors." He raised his voice to an imitation
of a woman. "Can I get you your pills, Aunt Hannah? Here's
a cup of tea, Hannah. No, no, don't get up, Hannah. I'll get it
for you."

"You're not being fair. She's had a major brain injury. You
heard what Mom said."

"Yeah, your mom said she might never be able to work again.
Christ, Joanne, does that mean she'll be living here when the
kids are in university?"

*My mom thought I might never recover?*

"Please, Jake. She can't live on her own. She's much better
here than in Mom and Dad's condo in the city. They don't have
the room for one thing."

"They could make room if they wanted to."

"The new doctor told her being in the country was good for
her. Apparently people heal faster among nature."

Jake snorted. "Send her to a nursing home where she can sit out in the garden all day with the other loonies."

"You can't be serious! She's my sister. What do you want me to do? What can I do?"

"If you won't send her to your parents, you can stop coddling her for one thing. And you can tell Lily to back off. What the hell do you think you're teaching our daughter? If she's weak and helpless everyone'll make a fuss over her?"

I felt tears gathering behind my eyes. I thought I was a great role model for Lily.

I had been. Once.

"She's hurt, Jake. People with her were killed, remember?"

"Yeah, and she'll be milking that until the day she dies. I can't afford to feed a useless mouth, Joanne."

"She helps out."

"Right, she collects the eggs. And heats up soup you canned. Anything else? Nope. She's damned useless. Even Connor trips all over himself to help her with the lunch dishes. All she accomplishes is to give you more work. No, hear me out. She's not trying to get better. She pops pills and sleeps all day. She's been here two months, Joanne. Long enough. Send her back to your parents or find a place that will take her. She's not my responsibility anymore."

I'd heard enough. I crept around the corner of the greenhouse and cut across the yard to the chicken coop, trying to stay concealed behind a tractor and the WWOOFERS' trailer. Tears streamed down my face. Omar laughed and echoed Jake. *Damned useless.*

As I was rounding the corner of the trailer, a car pulled up. I ducked down.

It was Connor's car, but he sat in the passenger seat. A man was driving. He had small dark eyes, short black hair, and a full beard. His eyes swept the farmyard as Connor got out. A bandage was wrapped around his left hand. The car backed up and turned into the road in a spray of gravel.

Joanne emerged from the greenhouse and walked toward Connor. Her footsteps were hard and her face set into angry lines. One didn't need to be eavesdropping to know she'd had a fight with her husband.

"Morning, Joanne." Connor lifted his hand. "All fixed up. I had an idea yesterday and want to talk to you about it."

"You're late," she snapped.

Connor shrugged. "Sorry. My cousin's car's in the shop so he needs to use mine."

"Liz is getting the produce bagged and labeled for tomorrow. Go and help her. And then I want you stringing the tomatoes. We're way behind this year."

"Yes, ma'am. Anything else, ma'am?"

"Mock me and you're fired. Get it?" She was not joking.

Connor's face fell. "Gee. Sorry."

I waited until everyone had gone about their business before coming out of hiding. I slipped back into the house and went up to my room. Where I lay on my bed and had a good long cry.

I *was* sick. I *was* trying. I *wanted* to get better. I *wanted* to go back to work. I *wanted* my life back. I was *not* a candidate for the loony bin.

I wanted to smash my fist into Omar's leering grin.

Rather than retreating, Omar regrouped his forces and crept forward. I gritted my teeth and determined that I was not going to give in.

I wasn't.

I grabbed my pill bottle and twisted the top open. I shook one into my hand. Not many left.

Could I stay here? If Jake didn't want me?

Joanne wanted me.

Did she? Or did she just feel she had to defend me to her husband?

I lay on my bed and cried some more.

I cried for Simon and for the child I would never know. I cried for my job and for all the lost women. I cried for Hila and her ruined face and dead family.

Hila.

*How could I possibly have forgotten about Hila?*

I rolled out of bed and went to the bathroom to splash water on my face. I peered at myself in the mirror. I looked, quite simply, as bad as I felt. Thick black clouds crowded the edges of my vision. I narrowed my eyes and tried to peer through a tunnel in the center as I made my way downstairs to get the piece of paper Grant had left with his phone number. I could hardly see by the time I got to the bottom.

The doorbell rang.

No one else, of course, was in the house to get it.

It was the police. An Ontario Provincial Police officer in dark blue uniform with a pale blue-gray stripe running down the pant leg. He was young, tall and lanky, and totally bald. His huge ears stuck out to the sides making it look as if he were preparing to take flight.

"Ms. Manning?" he said

"One of them. Is it about Hila?"

"Yes."

"She isn't…?"

"Ms. Popalzai has been reported missing. I understand Mr. Harrison came here yesterday looking for her."

"That's right. My brother-in-law searched the property and my sister phoned the neighbors. No sign of her."

"Are they home? We'd like permission to do a full search of your property."

"They're out in the fields, I think. I can call them and ask them to come in."

"Please," he said. "I'm Constable Graves, by the way."

"Hannah Manning." I pulled my cell phone out of my pocket. I called Joanne and told her what was happening. I thought it best to leave it to her to contact Jake.

I told the officer I'd meet him at the side door and went to put on my boots. A plain car pulled into the driveway and parked beside the farm shop. Two people got out. A woman, dressed in beige trousers, matching light-weight summer jacket, and black boots. The man wore a leather jacket over an open-necked shirt and chinos and dark sunglasses. The woman said something to Graves, but the man did not offer greetings. He studied the farm yard.

Jake arrived at a run. Joanne followed on her beat-up old bike. Liz was back at work after yesterday's illness, and she and Connor came out of the greenhouse to see what was going on. They kept their distance.

The police officer introduced himself, and he and Jake shook hands. The woman stepped forward and also took Jake's hand, but the man in plain clothes stood back. Jake's eyes flicked toward him, but he said nothing.

I didn't need to be introduced. I knew who, or rather what, he was.

"I'm Sergeant McNeil," the woman said to Jake and Joanne. "We'd like your permission to search your property. Ms. Hila Popalzai has been reported missing, and Mr. Harrison tells us she regularly walks in the woods that run behind your farm."

"That's right." Jake pointed at me. He did not look at my face. "Hannah there often went with her."

"There are snowmobile paths all through these woods. A maze of them. I suppose someone could get lost." I didn't add that one could get lost all right, for about an hour. This wasn't the wilderness. Roads, houses, and farms surrounded the small patches of woodland. Just keep walking and you'd come to a road before long. And a friendly local passing by would be more than happy to give you a lift.

Was Hila hurt, lying somewhere with a broken leg?

Had the friendly local turned out to be not so friendly?

"We have searchers out," McNeil said. "A dog's trying to find her path from the Harrison house. Unfortunately Mr. and Mrs. Harrison were all over the trails behind their house searching yesterday and the dog's having trouble getting the scent."

"I checked the farm last night," Jake said. "Didn't see any sign of her."

"Nevertheless, I'd like to have a look around. May I go into your outbuildings?"

Jake bit off the question. *What would Hila be doing hiding in the barn or the potting shed?* "Sure, go ahead."

"Mind the plants, please," Joanne said. "Don't trample them."

McNeil gave her a smile. "I won't." She hesitated and glanced behind her at the man watching. He jerked his head and McNeil and Graves set off. Liz had returned to her chores in the greenhouse, but Connor watched, arms crossed.

"Ms. Manning," the remaining man said to me. "I'd like a few minutes of your time."

"My sister isn't well," Joanne jumped in. "Perhaps you can come back later."

"It's okay," I said. The pill I'd taken was having no effect. My vision had narrowed to a pinprick and the pain was intense. "I want to help."

"Who are you, anyway?" Jake said.

"Rick Brecken."

"And you work for…?"

"The government," Brecken replied. "Why don't you give my buddies a hand? You wouldn't want them stepping on your lettuce, now would you?"

Jake bristled. Joanne jumped in before he could say something he might regret. "I'll help Hannah into the house."

Conscious of Jake and what he thought of me, I said, "Go back to work. I'm fine."

"I doubt that. But if you insist."

Jake glowered at Brecken, and then turned and followed his wife.

I headed for the office door. The sun was strong and bright and my head was full of pain. Brecken could follow me. Or not.

CSIS or RCMP? CSIS probably. The Mounties would be more likely to identify themselves. I didn't try to speculate as to what CSIS—the Canadian Security Intelligence Service—would want with a woman who'd not returned from an afternoon stroll in Prince Edward County. Hila Popalzai was from Afghanistan. She was a Muslim.

Enough said.

I kicked off my shoes and went into the kitchen. I dropped into a chair and closed my eyes. Brecken's boots pounded the floorboards as he followed.

"You're still having problems from the IED?" He'd pushed his sunglasses onto the top of his head.

I wasn't surprised he knew who I was. These people didn't care to find themselves in situations in which they didn't know who all the players were and what was going on. No matter, hadn't Maude Harrison said everyone in the county knew my story?

"Yeah."

"Tough."

"Yeah."

"Tell me about Hila Popalzai." He was in his early forties. Over six feet, well-tanned, short-cropped salt-and-pepper hair, close-shaven, chest broad, neck thick. His skin was pitted with the ravages of teenage ache, and his penetrating black eyes gave nothing away.

I kept my eyes closed against waves of pain as I talked. "I have nothing to tell. She lived with Grant and Maude Harrison. As you see, I'm somewhat of an invalid. She and I found we enjoyed walking together most afternoons."

"You talk much about Afghanistan?"

"No."

"No?"

"No. We didn't talk much about anything. I never even told her I'd been there. That I'd been injured there. That I lost…people there. She just knew. She never talked about her past either."

"I find that hard to believe."

"Tough. It's the truth."

"Was she happy with the Harrisons?"

"Happy? I doubt she knows what that word means. She was safe, that would have been good enough for any Afghan woman."

I opened my eyes a sliver. Brecken sat at the end of a long back tunnel. "At least, she thought she was safe. Was she? Is she?"

"She's gone missing."

"I know that. It's why you're here, right. You think something's happened to her."

"I think nothing."

"But you're here. Looking for her."

"If you didn't talk about Afghanistan, did she have much to say about her family?"

"Nothing."

"Again nothing?"

"That's right. She told me not one solitary thing about her family. And I did not ask."

"You must have told her something of your experiences in her country."

"Mr. Brecken. I said that I did not. Therefore I did not. No doubt you expect that because I'm a journalist I'd be digging around trying to find out her story, but I didn't meet her because I'm a journalist. I met her because I'm a woman who suffered a severe trauma and still gets incapacitating headaches. I find that walks in the woods help me. And it's better for someone who isn't always fully functioning to have company. *Comprende?*"

"What did she think about Grant and Maude Harrison?"

"Gee, you really don't get it, do you? I don't know what she thought about them. Because she didn't fuckin' tell me."

"No need to get upset, Hannah."

"I'm beginning to find your questions upsetting." *Arrogant fuckwit.* The expression Simon used whenever he ran up against military obstinacy. Simon had a deep inbuilt loathing of bureaucracy. This Brecken would have gotten under Simon's skin. An MI5-wanna-be. Probably took his tea shaken not stirred. For a moment my mind drifted, and I thought of Simon, yelling and stomping about our hotel room in Dubai because…I couldn't remember what he'd been so mad about.

"Did she seem happy there?" Brecken kept on.

"Sure. Like Buddy the dog seems happy. She didn't cower in terror every time they approached."

"No need to get sarcastic."

"No need to keep hounding me."

"Hannah, I'm not hounding you, and I apologize if you think I am. You seem to be the only person, apart from the Harrisons and the folks at the mosque in Belleville, who she spent any time with. Of course I want to know what you talked about."

"Nothing. Like I said. We talked about almost nothing. She told me about her studies. She's taking university courses online. I got the feeling, just a feeling, that she's content here. She liked the woods. We went to the beach a few times in May and she loved it. She said she'd never seen the ocean until she was on the plane coming here and Lake Ontario seems limitless, like the sea. But once the crowds started coming she didn't want to go any more. She smiled at Maude and Grant if they said something amusing, and she did seem fond of their dog, Buddy." She asked me what it meant to be free. I didn't tell Brecken that.

"Are your sister and her husband good friends with the Harrisons?"

"Not at all. We hardly ever see them. Grant Harrison was here last night, looking for Hila. He'd never been in this house before. I don't think his wife has either."

"Thank you, Hannah." His chair scraped across the floor.

"What's your interest? You're CSIS, Mr. Brecken. You don't normally spend your valuable time helping local cops search for adult women who've been missing for less than twenty-four hours."

The edges of his mouth turned up. It made him look almost human. "If you remember anything or can think of anywhere Ms. Popalzai might have gone, call the local O.P.P. detachment. They'll get a message to me."

"I have absolutely no doubt about that."

# Chapter Fifteen

Brecken left and I remained in my chair, trying to relax. The pain in my head retreated, ever so slightly, and the tunnel that was my range of vision expanded. When I heard voices outside I went to the living room and stood at the windows looking out over the driveway. Sergeant McNeil came back with Constable Graves. They spoke briefly to Brecken, then got into their respective cars and drove away without a backward glance.

"No sign of her," Joanne said from behind me. I hadn't heard her come in.

"I guessed not."

"They said they have a dog going through the woods. If she's…injured, he should find her."

"That's good."

"And they're checking all the properties along the road. Hannah, Jake and I have been thinking."

"I have too," I said quickly. She was going to tell me I had to move out. Go to Mom and Dad's. Or the *loony bin*. "I was considering seeing if I can move back into my condo early. Maybe pay the tenants off to get them to leave."

She reached out and touched my shoulder. "You can't live on your own. Not yet."

"You're probably right. Anyway, now that I'm seeing that doctor in Picton I wouldn't want to go back to Toronto. So, I've decided that even though you turned me down earlier, I'm going to start paying my way."

"No, Hannah."

"Yes. I'm still being paid by the paper. Seventy percent long-term disability insurance. I've nothing to spend it on out here. The rent from my tenant covers the mortgage on my condo." I gave her a smile.

She studied my face. "I won't say we couldn't use the money. Farming doesn't exactly lead to a lavish lifestyle. But we get by, and I don't want to be paid for helping my sister."

"I'm not going to pay you. Just help out."

To my considerable surprise she began to cry. I gathered her into my arms and held her. For the first time in a long while I was the one doing the sheltering, the comforting. Omar slipped away. "Gee," I said at last, "what brought this on?"

She pulled back and wiped a hand across her eyes. "We've been having some problems, Jake and me. Nothing big, mind, but it's hard sometimes working together all the time. Worrying about the farm. "

"Is the farm in trouble?"

She shook her head and rummaged in her copious pockets for a tissue. "Nothing in particular. Nothing new. It's a tough business. A couple of CSA shareholders dropped out this year. We rely on the money from the CSA to get us up and running before we start earning any cash from what we grow. All the expense is in the spring; all the profit in the fall. The WWOOFERS won't be coming. They got a better offer out in B.C. We need them. Jake's not happy with Connor. He says the guy puts up a nice front about wanting to be a farmer, but slacks off whenever he can. Disappears sometimes. Jake was planning to sack Connor soon as the WWOOFERS arrived. Now, I guess we're stuck with him. Lucky to have reliable farm help at all."

"I'm glad I can help out then."

"You'll make Lily very happy."

"Why?"

"She doesn't know, yet, but Jake's decided we have to sell the horses."

"Oh, no."

"Two useless mouths to feed, he calls them. Just another expense." She ran her hand lightly down my arm. "Maybe you could offer to support them?"

"Sure. Be glad to."

Joanne punched me. "You're not so bad, you know. For an older sister."

"You turned out okay, too."

"I gotta get back to work. Don't say anything to Jake, eh? Farmers get pretty upset at what they think is charity."

"I won't."

"Maybe mention you'd like to help Lily by paying for the upkeep of the horses."

She started to walk away and turned back to me. "You haven't been to the doctor in a while. You should, you know. I can tell you're not feeling well right now."

I shifted my feet and glanced to one side. "I'm okay," I mumbled.

"Make an appointment, Hannah. Please."

◇◇◇

Charlie was the first child home from day camp. He burst through the doors, scarcely able to talk around a mouthful of excitement. He'd seen police cars, lining the road outside the Harrison property. And policemen walking along the shoreline. And a boat, a big white police boat, searching the water. Could he go and watch, he asked his mother. Maybe he'd find a clue.

She sent him off with a DVD she'd been saving for a special occasion.

Lily, however, was not so easy to discourage.

"They're not even using Buddy," she complained. "Buddy will be able to find her. Buddy knows her, that police dog doesn't."

"The police dog's trained to search," Joanne said, "Buddy'll run off after a rabbit. Do you want juice or milk?"

"But…"

"Lily, please. Let the police do what they do, okay?"

"Aunt Hannah, have you shown them where Hila and you went walking?"

"Lily, drop it!" her mother ordered.

"But…"

"We understand that you care," I said. "I care and so does your mom. If the police want our help they'll ask for it."

She pouted. "I'll have another look around our land. Dad might have overlooked something. Dad's never met Hila, he doesn't know what she looks like."

Joanne knew when she was defeated. "Stay out of the vegetables and don't put a foot off our property. I have to get back outside, and I'll be watching, young lady. If I see a toe cross the boundary you'll be in trouble." She gave me a look, and I said, "I'll come with you, Lily. Two pairs of eyes are better than one."

Lily and I walked the perimeter of the farm. Lily kept her eyes on the ground, although I knew it was a useless exercise. Jake had searched, the police had searched, and the farm workers had been told to keep watch. Still, it made Lily think she was doing something to help her friend, and that was important.

Connor and Liz were weeding lettuce; Allison harvested eggplant. An airplane, painted dark gray with no markings, no doubt from the big military base nearby, flew overhead, drawing a white line in the soft blue sky.

We found nothing at all out of the ordinary.

Lily continued to worry. While I set the table for dinner and Joanne stirred the pasta, Lily called Maude Harrison to ask if there was any news. We would tell by the look on her face as she hung up the phone that there wasn't.

It was understandable, I thought, her anxiety about her friend. Neither of her parents had ever met Hila; thus there was no intimacy to their concern. I thought they didn't fully understand how this was affecting their daughter. Lily's a ten-year-old girl, loved, protected, cared for and nourished. Safe in her world.

I watched her twirling pasta in her fork and felt my heart break.

# Chapter Sixteen

Saturday morning I came downstairs to a pouting Lily and an exasperated Joanne.

"I can't take the day off whether you and Ashley are disappointed or not, and that's all there is to it," my sister was saying.

She was at the stove, stirring a pot of oatmeal. Lily stood by the French doors, glaring at her mother. She wore jeans faded with layers of deeply ground-in dirt. Her arms were crossed over her thin chest and, as the saying goes, if looks could kill…

"Problem?" I grabbed a mug from the drying rack. I could guess what the problem was. Last night after supper Joanne had tried to pull Lily out of her funk by talking about today's riding adventure. It had worked and Lily cheered up and began bubbling over with enthusiasm at the prospect of going riding with a friend and the friend's mother.

It worked too well, I suspected, as this morning the brown riding helmet sat on the counter, abandoned.

"Mom won't let Ashley and me go riding by ourselves," Lily huffed. "She says we're too *young*."

"Enough, Lily," Joanne warned, tasting the oatmeal.

The girl made a face, after first ensuring her mother's back was turned.

"What happened?" I rummaged in the cupboard for a tea bag. "You said last night your friend's mom was taking you girls out."

"That was Rachel, Ashley's mom, on the phone just now," Joanne said. "She fell in the night and twisted her ankle. The ride's off."

"Does Ashley have her own horse?" I asked.

"Yes."

"Then I'll take you," I said to Lily.

Her face broke into a wide smile. "Great!"

Joanne wasn't quite so enthusiastic. "You most certainly will not."

"Why not? You have two horses, so there's one for me. You have two saddles and all the equipment. I'd enjoy going for a ride."

"Don't be ridiculous. You can't ride."

"Of course I can. You must remember all the riding we did as girls."

"That was a long time ago. When was the last time you were on a horse?"

"As a matter of fact, it was the summer before last. When I went on a week-long horsepacking excursion in Alberta for my vacation. Six to seven hours a day on horseback, wilderness, steep mountain trails. Makes what you have around here a walk in the park."

"You sent pictures," Lily said. "That was so fantastic. You said you'll take me one year."

Joanne turned to face me, the large wooden spoon, dripping oatmeal, held up in front of her like a weapon. "And suppose you start feeling ill, Hannah. What then?"

"If that should happen, I'll bring the girls home. We aren't talking about going into the backcountry. We'll be what, a maximum of fifteen minutes, half an hour, from home at the most."

Lily was staring at her mother with wide, hopeful eyes.

"Besides," I said, "the doctor told me I need to get more fresh air and exercise."

"Lily," Joanne said, "go to your room for a few minutes. I want to talk to your aunt."

The girl jumped off her chair, smile back in place. "Does that mean yes?"

"It means I want to talk to your aunt."

Lily gave me a thumbs up and left the room.

"I can ride, Joanne," I said. "Very well. That's not an issue. I'm feeling good this morning." That was true. I'd had a proper night's sleep and my head was just fine. I'd been to the barn a couple of times to admire the horses, and I'd helped Lily brush them down and pour feed or water, but I'd had no interest at all in riding until I saw Lily's disappointed face and realized that in this one thing, at least, I could help.

Joanne let out a long sigh. "I don't know," she said. "I wasn't at all disappointed when Rachel called to say she couldn't take the girls. I'd prefer it if Lily stay out of the woods for a while."

"Why?" I asked, although I could guess.

Joanne lowered her voice. "Hila went for a walk. She never came back."

"If, and it's still an *if*, something happened to Hila, and some-one was…responsible, he'll be long gone. The police searched the woods thoroughly yesterday. Anyway, we're not one lone woman. We'll be three people on horses."

"I know that. Doesn't mean I like it."

"It might even do Lily some good. I'll tell her we'll keep an eye out for Hila. She's excited now about going riding, but she'll remember Hila soon enough and start worrying again. This way she can think she's doing something positive."

"I still don't know."

"I'll look after your daughter, Joanne."

She studied my face. "I know you will, but who's going to look after you?" She did not smile.

"Lily."

"Okay, I give in. Get her down here, and tell her to call Ashley with the good news. I absolutely have to get some work done on the farm accounts today. I promised myself last year I wouldn't let it all pile up. And there it is, piling up." Jake, I knew, had left before the sun was up for market day in Kingston. Liz and

Allison had gone with him and Connor had the day off. Charlie was in his room, head bent over his computer.

I sniffed the air. "The oatmeal's burning."

Joanne swore heartily.

It was a beautiful day for a ride, and I found my spirits lifting as we got the horses ready. It was nice to be in the barn, the scent of feed and hay and saddles and horses, light streaming in through the open door and the windows in the loft, small cats watching from the shadows, the clatter of equipment, the stomping of hooves. Reminded me of my childhood when I'd gone riding every chance I could get. Black Beauty and Tigger were waiting for us when we arrived, tossing their heads, and blowing in their eagerness, as if they knew what was ahead.

Lily gave Tigger an affectionate pat, but it was Beauty who clearly had the girl's heart. She stroked the long soft nose and the horse pushed against her hand asking for more. A barn cat jumped down from the loft, and Tigger snorted. "You'll ride Tigger, is that okay, Aunt Hannah?"

"Fine with me. He looks like a lively thing." Tigger watched me through enormous black eyes. He swished his tail and didn't look all that impressed. I opened the stall door and led him out.

I went through the familiar motions of getting the horses saddled and ready. Lily's equipment was old and well-used but she kept it clean and in good shape.

We were ready when Ashley's father arrived with his daughter and her horse. He unloaded the small white mare from the horse trailer while the two girls danced in circles in their excitement.

"Rachel says thanks for doing this," he said to me, throwing the saddle blanket over the mare's back. "Ashley was, to put it mildly, disappointed when her mom said the ride was cancelled." Short, tubby, and balding, he wore crisply ironed beige shorts and a blue golf shirt. Clearly not a farmer.

"I'm looking forward to it." I reached out a hand and touched the horse's neck. "What's this lady's name?"

"Snowflake," Ashley said, slipping the bit into the horse's mouth. Her dad held Snowflake steady while she mounted.

Effortlessly, Lily swung up onto Beauty, and I gathered Tigger's reins in one hand and grabbed the saddle. I lifted my leg and stepped into the stirrup. There I balanced, one foot in the stirrup, toes on the ground, and I felt a jolt of fear. Omar might react very badly indeed to this unaccustomed position. Did I want to take on the responsibility of leading these two sweet girls into the woods?

"Did you hear that Madeleine got grounded for a whole month for telling her mom she was going to a movie with the church group and instead going with Raquel?"

"No!" Lily said, "A whole month in the summer!"

"Madeleine's mom says Raquel's white trash." Beauty and Snowflake began to move. The girls' high-pitched voices faded. Tigger took a couple of steps. I had to hop after him.

"Something wrong?"

Ashley's dad was looking at me, his head cocked in question.

"Nothing. Just getting steady." I gave him a smile, trying to look confident, shoved myself off the ground, swung my leg over Tigger's wide rump and settled into the saddle. I shifted to find the right position and adjusted the reins. The leather saddle squeaked.

"Have Ashley call the house when she's ready to come home."

"Will do." Without being prompted Tigger set off after the other horses.

I had been highly optimistic when convincing Joanne that I was up to the trip and then in the barn with the horses, but now that I was actually mounted, I was having my reservations. I didn't know what the rhythmic up and down of my body matching the horse's gait would do to my head. I kept my eyes firmly on the two girls in front of me, hoping the sight of their young bodies and boundless enthusiasm for life would keep Omar from bothering me.

Whether it was that Omar couldn't bear being near the girls' joy, or that my head was healing itself in a proper scientific manner, I felt good. I was almost surprised to find myself relaxing and enjoying the outing.

The girls went ahead while we rounded the fields, and then fell into single file to enter the woods. Lily first, Ashley in the middle, and me bringing up the rear. The woods in Prince Edward County are not the great boreal forest, nor do they bear much similarity to the Canadian wilderness to the north. The trees are mostly hardwood—maple and oak, poplar and birch—with a scattering of pine and cedar. They were logged extensively, and little, if any, old growth remains. Thick patches of undergrowth and twigs and broken branches littered the forest floor. Birds, sparrows and chickadees and the occasional finch, darted between the trees, filling the air with cries of warning. In the open, the rising sun was hot on our heads and backs, but as soon as we passed under the green canopy the temperature dropped. The scent of the forest was all around us, the pungent decay of dead and dying vegetation, the fresh growth of new life. The girls stopped chattering, and other than the trill of birdsong and the steady tread of horses' hooves, all was quiet. I took a deep breath and felt good air pass through my lungs and was pleased I'd come.

We followed a winding snowmobile trail for about an hour. It would be hard to get lost out here—the snowmobilers had erected signs pointing out the directions. We travelled through deep woods and skirted fields planted in long straight rows. Being a farmer's daughter, Lily didn't have to be told to keep away from the burgeoning vegetation. My mind wandered and I thought about Hila. I'd overheard Jake telling Joanne, in a voice pitched low so the children wouldn't hear, that a description of Hila was going up on signposts all over town. No one had a photograph of her they could use. Traffic had been exceptionally busy up and down our road yesterday and again this morning, and we'd seen lights moving in the woods both behind the farm and on the lake side of the road last night. Divers and boats, Jake said, were being brought in.

I had little doubt she was dead. A woman like Hila wouldn't just up and leave the only home she had. She was so skittish she didn't like to be seen so much as walking down the open road.

The police weren't saying so, but I'd been a reporter long enough to know they were looking for a body. I glanced up ahead at the girls, saw their proud straight backs, their ponytails bouncing behind them, their pant legs thick with mud and horsehair. I heard their peals of laughter and spurts of excited gossip and murmurs of affectionate enthusiasm to their mounts.

I realized my hands were clenched so tightly around the reins they were hurting. Where was he now, the monster who'd taken one as innocent as Hila? Long gone, I hoped. Off to torment some other town, some other sweet young woman, goddamn him. Then I remembered Rick Brecken and who he was. CSIS. Intelligence. If a local woman had gone missing, the police probably wouldn't have come out in force until forty-eight hours had passed. If it had been a child, they'd be searching sooner, but not with the involvement of the security services, for sure. That Brecken was here, watching the police searching, meant they didn't suspect any random serial killer or sexual sadist was responsible for Hila's disappearance.

It had to be political.

Who was she? More than just an Afghan refugee plucked from the camps and given a rare opportunity to come to Canada?

I hadn't asked her about herself. Not that she was likely to have answered if I had. Somewhere, deep within my gut something moved, and I cursed myself for not showing more interest. The remnants of my journalistic self, which I'd thought long dead, perhaps. It's not as if I'd ever allowed an interviewee's reticence to stop me from probing before.

If Hila had been taken because of who she was, not just a random act of violence, then Lily and Ashley were safe.

As safe as young girls could ever be in this world.

Up ahead, Lily came to a halt. I was so deep in thought, Tigger almost ran into the back of Rachel's mount before I noticed and pulled him to a stop. He lowered his big head and immediately began pulling up weeds. As he munched happily, I peered around the girls and saw that we'd reached a road. Lily turned in the saddle and said, "Shall we cross?"

"What's the time?"

We'd been riding for almost an hour. I suggested we have a break and enjoy the snacks Rachel and Joanne had packed and then head slowly home. My head was fine, but I knew my legs and butt would be feeling the unaccustomed exercise soon enough. We tied the horses loosely to a couple of birch trees, and let them graze. Lily and Rachel threw themselves on the ground, and I found a rotting stump on which to sit. We drank water from stainless steel bottles and ate crackers and local cheese and carrots picked last night and homemade brownies. The girls laughed and talked, the horses grazed, and I closed my eyes and felt content.

"We'd better be heading back," I said at last. "You girls might be up to riding for the rest of the day, but I'm not."

As expected they protested but without putting much effort into it, and soon we were mounted and retracing our steps. Lily seemed to know where she was going, and if it took a bit longer to get back to where we'd begun, I pretended not to notice.

We came to a small but fast-moving stream not much more than a hundred yards from the edges of Joanne's pea field. Lily allowed Beauty to stop for a drink, and Ashley and I came up beside her.

"That was fun," Lily said, while the animals silently drank their fill. Water gurgled and splashed as it sought its way around the obstructions of boulders and horse's legs. "Can we do it again tomorrow, Aunt Hannah?"

I laughed, pleasure mixed with a groan. "I doubt I'll be capable of moving tomorrow. But it was fun, and yes I'd love to do it again."

Tigger lifted his head and let out a soft whinny. We heard a branch breaking and leaves rustling and then a single bark.

"Hey!" Lily shouted. "Buddy, here we are. Over here."

Buddy, the Harrison's old dog, broke out of the undergrowth and ran into the clearing, tail wagging furiously.

"Is anyone there?" I called. Getting no answer I said, more to myself than to Lily, "If people want to have a dog they should look after it."

"Buddy looks after himself, don't you?" Lily said.

I said nothing in reply. Bad enough they left the old mutt to wander through the woods, but the Harrisons also didn't seem to care if he walked down the road whenever he took a mind to.

Buddy was caked in mud and burrs, from his filthy muzzle to the tip of his ragged tail. A clump of burrs were sticking his single complete ear to the top of his head. Served the Harrisons right, I thought. Let the dog wander where and when it pleased, and you have to clean up after it. Even from the added height provided by the horse I could smell rancid old dog and muck and stagnant water and who knows what else. It hadn't rained much recently, and not for a few days, so the fields and woods were mostly dry. Stupid dog must have been cavorting in the stream or in the marshland further up behind the Harrisons' property.

"What's he got stuck to his tail?" Ashley asked.

It was a scrap of cloth. Black. As I looked, a shaft of sunlight broke through the gap in the canopy of trees and shone on streaks of dark blue thread. I sucked in a breath and swung myself off the horse.

Lily started to dismount, but I snapped at her to stay where she was. I approached the dog slowly, murmuring sweet nothings. I dropped to my haunches beside him. He sniffed at my hand, and I took a firm grip on his collar.

"What are you doing, Aunt Hannah?" Lily asked. I did not reply.

I grabbed at the cloth with my free hand. It was stuck to a clump of burrs in the dog's bushy tail. He whined and tried to pull his rear end away, but I was holding on and the cloth came free, along with a good bit of dog hair.

"Go straight home, both of you," I said to the watching girls. "Now. Tell your mother to call the police. I'll wait here for them." I tightened my grip on Buddy's collar.

"What is it? What'd he find?" Lily asked.

"I said go now. Don't argue with me."

I heard water splash and horses move and the girls' excited voices urging their mounts on. They broke into a trot and, after an initial burst of twigs snapping and hooves crashing on rocks, the forest fell silent once again. Buddy squirmed, trying to free himself from my grip. I held fast and murmured what I hoped were comforting words. Behind me, Tigger stamped his feet. He decided he'd rather follow his friends back to the comfortable barn and a fresh bag of oats than stay with this strange human, and he simply walked away. I paid him no further attention.

My sweater was a baggy old thing, much too big for me. Fortunately it came with a belt that I'd looped up behind and tied the ends together. I pulled the belt off and used it to secure Buddy to a sapling. He threw me a filthy look, and then sat down and began vigorously washing his private parts.

I studied the scrap of cloth I'd freed from his rat's nest of a tail.

I'd seen it before.

As Hila pulled her scarf across her face in an attempt to conceal her scars.

# Chapter Seventeen

I'd sent the girls away more because I didn't want them asking questions than to go for help. As soon as I had Buddy secured, I pulled out the cellphone Joanne had reminded me to take. In case of an emergency, she'd said. I figured this counted as an emergency.

I phoned the house and she answered before the first ring died away. "Everything okay?" she asked without even saying hello.

For a moment, I considered being offended that she'd be so quick to assume everything was not okay. Instead I said, "We're fine. The girls are almost home." I heard the door slam and high-pitched voices calling out. "I guess they are home. Call the cops, Joanne. I'm in the woods behind the peas. Buddy's found something. Something of Hila's."

"What?"

"Part of her scarf."

"Is she…"

"All I have is a scarf. Call the cops. Tell them I'm waiting here with the dog. And don't let Lily and Ashley come back out here."

I hung up before my sister could ask any more questions.

I settled down beside Buddy and for lack of anything better to do began picking burrs out of his long fur. He whined and tried to snap at my fingers, but I growled back and reminded him I was doing him a favor. I thought of how exposed and vulnerable Hila would feel out in the open without her head covering, and I shivered despite the warmth of the sun.

We didn't have long to wait. Buddy heard them first and sat to attention with a bark. Voices called out and I answered and then we were surrounded by men and women in uniform.

My head swam as I struggled to my feet, and I knew Omar was on his way. "The dog found something," I said to the approaching officers. I held the evidence out in front of me. "This belonged…belongs, to Hila Popalzai, I'm sure of it. It's part of her headscarf."

By the time a hand held out a plastic bag and told me to drop the cloth in, my vision had narrowed to a small circle of light, surrounded by black curtains. Nerve endings screamed. Omar chuckled.

"Do you know where the dog found this?" a man asked. I recognized Rick Brecken's voice. CSIS had arrived mighty quickly.

I didn't dare shake my head. "No. We found him here. I was riding with my niece and a friend. The dog knows us. He came up to greet us. It was stuck onto his tail by a burr. "

"This is the Harrisons' dog, right?"

"Buddy. He was friends with Hila. They went walking together sometimes. A lot of the time."

"Okay," Brecken said. His voice hardened. "I thought you people searched the woods. Looks like you didn't do much of a job."

"We did," a woman replied, her tone defensive. "There's a lot of ground out here and that's nothing more than a scrap of cloth. The dog could have found it anywhere. He might have even brought it from the house."

"I don't need excuses," Brecken snapped. "I need results."

"Then get the hell out of the way and let us do our jobs."

"If you don't need me any further," I interrupted, not interested in listening to their jurisdictional squabbles. "I'd like to go home now."

I took a step and tripped over an exposed root. I would have fallen had not a strong hand shot out and grabbed me. "Watch where you're going," Brecken said. "We don't need any broken bones out here."

"Thank you so much for your concern." I pulled my arm away. I might have heard the female cop swallow a chuckle.

"Constable Kowalski," Sergeant McNeil said, "will you see this lady safely home, please. Tell Joanne Manning that no one is to come this way until further notice. Watch where you put your feet. Thank you for calling this in so promptly, Ms. Manning. I'm afraid we'll be bringing our equipment in over your sister's fields. Can't be helped but we'll try to diminish the damage."

I let the young cop lead me away. As we left the cool of the woods, more police passed us. A big German shepherd, ears like satellite dishes, hips low to the ground, walked with them. Buddy, who'd been left behind tied to the tree, barked. The humans grunted a greeting to my escort, and he said something in return. The pain in my head was building and I could barely see, but as long as I kept my eyes fixed on the ground I could walk without assistance, picking my way slowly and carefully. We came out of the woods to the northeast of the house, passed through neat rows of burgeoning peas and tomato plants of all sizes, dwarfed by the six foot high iron stakes that were used to hold the string that would soon bear the weight of the growing vegetation. We skirted the greenhouse. Being market day, the yard was unnaturally quiet.

As my feet touched the gravel of the driveway, I smelled woodsmoke and heard the creak of a wagon's wheels. The tall poplar trees that lined the drive shrunk to roughly cut stumps. The shot of a rifle came from the far distance. I dared to look up, and glanced toward the young police officer beside me. The skin on his face was pure white, and the edges of his body softened and faded. He gave me a friendly smile and through him I could see the outline of massive trees, far larger than I'd seen here before. I dared to glance at the back of the shop. Through the clouds of my vision I could make out a shadow standing at the entrance to the root cellar. A strong wind came out of nowhere and blew toward us and brought with it the scent of clothes worn too long without washing. The shadow moved and I heard fabric rustle. Mist shifted in the wind and a hand reached for me. The fingers were long and thin, the nails broken. An ugly burn was fresh on the wrist, and a healing cut crossed the pad of the thumb.

"Thank you, Constable," I said. "I'll be okay now. It was the shock, you know. You go on ahead and deliver your message to my sister. She'll want to know what's happening. I remembered something I have to get from the shop."

"Are you sure?" His voice sounded as if he were speaking from the bottom of a swimming pool. "You seemed a bit wobbly back there."

I did not reply and began to walk toward the clump of bushes and the door that led down to the root cellar. The hand fell and the shadow turned and was swallowed up by the deeper shadows of the old building.

I followed.

◇◇◇

### January 6, 1780

Maggie was in the parlor, Flora cuddled on her lap turning the pages of a book, when Mrs. MacDonald knocked on the door. To Maggie's surprise the woman was dressed in coat and hat and outdoor shoes, as though she were venturing out to church or to market. But it was not the day for either of those things.

The house was cold and Maggie had dressed Flora in one of her new sweaters, delighted at the perfect fit, and had wrapped herself in the shawl that came from her mother.

"Begging your pardon, Ma'am," Mrs. MacDonald said. "I'm right sorry, but I'm taking my leave."

"What?" Flora tugged at a ringlet and Maggie pried the hand away. The little girl had been restless in the night, saying her throat hurt, and Maggie feared she was coming down with a cold. Not enough good food, a cold damp house.

"I can't work here no more, Mrs. Macgregor. This is a tory house and I don't dare stay no longer."

"But, but…that has nothing to do with me."

"Janie what used to be the kitchen girl told me yesterday I daren't be seen in this house any longer. She's a bit simple, is

Janie, but she knows things sometimes, 'cause people talk around her. It ain't safe, Janie said. And I believe her. A word to the wise, Mrs. Macgregor, 'cause you've been a good mistress. It ain't safe for you here no more either."

"Not safe! In my own home. My husband's parents built this house. Cleared the land. He joined Sir John's regiment because he felt it was the right thing to do, but what have I, a woman, got to do with this political foolishness?"

"Mrs. Macgregor, you'd do well to leave here. Now. You must not stay." And with that she left.

"Mamma?" Flora said, her sweet face crunched in concern at the words she did not understand, although the tone had been plain enough.

Maggie ignored her daughter. She looked out the window. Snow was falling, drifting in fat flakes onto the calm, silent woods. A knot of anger threatened to choke her. She tried and tried to convince herself that this war was men's business and she and Flora wanted no part of it. Mrs. MacDonald was obviously mistaken.

"Why don't we have tea, shall we?" she said brightly to Flora. "We might have some of that sugar left."

Flora sneezed.

They came in the night.

They would have known the servants had quit or run off, the master of the house had left to join the British, that the woman and child were alone.

She was woken by a yell. Followed by another and then another until the house almost shook with the force of them. Heart pounding, she sat up in bed. Her room was full of red and yellow light as firelight poured through the windows.

A rock came crashing through the bedroom window. Downstairs, wood groaned and splintered and glass broke.

Flora had moved into Maggie's bed at the beginning of winter. Easier and cheaper to heat just the one bedroom. She scooped her child up, wrapped her tightly in a blanket against the cold of the January night. As she ran for the door, she grabbed a small box off her dresser and stuffed it beneath the girl's blanket. Flora woke and, sensing her mother's fear, started to cry.

By the time they reached the top of the stairs, men were pouring through the shattered door. Maggie clutched her child to her chest, scarcely believing what she was seeing. She recognized some of them. Men from town, from the surrounding farms. Mr. Harper who owned the dry goods shop. Mr. Richardson the farrier. Mr. Stone who owned a farm almost as prosperous as theirs had once been.

"Stop. Stop. What are you doing?" she cried. Men were snatching pictures off the walls and carrying small bits of furniture outside. A fellow came out of the dining room, bearing the box of silver, now almost empty as the bigger pieces had been sold for food. She saw young John Wilson, who used to lift his cap politely when she passed and inquire after her health. "Johnny, tell them to stop."

He looked up at her. His eyes were red in the light cast by his torch. "Tory bitch," he said in a voice more like a snake than a man. Men climbed the stairs. She was shoved aside. She fell, hard, not able to use her hands to soften the fall. A jolt of pain ran up her back and spread through her body. A boot lashed out and kicked her in the shoulder. Flora screamed in terror. Maggie huddled on the step and clutched her child.

The house was soon full, and not only with men. Women ran through the upstairs rooms, grabbing hats and dresses, candlesticks and ornaments, even the lovely infant things she was saving in hope of Hamish's return and a new baby some day. Mrs. O'Reilly, who often sat near Maggie in church, approached her. Maggie raised a hand. "Mrs. O'Reilly. Help me." The woman pulled back her head and spat. Minutes later she ran past, Maggie's best scarlet gown in her arms.

Firelight glowed at the far end of the hall. At first Maggie thought it was light from the torches, shining through the windows. Then to her horror she understood that her house was on fire. They were burning down her house. She pushed herself to her feet, her arms wrapped around the screaming bundle of her child. She staggered down the stairs. Men and women pushed her out of the way. Someone yelled, "Traitor," and punched her, hard, in the back. She staggered and fell. Fortunately she had reached the bottom step. Flora flew out of her arms but didn't have far to fall. Maggie scooped the hysterical child up and staggered outside. Fire threw sparks high into the night sky. The carriage house and the barn, as well as the back of the house, were on fire. As Maggie watched, the barn roof collapsed in a roar of flame.

Maggie carried Flora into the grove of trees on the far side of the wide curving drive. There must have been fifty people in her yard. People she'd sat in church with, exchanged gossip with, whose babies she'd admired and whose shops she'd frequented. Men and women danced in the light of the flames as if they'd gone mad and carried what was left of Maggie's worldly possessions away into the night.

Red streaks were crossing the sky in the east and the snow changed to an unforgiving icy rain. The fires died down and eventually went out, leaving a scorched and stinking ruin. The barn was a lump of blackened cinders, the back of the house not much better. Parts of the front of the house still stood. The porch, the entrance hall, the parlor. The heavy maple dining room table that could seat twelve lay in the drive, legs sticking up into the air. Too heavy, perhaps, for someone to carry off in the night. No doubt they'd be back, soon enough, to pick over the carcass.

Maggie was dressed in a white cotton nightgown. Her feet were bare. Fortunately, she'd wrapped Flora in a heavy blanket. She would not go back into the house, not even to search for clothes. She could not bear it.

She shifted Flora and realized the little wooden box was still in place.

Maggie and Flora met up with other Loyalist families on the road. Some had escaped with a horse, a wagon if they were very lucky, a scattering of belongings. A woman rushed to offer Maggie a dress and an apron to replace the dirty, torn, white nightgown and ill-fitting boots to offer her feet some protection from the frozen ground. Maggie smelled smoke, but she didn't know if it was from the dress—a plain brown homespun she would once have torn up for rags—or from herself. She didn't care. She hugged Flora and walked on. The apron had a large pocket, and she slipped the box into it.

Overhead clouds were thick and the rain was mixed with ice and snow. The band of refugees slept at the side of the road, huddled under cloaks or shawls or blankets, and didn't have much to eat, although one or two of the men had rifles and were able to shoot the occasional rabbit or goose.

As the ragged group approached Albany, Flora began to cough in earnest. By the time they reached New York City, the little girl was dead. They buried her in a quickly dug shallow grave, while an old man said words over her and his wife bound two sticks of wood into a make-shift grave marker, and a wolf howled in the distance.

# Chapter Eighteen

A dog barked and a man shouted. All was dark. For a moment I didn't know if my eyes were open or closed. I moved my eyelids and a crack of weak light began to appear. I felt around inside my head. No sign of Omar, and so I dared to open my eyes. A shaft of light, as thin as a razor blade, outlined the door. I was sitting down, and the floor was hard and cold beneath my bottom. No headache but the rest of my body hurt. I touched the damp stone of the walls and struggled to stand, and it took all the energy I could muster to find my wobbly feet. Getting myself upright took a long time. At last I made it, and I leaned against the wall, concentrating on taking time to breathe.

The door flew open and sunlight poured in and I yelped in pain as the harsh rays hit my face. A hand grabbed me and a man said, "Take it easy." With my eyes tightly closed, I allowed him to lead me out of the root cellar. When I was outside, I blinked and tried to focus. A group of people were watching me. The parking area was full of marked and unmarked police cars. A dog was being loaded into the back of a black SUV.

Joanne ran forward and wrapped me in a fierce hug. "Oh, Hannah, you've given us such a fright."

My head felt like it was stuffed with cotton wool. Omar was there, smirking, but I had no pain. Just confusion. I'd gone down to the root cellar, but I wasn't sure why. To get potatoes? The horseback ride must have tired me out more than I realized, and I closed my eyes for a moment in that dark place. Then I remembered Hila and the scrap end of her scarf. Why were the police all standing around the farmyard, not out searching for her?

I pushed my sister away. "What's going on? Why is everyone looking at me like that? Have you found something?"

Rick Brecken broke from the crowd. "I suggest you people get back to work," he said. "It'll be dark soon enough."

It was only then I looked at the sky and realized the sun was hanging above the trees to the west.

People began to move away. Joanne, Brecken, and McNeil did not. "You think we have nothing more important to do today?" Rick Brecken asked me.

"What?"

"Hannah needs to come inside," Joanne said.

"Perhaps we'll all come inside." McNeil's arms were crossed over her chest, and she did not smile at me. She was in her late thirties, tall and lean, a runner's body, with blond hair cut short and almond-shaped brown eyes that seemed to want to penetrate my soul. I looked away and said to Joanne. "I don't understand."

"You…"

"Thank you, Ms. Manning," McNeil said. "We'd like to talk to your sister privately."

Joanne stared into my face, searching for something, and then she said, "Okay. Use my office."

"I think my office would be a better place." McNeil put her hand on my arm.

"What! You can't be arresting her," Joanne shouted.

*They were arresting me? For napping in the root cellar?*

"You are not under arrest, Ms. Manning," the cop said to me. "We have some questions for you, and this place is too public."

"You must be aware that my sister has suffered a serious brain injury," Joanne said, puffing up with indignation. "I won't allow you to take her away. Her doctors will not allow her to be interrogated."

"We're not going to interrogate anyone, "Brecken said. "Just a few questions. Not a problem; we can talk to her inside."

Before they could change their minds, Joanne grabbed my arm and almost dragged me into the house. Without even bothering to take off her muddy boots, she led the way into the dining room. The house was strangely quiet.

"Lily?" I said. "Oh, Joanne, you have to go and get Lily. I left her with Buddy."

"What are you talking about?"

"Lily's still in the woods, guarding the cloth. Hila's scarf. I'm so sorry, I forgot her. I shouldn't have left her." Panic rose in my chest.

Joanne let out a long puff of air. She stroked my cheek. "Oh, my dear. You're confused. Don't you remember? You sent Lily and Ashley to get me. You did the right thing."

"I did?"

"She told me to call the police. Ashley's father came and got them. Lily went home with Ashley."

"Oh. That's good, right?" I tried to stay calm, not to show panic. How could I possibly have thought I'd left Ashley and Lily alone in the woods? I tried to remember, to call up the scene. It was all just a jumble of sound and images.

I'll call and let them know you're okay."

"Why shouldn't I be?"

She didn't answer. Brecken and McNeil came in. I hoped they hadn't heard any of our conversation.

We took seats at the long wooden table, scratched and scarred with years of use, piled high with books, newspapers, mail. Joanne began to pull out a chair for herself, and McNeil said, "Thank you, Ms. Manning. You can leave us now."

My sister looked at me. She turned and went into the kitchen.

No one said anything for a long time. I studied the front page of the local paper—the MP was giving a check to some organization or another. I always wondered if these low-level backbenchers knew how smarmy they looked with their fake smiles and bored eyes. I heard Joanne's low voice and knew she was on the phone.

"Where did you put her, Hannah?" Brecken asked at last.

I was genuinely confused. "Put who?"

"I don't have time to waste running around in circles, and I don't like being led on a merry chase. The Harrisons' dog found the scarf, brought it to you. You couldn't just bury it, because your niece and her friend saw it. You knew you had to report it, and then you nipped back out and moved her. Checked for any more evidence that might point to you, maybe."

I blinked. I must have looked like the village idiot.

"Where is she?" Sergeant McNeil asked.

Silence stretched out again. The only sounds came from outside, as police and police cars came and went. Jake should have been back from market by now. Where was Charlie, anyway? I would have expected a seven-year-old boy to be eager to watch the police activity.

"I don't understand why you're asking me these questions. If you think I know where Hila is, I assure you I don't. She was my friend, and I'm concerned about what's happened to her."

"What have you been doing for the past two hours, then?" Brecken asked. "Since Constable Kowalski left you outside?"

*Two hours? I'd lost two hours?*

I must have fallen asleep in the root cellar. The muscles in my lower back, butt, and thighs ached. I shifted in my seat and rolled my shoulders. Sleeping on the damp earth floor wouldn't have helped much, not after the unaccustomed ride. How could I have been asleep, out there, for two hours? The clouds in my brain parted and I could see the woman standing in front of me. The woman in the many-times mended dress that fell all the way to her feet. I shuddered.

*Was I going mad?*

They'd said I might have hallucinations. That was all it was.

Hallucinations as my damaged brain tried to make sense of the world. Mistaking what I'd done with Lily? Confusion, too much happening at once.

"Aside from anything else," Brecken was saying, "we had to take officers off the search in the woods to look for you."

"And bring in outside resources," McNeil added. "We can't pull a dog suddenly off one search and put it onto another. Too confusing. We had to get Quinte West out to help with the search for you. They're not happy at finding you a few yards from your own doorstep."

"I'm sorry," I said. "I must have fallen asleep."

"Yeah, right," Brecken said, his voice dripping with scorn. "On a dirt floor in a cold cellar. When your own bed is a couple of yards away." He pushed back his chair so suddenly I jumped. He stood up and placed his hands on the table. He leaned over me. His breath was hot on my face. "You can save everyone a lot of time and bother if you tell us where she is. "

"But I didn't.... I don't know..."

"Ms. Manning," McNeil interrupted, the voice of sweet reason. "We know your story. About the attack in Afghanistan. I've heard that these IED explosions can do bad things to a person's brain. Did you think you were getting back at the people who harmed you, killed and injured your colleagues? War's a nasty business, and its consequences follow people home, soldiers or journalists."

I gaped at her. They thought I'd killed Hila in revenge for the Taliban killing Simon. For all they'd taken from me. She was telling me if I confessed they'd make sure the court understood I wasn't in my right mind.

"You're talking rubbish. Hila isn't Taliban," I said. "I liked her."

"Then what have you been up to for the past two hours?" Brecken said.

"I must have passed out." I touched my head. "As you said, I have had a brain injury." I tried to look ill. It wasn't hard.

"Thursday afternoon," Brecken said. "The day Ms. Popalzai disappeared. Where were you?"

"Here."

"Where's here?"

"At home. In the house." I thought back. "I wasn't feeling well, so I slept most of the afternoon."

"Not according to your sister," McNeil said. "She told us you left the house after lunch and she didn't see you for several hours. In fact, she took a break to check on you and looked in your room thinking you were having a nap, but you weren't there. She assumed you were visiting Ms. Popalzai and went back to work. Later that afternoon you were found lying on the ground. You claimed to have fallen. Is that how you got that bruise on your forehead?"

"I didn't claim to fall. I did fall. I hit my head. I must have blacked out for a few minutes."

"Was that after you led Hila Popalzai into the woods and killed her?"

"What the hell?" I turned to McNeil. "You can't let him talk to me like that. That's ridiculous. I liked her. I didn't kill her. I wouldn't have killed her even if I didn't like her."

"In that case," she said, "you won't mind telling us what you were up to on Thursday afternoon."

Pain was growing behind my right eye, and I knew I had to take a pill and lie down while I was still capable of moving. Omar chuckled happily at my predicament.

Could they be right? I didn't remember what I'd been doing on Thursday afternoon. I couldn't even remember what I'd been doing for the past two hours. Was it possible I'd mistaken Hila for Omar?

And killed her?

*Ridiculous.* Shy, quiet, gentle Hila. So smart, so strong. As different from Omar and his ilk as one could possibly be.

Had she said something in Pashtun and, my confused brain thinking I was back in Afghanistan, this time with the chance to save myself, I lashed out?

Had I killed her?

I started to cry. Tears ran down my face. I fumbled in my pocket for a tissue but couldn't find one. Rick Brecken leaned back, taking himself out of my private space. He had the beginnings of a smirk on his ugly face.

"Tell me how it happened, Hannah," McNeil said, her voice soft and gentle. Full of sweet understanding. "An accident was it? Tell me where you put her and we can all go home."

I could only cry. The pain wasn't too bad. Not yet, but if I didn't get to my pills soon...I wanted to confess, to get them to leave me alone.

What had I been doing on Thursday? Had I gone for a walk with Hila? Even if I didn't kill her, did I know something that could help the police? Something I couldn't remember?

What about today? I remembered leaving Lily in the woods, but Joanne said I hadn't.

How could I possibly have lost two hours?

I'd seen the woman in the root cellar. I'd watched her go about her life. She'd fled from her home, she'd buried her child.

*Was I going crazy?*

"I have to lie down," I said. "I'm sick."

"Tell us where she is, Hannah, and we'll have your sister take care of you."

I would have told them where Hila's body was.

Except that I didn't know.

McNeil's cell phone rang.

The doorbell rang.

McNeil scowled and grabbed for her phone. She glanced at the call display and flicked it open. "What?" she growled.

Joanne came into the dining room. A woman was with her. She took one look at me and crossed the floor. She faced Brecken from the other side of the table. "This woman is seriously ill and she is under my care. I'm ending this interrogation right now."

"Who the hell are you?" Brecken said. His hair almost stood on end and, through my misery, I was reminded of a dog defending its patch of territory.

"Doctor Rebecca Mansour." Brown eyes glittered like shards of broken glass. "Ms. Manning is my patient and I am telling you to leave. Now."

Brecken opened his mouth, but McNeil interrupted. "We'll be doing just that." She stuffed her phone back into her jacket pocket. She jerked her head at Brecken. "We're needed." His eyes opened a fraction wider.

Doctor Mansour reached down and touched my arm. She gave me a nice smile. "Let's go upstairs, Hannah. I'm going to check you over. You don't look good."

"Seems the cavalry has arrived," Brecken said. "Only a temporary reprieve. I will be back. Try and get your story straight before then, will you, Ms. Manning? And one more thing. Don't be leaving the area."

He stalked out.

# Chapter Nineteen

She lay in a shallow muddy puddle, beside a slow-moving stream, face down. Her nose and mouth were in water, but it didn't matter. She was no longer taking breath when she'd been put there.

Her shoes and baggy pants were missing along with her plain white cotton panties. Her black tunic was disheveled, her headscarf, the hijab, torn, the remnants wrapped around her neck. Her hands were bruised and scratched where she'd tried to defend herself, her lips and eyes badly swollen, and insects were already crawling into the vicious cut that exposed the lumpy gray matter of her brain. Her legs were spread, toes pointing toward the earth, and her virgin blood leaked slowly into the mud. The dog, they suspected, had had a taste before the burrs trapped on his tail snagged on the torn hijab. Tiny fish, not much more than flashes of silver, darted in and out of the wounds, feasting on what they found there.

Men and women moved through the woods. Birds watched them from the branches of trees, rabbits and foxes scurried for safety, and unseen deer slipped into deeper cover. It was July and the sun wouldn't be setting for a while yet, but it would set before they'd seen enough, and strong lights were being brought in over animal trails and snowmobile lanes by officers riding ATVs. Those same ATVs would take her out of the woods to the coroner's van waiting by the road.

The men surrounding the body stepped back as Brecken and McNeil arrived. No one said anything. McNeil grunted and dropped to her haunches, careless of swamp water and muck leaking into her leather boots and dirtying the hem of her pants.

Brecken stood on the bank watching, hands in his pockets. "Is it her?"

"Not much doubt about it."

"Why the hell didn't your people find her before this?"

McNeil didn't take offence at his tone. She studied the body and the soggy ground and marsh surrounding it before saying, "I don't think it was here."

"What's that mean?"

"She was killed someplace else. And brought here." Her eyes moved across the body, studying the damage. "Looks like she was given a good beating. Raped, maybe. So not Manning."

"Still could have been. Except for the raped part, and you won't know if that's what happened until the pathologist has a look. Manning's keeping a lot of secrets, and she's not right in the head. At least that's the impression she's trying to give. "

"Convenient the doctor showing up."

"Yes."

"Speaking of doctors, here's one now." She spoke over her shoulder. "Welcome to the party."

The pathologist began to take the tools of his trade out of his bag.

McNeil rose to her feet in one smooth movement. She stepped back. No need to see any more. She'd get the full report in due course.

She stood beside Brecken, lowering her voice so the others couldn't hear. "I'd still like to know what business this is of yours."

He didn't look at her. "I'm sure you would, Sergeant."

# Chapter Twenty

"I didn't kill her," I said to Rebecca Mansour.

"Shush," she replied. She guided me upstairs while Joanne ran on ahead to turn down the covers on my bed.

The room was close in the heat of the day. I lay down, shut my eyes, and felt the doctor's small frame settle beside me. Joanne pulled off my shoes.

"Your sister tells me you're not able to account for some time this afternoon," Rebecca said.

"I fell asleep, that's all."

"Outside? In the root cellar? On the ground? While people searched for you and called your name?" Joanne said. "I doubt that. And this wasn't the first time, either."

"Hannah?" Rebecca prompted.

"Maybe I like sleeping on the ground," I said, "reminds of me of some of the postings I've had."

I felt her cool hands on my forehead.

"And then there was the getting Lily wrong," Joanne said. "Doctor, Hannah told me she'd left Lily and Ashley in the woods. But she hadn't. That was just wrong."

"Hannah?"

"I get confused sometimes, okay? It's why I'm seeing a brain doctor."

"The passing out is worrying, indeed. But the memory mistake is understandable. It's called confabulation. Your brain is compelled to make sense of the world. Particularly in times of great stress or excitement, if a piece of information is missing— such as the whereabouts of your niece—you insert a detail which may not be correct. Most of us, most of the time, can simply say we don't remember, or ask for more information, but your damaged brain panics when pieces go missing."

I settled back into the pillows and closed my eyes as her voice drifted around me.

I slept, and my dreams did not trouble me.

◇◇◇

When I woke, I was surprised to see that it was still daylight. I lay in bed, warm and comfy under my thick, fluffy duvet. I thought about Hila, poor Hila. After all she had endured, to come here, to Canada, supposedly a place of safety, only to wind up dead in a patch of woods.

*Where had that idea come from?*

For a moment I was frightened. I slunk back under the covers. *How did I know Hila was dead?*

Get a grip, I said to myself. The cops are crawling all over the woods. Of course she's dead. I didn't have to be responsible to know that.

I thought about Hila. She didn't really smile, just the one side of her face could turn up, and she didn't laugh often. But when she did have a rare moment of amusement, it was all the more bright and infectious. She enjoyed learning the names of the plants and occasional animal we came across on our walks. Not that I can distinguish one tree from another or name the type of ducks that flew over our heads on their path between the marsh and the open lake. At the most I knew the difference between a maple and a birch, between a duck and a Canada goose, so I could tell her that.

I hoped she had not been too frightened in her last moments. Rick Brecken. CSIS.

The Canadian government was letting a few Afghans into to Canada. Those who'd worked for the Canadians in one capacity or another. Precious few, considering that if the Taliban returned, their lives, and the lives of their families, wouldn't be worth living. I'd assumed Hila was just an ordinary refugee. Maybe she'd worked as an interpreter for the Canadians, or her father had.

But CSIS wouldn't give a damn about any ordinary Afghan refugee.

Who *was* Hila?

I pushed the bed covers aside. Not my concern.

I smelled coffee wafting up from downstairs, and I heard Charlie yelling something and his mother's quiet voice in reply.

Coffee. That was strange. No one in this family ever drank coffee in the evening. At that moment I noticed the beams of light slipping into my room from beneath the blinds.

Coming from the east, not the west.

It was morning, which meant I'd slept around the clock.

What had Doctor Mansour given me?

Could I have more?

The family was at the kitchen table when I came in, sur-rounded by the Sunday morning smell of coffee, bacon, and maple syrup. Jake had the sports section of the Saturday *Globe and Mail* spread out in front of him and a cup of coffee, steam rising, at his elbow. Lily leapt to her feet and ran to give me a hug. She smelled of good soap and toothpaste and straw. She'd been out to the barn already. Jake looked up from the sports scores long enough to scowl at me and Joanne said, "Good morning. You've been asleep for a long time. Are you ready for pancakes?"

I sat down. Charlie was stuffing blueberry pancakes into his mouth as fast as he could. "Good?" I said. He grunted. "No pancakes, thanks. I'll just have tea and toast. Don't get up. I'll help myself in a minute. Are there any, uh, developments?"

Joanne glanced at her children. Charlie's head was down and Lily was at the fridge, pouring herself orange juice. She nodded, almost imperceptibly. Not good news then.

"What are your plans for the day?" I asked.

"We're farmers," Jake snapped. "We farm. Every day."

"Can I watch TV now?" Charlie asked. His plate was clean save for a small puddle of maple syrup.

"For a short while," Joanne replied.

"I must have been pretty darned tired," I said. "I slept all the night through. I didn't even hear Doctor Mansour leave."

"She's worried about you. These blackouts…"

"I'm not blacking out."

"If you say so."

Lily shut the fridge door and pressed herself against the back of my chair. Her arms came around me and she held me close. I reached up and patted her hands. Jake and Joanne exchanged worried glances. He pushed himself up from the table. "Come on, sweet-pea. You can give me a hand in the barn. "

She gave me another tight hug before unwrapping herself. "Sure, Dad."

When they'd left, Joanne also got up from the table. She filled the kettle and switched it on.

"Hila?"

"Yeah. They found her. Her body. Not long after those two were here, talking to you, and the doctor arrived. I guess that phone call Detective McNeil got told her they'd found her. It."

"Have you told Lily?"

"Yes. We felt that we had to. Fortunately the ambulance and the forensic van didn't have to come onto our property to get to…the place. There's an old road into the marsh and then trails from there."

"I don't suppose the cops told you anything?"

"No. One of them came to the house and told Jake a body had been found. A female, he said. He didn't say it was Hila, but who the hell else would it be?"

"Who indeed?"

My sister's hands were kept busy as she made me tea and toast.

"How's Lily taking it?"

"Hard to tell. She seemed a mite clingy this morning. First to me and then to you." The toaster popped and Joanne spread a thick layer of butter and last year's raspberry jam. She put the plate in front of me. I pushed it aide, and she said, "You need to eat."

"Yes, Mom."

She didn't smile. "This is going to be hard on Lily. Very hard. It was one thing when Jake's grandmother died last year. We'd prepared the kids for that. But a woman Hila's age?"

"I don't suppose the police told you anything about the cause of death?"

She shook her head and poured hot water over a tea bag. "No. I saw a news van last night, driving past. Fortunately it didn't stop here. Bloody reporters. That's all we need." She glanced at me quickly. "Present company excepted."

I didn't mind. Over the years I'd heard every insult known to journalists. "Perhaps you should get some counseling for Lily. I bet Doctor Mansour could recommend someone."

"I doubt Jake would like that idea. He thinks folks today spend too much time wallowing in grief for people they hardly know. Look, Hannah, I'm sorry he was so rude to you this morning."

"No problem," I said, wondering how much longer I could go on living here.

"All this disruption. The police, the…uh…search for you. It's put him behind, and he doesn't like that."

"The search for me," I said slowly. "You mean yesterday?"

"Yes, I do. You might want to tell yourself you're not having blackouts, but I don't think you can call it anything else, Hannah. We called the police for heaven's sake." She laughed without mirth. "It wasn't as if they had far to come. Jake got home from market as the search was beginning so he took Charlie away. He didn't get unpacked until it was late, and that made him angry. The cops were tramping all over the lettuce beds. They said they'd be careful, but they weren't. The new plants are tender, you know, and we lost quite a bit. Some of the peas too."

"I'm sorry, "I said. I glanced out the window. It was early still, and traces of mist were curling around the trees and drifting across the fields. A hummingbird hovered in the air beside its feeder, wings moving so fast they were invisible. Jake and Lily came out of the barn. They walked close together and he put his hand on his daughter's thin shoulder.

"I'm going to the Harrisons," I said. "To pay my respects, I guess. I think it would be good if Lily came with me."

"Why?"

"She knew Hila better than I did. She can't hide from her feelings, and it would be a mistake to make her." I lifted the tea cup to my lips and felt warm, fragrant air on my face. I took a sip. It was very sweet. I never used to take sugar in my tea. Joanne always added a hefty spoonful, thinking I needed the energy. "I might as well go over now. I'm sure they'll be up."

"You should phone ahead."

"That'll give them the chance to say no. I need the walk anyway. About Lily?"

"I guess that'll be okay. If you're having trouble, Hannah, don't keep it from me, eh?"

I pushed my chair back. "I won't."

"Don't," she shouted.

I hung halfway between seating and standing. "Don't what?"

"Don't you leave this table without finishing your tea and eating that toast. Every last bite." She glared at me with an expression that was so like our mother I dropped back down.

◇◇◇

There were no cars in the driveway at the Harrisons' but the door was opened almost immediately I rang the bell. Maude's face was red and blotchy and her nose and eyes swollen. She had no makeup on, and her hair was lank and unwashed. A fresh coffee stain marked the front of her pink T-shirt. She looked a good twenty years older than when we'd first met. She lifted a torn tissue to her nose. "Hannah. Lily," she said in a thick voice. "How nice to see you. Please come in."

Buddy ran to greet us, tail wagging. I thought of where he'd been and what he'd probably seen and my throat closed and my stomach lurched. Lily dropped to her knees and gave him a hug. He licked her face. I grabbed her arm and pulled her roughly away. Maude Harrison was leading the way to the sun room. I kept hold of Lily's arm and we followed. Buddy trailed happily along behind.

"Company, dear," Maude announced. Grant Harrison was sitting in the wing-back chair, a large book open on his lap. I glanced at it and could see pictures of golden statues and gem-encrusted jewelry. He gave the book a last, longing glance, politely closed it, placed it on the table beside him, and got to his feet. "I believe you're in time for tea," he said to me. "Lily, would you like tea or juice?"

"Juice," she said in a small voice.

"Juice it shall be."

It wasn't yet nine o'clock, so I doubted it was tea time for the Harrisons, but I said I'd enjoy a cup. "Why don't you give me a hand, Lily," Maude said. "I made a cake yesterday. Not too early for cake, is it?"

Lily agreed that it was not, and she, followed closely by Buddy, left the sun room. Birdsong and a warm, gentle breeze drifted in through the open doors.

After I was seated, Grant sat back down and folded his hands into his lap.

"They found Hila in the woods."

"Yes."

"I'm sorry. What happened?"

He let out a long breath. "They're telling us nothing. Except that they suspect foul play."

"Oh, dear."

We were silent for a long time. Grant couldn't help his eyes drifting back toward his book. I took a peek. *Afghanistan: Hidden Treasures from the National Museum, Kabul.*

"You're interested in antiquities?" I asked, although I need not have. The house, this room, full of art and artifacts from the couple's travels, was evidence enough.

"Maude and I collect what little pieces we can. This morning I've found that thoughts of Hila brought me to reminisce of her homeland."

I knew the story of the lost treasures of Afghanistan. At the beginning of the civil war, when the Soviets invaded, workers at the national museum scrambled to move and hide their artifacts, many of them dating all the way back to the first centuries B.C. They stored the precious, priceless things in the vaults of the national bank, and there they remained hidden for more than twenty years, until 2001 when it was considered safe to bring them out of hiding. Every seal was still in place. Every single one of the artifacts untouched.

One bit of good news from that tragic country.

Sadly, a great many of the other treasures could not be saved: stolen, vandalized, deliberately smashed by the Taliban or simply discarded.

"Why's CSIS interested?" I asked. In the kitchen, Lily and Maude chatted. Outside, birds darted amongst the almost-empty feeders. A huge crow, sleek black feathers glowing in the light of the sun, chased a chickadee off.

Grant pulled his eyes away from the book. "They told you they were from CSIS?"

"No. But I recognize the type. The O.P.P. doesn't seem too pleased at having them poking their nose into everything, criticizing, but I guess they don't have much say about it."

"I forgot for a moment that you aren't just a farm girl."

"These days, that's more than I amount to."

He leaned back and closed his eyes. "Hila's father Waheed was a good friend of mine. We met back in 1965, when we were at university in England. I was lucky enough to do a year at Oxford. He was studying archeology. It was his ambition to unearth the treasures of his homeland. Afghanistan has always been an important cross-road. It was part of the Silk Route, upon which traders from Europe, the Middle East, China travelled for hundreds of years. Traders don't just pass through; they leave objects behind. The Soviets invaded in 1979, and Waheed and I lost touch for a number of years. A great many Western-educated intellectuals fled the country, but he remained. When we'd been at school he was like all the other men of our circle. Interested in having a good time as much as political debate or his studies. He hadn't been religious or even particularly nationalist when we were young, but there's something about having your country invaded, your religion and culture mocked and derided that gets a man's backbone up. We began to correspond again, albeit infrequently, and I knew he'd achieved an important position in the national museum. When the Taliban came to power, I heard nothing more for a long time. I hoped he'd been able to get out of the country, for although he'd become more religious over the years he was by no means a fanatic. I knew he'd married late in life. He had one wife and three children.

"In the meantime, I'd joined the foreign service. I had a particular interest in Africa, and we were posted to South Africa, Kenya, Malawi. It was a good life.

"In March of 2002, I got a letter from my old friend. He and his family were living in Pakistan and very happy to see the back of the Taliban. His letter was full of optimism. He'd accepted a position with the new government, in the ministry of culture, and they were moving to Kabul. He was so excited about the future. For himself, his family, his country."

Grant shook his head. It was taking Maude and Lily a long time to make tea. No doubt Maude was keeping the child occupied while Grant told his tale.

"Anyway, to make a long, sad story short, it didn't turn out that way. I applied for a position at our embassy in Kabul. I knew that meant Maude wouldn't be able to come with me, but I hoped to get a chance to help Waheed. Help him and his country. I was there for two years and spent a good bit of time with my old friend. I never met his wife or his family. A Pashtun man doesn't introduce his wife or daughters to even his best of friends. I could see the despair settling in first hand. He'd come back to Afghanistan with such hope, such optimism. And he was seeing all his dreams fading in a nightmare of government corruption and incompetence. Not to mention the realization that of the millions upon millions of dollars being poured into the country by the West, more of it was going to make Western contractors rich than helping the people of Afghanistan. He was Pashtun, from Kandahar, but he had settled his family in Kabul. He was no supporter of the president, yet not on the side of the insurgents either. He said the only side he was on was the side of the people of Afghanistan. He always was pretty outspoken." Grant chuckled softly. "I remember in particular a bar brawl in Oxford. Some English toff made a racist crack and Waheed commented on the ancient history of Afghanistan versus the upstart British. He might have reminded the English guy about the retreat from Kabul in 1842. Someone took a swing and Waheed, as well as me and a number of our friends and erstwhile enemies, spent the night in jail. Ah, to be young again."

Maude and Lily crossed the emerald green lawn behind the house. Buddy was not with them. Maude carried a green plastic bucket, and Lily ran on ahead to take down the bird feeders. Sunlight sparkled off the clips in the girl's hair making it look as though sparks were shooting out of her head.

"He was angry and unhappy and one night, shortly before my posting was up, I suggested it was time to give up on Afghanistan and move to Canada. To my surprise, he agreed almost immediately. I set things in motion for him and his family to immigrate and then I left. After about a year, he sent word that his immigration status was approved and details of their pending arrival in Canada. I found them an apartment in Ottawa and a job at the Museum of Civilization for Waheed.

"The family were on their way to the airport. Waheed and his wife, their two sons, and the daughter. Hila. A suicide bomber drove a truck into their car."

I felt flames on my face, heard the cries of the dying and the screams of the wounded. I heard sirens and shouting and lamentation.

"I am telling you this," Grant said, "because you understand."

"I do."

"The authorities believe it was a targeted attack. Not random, not a case of the wrong place at the wrong time."

"Why would insurgents target an archeologist, do you suppose?"

"You know these people, Hannah. Why would they smash their country's heritage, destroy its culture; why would they blow up ancient statues?"

*Why indeed?*

"Waheed, his wife, the sons were killed instantly. Hila was injured, badly burned. Fortunately her immigration had been approved, so I was able to bring her to Canada when she got out of hospital." He spread his hands. "To Canada. Where everyone and everything was strange to her yet she felt she was safe, but some bastard attacked her and killed her. What a world we live in."

Outside, Maude and Lily had finished filling the bird feeders. They were crouched in the grass peering at something under a lush, full maple tree. A fat blue jay settled onto the feeder behind them.

"Which is a long answer to your question. Why would CSIS be interested in the death of Hila? I cannot begin to imagine. If she'd been a government official, maybe. But she was just a schoolteacher, like her mother. They ran a girl's school. They'd had threats, against the school, against the girls who went there. That was part of the reason Waheed wanted to get out of Afghanistan. If he was on his own, he probably wouldn't have tried to leave. But he was worried about the future and safety of his family, particularly his daughter. Better he should have stayed, I guess.

"I'd say CSIS is trying to make themselves seem important. They have to do something to justify their budget. They'll hang about for a few days, issue orders, shove the local police around, and then be gone. Back to their conspiracies and their paranoia. "

Just because you're paranoid, I remembered the old saying, doesn't mean they're not out to get you. When was the last time someone had been killed in the county other than by a relative or acquaintance?

Ever?

We jumped as tea cups clattered and Maude and Lily came into the sun room.

"We found a bird's nest," Lily said. "It was on the ground and empty. I hope the baby birds grew up and flew away."

"I'm sure they did," Maude said. "They would have had no more use for the nest."

"We put it back anyway," Lily said, "in case some other bird family wants to use it. Mrs. Harrison said we can come to Hila's funeral. I'd like that."

"So would I, dear."

"We don't know when the body will be released, but we'll let you know when we hear," Maude said.

She poured tea into beautiful china cups and apple juice for Lily into a glass of lead crystal. Maude noticed Lily eyeing Grant's book, and she said, "If you'd like to have a look at the book, dear, go ahead. It's about Afghanistan. Where Hila lived."

Lily needed no further invitation and she curled up in a corner of a big leather chair to look at the beautiful pictures. We chatted about inconsequentials, and before long Maude was the only one talking. Grant glanced longingly at his shelves of books, and Lily flipped pages. I drank tea. Maude told me about plans for a water garden and her work on the hospital's volunteer committee.

"Play with us, Hannah?"

I snapped to attention. I'd been thinking about Hila and had completely lost the thread of Maude's conversation. My tea cup was empty. I hadn't touched the lemon pound cake beside it, and Maude was looking at me with a question on her face.

"Play?" I said, sounding stupid to my own ears.

"Bridge. My Monday ladies' group often needs to complete a table. "

"Sorry. I don't play bridge." I put the cup down. "We've taken up enough of your morning. Lily, time to go."

"Look at this, Aunt Hannah." She uncurled herself from the chair and brought the book over. It was open to a full-page plate displaying a three-pointed crown of gold. The headgear was made of gold and covered in gold leaf with gold coins hanging from it. "Isn't it beautiful?"

"It certainly is." It was nothing short of stunning.

"If you'd like to borrow the book, Lily, you may," Maude said.

Grant looked like he'd swallowed a lemon, but he did not object.

"Thank you," Lily said, "I promise I'll take care of it."

"We have a couple of others you might like," Maude said. She went over to the bookshelves, studied the volumes, and selected two.

"Do you think Hila had beautiful things like this?" Lily said, flipping through the book as we walked home down the cool, shaded road, dust rising at our feet.

I laughed and touched the top of her head with my free hand. I carried the two other books. "Somewhat impractical, wouldn't you say, out working in the fields balancing that on your head."

"Hila and her family weren't farmers. They were city people, she told me. They lived in the capital, Kabul. Hila helped her mother teach, and her father was an important man in the government. I'll ask her…" Lily's voice trailed off. "I guess I won't be asking her anything, will I, Aunt Hannah?"

"No, dear. I'm very much afraid that you won't."

The sun was still bright and the birds were still singing, but it felt as if a storm cloud had settled over us. Lily's shoulders slumped and the bounce went out of her step. She lowered her head and the tears began to flow. We kept walking.

"It says in the book," she said, as we turned into our driveway, "that some of these things were funeral goods. What people wore to be buried in or to have with them after death. Do you think Hila needs to have fine things for her funeral, Aunt Hannah?"

"I suspect the objects shown in that book are very old, Lily. From long before Afghanistan was a Muslim country. The people who live there today don't take precious things to their grave, just the way that your great-grandma wasn't buried with her collection of cookbooks even though she cherished them so much."

Lily ran her fingers across the cover of the book, deep in thought. "Yeah. Great-grandma left her ruby ring for me to have when I grow up. She wasn't buried with it. Mom keeps it in her room and will let me have it when my finger's big enough. Why do you suppose in the olden days people didn't leave their things to their kids?"

"Perhaps it will tell you more about that in those books."

Lily took her treasure upstairs to her room and didn't come down for hours. The house was quiet; even on Sunday a farm family doesn't rest in planting season. I was tired from the walk, and emotionally drained from hearing Hila's story. It was no sadder than so many others I'd heard in the war-cursed countries I'd visited over the years. But this time it was personal. I'd gotten to know the woman. I'd liked her a great deal.

The doorbell rang, and I dragged myself out of my chair to answer it. A woman stood there, a tense smile plastered onto her face. She was dressed in designer jeans tucked into high-heeled leather ankle boots and a red leather jacket over a shirt so white it almost glowed. You didn't see clothes that clean in farm country much. Over her shoulder, I could see a man standing beside their car. He had a big camera in his hand and a black bag tossed over his shoulder.

*Oh, oh.*

The woman stuck out her hand. The nails were long and sharp and painted with deep red polish. You didn't see that in farm country either. "Hannah Manning. It's such an honor to be meeting you at last. I've followed your career with great interest. I was sorry to hear about your injury, but it's great to see you looking well. I guess you'll be back at work soon, eh?"

Her hand was damp and clammy. "Do I know you?" I didn't bother being polite. Obviously a reporter with her photographer in tow.

"Catherine Green. I'm so excited about meeting you. You've always been a hero of mine, you know."

I refrained from rolling my eyes. Catherine Green looked to be in her early forties, a bit old for the hero thing. "I don't give interviews." I began to close the door.

In true journalistic fashion she stuck her foot into it. "I know, otherwise I would have been here long before. I'm looking into the Hila…uh, someone…murder. Your name came up."

"It did?"

"My contacts tell me you're the one who found the body."

"Your contacts are wrong." If indeed she had any contacts. Probably fishing for an angle. "You didn't tell me what news-service you're with."

"Oh, didn't I?"

*No you did not.* I waited. She mumbled the name of a blog I'd never heard of. No matter. As I said, I don't give interviews. Out of the corner of my eye I saw the photographer lift his camera. I stuck out my tongue. "I have no comment." I shoved at the door. She shifted but didn't completely move her foot.

"The dead woman was from Afghanistan. You reported from Afghanistan. You were seriously injured in Afghanistan. Though you're looking great now," she added quickly. She lowered her voice. "Coincidence?"

"Not at all," I said. "I sought Hila out precisely because she was Afghan so we had something in common."

"Have you had much contact with any other people from Afghanistan since you've been back home?"

"No."

"The dead woman's father was President Karzai's right-hand man. He was executed by the Taliban on his way to the U.N. to negotiate a billion-dollar deal for increased aid for development projects, right?"

I shrugged. Not my place to enlighten her.

"His daughter was wounded in the attack and came to Canada to recover. I know all that. I also know she was to go to the U.N. in her father's place next month. The question is, did the Taliban follow her here? Did they bring their blood feud to our shores, and if so, who else might be in danger?"

"Better not let my brother-in-law find you poking around the farm. It's private property. And no pictures either. " I pushed at the door and she barely got her foot out in time. I stood at the living room window, watching them. Green spoke to her photographer for a moment. He replied, and then they got into their car and drove away.

CSIS.

Is that why CSIS was involved in what was otherwise nothing but a local murder? Did they think the Taliban were here? In Prince Edward County, Ontario?

Total nonsense. The Taliban, the true Taliban, care about nothing but their own patch of territory. They don't dress up like Westerners and try to infiltrate Western society. Most of them were so uneducated and provincial they couldn't even if they wanted to.

Home-grown terrorists? Perhaps. Canadian-born Muslims or recent immigrants have been suspected of having sympathy with the extremists. Could it be possible they came after Hila, not to stop her from going to the U.N., which she wasn't about to do, but in revenge against her father, who was a friend to the West? To finish what their compatriots back home had failed to finish?

My skin crawled.

Had the war followed me here?

# Chapter Twenty-one

We had returned from the Harrisons' in plenty of time for me to prepare lunch. When I called Lily to come down, she asked if she could take her food up to her room, and I agreed. She ran down the stairs, put the smallest of the books Maude had lent her on the table, saying, "You can read this one, Aunt Hannah," and dashed back to her room with a plate. Charlie had gone to the beach with friends for the day. I called Joanne on her cellphone and rang the big iron triangle hanging over the door to the side porch. The workers trooped in, today only Jake, Joanne, and Connor. Liz and Allison had Sunday off, but the plants didn't take a break for the weekend, so neither could the farmers. Jake and Connor had been laying long strips of black hose among the tomato plants. They needed water and there was no rain in the forecast.

"I've had an idea," Connor said, pulling a chair up to the table. He'd kicked off his rubber boots on the porch and was in stocking feet. "I'm staying at my cousin's. We're not getting on so well. He's a nice guy and all, but he likes to have people over, play music, and drink at night, and I have to get up early for work. We had a major blow up last night, and he's pretty much kicking me out."

"That's too bad," Joanne said. "Do you have someplace else to go?"

He grinned at her. "As a matter of fact, I might. How about the trailer?"

"The trailer?"

"Sure. That bunch of hippies aren't coming right? So the trailer's empty. I'll pay you for the use of it, same as I'm paying my cousin. I'll stay out of your way when it's not working hours, but I'll really enjoy the commute." He turned the full wattage of his smile onto me. "And the neighbors."

"I don't…" Joanne began, but Jake spoke over her. "That's a good idea. No point in that trailer standing empty. You'll be responsible for your own meals, other than lunch which is part of your wages."

"Great," Connor reached for a sandwich. "I'll get my stuff after work, I don't have much, and move in tonight. Now that's settled, I guess I should tell you that you folks are the talk of the town. No one was talking about anything else last night at the Acoustic Grill in Picton."

Joanne groaned. "That can't be good."

"Might be good for business," I said, passing around the salad bowl. "There's been a steady stream of cars pulling up outside and going into the shop. We're almost out of the lettuce mix."

"Connor, pick more after lunch and restock the shop."

"Sure, boss."

"When you've done that, there are some bags of potatoes in the greenhouse. The first of the fingerlings. Take them down to the root cellar."

"What are they saying in town?" I asked.

"A lot of wild speculation. Some people figure the terrorists are among us, and some are saying it comes of so many idle city people being here for the summer. Whatever your prejudice is, there's a theory to match it."

"A reporter was snooping around earlier."

"Oh, god. That's all we need," Joanne said. Jake growled around a mouthful of ham sandwich.

"She's with some online outfit. I sent her packing, but you might want to warn Charlie and Lily not to be talking to strangers. Liz and Allison too." I looked at Connor.

He lifted his hands. "For a million bucks I'll sell you guys down the river in a heartbeat. But I'll accept nothing less than that."

I laughed, but Jake did not. "I don't want those people on my property. And I'd better not find anyone talking to any reporters. You're not going to make a story out of this, are you, Hannah?"

"Give me some credit, will you, Jake." I pushed my chair back and got to my feet. "You might not like me much, and you might not want me here, but if you think that'd I'd betray my family as well as my professional reputation, then you're seriously lacking in judgment."

The thick cloud that had filled my head these days began to shift and suddenly I was angry. It felt strange, and I studied myself, wondering at the unfamiliar emotion. Despite all that had happened in the previous three months, I had not once thought to be angry.

"Jake didn't mean…" Joanne began.

"Helloooo."

"Not now," Joanne mumbled, as Jake said, "Mom, Dad. Hi." I dropped back into my chair.

Marlene and Ralph didn't bother with greetings. "What's this I hear? Barb from next door phoned me and said that murdered foreign girl was found on your property. You didn't think to call me and let me know?"

"It's nothing to do with us, Mom," Jake said. Joanne rolled her eyes, and Connor buried his curly head in his salad bowl. "She wasn't on our property. In that swamp land behind that's owned by the County. "

"Well my granddaughter found her, is what Nancy said, and I've come to take Lily and Charlie to my house until they've caught whoever did it."

"I don't think so," Joanne said.

Marlene whirled on her. "It's obviously not safe here."

"It's as safe as it was last week or last year. And Lily did not find the body. The police dog found it."

"Barb said…"

"I don't give a fuck what you and your gossipy friends say."
Joanne was on her feet now. Her face clenched and her eyes narrowed. "I won't have you putting fear into Lily's head."

"She has to know what's going on. That's what happens when
that kind come here. They can't leave their problems back in
the old country, oh no. Have to bring the fight to our shores."

"What kind is that?" I asked, politely.

"Foreigners. Those Muslims. "

"Well, if Hila was killed by someone from back home, then
Lily, and the rest of us, have nothing to fear, now do we?"

That took the wind out of Marlene's sails for a moment. She
took a deep breath prior to regrouping her forces. "We don't
know what that sort of people are capable of. Now, they're here,
in the county, who knows who they'll be after next. There's a
base here, you know." She meant Mountain View, the air force
training base which we passed going to the train station in
Belleville. When I'd first seen it, I'd laughed out loud to see a
military installation so minimally defended.

"No one's going to be attacking Mountain View," Jake said.

"That's my point." Marlene shrieked in triumph. "They can't
attack us head on so they'll go for the weakest point. And that's
our children."

"You're delusional," Joanne said.

"Don't go there, Mom," Jake said with a sigh. "Lily's perfectly
safe here with us, and that's the end of it." Jake's dad, Ralph,
shifted from one foot to another. Lunch finished, Connor looked
about for something, anything, to take his attention.

"We'll let the police do their jobs," Joanne said. "There's no
point in speculating."

"I said it before," Marlene muttered, "We don't need those
people here. Let them stay in their own countries. It's none of
our business."

"I thought you were all for us going to Afghanistan," Joanne
said, sweetly.

"To help them," Marlene replied. "So girls can go to school
and get an education. Not so they could come here and take

over our country. Refugees, ha. If they weren't so lazy, they could build something out of their own country. They're just here for a handout, most of them."

I'd heard it all before. How poor Hila being murdered meant that her countrymen were taking over Canada, I couldn't figure out. I stood up and began gathering dishes. Connor leapt to his feet, about as eager to get away from the conversation as I was.

"The tractor's got a rattle. Would you mind having a look at it, Dad," Jake said.

Ralph grunted in acknowledgement. They left.

"Back to work everyone," Joanne said. "While you're here, Marlene, I've been saving some seconds of the potatoes for you. Come and get them. And we'll have no more of this sort of talk around the children." She stalked out of the kitchen.

Marlene gave me an innocent shrug. "Really, I'm only trying to help. How are you, anyway, dear? You're looking well today."

"I'm fine, thanks."

"That's nice to hear," she said. "Is Lily in her room?"

"Isn't Joanne wanting to give you potatoes?"

"Mustn't keep her waiting. Give Lily a kiss for me. Tell her I'll have her around for a sleep-over soon." Marlene followed the rest of them out of the house.

Only Connor and I remained. He rinsed and stacked the dishes while I put the leftovers away.

I went to the bathroom, and when I came back, Connor was flipping through the book Lily had tossed on the table. "Nice stuff."

"It certainly is." If he'd been in the army, chances were he'd been to Afghanistan. I'd never asked, and he'd never mentioned hearing anything about me. He put the book down and turned to face me. He looked at me for a long time, and something flipped in my stomach.

"I hope you're okay with me moving into the trailer."

"It has nothing to do with me."

"I should have asked you first. But the opportunity came up and I took it." His blue Irish eyes were the color of the lake on a sunny day. He looked at me without smiling.

"Why would you ask me?"

"It's true what I said about my cousin. You'd think that after being in the army I'd be used to bunking with men, but we weren't getting on. But my main reason for liking the idea of the trailer is that I'd be able to see you more often."

Color rose into my face. I grabbed a cloth and wiped at invisible stains in the sink. "Sure. Whatever."

"Great. I'm going out to pick lettuce. Why don't you meet me in the greenhouse in half an hour and help me bag them, Hannah."

It might have been my imagination, but I thought his tongue lingered a bit too long over my name.

Nevertheless, I went out to the greenhouse in half an hour. The air was thick with the scent of stored compost, moist earth, fresh vegetables, and heat. We chatted as we bagged greens in sizes suitable for selling. Connor told me about his hopes for starting up his own farm. He had his eye on a piece of land near Lake Erie, not far from the cottage where he'd spent summers as a child. Formerly used to grow tobacco, the land had lain abandoned for several years, and he hoped it would still be available when he was ready to buy it. Joanne had told me Jake thought Connor wasn't a good worker. Hadn't she said he'd been ready to sack him at one point? Connor was strong, nice looking, full of casual charm. He seemed to be trying to charm me. Had he tried to charm Joanne? Had a jealous Jake simply thought he had?

We took the bags of greens out to the shop. In the paddock, one of the horses blew out a breath and the other stomped its feet. A car drove by, kicking up clouds of dust. The morning had been busy and not much was left in the store. While Connor arranged the goods, I emptied out the cash box.

"Hannah," he said.

I turned.

He was standing in the center of the shop, a lopsided grin on his face. "I know you're...well, ill. Perhaps one day, when you're feeling better, you'd like to go for a drink at the Grill, or maybe a latte at the cafe in the bookstore. Or dinner. Or something.

With me, I mean. You don't have to answer right now. It's going to be a long summer. Give it some thought, will you?"

He turned and walked out of the room.

Had Connor just asked me out on a date? I do believe he had.

As he said, it was going to be a long summer. And a long time indeed before I was ready to think about dating.

Still, nice to be asked.

A minute later he was back. "Oh, Joanne told me to put the potatoes in the root cellar. Where is it anyway?"

"At the back of this building. There's a gap in the bushes and you'll see a door, then a ramp going down. The door's never locked."

"Thanks. Catch you later." He winked, and was gone.

I looked around the shop. Light filled every nook and cranny; the fridge that contained frozen pies and soups gurgled softly; the floor was swept clean. It was so small. I thought about the people that had called it home, and had no doubt been pleased to have it.

Refugees. Like Hila. People for whom happiness was a concept long forgotten. For whom safety was the only thing that mattered.

What with the visit to the Harrisons' and learning the tragic tale of Hila's family, and the interruption by Marlene and Ralph, and then Connor's rather startling question, I hadn't thought much about what had happened to me yesterday.

Now I did.

Two missing hours.

Three hours missed on Thursday. The day Hila disappeared.

I felt nothing in the shop. I never had. No icy cold air, no foul smell. No dark-haired woman in a long, dirty dress. It was only the cellar beneath that seemed to affect me. But now that I was standing here, thinking about those long ago settlers, here in what had been their house, I wanted to know more.

I had no interest in Jake's ancestors' news about buying new coats or the cost of fixing the truck, and so I hadn't bothered to venture back up to the attic room for some time. Perhaps if

I dug deeper into the boxes I could find something from the 18ᵗʰ century.

Not that I thought I'd actually seen one of the house's original inhabitants.

◇◇◇

**August 4, 1780**

"Someone's at the door, asking for you, my dear."

Maggie jumped from her bed. "A man? Is it a man?" Her heart pounded.

"Yes, but not a young man, my dear. Don't get your hopes up."

Maggie ran. Hope was all she had.

She had been taken in by Mr. and Mrs. Van Alen, the elderly couple who had prayed over sweet Flora's grave. Not that they had much to spare, but the man's brother owned a small house in the city and they all squeezed in somehow.

New York City was full to bursting and still they came. Refugees. Loyalists. From all over America, streams of men and women and children poured into to the city, many with nothing but what they could carry. It seemed as if the entire Continent was in flames, and everywhere anyone suspected of having tory sympathies, or of not having enough patriotic fervor, were being chased from their homes, their farms, their businesses. Their property—often their lives—confiscated.

Maggie guarded her little wooden box carefully. The people in the house where she lodged seemed honest enough. But she had thought the same of her neighbors, once. She spent a few of her mother's coins on a new dress for herself so she could get out of the over-large homespun, boots so she needn't walk the filthy streets of New York on feet torn and blistered from ill-fitting shoes. She bought food for the household, trying to do her share.

Her bed was in what had once been a servants' room, in the attic, as hot as Hades in the humid August heat, with dormer windows which looked out over Fifth Avenue onto the restless crowds passing back and forth day and night. The war was not going well, everyone knew that.

As for Maggie, she didn't much care who won and who lost. She spent her days hanging around the fort, begging the authorities for news of Hamish, and stopping soldiers on the street, searching for anyone who might be able to tell her where he was.

She met men who knew of him, who'd seen him, maybe a year ago in Montreal, or was it two years ago in Niagara? They shook their heads sadly, and walked away.

She did not know the man who stood waiting for her at the door. "I'm Mrs. Macgregor," she said. "Do you have news? My husband?"

"Do you not recognize me, ma'am," he said. He took off his cap with his left hand.

She looked closely. She sucked in a breath.

Elijah Taylor who'd been one of their tenant farmers. He'd been a round man once, with fat red cheeks, and a twinkle in both eyes, and a roar of a laugh. He stood on the step, perhaps a hundred pounds lighter, his back stooped, a cut running from his hairline, through an empty eye socket to end in a twist of a lip. His right sleeve hung at his side. Empty. He'd gone with Hamish to join the King's Royal Regiment. His family, mother and wife and seven children, had left with Mrs. Dietrich.

"Oh, Mr. Taylor," she said.

"Aye. It's me. What's left of me. I've got news of Mr. Macgregor. And it's not good, I'm sorry to say."

The sun disappeared from the sky and a cold fog settled over her. Her heart stopped beating.

"Tell me," she said.

At one time a man such as Mr. Taylor would have taken his time to give a lady tragic news. Today he said, "Mr. Macgregor's dead, ma'am. I saw it myself, and I heard word his wife was in town, so knew it was my duty to tell you. It was last month, July. We were captured by the cursed Rebels in the spring. Taken to Simsburg." His one eye looked into hers. "You know about Simsburg?"

"Yes." Everyone knew about Simsburg Mines. Turned into a prison for Loyalist soldiers. The Rebels recognized British soldiers as soldiers, and treated them not unwell, subject to exchanges and pardons. But the Loyalists they threw into the depths of the mines. To rot.

"We were there together. Me and Mr. Macgregor and some of the other men from the Valley. It was a hellish place, ma'am." He touched his loose sleeve and his face twisted with remembered pain. "We knew we had to get out of there, or we'd die without ever seeing the sun again. Six of us made the break. Mr. Macgregor, he was a good man, a real leader, unlike some others I could mention. He came last, after making sure the rest of us were well away. He didn't make it, ma'am. Shot in the back by a rebel bastard."

"Are you sure? Perhaps he was only wounded. Perhaps he'll recover from his injuries and try to escape again?"

He shook his head. "I'm sorry, Mrs. Macgregor. But no. I've seen battle, though I wish to God I hadn't. I know a deadly shot when I see one. That's all I've come to say. I wish you well, ma'am, and I'm right sorry to have to bring you this news."

"Thank you," a voice said. Maggie felt an arm around her, although she hadn't heard anyone approach. The front door was closed silently, and Maggie was led into the kitchen. A cup of tea, fortified with an extra teaspoon of valuable sugar, was placed in her hand.

◇◇◇

**September 22, 1783**
"Mrs. Macgregor."

"Yes?"

Once again Maggie stood in the doorway, facing a man she did not know.

The Van Alens had left for England, although they had never been to that country and knew no one there. Maggie had wondered what she would say if they asked her to accompany them, but they did not. She lost her room in their relative's house, but with the last bit of money from the sale of her mother's emerald brooch, she found new lodgings in a house on Broadway, not far from the fort.

She had been in New York City for three years. Time passed in a blur as she mourned all she had lost. She lived with three other childless women, the others waiting to join their husbands whose regiments had gone ahead to Canada. The war was lost, everyone knew, and the British commanders werepreparing to evacuate the city. Any Loyalist who wanted to leave would be given passage.

The victors were unforgiving in their triumph. There would be no mercy, no forgetting or reconciliation. Old grievances were resurrected, and theft, pure and simple, became the order of the day when one party could be accused of treason simply for following the laws or norms of the pre-Revolutionary society.

Tents and make-shift huts were thrown up on every bit of vacant land in and around the city. All summer long ships left, loaded with some of the more than thirty thousand refugees that Sir Guy Carleton, the last governor, had sworn to protect.

She had not wanted to believe what poor Elijah Taylor had told her. Perhaps he was mistaken and Hamish was only wounded. Men said the chaos of battle could be a confusing thing. But as the months, and then the years, passed Maggie accepted that Hamish would not be returning to claim her.

She wrote to her mother. She did not ask to be allowed to come home, had merely stated her situation in prose as stiff and formal as a business communication, and waited for a reply which never came. Either her letter had not arrived, or her father had intercepted and destroyed it. All over New York everyone had stories the same. Adult children estranged from parents, brother from brother, father from son. Best friends, turned the bitterest of enemies.

One of Maggie's roommates, a hearty Scotswoman almost as round as she was tall named Fiona, had been a cook in a big house. These days she made a living cooking for soldiers tired of military rations or single men needing a good meal. Not that the facilities, Fiona constantly complained, were anything like the kitchen she'd had in the house in Philadelphia. "Ye could turn an ox on a spit, the hearth was that wide," she said. "I had three young lasses to give me a hand, and more help they were than this useless lot, ye ken." Maggie helped by tending the fire or chopping onions—at which she'd almost sliced off the tip of her index finger—and slowly began to learn. Not only to cook, but to shop, to clean. One of the women took in laundry, and Maggie learned more than she'd ever wanted to know about soap and about the filth that could get into men's clothing. Her skill with a needle, learned only so she could embroider her trousseau and baby clothes, earned her some extra money sewing for the wives of British officers.

The days full of hard work passed as they waited to find out when they'd be evacuated. Maggie scarcely knew whether or not she wanted to leave New York City. Her friends were going; she had nothing to stay here for. There was no point in going home, back to Hamish's farm in the Mohawk Valley to try to rebuild. As his wife she had no rights to his property. Not that there was anything to inherit. Word had come that all Loyalist property had been confiscated.

Stolen, more like it.

She'd put her name on the list and waited.

"Yes," she said to the man standing at her door.

"Mrs. Hamish Macgregor?"

"Yes."

"I'm so glad to have found you at last." He took off his cap to reveal a shock of blond hair and gave her a big smile. He was quite handsome with most of his teeth, good skin, and unusual gray eyes. "My name is Nathanial Macgregor."

"Yes?"

"Your husband, Hamish Macgregor, was my cousin. Our fathers were brothers."

Maggie's stomach rolled over. "You're Hamish's cousin?" She desperately searched his face, looking for something, anything, familiar. She did not find it.

"Don't stand there gossiping, lass," Fiona shouted from behind a cloud of steam. "I've got cabbage boiling over here."

Only a few years ago Maggie would have been mortified to be found answering her own door, clad in a ragged second-hand dress with a dirty apron tired around her waist, being summoned to strain boiled cabbage. She had no pride left, and her circumstances were not much worse than most of the refugees trapped in New York City.

"If you don't mind waiting a moment," she said to her visitor. "I'll finish the cabbage and be right out." There was no room in the crowded house to entertain a visitor. They'd have to stand in the street.

# Chapter Twenty-two

At dinner that night Lily toyed with her sausage and then asked, "When you die, what will happen to the farm?"

"What on earth brought that question up?" Joanne threw a worried look at Jake. Lily had spent the day upstairs in her room with the books she'd brought home from the Harrisons'. Clearly death, in the form of not only Hila but funerary relics, was on her mind.

"I'll run it," Charlie said. "You'll have to live out in the trailer and do whatever I say." He'd had way too much sun at the beach and the top of his pert little nose was very red.

"I will not."

"First of all," Jake said, "We aren't about to die any time soon."

"Hila did."

Joanne put down her fork. "What happened to Hila, sweetie, is hard to understand. But you have to remember that we're upset precisely because Hila's death was shocking and unexpected. That's why the police are working so hard on finding out what happened to her."

We'd been told we weren't to go into the woods, and all day we'd caught glimpses of police moving through the trees. Lily's bedroom faced the back, looking out over the forest, and it had a window bench, a comfortable cozy spot piled high with brightly colored pillows, where she liked to curl up and read. She would have had a good view, from up there, of the comings and goings.

I hadn't been questioned again, but Jake and Joanne, Connor, Liz, and Allison had. Even Lily, in her parents' presence, had been asked what she'd seen on our ride.

"We aren't planning to die until we're very old, like your great-grandma did," Joanne said. "When we do, you and your brother will inherit the farm. Together."

"Why doesn't Aunt Hannah get it?" Lily asked.

"I doubt she wants it," Joanne replied. "But even if she did, she can't have it. You are our children, so all that we own," she spread out her arms to encompass the kitchen, the house, the farm, "will be yours."

"Not that that amounts to much," Jake grumbled.

"It amounts to everything I want in this world," Joanne snapped back.

Tensions were growing between those two, and the disappearance and death of Hila wasn't helping. Jake was furious at the amount of working time he was missing and at having to pay his employees while they answered police questions.

Jake had grunted his thanks after Joanne told him I'd pay the horses' expenses and for my own keep, but his gratitude hadn't lasted long. My presence wasn't helping this marriage any, but where could I go? To Mom and Dad's? They'd take me in, of course, and make room, pretending it was a delightful idea.

I thought about their two-bedroom condo on Collier Street in downtown Toronto. Right near Bloor and Yonge, perhaps the busiest intersections in the whole country. The lights, day and night, the traffic, the crowds, the pollution, the noise.

Brecken had told me I couldn't leave, but I didn't much care what he said. The police might be letting him take the lead, but he had no authority over me. Made a nice excuse to stay, though.

"The farm's important to me, too, okay." Jake made an effort to smile at his daughter. "Your mom and I worked hard to buy this place. To bring it back into my family. I hope it can stay in the family, and that means you and Charlie."

Lily's forehead crunched up in thought. "What if people die who don't have children? What happens to their stuff?"

"It usually goes to their brothers and sisters. Cousins maybe. Even the government, if they don't have a will or any obvious heirs."

"What's a will?" Charlie asked.

"A legal document providing for the disposal of one's property and possessions in the event of death," Jake said.

"Oh," Charlie said, not understanding and not caring. He reached across the table and grabbed the bottle of ketchup. He squeezed a generous amount onto the plate beside his sausage. He drew a face—a circle, eyes, a smiling mouth. Then he dragged a slice of sausage through it, smearing the remains of the face into a lumpy red mess. My stomach lurched, and I felt my own few bites of sausage, cabbage, and mashed potatoes rise into my throat. I looked quickly away.

"Dead peoples' things belong to their family?" Lily'd put down her knife and fork and her face was intent.

"Yes," Joanne replied. "That's why you have Great-Grandma's ring and why you and Charlie and your children will have the farm someday. My cousin Jennifer, who was always close to my grandmother, has her pearl necklace and I have her cookbooks. People can also leave things of value or sentiment to their friends or the children of their friends, if they wish."

There was, of course, a lot more to the laws of inheritance than that, but Lily gave a satisfied nod and turned her attention back to her meal.

We were finishing up dessert, freshly-picked blackberries over ice cream, when the doorbell rang.

Jake got up to answer it and came back with Rebecca Mansour.

"I'm sorry," the doctor said. "I don't mean to interrupt your dinner, but I was nearby and thought I'd pay a house call."

"You're in time for tea," Joanne replied. "Please, join us."

Rebecca gave her a smile and took the spare chair.

"Would you like some ice cream and berries?"

"Don't mind if I do." She turned to me. "You look well, Hannah. How are you feeling?"

"Okay."

She pointedly eyed the bowl of melting ice cream in front of me. "Eating well?"

"Yes," I said.

"No," my sister said. "She doesn't eat enough to keep a bird alive."

"I eat when I'm hungry."

"Which is precisely never."

"Come on, Lily," Jake said, getting to his feet. "Time to get the horses in for the night. "

"Can I watch TV?" Charlie asked.

"No," Joanne said.

"You can help me, buddy," Jake said. "Let's go."

"Any more trouble since yesterday?" Rebecca asked as Jake and the kids left and Joanne made more tea.

"Not a bit. "

"Is that right, Joanne?"

"Hey. I'm the patient here. You don't ask someone else for a diagnosis."

"I will if I have to. If you won't take your injury seriously enough to let your doctor help you."

"Time, isn't that what you and your colleagues keep saying I need, time? Well in the time that's passed since yesterday, I've been perfectly fine." To my horror, I felt tears behind my eyes. I got to my feet to help Joanne with the tea.

"Why don't we take our tea outside," my sister said. "The mosquitoes haven't been too bad this year."

"Good idea," Rebecca said.

"Hannah, would you get the cushions?"

I found the blue and yellow patio cushions in the office and brought three outside while Joanne prepared a tea tray and an extra serving of dessert.

We settled ourselves and Joanne served. The sun was almost set. A gentle breeze stirred the humid air.

"Oh, look," Rebecca said as the first flashes of white light danced in the bushes and across the fields. "Fireflies. I love them."

We fell silent, watching the sparks of light.

"You're impatient, Hannah," Rebecca said, picking up her spoon. "If you've been told you need time, it's because it's true. You will get better, but you have to take care of yourself. Or at least allow your sister to do it for you." She smiled at Joanne. "If you have any more blackouts, you simply have to tell us. In the meantime, I want you to have another MRI. I'll schedule the appointment for you on Monday."

"If I must."

"You must."

"Do you hear anything in town about...you know, about what happened out here?" Joanne asked.

"Rumors are running wild. Some people say it's a serial killer and we have to lock up our daughters, some say it's the Taliban and we'll all be slaughtered in our beds." Her short black hair bounced as she shook her head.

"That's pretty much what Connor said he was hearing."

"It's got people looking over their shoulders, and that's never a good thing. Not in a close-knit community like this one."

"And not at tourist season, I'd imagine," Joanne said, cradling her mug in her hands. Her fingers were long, nails chipped and broken, scratches climbed up her arms, and a Band-Aid was wrapped around her thumb. Hardworking hands. Hands that grew food and raised children and cared for sisters. Impulsively, I reached across the table and touched her arm.

Jake and the kids came out of the barn. Charlie first, then Lily dashed off after him, chasing the fireflies. Jake stopped to watch them, hands on his hips. The children's cries of glee filled the soft night air.

"There's been some talk about tourists leaving and reservations being cancelled. But it'll all blow over soon enough, I suspect. I hope," Rebecca said.

"Unless..." Joanne began. She didn't finish the sentence because the doorbell rang once again.

"Busy night," she said, getting up to answer it.

Rebecca Mansour sipped at her tea, and we watched the children play.

Joanne led Maude Harrison out to the deck. She was twisting her hands in front of her and her eyes were wide with fright and her face was bloodless.

Rebecca leapt to her feet. "Maude, what's happened?"

"I don't know where to go. I don't know what to do. I saw your car go by earlier, Doctor, and guessed you'd be here."

Joanne gestured toward a chair. "You need to sit down."

Maude shook her head. "It's Grant."

Rebecca headed for the door.

"No," Maude said. "He's okay. I mean he's not hurt. I mean… he's been arrested. The police have arrested him for Hila's murder." She burst into tears.

# Chapter Twenty-three

It was after midnight when Grant Harrison came to collect his wife. Rebecca Mansour drove him.

Joanne had insisted Maude couldn't go home by herself and ordered Lily to vacate her room for the night. She'd made up the bed with fresh sheets and put a sleeping bag on the floor of my room for her daughter. Rebecca had gone to the police station to find out what was happening, having ordered Maude to remain here. Jake went to bed, but Joanne and I waited with Maude who insisted she couldn't sleep. We sat in the living room, drinking tea. The forecast had been wrong and it had started to rain. High winds lashed the trees and water streamed down the windows. Small branches swayed and large ones groaned and debris scratched against the glass. The chimney of the propane fireplace in the living room squeaked as it moved.

The house lights flickered, but before we could react, they came back on. I thought for a moment of the people who'd lived in this house when it was first built. A storm at night would be a terrifying thing, with nothing but tallow candles and burning wood to keep creatures of the dark at bay.

When a curve of headlights swept up the road, we were at the side door before the car engine was even switched off.

Two people got out, and Maude slumped in relief. Grant glanced toward us. He would have seen three women bathed in the light that burned over the door, but he headed straight for Maude's car. He climbed inside, taking the driver's seat, and sat there, staring straight ahead. Presumably he did not have the keys.

"Thank you for your kindness," Maude said. "Just a misunderstanding." She dashed for the Toyota, holding her hand over her head as feeble protection from the storm. The engine roared to life and they backed up the driveway and sped off into the night in a spray of water from under the wheels.

Rebecca Mansour joined my sister and me. She was drenched right though.

"They aren't holding him?" Joanne asked. "I'm glad."

"He wasn't arrested. Just questioned."

"Well, I'm going to bed, morning comes early."

"Would you like a cup of tea before you leave?" I said. "You need to dry off a bit."

"Tea would be welcome, but I don't want to keep you up."

"As my sister will tell you, I don't sleep all that well most nights."

"I'm not surprised to hear it." Rebecca kicked off her wet, muddy running shoes. Joanne thanked her for her help and made her way to bed. Her footsteps were slow and heavy on the stairs.

I plugged in the kettle. "Would you like something a touch stronger? There's a bottle of Drambuie in the cupboard, and I think there's some Jameson's as well."

"Jameson's did you say? *Faith and begorrah.*" She put on a hideous Irish accent. "The answer to a lady's prayers. Just a splash mind as it's an ugly night to be out."

I found the bottle in the back of the cupboard. "Ice?"

"Heresy. A drop of water will do."

I poured her drink and made tea for myself. I sat across from her at the big kitchen table.

"Cheers," she said.

"Cheers."

"Do you know what the police wanted to talk to Grant about? He was gone for a long time."

"They wouldn't tell me anything. Left me cooling my heels in an interview room. I had a couple of medical journals in the car, so at least I had something to read. Grant was pretty tight-lipped on the way home."

"Do you know them well?"

"The Harrisons? Him, I don't know at all, but Maude's a dynamo with the hospital volunteer committee. I met him once at a fundraising dinner. The word taciturn was invented for Grant Harrison, I'd say."

I nodded in agreement.

"I guess he felt he had to tell me something, as I'd come to fetch him. The police are interested, he said, in anyone who might have come to visit Hila while she's been staying with them. No one, apparently, had. She had no visitors. Grant seemed surprised that the police didn't believe him. When he insisted, they asked about letters. None, he replied. She didn't even get junk mail. They confiscated her computer and are searching to see who she's been in touch with."

"She was taking university courses on line. Probably had lots of e-mails to do with that. Police. You said he was questioned by the police. Was anyone else present?"

"Like who?"

"CSIS is poking around. If the cops are looking into Hila's friends and contacts, then they don't suspect it's a random attack sort of thing."

"I'm sure they're looking into everything, Hannah."

"I guess. I don't actually know anything about how the cops operate. I've never been on the," I wiggled my fingers in the air, "crime beat."

"As for who was questioning Grant, he just said they and them."

"I may not know anything about the crime beat, but I do know a thing or two about intelligence operatives. Normally, they would have as much interest in the death of a Prince Edward County woman as in a farmer's cow. So what's brought them here?"

I didn't answer my own question. I wasn't a journalist these days. I was a woman trying to get her head on straight and her life back. "No matter. It won't do Grant any good if the townsfolk hear he's been brought to the station and questioned. Rumor doesn't need much to get it started."

"From what I know of Grant, he won't give a rat's ass, pardon the expression. But Maude, yes, it will upset Maude a great deal."

She finished her whiskey. When she put the glass onto the table a smile touched the edges of her mouth. I found myself smiling back; I liked this woman very much. In another life, another place, we could have been friends.

We both jumped at the sound of a clatter and glanced toward the deck. I got up and peeked outside. The wind had knocked over a decorative metal flamingo and thrown it against the wall. The yellow light over the deck shone on sheets of rain, and the glass table top rattled. The wooden planks were littered with leaves and small branches. We'd forgotten to bring the cushions in. They'd be soaked in the morning.

A chair scraped the linoleum behind me and I turned.

"I'd better be going. Morning comes early at the hospital." Rebecca studied my face. "Take care of yourself, Hannah. And if you can't do that, will you at least let your sister take care of you?"

"Sure."

"Why don't I believe you? Come and see me tomorrow morning at the hospital."

I stood in the doorway for a long time, watching the red lights of her car disappear into the storm. Then I came back inside and switched off the kitchen lights. I walked through the dark house listening to the sounds all around me. Outside the storm continued, unabated. The old house groaned, but it had withstood far worse weather than this, and it would for a long time still to come. Inside we were all warm and snug. Well-fed, well-loved children tucked up safely in their beds. Farmers sleeping soundly before heading out to another day's work. The horses and chickens and barn cats would be restless, but even they would know they were safe.

I was restless and knew sleep would not come. I climbed the second set of stairs and went into the attic. I switched on the lamp and settled myself into the ratty old chair.

◇◇◇

"Finding anything?"

I jumped. Weak morning light spilled through the uncurtained windows.

"You frightened me," I said to Jake.

He leaned against the door frame. He was barefoot and dressed only in his pajama bottoms, riding low on thin hips. His arms bulged with muscle earned over days spent at a physical job. His chest was white, covered with sprinkles of black hair, but his neck and arms were as brown as the wood of the kitchen table. My sister was a lucky woman, to have that to keep her warm at night.

"I'm enjoying the old letters," I said. And I was. I'd taken the bunch off the top, put them to one side, and burrowed back in time. I stopped around 1820 and began reading a stack of letters between a woman by the name of Emily and her friend Sarah, both of them highly excited about the construction of Sarah's new house and the purchasing of furniture and hiring of servants. The letters were out of order, with many gaps indicating where letters had either not been written or had been lost. Emily had beautiful handwriting, and I could understand every word. Sarah's hand was small and cramped and difficult to decipher, but I knew that the trouble reading them was due to her penmanship, not to my brain injury, and that made me very happy indeed.

"Anything interesting?"

"Day-to-day life. Lives so different from our own. What are you doing up here, anyway?"

"It's my house. I can go where I like."

"I know that, Jake. I'm just asking."

"I saw the light and thought one of the kids might have left it on. You're dressed. Haven't you been to bed?"

"You know Grant was released, right?"

"Joanne told me when she got into bed."

"I couldn't sleep, so came in here."

"Must be nice."

"What?"

"Sit up all night. Sleep all day. While people work all around you."

I felt as if I'd been struck across the face. "What's your problem, Jake? I'm paying my way, aren't I? If you want me to leave, tell me to my face, and I will."

His eyes slid to one side. "Sorry, Hannah. Joanne loves you, I know that. She won't hear of you leaving."

"And I love her. And Lily and Charlie. And you, Jake."

"Be sure and turn off that light when you're done here, will you." He left.

I let out a long breath before bending my head once again over the papers.

# Chapter Twenty-four

"You think she went off her rocker?"

"I think it's a possibility," Rick Brecken said.

"Can't say I'd be sorry to see the bitch get what's coming to her."

"You've met?"

"Once or twice. Tell me what you have on her."

"She doesn't have an alibi for two important time frames. Thursday afternoon, when Hila disappeared. She won't say where she was, and no one seems to be able to place her, try as they might. Again on Saturday after she found the remnants of the scarf and called the cops. Another couple of hours without an alibi."

"Manning's not stupid," McNeil sipped at her beer. "She's a journalist, of all things, a successful one. If she killed Hila, or knew what had happened to her, she'd at least have come up with some story for where she was at the time in question."

The newcomer's name was Gary Wolfe. He was with military intelligence. Not the sort of role that should have him looking into a small-town murder. But as soon as the name Manning crossed his computer screen, he was on the phone, calling for details. Two hours later he was on the road out of Ottawa, heading to Picton. He thrust his hand into the tin of nuts and sorted through them, looking for cashews and brazils, throwing the peanuts aside. They were in his motel room, gathered around a six-pack of beer and bags of nuts and potato chips. "Rick?"

"Precisely the point, I'd say. There's nothing rational about Manning killing Hila Popalzai. If she wasn't acting rationally, she wouldn't have thought rationally enough to be able to cover it up. I've seen her medical records…"

"Wow. How'd you ever get those?" McNeil said, impressed.

He didn't bother to answer. "TBI they call it. Traumatic brain injury. Severe trauma to the occipital lobe, among other injuries, resulting in a massive concussion, all of which can lead to seeing things that aren't there as well as vision and perception problems. Did her mush of a brain think Hila was coming after her? And lash out?"

"I don't see it," McNeil said. "Remember the autopsy? Hila was beaten. Pretty severely. Almost certainly tied up while they were having a go at her. If Manning was having some sort of delusion, she might lash out, sure. But carry the woman away, conceal her, rip off her underclothes, and tie her up?"

"She wasn't raped, or even molested, so no need to think it wasn't a woman. And who knows what Manning might have been thinking." Brecken took a long drink.

"Well, I don't buy it," she said. "Hannah Manning couldn't…. wouldn't…have done all of that on her own."

"That sister of hers is mighty protective. Suppose the sister came across Manning with Hila, realized what had happened and helped get rid of the body. Hila might not even have been dead yet, and the sister knocked her around to make it look like a beating and then whacked her over the head to get it over with."

"Now you're really stretching. If the sister had had anything to do with it she would've folded the first time an officer questioned her. She's just a farm wife, for god's sake. You've spent too long in the netherworld."

"The netherworld, as you call it, is why Hila was here. In Canada. Don't forget, her family was murdered in Afghanistan. She's the only one who survived. And then she ends up murdered? You think that's a coincidence?"

"You can't possibly suspect Hannah Manning is an Islamist sympathizer? She's an educated Western woman for god's sake."

"That means nothing when these religious fanatics get hold of them. But no, Manning isn't a friend of the Taliban, I'll give her that. If nothing else. But she's a reporter, and they have their own agenda, always after 'the story.'" Wolfe made quotation marks in the air with his fingers. "No matter what harm that story might do to their country's interests. Scum of the earth, most of them."

McNeil put down her beer, unfinished. "You're saying Manning killed her in a fit of insanity, then you're saying it was politically motivated. Can't you get your story straight?"

"At first I figured it was political, yes," Brecken said. "Someone finishing what the Talib failed to do to Waheed Popalazi's family. That's why I'm here. But now, yeah I'm considering Manning. And her sister. And a passing serial killer. But hey, you're the cops. Aren't you the ones supposed to be looking at all the angles?"

"We're doing our jobs, thank you. And we'd be better off without any unofficial help. She got to her feet. "Be seeing you."

"Take the sister to the station tomorrow," Wolfe said. "Put the pressure on. If she knows something, she'll crack soon enough. If she doesn't know anything, it'll up the pressure on Manning. And, if it is Islamic extremists, maybe'll they'll think the heat's off and relax. When people relax they make mistakes."

"I don't take orders from you."

He tossed another handful of nuts into his mouth. "The orders will be on your desk before you get home."

She slammed the motel room door on the way out.

Rick Brecken leaned back in his chair. His feet were on the bed and he lifted his bottle of beer. "You don't need to antagonize the locals, Gary. We need them."

"We don't need anyone. Let them run around in circles with their little investigation. Manning did it, pure and simple."

"If Manning killed Hila, and I concede that's a possibility, but only one of several, you must know she'll get off for diminished responsibility. Her doctor, her medical records, her media friends will make sure of that."

"So then it's up to me to make sure this is handled as a national security matter. I don't intend to see it go to court." Wolfe threw a peanut onto the floor.

Rick Brecken grinned. "What the hell'd she ever do to you?"

# Chapter Twenty-five

When I came downstairs, having not gone to bed, Jake's mother was sitting at the kitchen table, nursing a mug of coffee.

Joanne stood at the counter, making the children's sandwiches. She looked tired. Dark bags had formed beneath her eyes, and the skin around her mouth had fine lines that hadn't been there a few weeks ago.

"Bad business," Marlene said. Her mouth twisted as if she were sucking on a lemon. "No good comes from letting them into our county. They bring their fights with them."

"Yes, yes," Joanne said. "You told us that already."

Marlene turned her attention to me. "Jake says you've been poking around in our family letters."

"Not poking. Reading them. I find them interesting."

"I suppose that's all right then. Mind you take care of them. They're very important to us."

*So important they'd been sold along with the house and left to the attentions of mice and mold.*

I didn't say the words, just smiled politely.

But Marlene was never one to let things lie. "I suppose it gives you something to do, Hannah. The days must get quite long and boring. Things are different from when I was a girl. I remember the time I broke my arm. My dad insisted that I still did my chores and help Mother around the house as best I was able. We didn't believe in all this modern mollycoddling back in my day. Don't work; don't eat, my father always said." She looked at me, expecting a retort.

I didn't care enough to bother to reply.

"Did you know that they uncovered six tombs at Tillya Tepe, but didn't have time to open the last two before the war, and when they went back everything had been looted?" Lily said from the doorway. She had her book in her hands, open to a colorful illustration. "Why would people steal stuff like that?"

Joanne had warned her not to bring Maude's book to the table, so Lily had bolted her breakfast and run into the living room to continue reading.

"Shouldn't you be getting ready to go?" Marlene said. She turned to Joanne. "Lily's old enough to help around the farm. You shouldn't be wasting money on that day camp. My father expected us to put in a good day's work on summer vacation."

The morning didn't get any better. The police were soon back. They arrived in three cars. Two cruisers and one plain black SUV. Two officers took Liz and Allison out to the greenhouse to interview them, one more time. Jake tried to argue, fuming about having to pay his workers when they weren't working, and Joanne tried to calm him down. Jake was not in a good mood when Sergeant McNeil said she needed to talk to him again. He muttered something about wanting compensation for the loss of work time and the damage to his crops. She replied that if he'd prefer they took everyone down to the police station, that could be arranged.

She ordered Joanne not to leave the house, and she and Jake went into the office and shut the door. They were there for a long time. Marlene hovered and made excuses to stay, and eventually Joanne almost ordered her to go home. She left, in full snit.

"Is she always so difficult?" I asked. "Or is it me that gets under her skin?"

"She's never been easy. Nothing she loves more than to climb up onto her high horse. She was so excited when Jake and I bought this house. I do think she wanted to take up residence as dowager lady muck. It's not even her old family property, it's her husband's. Like many families around here, the Stewarts had their ups and downs over the years. For a while, back in the mid-nineteenth century, they were quite well off. Marlene thinks we should continually remind people of that." She grimaced. "She's hoping we'll find some valuable things in the attic that will get her on the *Antique Roadshow*. She loves that program."

"Nothing up there but letters and farm accounts, from what I've seen."

"Yeah, Jake did check." Joanne let out a long puff of air, sounding much like one of the horses. "Marlene's a good grandmother, I'll give her that. The children love her. Her and the long-suffering Ralph. They'll always help out when needed. After a lecture about how things were done in her day."

Joanne did not look well. She'd been up late last night, sitting with Maude, and out of bed at her usual time this morning. She saw me watching her and tried to smile. "This isn't good. I'm sorry for Hila, I really am. I want the police to catch whoever did it, but why couldn't it have happened in winter, when we aren't so darn busy? If we don't get today's produce to the restaurants in time for them to start lunch, they'll consider us unreliable. And today's CSA day."

"I'll help you with the restaurant deliveries, when the cops are finished here. I'll call the CSA people and explain. They'll understand."

My sister eyed me.

"I want to help out," I said, "when I can."

"When you can," she repeated. "That's the problem isn't it? You never know when you're going to be struck by a headache."

"I usually have some warning."

"Usually."

The office door few open, and a black-faced Jake stormed out.

"Ms. Manning," O'Neil said to Joanne. "I'd like you to come into town with me."

"What the hell!" Jake whirled around.

Color drained from Joanne's face. "You must be kidding me. I can't do that. I have to take my daughter to summer camp. And pick up her friend on the way. We're already late."

"Your husband will have to do it."

"Are you nuts? My wife has work to do. Why can't you talk to her here, like you did with the rest of us?"

McNeil glanced at me. I was sure it was involuntary. She didn't want to risk me listening in while she was talking with Joanne. I didn't know why, but figured that wasn't good.

"Are you arresting her?" Jake demanded.

The children had come into the hall, attracted by the noise. Charlie began to cry. Lily looked from one adult to another.

"Please look after your children, sir," McNeil said. "Your wife is not under arrest, but I have my reasons for wanting to talk to her in a private, secure place. Now, shall we go? Or would you prefer that I formally detain you, Ms. Manning?"

"Look," Jake said. "This is nuts. I told you I didn't see Joanne the afternoon Hila disappeared. That means nothing. We don't live in each other's pockets, you know. I don't see your husband following you around when you're working. Joanne was busy around the farm, like she always is, right Joanne?"

"You can't think…" Joanne's voice broke. She coughed and said, "Lily, Charlie, off you go with your dad. It's always so busy around here, I'll enjoy getting away for a few hours. I'll grab a latte in town later."

I slipped my hand into Charlie's small one. His backpack was slung over his shoulder. I took him into the kitchen and found the bagged lunches Joanne had prepared. "Here you go, big guy," I said. "Lily, come get your lunch. "

The children did not look at all appeased, but they did as they were told.

I led the kids outside and Jake helped them into his truck. None of us looked as Joanne climbed into the back of the police vehicle and O'Neil pulled away.

At least she didn't put the lights and sirens on.

◇◇◇

We passed the remainder of the morning in an agony of unease. Jake dropped the kids off at their respective day camps. He ordered Connor and Liz to make the restaurant deliveries, but his mind clearly wasn't on giving instructions, and I suspected that some of the restaurants would end up having to scramble to rearrange their menus.

I went into the office and phoned the CSA holders. Fortunately Joanne kept their records in a neat folder—names and numbers hand-written—so all I had to do was dial one number after another. I explained, quickly and succinctly, that police investigation in the vicinity of the farm had impeded work for a couple of days, but their boxes would soon be ready and I'd call again.

I hung up before the person on the other end of the line could get in a single question.

It was dark and cool and quiet in the office. Jake had gone out to the fields, and Allison was busy in the greenhouse.

I debated calling my own mother. She'd be absolutely furious if I didn't let her know what was going on, but I hoped I'd have better news soon. Besides, she had a full schedule of patients and hospital rounds of her own. My dad wasn't teaching over the summer, but he'd gone for week's fishing trip to the Nahanni River. A long way away.

Wandering into the kitchen, I dropped into a chair at the table and idly leafed through the book Lily'd left there. The ancient treasures of Afghanistan. Pages and pages of photographs of stunningly beautiful, priceless things. Many of them gone now, smashed by the vindictive Taliban or by mindless looters. A legacy of over two thousand years, destroyed in minutes by uneducated thugs and religious fanatics. In my head, Omar remained still.

I'd been told by every doctor I'd seen that it was important that I stayed quiet and calm while my brain worked to heal itself. "Don't let anything upset you," one fool had said. As if I, or anyone, could control what upset us and what did not.

Leafing through this beautiful book, remembering Hila, thinking of my sister being marched off to the police station, all that upset me.

Yet Omar stayed away.

Maybe a good upset was what I needed.

I was preparing lunch, thinking it best to continue with the routine, when I heard a car in the driveway. I ran through the house to the front door. It was a police car, a cruiser. A uniformed officer was in the front with Joanne beside her. The officer stayed in her seat while Joanne climbed out. My sister slammed the door and walked to the house, her head high, her neck stiff. She did not look back.

I wrapped my arms around her. The patrol car backed up, turned into the road, and sped away.

"All okay?" I asked.

"Yes."

"I'll call Jake. Let him know you're back."

"Not right now. I have to talk to you first."

"What about?"

She let out a long sigh. "They think you killed Hila, Hannah."

"Who cares what they think. I didn't do anything of the sort. You know that. Don't you?"

"Of course. That Sergeant, McNeil, her questions were all about you. What you'd done on Thursday and then again on Saturday after you found Buddy with the scarf." My sister studied my face. "I couldn't tell her, Hannah. I don't know where you were or what you were doing."

"So? You have a farm to run. No one expects you to be hovering over me all day long. I hope you told her that."

"I did. She asked what you'd told me you were doing. I couldn't answer, Hannah. Because you haven't said."

I took a deep breath. "Joanne. My head doesn't work right, okay. That's why I'm here. That's why I'm not in my own home or out doing the job I love. I don't sleep for days on end and then I fall asleep at the strangest moments. Sometimes I feel exactly as I did before the explosion, and decide I'm ready to go back to work. Sometimes I don't even know who I am. I stand beside myself, wondering who is that strange woman who could stand to put on a bit of weight and get some exercise and pull herself together. And for god's sake do something about that ragged mess of hair and put some make up on." I wiped at my eyes.

Joanne was crying also. She wrapped me in her arms and we clung to each other.

"I might not be able to account for where I am all the time," I said when we pulled apart, "but I know I didn't kill anyone. Certainly not Hila. I cared about her a great deal."

"I'm sorry. I guess I just needed to hear that. It's not fun, being interrogated. Everyone stared at me when I came in. Lucille Roszak, who's one of our CSA shareholders, works at the police station. She won't tell anyone, of course, but she knows I've been questioned."

"You guys okay?" It was Allison, standing at the office door.

"No," Joanne said, "but we'll live. What's up?"

"Nothing. I saw you were back and came to check, that's all."

"This is such a goddamned mess." Joanne rubbed her hands through her hair.

"Everyone's feeling it," Allison said. "My friend Jodie works at the hospital. She's a receptionist in the ER. She said a patient refused to let Doctor Mansour treat her yesterday."

"What?"

Allison nodded. "It was a local. Jodie said she's seen her around town. She came into the ER with a bad cut on her hand, a kitchen accident. She wouldn't let Doctor Mansour touch her, insisted on another doctor. She said she wanted a Canadian doctor, not some unqualified foreigner."

"I hope they told her to go home and treat herself if she's so darned fussy."

Allison shrugged. "I didn't hear how it turned out."

"I just want this to be over," Joanne moaned. "What are you working on now, Allison?"

"Harvesting lettuce seeds."

"Better get back to it then, hadn't you?"

"Okay."

When she was gone, I said, "I'll call Jake. Let him know you're back. He's so worried he sent Connor to do the restaurant deliveries."

The edges of Joanne's mouth turned up. "I'll go out and find him myself. I know Jake's been sniping at you, but I love him, Hannah."

"And he loves you back. I can see that."

"Did the kids get away okay?"

"Yes."

She stopped at the entrance to the kitchen and looked back at me. "A man was there, Hannah. I didn't know who he was or what to think, but I didn't like him."

"A man? Where?"

"In the interview room at the police station. Sergeant McNeil asked all the questions. He stood in a corner, watching and listening. He didn't say a word."

"She must have said his name and rank or position when she began the recording."

Joanne shook her head. "I don't think so, but I could be mistaken. I was confused, upset. Frightened."

"Rick Brecken? The guy from CSIS? He's been here with the cops."

"No, I remember Brecken. This guy was big, tough looking, with a bald head and small black eyes, and a vicious scar down his right cheek. He's either dark skinned or has a heavy tan. He didn't say a single word, Hannah. Just looked at me. I thought…"

"What, what did you think?"

"I've never seen him before in my life. Yet for some reason I thought he hated me."

# Chapter Twenty-six

They came after lunch.

Connor and Liz and Allison came in to eat, but Jake and Joanne did not. I hoped they'd found a quiet private place where they could talk. Lunch was a gloomy meal. No one said anything more than pass the mustard or thank you.

I pushed lettuce leaves around on my plate and thought.

The man who'd watched the police interrogation of my sister bothered me a great deal. He sounded like one of the men I'd met in the course of doing my job.

One in particular.

Journalists and security officials don't always see eye-to-eye.

He might have not had anything to say to Joanne, but I was pretty sure he, whoever he was, had orchestrated the whole thing. They had, I suspected, taken Joanne to the station, instead of interviewing her here at the farm like they did everyone else, to rattle me.

Me, they'd have trouble badgering. All I had to do was call my doctor, and she'd put an end to it. I was still on the paper's payroll, and I'd have access to their lawyers who'd shut down any fishing attempts on the part of the police fast enough.

Liz and Allison finished lunch and went back to work, and Connor carried the dishes into the kitchen. "Everything, okay?" He asked me. "I saw Joanne heading toward the back fields, so I guess the cops didn't...uh...detain her."

"Arrest her for the murder of Hila, you mean. No they didn't."

"I didn't mean it like that, Hannah. It's got us all spooked. Cops poking around all the time. People in town are talking about nothing else. Do you know why they wanted to talk to Joanne?"

"They couldn't interview her here properly," I said. "Not with her children around and all that goes on during the day. They wanted some privacy. That's all."

"If you say so. Do you have any ideas yourself? About what might have happened, I mean?"

"Me? Heavens' no."

"It's gotta be terrorist sympathizers." Connor leaned against the counter and crossed his arms over his chest. His blue eyes burned with anger. "A threat, maybe, to any Muslim who tries to settle in the West and become Westernized."

"I can't see it. I haven't noticed any swarthy Middle-Eastern men around here lately, peeking out from behind bushes."

"Don't be naive," he said. "They don't have to be dressed in *salwar kameez* and *keffiyehs* to be terrorists. Plenty of homegrown ones, Canadian and American and British. They look just like us, many of them. Jake's mom's right. We don't need them or their ancient squabbles here. Shouldn't be letting them into our country; they've made enough of a mess of their own."

I wasn't about to get into an argument. Hila hadn't brought her country's problems here. She just wanted to live a quiet life and be left alone.

*Or did she?*

What did I know about what Hila wanted or did not want? All I knew is what she'd told me, and what Grant Harrison had said about her father. Maybe she was involved in Afghan politics up to her neck.

*Could this have been a political killing?*

"I don't know, Connor. Right now I just want it to go away."

"I'm sure it will," he said in a kind voice, his eyes on my face. "How are you finding the trailer accommodations?"

"Great. No one cranking up the music at two a.m. and yelling at me to come join the party. Nice to roll out of bed and walk all of five yards to work." He shifted his feet and hesitated. Then he looked up abruptly, into my eyes. "Maybe…uh, some night after supper you can come out and get me and we can go for a walk or something. Would you like that?"

I felt heat rising in my face. I must have turned a brilliant red, the color of one of the ever-bearing strawberries sitting in a bowl on the counter. "A walk. Yes, that would be nice."

"Good." He returned his attention to the floor, an embarrassed grin turning up the edges of his mouth. "Take care of yourself, Hannah. You don't look too well. I'd better get back out there."

I was starting to feel my lack of sleep and knew I'd better lie down before Omar roared to life. The office door slammed as Connor let himself out, and I was heading for the stairs, thinking fondly of my bed, when the doorbell rang. Suspecting it was Connor, back with another invitation for a 'walk', I hurried to answer it.

"Well, well, well, if it isn't Hannah Manning." A man stood there, a big grin plastered across his ugly face. My stomach rolled over and my head began to swim.

Rick Brecken was beside him, looking somewhat pleased with himself. "Afternoon, Hannah. We'd like to talk to you for a bit, if we may. Your doctor's not around? That's too bad."

I ignored him. "Gary Wolfe. I won't say it's a pleasure." I had known Wolfe in Afghanistan. We were not, to say the least, friends.

"Mind if we come in?" Wolfe said. He didn't wait for an answer, but stepped forward. Instinctively I moved out of the way, and they were in the house.

"It was you at the police interrogation of my sister earlier, wasn't it?"

Wolfe studied his surroundings. A typical modernized, nineteenth-century Ontario farmhouse, full of family pictures and mementos, children's shoes and toys, insignificant art and cheap souvenirs, books and magazines. All the stuff of an ordinary family living an ordinary life.

I did not want Gary Wolfe in this house.

"I'd like you to leave."

"You don't look too bad," he said. "Bit on the thin side, and I don't like your hair that way. Other than that, you look almost…normal."

"I'm surprised to see you here, Wolfe. What, you've been given a well-deserved demotion and are now investigating small-town murders?"

His eyes flared. "Hila Popalzai wasn't any ordinary small-town woman."

"No."

"Afghan refugee. From an important family. Did you know her back in Kabul?"

"No."

"Why'd you kill her?"

"Don't give me your bull, Wolfe. I'm not answerable to you." A headache was moving in, bringing clouds over my mind, and my range of vision was narrowing. In a battle of words and wits, I'd be no match for Gary Wolfe.

"You're as answerable to me as anyone else, Manning. I've seen your medical records. I know your mind's a ball of pure mush. You'll never work again. You can't write a sensible sentence, can you?"

"Leave now." I said. It came out like a plea, not a demand as I'd intended.

"Not that any of your treasonous diatribes were worth the paper they were printed on in any event."

To my horror I felt tears behind my eyes. I fumbled in the pocket of my shorts and my fingers found my cell phone.

He leaned forward and leered into my face. I smelled tobacco on his clothes and the hamburger he'd had for lunch on his breath. "I'm only sorry it wasn't me who got you. At least the Taliban were good for one thing."

"Gary, back off." From the dark edges of my consciousness, I heard Brecken's voice tinged with alarm . Wolfe was going too far. "Let's go. She doesn't look good. Anything she tells you will be suspect."

Waves crashed into my head. Omar laughed. I narrowed my eyes and tried to focus on the phone in my hand to pull up Joanne's number.

"Calling your doctor?" Wolfe asked, his voice low and menacing. "What's her name? Oh, yes. Mansour. Now, what kind of a name's that, I wonder?"

"Gary, let's go. This isn't helping."

"Sure." Wolfe sounded cheerful now, friendly. "Thought I'd drop in on an old war acquaintance and say hi. Sorry to hear about your injury, Manning. Next time, I'll bring flowers. He paused. "Calla lilies, I hope."

I heard footsteps and the door closing. My legs trembled beneath me and I crumbled to the floor. I lay there for a long time, while Omar danced the jig across my eyeballs.

Gary Wolfe was a major in the Canadian Army. He was with the Intelligence branch, and our paths had crossed more than once in Afghanistan. I was a reporter. I had a job to do and stories to tell. He was a military man, with secrets to keep. Personal secrets as well as military ones.

I'd written a story about a warlord, a big man in a small district. The warlord was supposedly our ally in the war on terror. I thought he was worse than the enemy. Everyone knew he was deep into the drug trade, and that he had a fondness for boys—the younger and more cowed the better. He kept a fully equipped torture chamber (which I had, fortunately, never seen) in the cellar of a mansion so over-decorated it made mad King Ludwig's palace look sedate. My story laid it all out—the drugs, the debauchery, the cruelty.

I also suspected, although couldn't prove, that he slipped drug money to one Major Gary Wolfe. That part of it I did not include in my story.

Military intelligence got wind of what I was investigating and ordered me to stop. They sent Wolfe around to badger me. Until then I'd merely suspected the major was taking bribes from the warlord. When I saw the fear and hatred in his eyes, fear of being discovered, hatred of me for uncovering his secrets, I knew it.

Threats were made, on Wolfe's part, not mine. I refused to withdraw the story.

The brass went to my bosses, demanding the paper not print the story, saying it was a threat to national security as our army needed the warlord's good will.

The paper pulled the story.

I never quite forgave them for that. I could understand their point of view, but how we were winning the hearts and minds of the people of Afghanistan by letting someone rape their children and torture their cousins and brothers, never mind act as a conduit for hard drugs flooding the cities of the West, was beyond my understanding.

I'd been angry at the paper, for giving in and not standing up for what was supposed to be their responsibility, but in a way I understood and I'd moved on. I hadn't exposed Wolfe, which I wouldn't do without proof, and heard he'd been posted back to Canada shortly thereafter.

I remembered the way he spoke to me that day in Kabul. As if me, my job, was a personal affront to him. He'd spat words like treachery and sedition and sworn he'd see me ruined.

I've found that, no matter where or when, once the language gets ratcheted up to talk of treason and liberty there can be no compromise. Particularly not when it was used to conceal an underlying fear—fear at being exposed and disgraced.

All that had happened a year ago. I'd forgotten about Gary Wolfe and that petty warlord. Clearly Wolfe hadn't forgotten me. He must have been following me: my career, my injury, my recovery. There was no reason at all anyone in military intelligence would be concerned with the murder of Hila Popalzai. Only, Wolfe, who'd never forgotten me.

Or how much he hated me.

◇◇◇

I woke up on the living-room floor. My head full of pain. I couldn't let Joanne find me here, like this. Certainly not Lily or Charlie. I rolled onto my stomach and slowly, very slowly, pulled myself as far as to my hands and knees.

I opened my eyes only enough to see the patch of floor in front of me, and I crawled up the stairs. Like a baby or an old dog. I felt my way to my room, and then to my bed. It took all the strength I had to pull myself to my feet and roll onto the bed.

The air conditioning was off and my room was overly warm. It didn't matter as I didn't have the strength to crawl under the covers. Only a few hours ago, I'd told Jake I'd move out if he wanted me to. I'd been somewhat optimistic, to say the least.

I lay on the top of my bed for a long time, wrapped in pain and misery.

And fear.

Hila's death was a terrible thing.

But it had nothing to do with me. With us. With my sister, my family.

Was Gary Wolfe going to make it about me? Just because he could?

Why not? If Hila's death was an ordinary murder, someone who saw her on her own and took advantage of the opportunity for a bout of rape and murder, Wolfe wouldn't care. It wouldn't matter to him if the perpetrator got away. If he could nail me for it, he'd consider it a job well done.

He didn't even have to have a case to take to court. A security certificate maybe, restricting my contacts and movements, perhaps even an involuntary confinement in a psychiatric hospital.

I reminded myself that I was not without resources. My mother was a doctor; she and Rebecca Mansour would ensure I wasn't declared insane.

Wouldn't they?

I was thinking of the missing hours, the hours when even I couldn't account for my whereabouts or actions, when I fell asleep.

◇◇◇

## November 3, 1783

In November 1783 the British abandoned New York and America forever. Ships packed with refugees left with them. Many returned to England, many went south to the warmer colonies of Bermuda or the Bahamas, but more than half went north, to the largely unsettled areas of Canada. Maggie accompanied Nathanial Macgregor and his family and the group heading to Upper Canada with Captain Peter van Alstine.

She went because, quite simply, she had no place else to go.

She didn't care for Nathanial's wife, a whiny self-pitying thing with airs beyond her station, and Maggie glimpsed a cruel streak in Nathanial, which he managed to keep hidden, most of the time, behind a façade of charm.

But what choice did she have? Her friends were joining their husbands, starting new lives of their own.

Maggie had no one else in the world to offer her protection. If she travelled alone her reputation, not to mention her personal safety, would be in great danger. Nathanial had assured her there were plenty of men in Upper Canada in need of a wife. Disbanded soldiers who decided to stay on in the colony rather go back to England or Germany; single men or widowers eager to take up the British offer of land of their own.

She met men in search of a wife on the ship and in Montreal where they prepared for the journey west. But she turned aside their feeble attempts to court her. She knew she had to get over the loss of Hamish and Flora and all they had. She needed to start a new life, a new family.

In a new county.

But whether it was because Maggie couldn't bear the idea of man who was not Hamish coming to her bed, or because Nathanial was hostile to any potential suitors, by the time Maggie arrived in Fifth Town in July of 1784 she was a servant in all but name to the Macgregor family.

◇◇◇

**July 15, 1786**

It had been a hellish journey. First the overcrowded ship, packed beyond civilized endurance with families consisting of everything from screaming babies to confused grandfathers. Rations were poor, tempers were short, the weather poor. As the creaky old ship tossed on the waves the stomachs of many of the passengers, a great many of whom had never even seen the sea, much less been cast adrift upon it, tossed as well.

They disembarked on shaky legs and were loaded onto more boats for the journey up the river to Quebec. They could not stay in Quebec; it was an English colony but still French, French laws and customs and language. The English-speaking refugees were not wanted there, nor did they wish to stay. They wintered in Lachine, north of Montreal, and a cold, lonely, boring, miserable winter it was, everyone waiting. Waiting. To be on their way to their new homes. Babies were born and old people died. Children died too, and strong young men and women, of accidents and infections and of despair. They almost lost Marie and Nathanial's daughter Emily to the fever, but Maggie put everything she had into saving the little girl, and one day, while a blizzard raged in the night and the last of the candles burned low, Emily opened her eyes, bright and clear, and said, "I'm thirsty."

Spring came at long last, and they set off, up the river to Upper Canada. More than a thousand of them, a motley pack of refugees, many of them ex-soldiers, in a party led by Captain Peter van Alstine, formerly of New York. The British government had granted every Loyalist family a plot of land, hundreds of acres, and supplies. Maggie, of course, got no land of her own. Bateaux were loaded with men and women, cows and oxen, chickens and children, and all they would need to carve a life out of the vast wilderness. Maggie looked at the pile of supplies that were to get the Macgregor family started and thought it pitifully small.

Her heart lifted the moment she saw the lake. Blue water, stretching farther than the eye could see, sparkled in the sunlight. As vast as the ocean, yet not tempest-tossed but calm and peaceful. Trees, taller than the masts of the ship that had taken them from New York, wider than the boat on which she perched, lined the shore. At the edge of the water, everything was green and bright and sun-touched, but beyond the first line of trees the forest closed in, dark and foreboding. Trees had stood here for hundreds of years, growing tall and broad without ever hearing the sound of an axe or feeling the touch of fire save from an Indian hunting party's small flame.

Yet this band of refugees, soldiers, blacksmiths, shopkeepers, innkeepers, cooks, only a few farmers, were to work this land and make a living from it?

Each night they pulled their boats up to shore and made camp. Firelight flickered against the dark, impenetrable forest, and ex-soldiers and townsmen kept watch and no one dared venture far.

"You seem like an educated lady," an elderly woman said to Maggie late one night, as the last of the men extinguished their pipes and the solders among them changed guard and the women lay down beside exhausted children. She sat on the ground watching the flames of the communal fire and tried to remember Hamish and the face she had loved so much.

"I have little formal schooling," Maggie replied. "But my mother and father loved to read and our library was considered quite grand."

The old lady reached into the depths of her shawl and pulled out a small book. She handed it to Maggie with no expression on her face. Maggie took it. It was small but very fine, good quality paper bound in black leather. She opened the book and flicked through the pages. It was a ledger, the sort that a shopkeeper might use to record sales. The first several pages were full of small cramped writing and neat rows of numbers, the rest of the book was empty, still waiting the touch of a pen.

"It's very nice," Maggie said, passing the book back. From the edge of the woods an owl called. Small yellow eyes blinked at them from beyond the rim of firelight.

The lady shook her head. "Keep it, my dear. It belonged to my late husband. We had a dry goods shop in Albany. Our neighbors killed him for continuing to stock tea. I kept the book, thinking I might use it to make a record of my journey." She fumbled in her pockets with crooked fingers and coughed. "But my journey will not be a long one and books will be rare where we are headed. I'd like you to have it." She pulled out a small bottle of ink and passed it over.

"Me? Why are you giving this to me? I don't even know your name."

"That is of no importance. I've been watching you and I know you will take care of it. Use it carefully; perhaps someday someone will read the story of your journey."

She got to her feet as if every movement was an effort. "Good night, my dear. Travel well." She disappeared into the night.

Maggie was pleased with the gift and tucked it safely away with her small bundle of belongings. She lay down on the rough ground, pulled her blanket over her and slept.

The morning was, as always, a chaos of breaking camp and loading everyone back onto the boats. Several days passed before Maggie thought to seek out the kind woman and inquire as to her health.

The light had been poor around the fire, shapes shifting and shadows deep, and Maggie could scarcely remember what the old woman looked like. She probably wasn't even all that old: the war, the journey, had taken its toll on them all. She didn't find the woman, and soon forgot her, as word spread that they were approaching their destination.

After a month on the river, having left some of their party in various places along the route, the ragged band of refugees crossed the bay and landed on a peninsula of untouched wilderness, jutting into the great lake. Lots were drawn, land assigned, and the new settlers set about making a home. They worked in groups at first, cutting down sufficient of the giant hardwood trees to clear a patch of land for the first crops and harvest wood to build a rude shelter for the coming winter. Then it was on to the next farm and a home for the next family.

All the money Maggie's mother had sent her, all of her earnings in New York, her mother's jewelry, even the wooden box itself had been sold long ago.

As well as the half-used shopkeeper's ledger and bottle of ink, Maggie's worldly belongings consisted of two dresses, one for every day and one for the rare occasion to attend church services, one pair of sturdy, although worn boots, a couple of blankets, a heavy shawl, two lengths of hair ribbon—one blue and one cream—a white nightgown with lace many times repaired, a set of sewing needles and thread, one pot and one frying pan that Fiona, the cook, had insisted she have as her share for working in the kitchen. Flora's soft baby blanket, from which the scent of the little girl had faded long ago, she used as a pillow.

And the diamond earrings Hamish had given her on the occasion of their wedding. She kept the earrings, tied together, pinned to the inside of her dress, out of sight.

Someday, she continued to hope, she would be able to make a life of her own, away from Nathanial and his stifling wife.

Nathanial never behaved improperly toward her, but sometimes she saw something in his eye, the way he watched her, which she did not care for.

The first winter in Fifth Town had been long and bleak. As snow fell the family, and Maggie, huddled in the small log house they'd built around the few pieces of furniture Nathanial and his sons managed to make out of logs and stumps. They had a few chickens, which didn't lay well in the dark days, and a single small red and white cow Nathanial had managed to purchase in Lachine provided milk for the children. Otherwise their diet consisted of their allotment of rations from the government: a great deal of salt pork. Some of the men were able to supplement their family's rations with deer or geese they'd hunted with muskets they'd brought with them from the army. Nathanial had no weapon, and his attempts at setting snares and traps were rarely successful. Caleb was able to catch some of the gray squirrels brave enough to nose around his traps. They were tough and unappetizing, but the squirrels were meat and enough of them could feed the family. Heavily salted they could be stored for leaner times.

A baby boy was born to Nathanial and Maria in the spring of 1785, but it was blue and thin and its breath came in ragged gasps; it hadn't lived a week before being buried in a tiny home-made coffin in a piece of land hastily cleared to provide a small cemetery. No preacher was in the area, so Nathanial himself mumbled the words over a simple cross made of green wood while his family and Maggie watched. Maggie stood beside the grave, her arm around little Emily, and wondered how many more would be laid to rest beside the infant.

Nathanial and his sons planted wheat between the stumps of mighty trees they'd felled the previous year, and Maggie began a vegetable garden in the rocky soil. She planted turnips, kale, Indian corn, peas, potatoes, and pumpkin. In a corner she put in a few of the herbs that Fiona in New York had taught her to use to liven up her cooking: some rosemary and mint. Beyond the little circle of the homestead clinging to the shores of the great lake, the forest loomed thick and dark and foreboding. They'd almost lost young Caleb, who'd gotten lost searching for the wandering cow. He, and the cow, spent a cold fearful night in the deep woods before stumbling onto the lakefront and following it to a neighboring farm.

A widower by the name of Rudolph Mann owned the plot three over. He had six sons and thus, because families got extra land for their children, had the potential to become one of the more prosperous in the area. Mr. Mann and his sons were ferociously hard workers but, as everyone knew, no matter how many sons there might be the family needed someone to do women's work. Rudolph been a tenant farmer in Pennsylvania and was happy and proud to now have a sizable holding of his own. Land for his sons to inherit. Land on which generations still to come would grow and prosper.

The new settlers, many with no experience living in the countryside, never mind the wilderness, were dependent on each other and, with few exceptions, were close. The experienced farmers among them were quick to give a helping hand or the benefit of their advice to the struggling new ones. Rudolph Mann came regularly to the Macgregor place with an offer of advice or assistance. He'd doff his cap politely to Maria and Maggie, and one hot summer's day, his face as red as the cardinal watching them from the branch of an oak, he dared to ask Maggie if she'd care to go for a stroll.

Rudolph was not a good-looking man, and he was considerably older than Maggie. His English was poor, his manners were rough, and his words few. He was not Hamish. But he had a nice smile and a kind heart, and his sons were always unfailingly polite.

He would soon ask Nathanial for Maggie's hand, she was sure. After their wedding, she'd give him her earrings. They had been a gift from Hamish, and were, she sometimes thought, more important to her than life itself. But she would use them as Hamish would have wanted her to, to make a new life for herself.

And any children she and Rudolph might have.

She was twenty-eight years old but there was still plenty of time to have more children. The first son would be named Hamish.

Maggie Macgregor and Rudolph Mann stood on the shore of the lake, so vast they could not see the other side. The reflection of the sun on the brilliant blue water was painful to their eyes. There was no wind and the surface of the lake lay still and calm. White birds circled above the water, screeching to their fellows, and a family of ducks paddled by staying close to the shore. Maggie's dress clung to the small of her back and sweat gathered under her thick hair.

Rudolph shifted from one foot to another. He took off his cap and twisted it in his big, scarred hands. He'd gone to some trouble to clean up this morning, she'd noticed, and most of the dirt was gone from beneath his fingernails. She hid a smile, waiting for him to speak.

"Mrs. Macgregor," he said at last. He paused and cleared his throat.

"Yes," she said.

A raft, rough logs looped together, rounded the point bearing two men and a mangy dog. The men lifted their caps. The dog seemed to be enjoying the cruise.

"Mrs. Macgregor," Rudolph repeated when the craft had passed.

"There you are." Caleb, the eldest of Nathanial and Maria's surviving children, came out of the trees. He walked across the rock toward them. "You shouldn't disappear like that, Maggie."

"I have scarcely disappeared," she replied. "As you have found me." She was technically this boy's father's cousin's wife, and thus deserving of the respect shown to an older family member. However, the boys, like their parents, had come to regard Maggie as more of a servant than a relation, and usually spoke to her as such.

"Pa sent me to look for you. You've chores to do at home. Today's washing day, you know."

"I am aware of that, Caleb. I'll be along shortly."

Caleb stood his ground. Rudolph shifted from one foot to another, and then he put his cap back on his head and said, "I'll be back to my own chores. Can we walk another day, Mrs. Macgregor?"

"I would like that, thank you."

"When she's finished her work," Caleb said. He turned and walked away, leaving Maggie to follow. She hiked her skirts to keep the hem out of the water lapping at the edges of the rocks. The settlers erected their buildings close to the lake, as there were no roads, and their acres ran in a long strip through the dense forest.

"Caleb," Maggie called after him. He stopped and waited for her. "That was rude of you. Mr. Mann and I were engaged in a private conversation."

He had the grace to look embarrassed. "Sorry, Maggie. But Pa told me to fetch you right away."

The big vat of water placed over an open fire in the yard had not even come to the boil. Marie was sitting in her chair beside the pile of laundry, shelling peas. She watched Maggie approach with narrow eyes. "I'd like a cup of tea."

"So would I," Maggie said.

Nathanial learned against the rail fence surrounding the vegetable garden, erected to keep deer from the tender plants. He watched Maggie, but said nothing.

She felt his eyes on her back as she went into the house. She would have to make the tea. No one else would.

It was July, and the bounty of the farm and the forest was providing welcoming food. For supper that evening, Maggie roasted rabbits the boys had trapped, and served the meat with little round potatoes and bright green peas picked fresh from her own garden. She'd even made a pie with brilliant red berries she and Emily had collected by the bucketful at the edge of the forest. Maggie had learned to bake in Fiona's kitchen in New York, where they made pies sweetened with expensive sugar for customers who could afford to pay. This crust was tough and lumpy, the berries sweetened with a touch of honey, but the family dove in with enthusiasm.

Nathanial got up from the table with a grunt. "Going out for a bit," he said to his wife. And he left.

The men rarely socialized with their neighbors in spring or summer. The working day was long and hard, and most wanted nothing to do after supper but to go bed to rest up for another day that would be exactly the same as every other.

Maggie boiled water over the fire, not much caring what Nathanial did with his evenings. She washed up the dishes, and took the dirty water outside to throw under the trees.

It was July and it took a long time for night to fall. Maggie stood in the clearing, enjoying the quiet of the dusk, as soft and warm as a black velvet robe she had owned long ago. Pricks of light began to appear, first one, then three, then many lights, quick as a blink, darting amongst the vegetables, flittering between the branches of the trees. Emily chased them, her braid streaming behind, arms outstretched, laughing. The lights danced around her and try as she might she could never catch one. Fireflies, one of the most delightful things Maggie had ever known.

The next morning, the new calf was gone and when Maggie came across its bellowing, searching mother and ran to tell Nathanial, he said he'd sold it and she was to mind her own business.

Rudolph Mann did not call on Maggie again.

# Chapter Twenty-seven

I'd never before had a doctor who made house calls. Definitely not one who just dropped in to see if I needed anything.

I'd been in the greenhouse, placing eggs into cartons for CSA delivery and to put in the shop fridge, when I heard a car drive up. I stuck my head out and saw Doctor Mansour picking her way across the lawn to the side door.

She turned and waved at my call. She was dressed in a linen navy suit, the skirt cut precisely at her knees, the jacket perfectly ironed, the white silk blouse underneath as crisp as a newly made hotel bed. Her shoes were sexy strappy sandals with stiletto heels. No wonder she was having trouble navigating Joanne's patchy weedy lawn.

"You look nice," I said, walking out of the greenhouse to greet her.

She made a face. "Business meeting in Toronto. I have to look the part. Can't wait to get back into scrubs."

"If you're looking to buy eggs, I have lots."

She smiled. "I was thinking about you as I drove back from Toronto and thought I'd stop by and check up. You missed your appointment on Monday."

Monday. When the police took my sister in for questioning and Gary Wolfe practically accused me of murder. I had other things on my mind that day.

"Sorry. You were thinking about me?"

"I had a breakfast meeting with one of my former colleagues—thus the attire. He's an old guy and a stickler for dressing the part. I brought up your case. No names, of course. I hope you don't mind, but I did want to get another other opinion. I've been out of the loop, neurologically speaking, for some time."

As we talked we gravitated toward the house. "Would you like something to drink? Tea, juice?"

"Tea would be nice."

I set about filling the kettle and laying out the tea things while the doctor settled herself at the table.

"Did your friend tell you anything, about me? I mean, my 'case'," I wiggled my fingers in the air.

"Little I didn't already know. Time is the great healer. He always says that. How have you been?" She slipped off her jacket and hung it on the back of the chair.

I poured boiling water into the tea pot. "Good."

"He also says that total honesty between patient and doctor is another great healer."

I made myself busy. I hadn't told anyone about the visions I'd been having, the hallucinations. Quite simply, I was afraid to. I had suffered physical damage to my brain which required extensive surgery. All of which, as Rebecca's mentor believed, took time to heal. But hallucinations were another matter.

That was crossing over into mental illness territory and I most certainly did not intend to go there.

Just an overactive imagination. I'd led a busy life, full of excitement, new experiences, responsibility, even times of constant danger. Now my mind was finding itself with nothing much to do. Bored, it was taking what I'd been learning about the Loyalists and the earliest residents in this house and turned it into some sort of a mental play for my amusement.

I smiled at Doctor Mansour, pleased with my reasoning.

"He reminded me that it's sometimes difficult for patients with brain injuries, such as yourself, when the people around them don't truly understand. I suspect that's happening to you."

I shrugged.

"You look good; you look perfectly normal. Your hair's obviously shorter than you might normally wear it, but it's growing back, covering up the scars in your scalp. It can be difficult for people to understand that you are ill, very ill, when they can't see any visible wounds. Easy for them to suspect you're not as sick as you make out."

"We're doing fine," I said. I changed the subject. "I heard you had some trouble at the hospital recently."

"I did?"

"A patient refused to let you treat her. Does that happen often?"

"Not often. But more than I'd like." She held up one arm. We both studied the smooth brown skin. "Either people of this color are uneducated—despite our qualifications—or terrorists going to inject them with some sort of slow-acting poison. Take your pick." She stirred a generous amount of sugar into her tea.

"What are you doing here anyway?"

A flash of anger crossed her face. "What am I doing here? I was born here. In a hospital in Mississauga. I'm as Canadian as you are, Hannah. My parents came from Egypt in the early '50s. We're not even Muslim. We're Coptic Christians. Is that good enough for you?"

"Whoa, Nelly! Your family origins are no interest to me. Unless they were United Empire Loyalists, which is something I've been learning about lately. I meant, what are you doing here in Prince Edward County, a bit of a backwater medically speaking, working in the ER? You're a neurologist. Doctor Singh, who referred me to you, said you were at the top of that distinguished group. You don't have to tell me if you don't want. I'm curious that's all. I am a journalist, remember, and I'd have thought that as my doctor you'd be pleased I was showing some signs of my profession."

"Sorry," she mumbled into her tea. "Looks like I was more upset by that incident at the hospital than I thought. You'd be surprised how often I get asked where I'm from. Mississauga, I say, and they usually look surprised. I'm here, working in Emerg, because I need a break. I was with Doctors without Borders for a couple of years. In Africa."

"Tough."

"Yes. I was in South Sudan during the civil war, then in Congo for a while. Too many heads split open with machetes. Too many deliberate amputations. Too many women raped so many times they'll never function normally again." She sighed. "Children. Little children. Too much."

"Yeah," I said. "I know."

We drank our tea in silence. Outside it was a fabulous Ontario summer's day. Hot sun, blue sky, soft breeze, crops growing. Inside, death and despair had slipped in.

"A friend of mine from med school was working here and when she went on maternity leave I thought it would give me a chance to sort out what I want to do with my life."

"And has it?"

"No. My husband wants me to return to Toronto. We're separated; he wants to get back together. I just don't know."

"Is he a doctor also?"

"Orthopedic surgeon. We've been together since first day at university. He's lost the passion for the job. He's still a good doctor, a great surgeon, but patients are like things to him now. He might as well be a motor mechanic. Me, I still feel their pain.

"Good heavens! What am I saying! I came to see you because you missed our appointment and wanted to check up on you, and now I'm confessing as if you're my psychiatrist. Is that why you make such a good journalist?"

I grinned at her. "Yup."

"I'd better get going. I'm on this afternoon, and," she touched the collar of her immaculate white shirt, "this is not something I want to be wearing when some kid comes in with a nosebleed that won't let up."

We walked together out to her car. It was a fancy red thing, slung low to the ground, paint glistening in the sun, convertible top down, white leather seats.

"Nice wheels," I said.

"My one indulgence in life. Thanks for the tea, Hannah. I enjoyed talking to you."

"I did, too." And I had. It would be nice to have a friend out here.

◇◇◇

Black Beauty tossed her head and stamped her feet. Lily stroked the horse's soft velvet nose. "Come on, girl," she said. I had hold of Tigger's bridle and followed Lily and her horse into the barn. The scent of fresh straw and ammonia and aging wood. Lily led Beauty into her stall and came back for Tigger. I turned on the tap and filled the water trough from a hose while Lily poured the nightly treat of oats into the feeding pails. The horses lowered their big heads and began to munch. As they ate, their powerful muscles twitched to get rid of settling flies. A scrawny barn cat, as orange as a Halloween pumpkin, climbed a bale of hay and began washing its whiskers. I waited at the barn door for Lily, who said good night to her animals and gave them and their surroundings one last affectionate look before closing the doors. We walked slowly across the yard. A length of straw was trapped in her braid. I pulled it loose and let my hand rest on her shoulder.

We'd had a barbeque for dinner, and the scent of hot coals and roasting meat lingered over the yard in the long summer twilight. A mosquito buzzed around my ear, and I waved my hand in the air. A soft wind stirred the leaves of the maple trees, and a dove cooed from atop a telephone wire. The setting sun turned the clouds shades of baby blue and pink and the fields glowed with the last lingering light. Jake tossed a ball to Charlie, while Joanne stood on the deck watching them, a wine glass in her hand.

A wave of contentment washed over me. It had been a long time since I'd felt this well. Even when I was healthy and whole, the job was everything in my life, leaving little time to relax and enjoy my surroundings and think about all that was good.

Hila's funeral had been today. We had not gone. Muslims bury their dead as soon as possible. The police had released the body yesterday, after the autopsy and further investigations.

Whatever that meant. The Harrisons then contacted the small Islamic community in Belleville and the job was done.

I'd been invited, but Rebecca Mansour had advised against attending. The press of people, the emotion. I said I'd risk it, and she said, with considerable frankness, did I want to collapse and take the attention away from Hila, where it belonged?

I regretted not going. I needed to say my good-byes. I missed Hila; I missed her silent presence as she walked beside me in the summer woods. Her strength, I now understood, had given me strength. Would I be able to find it again, on my own?

The police hadn't been around for a couple of days. According to the paper there had been no new developments, and according Connor, who regularly reported from the bars in Picton, the cops were looking for two young white men, seen driving around the countryside in the days prior to Hila's disappearance.

Lily went to join her father and brother in their game, and I climbed the steps to the deck. The phone rang, and Joanne slipped into the kitchen to get it. I kicked my farm boots off and followed, intending to put the kettle on. I eyed the open bottle of wine on the counter longingly. I'd loved red wine once, too much sometimes. It didn't go with my medication and even if it did, I dared not give Omar any additional opportunity to find me not in control of myself. Joanne answered the phone and her voice registered alarm. "I'll be right over."

"What's the matter?"

"That was Maude Harrison. Their house has been vandalized. Grant's not there, and she sounds frightened."

"I'll come with you."

"No."

"Yes," I said, heading for the porch in search of shoes.

Joanne yelled to Jake that she was popping out for a moment. I was waiting for her by her car, and we drove the short distance to the Harrison home.

Maude met us at the front door, Buddy at her side. Her eyes were large and dark in a pale face. She twisted her hands in front of her. As we approached, she turned without a word and led the way into the house.

The art had been torn off the walls, books pulled from bookcases, cushions tossed off couches, drawers opened and contents dumped out. Broken china, pottery, and porcelain littered the floor. An African mask swung silently from one hook.

So many of their lovely things, the accumulation of a lifetime, a broken mess.

The Royal Doulton China, on which I'd been served tea, was a jumble of fragments.

"Have you called the police?" Joanne asked.

Maude shook her head.

"I'll do it."

"No. I don't want them here, poking around. Causing more trouble. Taking Grant away again. "

"Trouble's here, Maude," I said, "whether you like it or not. Where's Grant?"

"We went to Hila's funeral in separate cars. After, he went to Kingston to have dinner with an old friend, and I came on home."

"You'd better call him."

She shook her head. "He keeps a cell phone for emergencies, but otherwise never turns it on. " She crouched down and picked up an African carving. Made of good strong wood, it was undamaged. She put it carefully onto the table.

"Where was Buddy when this happened?" I asked. He was sniffing at the rug. Too bad he couldn't tell us what he was finding there.

"There's a small room off the kitchen. We leave him in there with his bed and food and water when we go out for any length of time."

"Is anything taken?" Joanne asked.

"I've hardly had time to notice, but it doesn't look like it. Sheer vandalism. Sheer meanness."

"Probably," Joanne said. "Talk in town is of Islamic terrorists running amok in the county, although no one has actually seen such a thing. There was at least one incident at the hospital when someone refused to let Doctor Mansour treat them. Maybe a couple of guys got drunk and figured you and Grant for terrorist sympathizers."

I thought it more likely common-or-garden thieves than drunken old boys out for some fun. The Harrisons had been in the news lately; everyone knew Hila had been living here. Easy enough to find out today was her funeral and assume Maude and Grant would be out, the house empty and ripe for a bit of thieving.

The beautiful Afghan rug I'd admired on my first visit to this home had been pulled up and tossed aside. Nothing underneath but plain plywood flooring. The rug was undamaged. I didn't like to tell Maude she'd been lucky. Nothing lucky about what had happened here. But the damage was a lot less than it could have been. The house had been ransacked, but I saw little of the mindless destruction there could have been. Some pieces were broken, but only because they'd been thrown to the floor. I'd seen vandalized homes before. Sometimes all that remained of precious objects would be a pile of colored dust. Destruction for its own sake.

"Have you had a look in the bedrooms?" I asked. "Your jewelry? What about electronics, computers and things?"

Maude led the way down the corridor to the master bedroom at the back. The overwhelming scent of spilled perfume drifted toward us. Clothes had been tossed out of the closets onto the floor; drawers ransacked. Several pairs of lacy panties and skimpy bras were tossed on the bed, and I almost chuckled in surprise. Wouldn't have thought prim and proper Maude had it in her.

A wooden box with numerous small drawers lay on the floor. Maude scooped it up and gave it a shake. It rattled. "I don't have much in the way of good jewelry. Other than my rings." A row of diamonds glittered on her left hand and a blood-red ruby graced the right. "Grant and I prefer to spend money on our collection. I guess whoever did this didn't think my stuff was worth taking." She pulled out a couple of long glittering strands. Big colorful stones, obviously glass.

We checked the den next. Not too much damage. Papers on the floor, paintings and photographs torn off the walls. A large wooden desk was up against the windows, looking out over the side lawn. A flat-screen monitor, keyboard, and mouse were still in place. A gaping space where a laptop had sat.

"They took the computer," I said.

"No. Grant has it with him. He thought he might be early for meeting his friend and if so wanted to get some work done."

"What's he working on?"

"He has a contract with the department. Some research project or another to do with the Afghan national museum."

"The department? You mean DFAIT?" The Department of Foreign Affairs and International Trade.

"Yes."

I studied the floor. Piles of CD cases had been swept off the desk shelves and scattered across the floor but few were broken. "I don't suppose you can tell if any of his computer accessories are missing? Like backup CDs or a thumb drive?"

"What's that?"

I explained, and Maude shrugged. "Don't think he has one of those."

She turned and left the room. Joanne and I followed. Maude stopped at another bedroom. She rested her hand against the open door. "Hila's room."

It was a small room, made smaller by the jumble of books and bedding and black clothing. The mattress on the bed and the top of the desk were bare, sheets and blankets a heap on the floor.

"I haven't cleaned up her things yet," Maude said, and her voice caught.

"Her computer?" I asked.

"The police took it, along with all of her CDs and her notebooks. They haven't brought it back yet. Her iPod is there." Maude pointed to the white wires underneath a pillow.

Joanne picked up a headscarf. We three women stood in silence for a long time. Outside birds called to each other from the tops of trees. It was getting late. It would be dark soon.

"Her Koran!" Maude dropped to her knees with a cry.

"What about it?"

"Where is it?" Maude scrambled across the floor, throwing clothes and sheets aside. Joanne and I joined her, and Hila's bedroom was soon a blur of flying cloth and papers and weeping women. There were lots of books, from modern mysteries to classic English novels to grammar guides to mathematics texts. But no sign of the holy book.

"It's gone." Maude sat back on her heels and wailed.

"Are you sure she left it here?" I asked. "Maybe the police took it with her computer and things?"

"It was right here this morning, on the bedside table. I was in earlier, before we left for…the funeral. I…I find it hard to believe she's gone." Maude began to cry. Great gulping sobs as the tears ran down her face and her nose streamed. Joanne went to the bathroom and returned with a box of tissues. Maude held one to her face and talked, words muffled by tears and tissue. "She seemed so quiet and reserved, but in this house she was a life force. She was shy around Grant, as could be expected, but when we were alone, she and I, she was nothing but a bundle of questions. Always questions; always wanting to know. About Canada, about living in the West. She was fascinated by you, Hannah, did you know that? So interested in the places you'd been and the work you'd done. And Lily, she adored Lily. She would watch Lily sometimes as if she couldn't believe a girl could be so happy. So full of fun. So free." Maude dropped to the bed. Joanne and I sat on either side of her, our arms around her. We cried together. Buddy pawed at Maude's legs, but she paid him no attention.

"She wanted so much to go to Vancouver. She read about it, and began looking at pictures on the Internet. She was excited, thought it must be the most beautiful place on earth. She'd never seen the ocean, thought Lake Ontario was magnificent." Maude wiped at her eyes and blew her nose. "I'll never look at the lake the same way again."

I began to get to my feet, but at that moment Maude remembered what had brought on this bout of tearful remembrance. "Her Koran. It was precious to her. The only thing she had left in the world that had been her family's. It was found in the wreckage of their car and brought to her in hospital. I saw it this morning, I'm sure of it. It's been stolen. Of all the things in this house, why would someone take that? It wasn't a valuable book, nothing out of the ordinary. Only valuable to Hila."

*Hate*, I thought. Pure hate. Because someone had said the word 'terrorist' and they had to destroy what they could not understand. No doubt Hila's precious Koran was in a bonfire right about now.

While a couple of drunken louts danced about and compared the size of their pricks.

Another thought struck me. Might it be the exact opposite?

Had the Koran been taken because it didn't belong in the house of the Infidel?

◇◇◇

Finally, Maude agreed to call the police. As nothing of any sizeable value had been stolen, she was reluctant, but Joanne told her that nothing being stolen was not a good sign. It meant they'd done it for fun. Because they could.

And maybe they'd want to do it again.

"Besides," she added with a shrug, "You have to tell the insurance company, and they'll insist on the police being called."

Maude took Buddy to his room off the kitchen so he'd be out of the way. We waited for the police to arrive, while the dog scratched at the door and whined to be let out.

It didn't take long, and I wasn't surprised to see Sergeant McNeil pull in behind the patrol car. A couple of minutes later a black Suburban came down the long driveway in a spray of dust and screeching breaks and aggression.

Rick Brecken and Gary Wolfe.

Wolfe gave me a look of pure contempt and went to talk to McNeil. Brecken came up to where Joanne and I stood with Maude. "You ladies can be going home now."

"I don't…" I began, but Maude put her hand on my arm. "Thank you. Thank you for being here. I'll be all right now. Grant will be home soon." While we'd waited for the police, she'd splashed water on her face and retied her bundle of hair and settled her face into calm lines.

Knowing we'd been dismissed, Joanne and I walked to her car. I felt Gary Wolfe's eyes on my back, and I shivered. The police officer had to move his vehicle so we could get out of the driveway.

A large van was parked at the side of the road, and a man and a woman were unloading TV cameras and sound equipment. "Oh, no," Joanne said.

I ducked my head. Fortunately night had arrived and the road was dark. I didn't think they'd recognized me.

I hoped they hadn't recognized me.

"How awful for Maude and Grant," Joanne said. She couldn't help glancing at the TV people in her rear-view mirror. "First Hila's death and then this. Maude seems okay, but it'll hit her soon enough when she has to start cleaning up the mess. I'd like to get my hands on the miserable buggers who did this."

I smiled to myself. "You'd give them a stern talking to, I'm sure. Before you turn into our driveway, make sure no one's following us, Joanne."

She gasped. "You think…"

"No, I don't think the vandals are after us. But those reporters will be if they know it's me in this car."

She drove to a house further down the road and then made a circle in their drive. No one appeared to be following us.

At the farm, yellow lights burned over the front and side doors; brighter lights were on by the barn and the greenhouse. The warm night air was like velvet on my skin. The distant noise of a TV coming from Connor's trailer broke the deep silence. A man stood up and crossed in front of the window. Connor's cousin, probably around for a couple of beers and a movie.

Jake was in the kitchen with Lily and Charlie, giving them a bedtime snack. The kids were in their pajamas, skin scrubbed clean from their baths and hair shiny with brushing.

"You were gone a long time?" Jake said in question.

"At the Harrison's. Someone broke into their house while they were out, and Maude came home alone. The police are there now."

Jake swore, and then gave his children a guilty look. "Sorry. I can't help wondering what's going to happen next."

"Nothing. It's over," Joanne said quickly. She plugged in the kettle. Lily opened the fridge and reached for the jug of orange juice.

"They take much?" Jake asked.

"Nothing. Just ransacked the house. Made a heck of a mess."

"They stole only one thing," I said. "Far as Maude could see. From Hila's room."

We jumped at the sound of shattering glass. Orange liquid sprayed across the linoleum. Lily stood at the open fridge door, juice pooling at her feet.

Charlie laughed and his father snapped at him.

"Did they…did they steal Hila's things?" Lily said, her voice small.

Joanne sat down and pulled her daughter to her. Lily climbed up into her mother's lap. At ten years old she was getting too big for lap-sitting, but she buried her head into Joanne's chest. "Some of their nice things were broken but nothing seemed to have been taken. Other than Hila's Koran. Mr. and Mrs. Harrison don't have a lot of jewelry or electronics. That's the sort of stuff thieves are after, usually. Things they can get rid of easily. They weren't smart enough to know that some of the paintings and carvings are worth a lot, and they wouldn't be able to sell them anyway."

"Will thieves come for our things?" Charlie asked.

"No," Jake said, very firmly.

"Okay," Charlie said, satisfied. "Can I have a cookie?"

Jake handed his son the tin. Charlie took one. Seeing that no one was paying him much attention, he snuck another.

Nice, I thought, to be able to be so reassured by one word from your father. I glanced at Lily. Far from being comforted her face was pure white under her tan and her eyes were round with fear.

# Chapter Twenty-eight

Lily came into my room on her way to bed. She was ready for sleep, dressed in cheerful yellow pajamas, smelling of toothpaste and shampoo overlaying a lingering trace of horses and hay. I was sitting in bed, listening to an audio book. The library history books were piled beside me, but I'd been unable to follow the words and had discarded them in anger. I pulled the ear buds away and patted the duvet.

"Good night, Aunt Hannah." Lily sat on the bed and gave me a big hug.

"Good night, dearest. What's on for tomorrow?"

"Nothing much." She picked up the top book and flicked through it without interest. She stopped at a picture, a drawing of an eighteenth century couple standing in front of a log cabin.

"Aunt Hannah?"

"Yes?"

"I overheard Mom telling Dad you shouldn't go into the root cellar. She said it has a strange effect on you. What'd she mean?"

"The bright light in that enclosed space hurts my head."

"Is that all?"

It certainly wasn't all. "Yes, that's all. Why do you ask, Lily?"

She was silent for a long time. She ran the tip of her index finger across the picture in the book, tracing the outline of the woman's dress, the neatly-tied bonnet.

"When I was little," she said in a slow, soft voice, "my cousins Mike and Louise came to visit from Vancouver." She stopped talking and I waited her out. She had something she wanted to tell me but she needed to tell it in her own way, in her own time.

"Louise is nice, but Mike's mean. I don't like him. He's older than me and is really bossy. One night, after dinner, we were playing hide and seek outside. I didn't want to play, but Mom said I had to. I hid in the root cellar. Mike found me and instead of yelling to tell Louise and Charlie where I was, he locked me in."

"How awful. There isn't a lock on the door, is there?"

"No, but he leaned up against it so I couldn't get it open. I could hear him laughing and laughing. I was there for a long time. Louise and Charlie gave up on the game and went back into the house. It was really dark. I was too small then to reach the string for the light."

"You must have been terribly frightened."

"I was. At first." She hesitated. Her fingers plucked at a loose thread on the cover of my duvet.

"At first?"

"The lady came to me. I could see her, even though it was dark. She wore a long dress just like that one." Lily's finger stabbed the page. "She had the same sort of hat tied under her chin. She didn't smell good, like she hadn't washed in a long time. She wasn't pretty, like a fairy, just an ordinary lady. She was nice. She told me I wasn't to be afraid. She said I was safe. And then I wasn't scared any more."

I realized that I'd stopped breathing. A cold chill reached down my spine. I stroked Lily's hair. "I'm assuming you got out of the root cellar eventually."

"Stupid Mike gave up and went into the house. The lady told me I could leave now, and I did."

"Did you tell your mother?"

"I told Dad. He said I was imaging things, that there wasn't any lady living in the root cellar. He got mad at Mike, though and sent him to bed early."

"Have you seen her again, Lily, this lady?"

She shook her head. "I heard music once, when I went down there with Mom. As if a woman was singing. I asked Mom what it was, and she said I needed to have my ears checked. That was the last time. I forgot about her. Until now. I was wondering if you'd seen her, if that was why Mom said you shouldn't go there."

*Children and idiots see ghosts where no one else can.*

Had Lily seen a ghost, heard a ghost, down in the dark, dank root cellar? Clearly she believed she had, and the memory hadn't faded like a childish dream. I remembered icy wind against my legs, the stench of unwashed clothes, wood smoke, and drifting fog. Images where no one stood and voices coming out of the mist.

I fell back against the pillows, heart pounding. Lily'd seen something she didn't understand.

As had I.

Did that mean I wasn't going crazy?

Or had Lily's childish brain simply interpreted a set of information in exactly the same way my damaged one had? Perhaps she'd been studying the Loyalists in school before the incident, in the same way I'd been reading up on them. In a frightening situation we'd both sought solace by dragging up images.

I didn't know what I wanted more. To believe we'd imagined things. Or that someone…something…was down in the root cellar.

I didn't answer Lily's original question. Instead I said, "Off you go. Bed time."

She kissed my cheek. "Night, Aunt Hannah."

"Sleep well."

Memories forgotten, she bounced off the bed and ran out the door. Lily was a great deal deeper than she appeared, I suspected, and things bothered her intently. Having me living here, clearly not quite normal, the increasing tension between her parents, the death of Hila hanging over everything.

I didn't switch my book back on. I lay in bed, staring at the ceiling, deep in thought.

# Chapter Twenty-nine

Talk at lunch on Thursday was all about the break-in at the Harrisons' home. Reporters and TV people had been in town after Hila's funeral, and they'd salivated when word of the break-in began to spread. Liz told us she'd been in a bar with a group of friends when a man approached her and offered to buy her a drink.

Jake growled before she could finish her sentence. "I hope I made myself clear that anyone found talking to reporters or spreading gossip about what goes on at this farm, or at the neighbors, will be out of a job."

"Give me some credit, will you. Besides," Liz wiggled her eyebrows at Allison, "he was old and fat. A newspaper reporter, not a TV guy."

A tall fan stood in the corner, stirring the humid air, trying to cool the room down a fraction. They were calling for record temperatures again today, but no rain.

"So," Allison said, as if she didn't really care, "What did happen at the Harrisons?"

"A break-in," Jake said. "Vandalism, nothing stolen, but lots of damage."

"I've heard of that happening," Liz said. "People read the obits to find out when funerals are, then raid the house when everyone's out. I can't image much lower scum-balls than that."

I picked at the salad on my plate. I'd called Maude this morning to check up on her. Grant had answered and said she was resting. He sounded tired himself, tired and worn down.

"Any more gossip in town about what happened to Hila?" I asked.

"Consensus is home-grown terrorists," Connor replied. "They've done what they came here to do and slipped away into the night, back to their dens of iniquity in the big cities."

"Least that's what the shop-owners and property developers want everyone to think," Liz added. "It's perfectly safe here. Nothing to worry about."

"It *is* perfectly safe here," Joanne snapped. "Everyone needs to get a fucking grip."

We finished lunch in silence.

Disturbed only by a knock on the door to announce the arrival of Rick Brecken and Sergeant McNeil.

◇◇◇

Fortunately the cops hadn't stayed for long. They wanted Joanne and me to go over what happened last night. As we hadn't arrived until long after the break-in, and had done nothing but look around and suggest Maude phone the police, we didn't have much to tell them and they soon ran out of questions. As usual, Brecken had little to say, stood in the corner with his arms crossed, watching. Sergeant McNeil had edged toward the fan and tried unobtrusively to allow some of the blowing air into her dark blouse and jacket. Joanne did not offer them tea or cookies. When they left, she'd sighed and said, "I don't know how much more of this I can take."

I watched her head back to work, knowing I could do nothing to help.

I'd promised Lily I'd check on the horses in the early afternoon. She was worried they'd run out of water in the heat. Their heads were down in their paddock, searching for some leaves or tough grass they might have overlooked, tails constantly moving and muscles twitching against the onslaught of deer flies. They came to the fence to greet me, but only Beauty stayed for a pat and a scratch after I'd filled the trough. Tigger, I was beginning to suspect, did not like me.

I crossed the yard, heading back to the house. A minivan pulled up, and a family—Mom, Dad, three sunburned children—got out and went into the shop. At least Mom and Dad went into the shop. The children began chasing chickens.

Not wanting to have to make conversation, I detoured by way of the back of the equipment shed. The wall was lined with hooks on which were hung a myriad of farm implements—shovels, pitchforks, rakes, hand tools, garden hoses. Connor was bent over the sink, T-shirt tossed to one side, pants slung low on slim hips. He had a hose in his right hand and sprayed his head and neck. He straightened up, leaned back, and shook a head full of wet curls. His bare chest was slick with water and sweat, thick with muscle. A tattoo of a snake curled around a bulging bicep. He sensed me watching and turned with a grin. "Hot enough for you?"

Something moved, low in my belly. Something I'd thought had died on a roadside in Afghanistan. I mumbled words of agreement, said it looked like I had customers to attend to, and hurried away, the hot feel of Connor's eyes following me.

Or perhaps they weren't, because when I glanced back, he was gone, the hose was hung up and the parched ground was soaking up water.

# Chapter Thirty

"Hannah Manning might present a problem."

"Nah."

"She's a journalist. A reporter. A good one, I've heard. Can't keep her nose out of everyone else's business."

"Don't worry about her. Her mind's not all there. She has blackouts, whole periods of time when she doesn't know what the hell's going on. It frightens her so much, she'll believe whatever anyone tells her. She's as malleable as a kitten."

"Even kittens have claws."

"Not this one. Forget about Manning, will you? Let's get this done. I'm sick and tired of all this waiting, watching."

"Patience, my friend."

"I'm not your friend, and I'm running out of patience. I'm ready to move, and if you're not, too bad."

"I don't like it."

"I don't care if you like it or not. It's time."

"Very well."

# Chapter Thirty-one

After the children were in bed, Jake and Joanne put a movie into the DVD player. It was something of Jake's, and the cover promised guns shooting and cars exploding. I made my excuses, pretending not to notice the look of relief on Jake's face, and went upstairs.

The house was hot from the heat of the day, and I wanted to have a shower to cool down. I tilted my face and held it under the water for a long time, allowing the streaming water to stroke and caress and carry away my worries. Then I slipped into my nightgown and crawled into bed. The shower had refreshed me, physically, but my worries had not swirled down the drain with the water as I'd hoped. Rick Brecken had stood in our kitchen, watching me, hoping I'd...do what? Crack, break down, confess to murdering a lovely young woman?

There were times I got facts muddled, times when I could scarcely tell up from down. Times when I saw a woman in the root cellar or thought papers cracking with age were speaking directly to me.

But I knew, I knew, I had killed no one.

No matter what happened. No matter how Rick Brecken looked at me, or Gary Wolfe taunted me, I had that to cling to.

I'd gotten bored with the audio book and had brought a book of Joanne's with me to bed. A Scandinavian bestseller that I thought I'd enjoy, but once again I couldn't follow the story. The letters lined up in formation; they blended into words and the words grouped themselves into sentences with a capital letter at the beginning and a period at the end and a handful of commas in between.

None of which made any sense to me.

I threw the book against the wall, swallowing a cry of frustration. Yes, yes, a consequence of my brain trauma. *Give it time, give it time.* I'd always been a voracious reader, and over the years when I'd been so busy with the job, I'd missed having time and leisure to get lost in a good book. Now here I was with all the time and leisure in the world and I couldn't read the blasted thing. I would have screamed, had I not been aware of Jake and Joanne below and the two children sleeping nearby.

I switched off the bedside light and threw myself back into my pillows. My duvet was bundled at the bottom of the bed, but it was too hot to pull it up. The ceiling fan turned.

As I lay there, I gradually felt a deep cold seep across my exposed chest and neck, reaching under my thin white cotton nightgown. I scrambled to pull the duvet up to my chin. I shivered. Only a short while ago it had been hot. A sultry summer night.

Deep inside my damaged head it felt as if something was moving. I braced myself for a visit from Omar, but there was no pain, not even the threat of pain. How strange, I thought, to be able to feel the brain healing itself.

I lay on my back, eyes wide open. Thoughts jumped around in my head, unbidden. Memories that were not mine. People I had never known.

Traces of white mist formed patterns in front of my eyes. I blinked. They were still there. I'd shut my door and the room should have been completely dark. Yet I could see tendrils of white, stirred by the fan, dripping along the walls, curling across the floor. I shuddered in the cold.

<> <> <>

**August 20, 1786**
An itinerant preacher arrived in Fifth Town, and everyone gathered for services with as much excitement, if not more, at the

opportunity to socialize with neighbors as to hear the word of God. A building to house a church had not yet been built, so one of the settlers offered his yard for the purpose. The sermon was long and boring, and it was stifling hot in the strong sun. Children shifted, their mothers shushed them, and the occasional sound of a slap could be heard. Women fanned themselves with hats and whatever else came to hand, and men wiped sweat off their brow with shirt sleeves. Young men eyed young women, young women peeked out from under their lashes, and old men snored until their wives delivered a sharp elbow to the ribs.

After the service, a picnic was served on the rocks at the edge of the lake. The men talked about farming while those lucky enough to have tobacco smoked their pipes, and women sat in the shade of big oaks and gossiped. Children ran and played and splashed in the water, and everyone was delighted to have the chance to stop work for a few hours.

Maggie leaned back. The bark of a tree was solid against her back, the sun warm on her face, and the light breeze off the water stirred her hair. It felt so wonderful not be working. All around her women chatted.

"Everyone knows she's simple," said Mrs. vanden Hovel, an older woman known to have a vicious tongue. "I suppose as long as she can keep house and bear children nothing else matters."

"She's very young," someone replied.

Maggie kept her eyes closed and tried to shut out the woman's voices.

"Sixteen's not young. I was fourteen when I married my Gerrit. God bless his soul."

"It's a good match," another woman said. "He's going to do well, everyone says so. With six strapping sons they're clearing their land so such faster than any of the rest of us can. Why he even came into possession of a new calf recently."

Maggie opened her eyes. "Who are you talking about?"

Mrs. vanden Hovel opened her mouth to answer but Marie got in first. Her eyes glittered with malice. "Mr. Mann, of course.

He's been looking for a wife with that pack of sons to feed. I'm not surprised he decided to favor a *young* woman."

*So, I now know my worth*, Maggie thought. One calf.

◇◇◇

## December 22, 1786

It had snowed in the night, and this snow looked as though it intended to stay. Maggie had risen twice to stoke the embers of the fire back to a flame, put on more wood, and to check that sleeping Emily was well wrapped. The logs that made up their house didn't fit perfectly together and the dirt and straw used for chinking was coming loose in places. Snowflakes had drifted in on icy winds to settle on top of Jacob and Caleb's blankets, but nothing ever seemed to disturb their sleep.

Maggie wrapped herself in her shawl and made her way toward the chicken coop. The nights came early and the mornings late and chickens wouldn't lay well for many months to come, but they had to be fed if the family was to eat eggs in the spring and enjoy a treat of roast chicken for a special dinner.

She was almost at the henhouse, the cold ground biting through the soles of her boots, when she remembered that she hadn't hung the kettle back on the hook above the fire. Better do that if she wanted a warming drink later.

She didn't intend to be quiet, but the snow muffled her footsteps. The door opened and Maggie saw Marie, still in her nightgown although the pale winter sun was rising in the east, in the corner where Maggie and Emily slept, bending over the shelf where she, Maggie, kept her few possessions.

"What do you think you're doing?"

Marie leapt back. "Nothing. I can't find my best candlestick. Have you taken it?"

"It's on the mantle. Where it is always kept." Maggie placed her hands on her hips. She stared Marie down.

The woman had the grace to flush. "Oh, I must have missed it. Thank you, Maggie." She scurried back to her alcove and pulled the blanket to.

Maggie waited, while Marie dressed and went outside, head down, shoulders hunched, to use the privy. Then, heart pounding in fear, Maggie dove into her small bundle of possessions. The earrings, the most precious things she owned, were still tucked safely into the pocket of her Sunday dress. Maggie let out a long breath. She kept them hidden and rarely took the jewels out. She stroked them sometimes, through the cloth, but dared not look at them. If Nathanial and Marie knew she had such things, they would take them. And no one would help her get them back. Didn't everything she had belong to Nathanial, her "guardian"?

She slipped the earrings into her pocket and went to the root cellar on the pretext of getting potatoes.

The cellar had been dug out of the forest floor, rocks (they had plenty of those) piled around the sides to make the walls, small stones packed into the cracks, and dirt pounded down to make a floor. Maggie pried a loose stone out of a fissure between two large rocks. She'd brought a knife which she used to cut the pocket from her dress, and then she wrapped the earrings in the cloth. She stuffed the precious packet into the crevice and tapped the stone into place. Leaning back on her heels, she inspected her handiwork. Nothing at all out of the ordinary. It was so gloomy down here, even in the flickering light from the poor tallow candle, no one would notice that anything had been moved. She marked the exact spot in her mind, collected the potatoes in a bowl of her apron, and went back to work.

◇◇◇

## March 28, 1788

After a poor supper of stew made with dried fish and sprouting potatoes, Maggie walked to the Ostrander house, their nearest neighbors, to trade the last of her carrots for a bit of butter. Mrs. Ostrander, a red-faced cheerful woman not yet twenty, lifted the kettle from where it hung over the roaring fire. She'd been quite plump, Martha Ostrander, when they arrived in Lachine. Now she was almost as thin as Maggie herself. Young Mr. Ostrander, all knees and elbows and bobbing Adam's apple, gave Maggie a shy nod, lit his pipe, and headed out to the barn to check on his cow.

They'd nearly starved that winter. Some people had starved, and a few died of it. The government stopped giving the settlers rations and supplies in the summer of 1787. They were now on their own. But with so much land still to be cleared, so few crops planted, so little put aside for the long cold winter, the settlers had suffered greatly. The Macgregor family among them.

When the children complained that they wanted milk, Maggie thought it too bad they no longer had a cow. The skinny calf Nathanial had given to Rudolph Mann as payment for not marrying Maggie had grown into a good-sized beast, and its meat had gone a long way toward keeping the large family fed over the winter. In late summer, the Macgregors' cow had broken through the flimsy fence and disappeared. Taken by a wolf, likely, or one of the less honest of the neighbors. As the family's fortunes declined, Nathanial Macgregor sought someone to blame. His sons, Maggie. Soon Caleb and Jacob were avoiding their father wherever they could, and Maggie's face became accustomed to receiving a sharp slap if she didn't dodge fast enough.

"I have something I must show you," Martha Ostrander said, bustling off to the back room. Maggie ran her fingers across the smooth wood of the table. Mr. Ostrander was a deft hand with woodwork and everything in their home had been carved with an extra touch of pride and no lack of skill. Martha came back, carrying a small flat square object. She was young and pretty and joyously happy with her strapping young husband and brand-new baby. She was Maggie's only friend.

"This came just last week. The preacher brought it, a gift from my sister in Niagara. Her husband was in Butler's Rangers, you know, dear, and they're doing ever so well. Imagine, having money for trinkets such as this. I'm quite jealous." She smiled at the baby asleep in its basket by the fire, her fond expression belittling her words. "Have a look."

It was a mirror. A beautiful silver hand mirror, of the type Maggie used to have on her dressing table.

She held it up to her face. For a moment she scarcely recognized the woman looking back at her. When had she last seen her reflection? Probably not since New York, a glimpse of herself as she'd waked past a glass window. No one here had glass for their windows; a bit of oiled paper set in the frame to let in some light was the best they could do.

She was so old. The paper-thin skin beneath her eyes was the color of the sky before a thunderstorm broke, tiny lines radiated out from her mouth, skin hung loose at her throat, and sharp bones protruded above sunken cheeks. She lifted a hand and touched her hair. More than a few silver threads were woven among the black.

So old.

Mrs. Ostrander read Maggie's mind and laughed. "I thought the same, my dear. Time and this hard land are written on our faces."

Maggie put the mirror face down on the table.

Time. Once she had measured the passage of time by days. Friday piano lessons, Tuesday the art tutor came, Sunday Father led the family to church, Wednesday Mother entertained ladies to tea. At the most they marked the months: July they visited Father's sister in Philadelphia, and Mother's parents came to the house in the Mohawk Valley for the entire month of December.

Time is now marked by the seasons. The first white flower in the woods grabbing the light of the sun before the foliage grew in meant there would soon be good food to eat; stifling summer when the air was as thick as a raincloud; the harvest which brought so much work; the first snowflake, sign of hardship to come.

Time was passing her by.

When she allowed herself to think about it, she was sorry she had not married Rudolph. Sorry he'd preferred a cow and a young wife to her. She hadn't loved him, but she knew love was a rare bonus in most marriages, particularly on the frontier, where marriage meant survival for a woman on her own. The best a woman could hope for was that her husband be kind to her.

Jane had given birth nine months after her wedding to Rudolph Mann, a healthy girl, and another was on the way.

Martha's baby grizzled and stretched, and the young mother hurried to its cradle.

"I'd best be heading back," Maggie said, getting to her feet. "Work will still be waiting."

Martha gave her a smile. "So it will. You take care, won't you, my dear." She picked up her baby, and Maggie showed herself out.

As Maggie had watched the snow fall in the dark still forest, she made up her mind at last. Come spring she would be leaving. The fact that a woman such as her, of her age and her still attractive looks (or so she thought until she looked in that mirror), with good breeding as well as skill in the kitchen and with a needle, was still unwed, could only be because Nathanial Macgregor discouraged any and all potential suitors.

His wife liked having a servant, and goodness knows the family needed someone to do the hard work in the kitchen and the vegetable garden.

It would no longer be Maggie Macgregor. Her heart would break to leave sweet little Emily, who regarded Maggie as a mother. But as much as she loved Emily, the girl was not her own child, and Maggie would not give up hopes of a better life for herself.

Time, as she saw in Martha's mirror, was passing. She was thirty-one, and her chances of making a good marriage were likely gone. If she didn't leave, she'd stay here, Marie's servant, Nathanial's...what? Marie was pregnant again, complaining constantly about the ache in her back or the tiredness in her legs, and Nathanial's usual black moods were getting blacker.

Many of the other settlers had added onto their initial shanty, expanding rooms, adding some nice, although rough, furniture. Some had even built—with the help of their neighbors—log barns and outbuildings. Slowly, very slowly, trees were being cut down, land cleared, crops planted, livestock breed.

The Macgregors, however, were falling further and further behind. Caleb was a good worker, but Jacob could be counted on to disappear whenever a strong back was needed and now that he was almost seventeen was muttering about wanting more out of life than a hardscrabble farm in the wilderness and a father too quick with his fists.

Nathanial was a stubborn man, quick to take offence, too proud for his own good. He rudely turned aside advice he would have been well-suited to accept.

And Marie—everything was too difficult, too much trouble for Marie.

Their house still had nothing more than the one original room with an alcove for the parents' bed. One room where the family cooked and ate, rarely entertained visitors, and where Maggie and the children slept. Maggie knew most of what went on in the bedroom, and she could hear, although she tried not to, Marie complaining when her husband came to bed that she was unwell and besides, he mustn't take the chance of harming the baby.

The baby was due to arrive in the fall. Could Maggie stay one more winter? Her help would be needed. She'd happily leave Marie and Nathanial on their own, to survive or not. But Emily? Dear little Emily, who snuggled against Maggie in the dark cold nights and had a ready smile when she knew Maggie was feeling down. Realizing that lazy Marie had no inclination to educate her daughter, Maggie took it upon herself to teach Emily her letters. They had no books, but some of the settlers had brought one or two with them, and books were freely lent. The previous autumn Maggie had traded her frying pan, one of the last of her own possessions, for a stub of chalk and a small slate on which the girl could practice forming letters. She'd come to realize that Emily was exceptionally bright and felt a stab of pride, as if she, Maggie, had had something to do with it. The leather-bound ledger and small bottle of ink was brought out only as a special treat when Maggie allowed Emily to record something permanent on the precious paper.

It would be hard to leave Emily. She wouldn't miss the boys, though. Caleb and Jacob, who as they grew into men followed their father's lead and turned increasingly dictatorial with Maggie.

All winter and early spring Maggie had dithered.

That night she made up her mind.

The house had one large fireplace used for cooking and for heat. They tried to keep the fire burning all the time, as it was difficult to start a new one using flint and a short iron bar. It was Maggie's job—everything in the house and garden was Maggie's job—to ensure the fire was well banked overnight so there would be sufficient live embers in the morning to begin a new fire.

By late March, winter was not yet over and that night the temperature dropped sharply, and they were hit by an unexpected fall of snow. Maggie, exhausted as she usually was, slept deeply. Emily snuggled closer, and Maggie wrapped them both tighter in their blankets without waking.

Nathanial's roar of rage had Maggie sitting up in bed, blinking away sleep.

"The fire's gone out, you bitch," he yelled. He crouched in front of the hearth, a length of firewood in his hand. She pushed Emily aside and clambered out of bed. Her nightgown bunched around her legs.

"Let me see," she said, "there must be some embers left."

"You think I can't check for myself?" He rose to his feet. His hand tightened on the wood. "You lazy, ungrateful bitch. I put a roof over your head and food in your belly, and you can't do a simple job like tending the fire."

Emily began to cry. Marie got out of bed and came to see what was going on. In their corner, the boys sat up, watching silently.

"We'll get it started again," Maggie said, turning. "Jacob, get dressed quickly and run to Mrs. Ostrander and ask for some embers from her fire. You can carry them back on the shovel."

"You don't give orders to my son," Nathanial yelled. "He's his own work to do, not yours."

Out of the corner of her eye Maggie saw something move. She lifted her arm as the wood descended. She fell back with a cry and fire raced through her shoulder and down her arm. She tripped over a bench and crashed to the floor, landing hard on her back. Shock filled her head and her vision swam. Nathanial stood over her, staring down. His eyes burned so fiercely he might be able to start the fire with a glance and, still clenching the log, he lifted his leg and kicked her, hard, in the side. Her shoulder felt as if it were burning, and she struggled to suck in air through her aching ribs. If she hadn't seen the blow coming the log would have struck the side of her head.

As she fell, her nightgown rode up, over her thighs. Her legs were braced on the floor, feet planted and knees bent as her head swum and she struggled to breathe. She looked into Nathanial's face and saw his eyes move. They traveled down her body and rested on her exposed upper legs. His face grew slack and his lips opened and a bubble of saliva formed at the side of his mouth.

"No, Papa, no." Then Emily was on the rag rug beside Maggie, trying to shield her with her little body.

Nathanial lowered the log and stepped back. He dragged his gaze up her figure to rest on Maggie's face. "Jacob," he said. "Go to the Ostrander's for fire. Marie, get your daughter dressed. And you," he touched Maggie's leg with his toe, "get off the floor and get yourself decent. My sons and I have work to do and we can't waste time sitting around waiting for our breakfast because a useless slut can't keep a fire going."

Maggie got to her feet, slowly, full of pain. Emily helped her, but no one else dared to step forward. Jacob pulled on his trousers and ran out the door. Marie went back to her alcove, pulling the blanket door after her. Caleb followed his brother outside.

Nathanial threw the wood to the floor and sat down at the table. He watched Maggie with dark eyes as Emily led her toward her bedding and her few belongings.

Her shoulder was not broken, nor were any ribs, as she'd feared at first. Her body ached and her skin was a mess of black and purple bruises for a few days. They soon began to fade, but the look in Nathanial's eyes did not.

He'd tasted blood and power, and he wanted more.

Maggie had no money but she had the skills she'd learned in New York and on this farm. She'd go to the city of Cataraqui at the head of the St. Lawrence River. As the countryside opened to settlers the town was growing into a major center. The sale of Hamish's earrings should net her sufficient money to live for a while. She could get a job with the garrison, doing laundry, sewing, cooking. If the town continued to grow, one day there might even be an opportunity to open a restaurant. Perhaps she'd be able to purchase a house in which to take boarders.

She had to leave this place. She would make her own life, to succeed or to fail come what may.

She rarely thought of her family, her mother and father and brothers. *What would her mother think of her now?* Of what she hoped to become? A woman on her own, a businesswoman. Through her pain, Maggie smiled at the thought.

If she was successful enough, able to provide for herself, why she might not even have to get married.

The thought was so liberating she found herself warming from inside as the days got longer and the snow turned to rain and the fields to seas of mud and she made her plans.

# Chapter Thirty-two

I woke with a start, my heart pounding, drenched in sweat. For the briefest of moments I couldn't quite remember where I was. I wasn't even entirely sure *who* I was. A car came down the road, its headlights sweeping across my windows, and I could see my room. My bedroom in my sister's house. Not a fire burning in the fireplace, but an electric bulb hanging from the ceiling.

I was safe here.

Panic subsided, and I lay back against the pillows. The sheets were damp and wrapped around my legs like a shroud. I'd had a strange dream, something about an unhappy woman in a long dress looking out into a forest of giant trees.

I tried to fall back to sleep, but slumber would not come. Thoughts of Hila, her death, the vandalism in the Harrison home, Gary Wolfe and Rick Brecken, filled my mind. I tossed and turned, worried, angry, frightened.

In my past life, on the rare occasion I'd not been able to sleep, I'd read in bed for a while until I drifted off, but reading a book these days was not relaxing; it was hard work.

I remembered something I'd been able to read.

Sipping out of bed, I padded down the hall in my bare feet. Thin strands of cold white mist drifted before me, but it didn't even occur to me to think of fire. This was not smoke. The nightlight burned in the bathroom. The house was quiet.

I switched on the light at the end of the hall, and carefully made my way up the stairs to the attic room. I stood in the doorway for a moment sniffing the air and looking at the dark. Then I turned on the light and sat down in the comfortable old chair beside the wooden tea chests. I shifted papers aside, and thought I could detect the fait odor of Earl Grey, of Indian tea plantations, dusky-skinned women bent over green plants with wicker baskets on their backs. The white mist dissolved and I felt the stuffy warm air of an overheated attic room.

I took out layers and layers of envelopes and boxes. As I dug my way down, excavating, the paper got yellower and frailer, the ink fainter. Some pages practically dissolved at my touch, yet I kept digging. Reaching the bottom, I unearthed a small leather- bound book, tied with a frayed leather cord.

The leather was dry and full of small cracks. Pieces crumbled and a fine red dust covered my hands. I gently undid the cord. A couple of inches broke off. I fingered the binding, hesitating. I should take this to a professional, someone who knew how to handle it to allow the minimum amount of damage. Impatience won, and I finished untying the cord with as much care as I was able. I opened the cover, holding my breath, but the paper held. I read the first page and was crushingly disappointed. Columns of numbers. Some sort of shopkeeper's ledger probably. I turned the pages. The numbers ended and a child's handwriting began. The ink was faded and the paper old, but most of the paper was intact.

*The Journal of Miss Emily Macgregor* was proudly printed across the top of a fresh page. I glanced quickly over the neat lines of handwriting. Something about Mother being ill and Father telling her she was a naughty girl.

Boring.

I wasn't interested in this, but Jake and his mother might be, although they were not named Macgregor. I yawned. Time to go back to bed. I began to close the book.

My hand hovered in the air. The white mist returned. It swirled around me. Outside, an owl called. I turned more pages, feeling almost compelled to do so.

The handwriting changed. No longer a child's big letters but an adult's excellent penmanship. I bent my head and began to read.

◇◇◇

**March 28, 1788**

*I am trying to preserve as much of this paper as I can. Who knows when we will be able to get more. Even should some arrive, we would not be able to afford it. I am trying to encourage Emily to work on her letters, and I permit her to write in this book as a small reward for a job well done. It would be nice if Emily has a journal to pass on to her own daughter someday.*

*Something happened today and I feel compelled to record it. Mrs. Ostrander, who has become my good friend, received a gift from her sister. A beautiful silver mirror, of the sort I used to have on my dresser. I looked into it and could scarcely credit what lay before me.*

*For a moment I did not recognize the woman looking back at me. When had I last seen my reflection? Probably not since New York, a glimpse of myself as I'd waked past a glass window perhaps. No one here has glass for their windows; a bit of oiled paper set in the frame to let in some light is the best anyone can do.*

*I am so old. The paper-thin skin beneath my eyes is the color of the sky before a thunderstorm breaks, tiny lines radiate out from my mouth, skin hangs loose at my throat, and sharp bones protrude above sunken cheeks. More than a few silver threads are woven among the black of my hair.*

*So old.*

◇◇◇

**May 12, 1788**

Freedom.

What did that mean?

Maggie thought a lot about freedom that spring and her determination to become free strengthened. She would be free from the whining demands of Marie, the brooding ever-watching Nathanial, their rude sons.

Men had fought and died for what they called freedom. They waged war, destroyed lives, decimated the countryside, burned towns, all while shouting slogans of freedom or loyalty. Maggie had never even stopped to consider what the word meant. As a woman, nothing was expected of her but to do as her father and husband ordered and smile while she was doing it. If she were unfortunate enough not to marry, then she would do as her master, or what relatives would reluctantly agree to take her in, instructed.

If—when—she went to Cataraqui and tried to support herself, the only loyalty she would have would be to herself. The only freedom she might be granted was the freedom to starve to death.

Perhaps that was all that freedom was. Here, everyone worked so hard (well, almost everyone, and no one would call Marie free). The men had no master and were far from the regulations, and support, of the government. Life was a never-ending struggle, and people had died, seen their children die, for lack of food or heat over the winter.

*Was that freedom?*

No matter. The travelling preacher was here, and a barn raising was planned for tomorrow. After the work, when everyone paused to eat together and the young people might even begin a dance, Maggie would beg for a ride on the back of the preacher's horse.

It was baking day, and Maggie covered the bread dough with a damp cloth to allow it to rise. Emily was having a rare day of play at a friend's house; Marie, complaining that the forthcoming baby had kept her awake all night, was lying down; Nathanial and Jacob had gone to collect the two oxen jointly owned by a group of farmers that would help them plough a new field; Caleb was in the shed, attempting to repair a pot with a broken handle.

Dreaming of her new life—Maggie had decided that operating a boarding house might be her best option—she lit the stub of a tallow candle from the fire and headed out to the root cellar.

Every family had a cellar built under their house. A cool place where they could store excess crops away from the heat of the kitchen and the icy cold of the outside. The root cellar was dark and dreary, and she did not care to spend more time there than necessary. The hard-packed earthen ramp led to a roughly hewn plank that served as a door. She felt her way carefully. She pulled the door ajar on ill-fitting hinges and, holding the candle high, went in, her back bent as the roof was low. She sang softly, a song from long ago, a song her own mother had sung, to chase the darkness away. Long shadows leapt across the almost empty room. As they ran out of winter stores, the weather began to hint that it might begin to warm, and geese and ducks and pigeons traveled across the lake, heading north, sometimes in flocks so numerous they darkened the sky and the air was full of the sound of their cries and flapping wings. The men were out most of the day hunting. Even Nathanial had managed to bag a few tough old geese.

Maggie stopped her song and stood still, holding her breath, listening. Listening for the sound of footsteps, a voice, someone coming. Marie never came down here; she said it frightened her. It frightened Maggie, but she came anyway. Emily wasn't allowed, because Marie thought it unsafe. The boys and Nathanial would come in the autumn, bearing heavy loads of vegetables or salted meat to lay by for winner storage, but never in the spring. Nevertheless, she waited until she was sure she would not be surprised.

She dropped to her haunches and pulled aside the stone. Her small bundle was safely tucked in place. She picked it up, unwrapped the cloth. Hamish's gift. Her new life. Diamonds sparkled in the light cast by the candle. She closed her eyes and tightened her fingers around them, seeking strength and courage. She whispered a prayer that Hamish had found peace.

"Tomorrow," she said. "Tomorrow." She put them away, where they would be safe.

◇◇◇

## May 13, 1788

Maggie made long slow strokes though Emily's brown hair while the girl turned the pages of her book. She separated the hair into three strands and deftly twisted it into a braid which she secured with a faded yellow ribbon.

"There you go. As pretty as a picture," Maggie said and the child turned to her with a beaming smile. "I love you, Maggie." Emily threw her arms around Maggie and hugged her hard.

A lump rose in Maggie's throat. She pushed the girl away, a bit roughly perhaps. "None of that, now. Time to be off."

The family had assembled to go to the barn-raising. Marie's pregnancy was a small round bulge in her dress and she stood with her hand pressed into the small of her back as if the load she bore were a great weight. Maggie had tamed Marie's hair into ringlets, and the dull brown curls fell around her pale, pinched face. She wore a blue bonnet and a forest green dress. The colors, Maggie thought, did not match.

But, Maggie knew, she herself did not look much better. Her dress was definitely looking its age, and her mother would be shocked to see the condition of her bonnet and the state of her shoes.

Then again, Maggie thought, her mother would be shocked to see the condition of her daughter.

No matter. She looked like the maid she was. Soon, all going well, she would be in Cataraqui and look like the woman of independent means she intended to be.

Nathanial examined his family, seeking flaws. His eyes settled on Maggie, standing at the back, her hands loose at her side. He studied her for a long time, and she did not look away.

He turned and led the way out the door.

"Oh, dear," Maggie said, hesitating on the threshold. "I've forgotten to put the chickens in. We might not be home until after dark." She couldn't, of course, accompany the family to the neighbors carrying all of her worldly goods. She'd get her things and follow, leave her bundle hidden in the woods until time came to approach the preacher. She'd heard, from local gossip, that he was needed elsewhere and would be leaving immediately after the communal supper.

She planned to tell him that she had heard, finally, from her brothers and they were anxious for her to return to the bosom of her family. He might still refuse her the ride, in which case she would walk.

Marie muttered something about chickens and stupid girls and leaned against her eldest son for his support. Emily wiggled her fingers at Maggie, and Maggie wanted to leap forward, grab the girl and never let go. But she did not. She dutifully went out to gather up the chickens, which she had deliberately not done earlier. Then she came back into the house, took a seat at the table, and waited. When sufficient time had passed that none of the family were likely to return to collect something they'd forgotten, she packed quickly. A loaf of yesterday's bread, a hunk of salted squirrel, as foul tasting as that was, some of the willow tea, a newly made tallow candle and a piece of flint, a sharp knife, the smallest pot. Miserly payment for her years of labor in this house, but she could only take what she could carry with ease. She spread her shawl on the table and piled everything on top of it. She brought the edges of the shawl together and tied the corners to make a bundle. She picked up the pathetically small package and left the house for the last time.

All she had to do now was collect the earrings and she'd be on her way.

A free woman.

# Chapter Thirty-three

"Hannah!"

I jerked awake. I cried out as my arms flew up and my body stiffened. The book fell onto the floor with a thud.

Once again it was my brother-in-law who found me in the attic in the morning. I'd fallen asleep, the leather-bound journal open on my lap.

"Sorry," he said, "were you asleep?" He didn't look, or sound, at all sorry.

"Just resting."

"You've been spending a lot of time up here."

"I don't sleep well, as you know. It's dark. It's cool."

It was anything but cool in the enclosed space. Heat rises, of course, and all the heat of the house was in this room. Had I really been cold last night? Had I really seen swirling white mist and felt that someone was reaching into my brain?

Perhaps I had. After Lily had told me of her encounter with 'the lady,' I was not so quick to dismiss my own experiences.

I got to my feet. My body stiff after sleeping in a chair.

"What's the plan for today?" I asked Jake.

"Work. As usual."

He walked into the room. He was dressed in jeans and a loose blue shirt over a Toronto Maple Leafs T-shirt. His face was freshly shaven and his hair damp from the shower. He bent over and picked up the journal. He flicked through it, and a flash of interest crossed his face.

"Wow, this is really old."

"It is. There's an entry from 1788."

"You're kidding me?"

"True. Looks like the book belonged to a shopkeeper or merchant of some sort initially. Then it was used as a journal or something. By the people who were here the day the land was being cleared. You should take it to the library, Jake. They have archives there, and they'll know how to take care of it. It's in pretty good shape, considering how old it is. The paper's been protected by the leather, I'd guess. And down near the bottom of this box with all that stuff on top."

He ran his fingers over the cover, a look of awe on his face. "Imagine. Here all this time and we didn't know. I never got all the way to the bottom of the boxes."

"I'd guess your ancestors started throwing their letters and accounts on top and everything piled up. You're lucky the new owners didn't chuck it all out when they bought the house. "

"Lucky. Yes. Did you read anything interesting?"

"There was a woman…I almost feel I know her. She had a hard life, made harder by…"

"By?"

"By the circumstances. They were Loyalists, like you told me." *How did I know that?* I'd only read the scribblings of a child complaining about her parents and a woman thinking she'd turned old.

A thin line of light was touching the edges of the window. The household would be up soon. I rolled my neck, trying to work some of the kinks out.

"We've wondered," Jake said, picking his words with care. "If there's anything valuable lying around up here. Something from the old settlers, I mean. They were quite wealthy in the States, a very prominent family, before they had to leave. We, Mom and I, have never had the time to properly go through everything."

"If they did bring anything with them, they would have sold it to survive, I'd think. That book's valuable. Not in money, probably, but in history. In knowledge."

"I guess that's good enough."

I got to my feet. I held out my hand for the journal.

"I'll keep this," Jake said. "Put it downstairs. Someplace safe."

"I'd like to finish reading it."

"Later." He left and took the book with him.

I wondered if I'd ever see it again. If Jake showed the journal to his mother, she'd snatch it out of this house before you could say *greedy*.

I dressed in the lightest of clothes, shorts and a tank top, and went downstairs as the family was beginning to gather. Lily sat hunched over her cereal bowl, flicking through one of the books on Afghanistan. Joanne pulled out the frying pan. I filled the kettle and glanced outside while waiting for it to boil.

The sky was a brilliant blue and not a leaf stirred in the trees. The two horses galloped across the paddock.

Connor came in. In the last couple of days, he'd somehow started appearing at breakfast every morning. Joanne seemed okay with that, and was even going out of her way to prepare a more substantial meal than the family was used to on weekdays. She considered dinner to be important family time, but I thought it wouldn't be long before he was pulling up a chair then too.

"Morning all," he said. He ruffled Lily's hair, and she pulled away.

Connor came to stand beside me. "Morning, Hannah. Sleep well?"

"Yes," I lied.

Without asking, Joanne passed him a cup of coffee. Black. No sugar.

He thanked her and gave me a smile. A private smile, and reached out with his free hand to lightly touch my arm. A jolt of lightning passed through me, and I glanced away.

Charlie bounded into the kitchen. Connor picked him up and swung him around. The boy screeched with laughter, but Joanne said, "Hey, I'm cooking here. Careful."

Fat sizzled as she tossed bacon into the frying pan, and the toaster popped up two brown slices.

I watched the scene, feeling a smile cross my face. The ballet of breakfast. Joanne flipped bacon and eggs, Connor tossed hot toast onto a plate, Charlie put the brown paper bag containing his sandwich and juice box into his backpack, Lily ate cereal and flicked pages, and Jake took jam and marmalade out of the fridge.

"How about we go for a horseback ride when you get home, Lily?" I said.

Her face lit up, but her mother's did not.

"The police are finished in the woods, right?" I said. "They told us we could go wherever we like. I'd like to go for a ride."

"Good idea," Jake said, with a glance at his daughter. "If it's a short one."

Lily beamed.

"Short's good for me," I said.

Joanne piled fried eggs and bacon onto two plates and put them in Jake and Connor's places. Then she served a smaller mound of food to herself and Charlie and sat down.

"I was at the Grill last night. There's nothing new, so they say, on the break-in at Harrison's place," Connor said. "Troublemakers and shiftless lay-abouts seems to be the general feeling." He snorted. "All would be solved, I'm told, if they brought back the strap."

"Hello!" A shout from the door. Liz and Allison.

"Good morning." Allison had a big smile on her chubby face.

"You're in a good mood," Joanne said.

"Aaron's here," Allison said.

Liz rolled her eyes. "The reunion of the lovebirds was positively sickening to behold."

Allison stuck out her tongue. She wasn't a pretty girl: her cheeks too round, her chin too small, her nose too big, but this morning she glowed with health and youth and happiness. "A whole weekend of sheer unbridled debauchery lies ahead."

"What's debauchery?" Charlie asked.

Allison gasped and clapped her hand to her mouth. Connor laughed.

I glanced at Lily, but her head was down, lost in thought.

"It means to have fun," Joanne told her son.

"So, I'm going to have debauchery at Ryan's cottage this weekend?"

Connor roared with laughter, and Jake gave him a dirty look. "I completely forgot, Allison, I gave you the weekend off, right?"

"That's right." She lifted her arms and spun in a circle.

"Why did you do that?" Joanne said. "It's the middle of July, one of the busiest market days. You can't manage on your own."

"I can't change my plans," Allison wailed, horror-stricken. "Aaron's come specially. He's working up north for the summer, planting trees."

"You don't have to," Jake said. "Connor can come to market with me."

"Me?"

"Yes, you."

"I don't know anything about selling vegetables."

"You don't know anything about growing them, either," Jake snapped. He threw his napkin onto the table and stood up. "Doesn't stop you taking a wage, though."

Connor straightened in his chair. A vein pulsed in the side of his neck, and his eyes narrowed. "I do my work."

"When I'm watching you."

"Hey," Joanne interrupted. "Leave it. If you have issues, sort them out later. Right now, we all have work to do."

Jake and Connor stared at each other across the breakfast table. Even Lily pulled herself out of her funk to watch them. Jake turned away first. "I've ordered a load of hay for those damned horses. I have to go and pick it up later. Connor, be in the greenhouse at five tomorrow. We leave for market early." He stalked out of the kitchen.

Connor sat back down and sipped at his coffee. Joanne spooned up her eggs quickly. "Come on, everyone, time to go. Charlie, you didn't take anything out of that backpack after I closed it last night did you?" After camp, he'd be going to a cottage with his best friend Ryan for the weekend.

"Nope."

"Good. Finish your breakfast. It's time to go. Lily, run upstairs and comb your hair. It's a mess. Connor, eat up. We have a full day's work to do."

"Yes, boss."

# Chapter Thirty-four

When she got home from day camp, Lily ran through the house in a blur of pink and blue and dashed upstairs. She was back in minutes, dressed for riding in black stretch pants, helmet tucked under her arm. Earlier, I'd changed into jeans and thick socks and was ready to go. I'd packed cheese sandwiches and juice boxes and had been out to gather the horses and tie them to the railing at the side of the barn.

"Ready?" Lily said, her beautiful face bright with anticipation. She'd gotten a lot of summer sun, and a patch of freckles had seeded itself across her nose. Her hair hung down her back in a sun-kissed braid.

I considered teasing and telling her I'd changed my mind, but I couldn't be that mean. "Let's go."

Allison and Liz were in the greenhouse, working with long neat rows of miniature lettuce seedlings, and Joanne was rinsing out the boxes they'd use to take produce to market. The women's T-shirts were stuck to their backs and chests with perspiration, their hair was damp, their faces smudged with dirt mixed with sweat. Lily dashed in to tell her mom we were going, and then we walked together to the barn. A couple of chickens began to follow, but they soon found more interesting things to take their attention and dropped away.

Beauty saw us coming, tossed her mane in greeting, and stretched out her head. Lily touched the horse's nose with her forehead, lifted both hands to stroke the powerful neck, and told her we were going for a ride, and wouldn't that be fun. Beauty tossed her head up and down in agreement. Tigger eyed me as if to say, "Not you again."

Lily dashed in and out of the barn, collecting saddles and blankets, and I stuffed our snack into saddlebags. We prepared the horses as Lily chatted happily to Beauty, and Beauty listened, her head bent and pointed ears held high.

"You'd better give that girth an extra tug, Aunt Hannah," Lily advised. "Tigger's a clever boy and he knows to puff up his stomach at just the right time." She walloped him on the rump, he blew out air, and sure enough I could tighten the strap more.

Lily swung up into the saddle, and I'd swear Beauty laughed with joy. I mounted with considerably less ease, hopping on one foot, trying to fit the other into the stirrup as Tigger tried to dance out of the way.

Directly above us the sky was as blue as in photographs advertising Caribbean vacations, but clouds, thick and black, were gathering low in the east, portending a break in the heat. I'd added ponchos to the saddlebags in anticipation of rain. We walked slowly across the fields, letting the horses have their heads, the sun baking my legs through my jeans. The moment we entered the green shade of the woods the temperature dropped delightfully. Lily chatted about the various goings-on in her life. Ashley, her best friend and usual riding buddy, had gone on vacation for an *entire* month. Lily had wanted to be a journalist, like me, but now she was thinking she might be a vet. Did I think being a vet was okay? I did. Charlie, to Lily's delight, wouldn't be home from Ryan's cottage until Sunday night. Lily would like to have a cottage, but it was hardly possible, was it, when her parents were farmers and had to work all summer. Her friend Mary Ann was dating a boy. Lily would like to have a boyfriend, but her mom said she had to be thirteen at least. Did I think thirteen was too old for a first boyfriend?

Boyfriends.

Simon.

Connor?

Connor had been sending strong signals my way, but I hadn't been interested in responding. I wasn't ready to enter into a new relationship. I didn't think of Simon often, and when I did it was with a sense of guilt that I wasn't deeper in mourning. But aside from that, I wasn't sure about Connor. He was charming and cheerful, but something lay beneath. He didn't get on with Jake, probably because he didn't like taking orders, and I thought I caught the occasional glimpse of pent-up anger and potential violence.

But he did look awfully nice half-dressed and soaking wet.

I gave my head a mental shake and gave Tigger a nudge to get him moving.

We were relaxing on a patch of grass beside a small stream, letting the horses drink their fill and munch on waterweeds, eating our sandwiches when Lily said, "If someone dies without any family, who gets their things?"

Death had been on her mind lately. Understandable in light of Hila's death and all the turmoil following it. I thought Lily should have been allowed to go to the funeral. To say her good-byes and begin to move on. But her parents said it would be too upsetting for her, and it was not my place to argue.

"Lots of people leave their estate—that means all their possessions—to charities. Maybe to a close friend or someone who looked after them if they were sick for a long time. Why do you ask, Lily?"

"Just wondering. Hila didn't have many possessions, did she?"

"No, dearest. She lost everything when her family was killed. I suppose Mr. and Mrs. Harrison will keep her computer and her school books and stuff like that. They might belong to the Harrisons anyway." I thought of the Koran. The only thing Hila owned. Stolen.

"The Harrisons will inherit her things?"

"I guess so. They were the closest people she had. I don't think she was in contact with any of her relatives back in Afghanistan."

Lily picked up a round white stone and tossed it into the slow-moving water.

"Lily, Is there something you should tell me? Or your mother? About Hila?"

At that moment a flock of ducks swooped down to land on the surface of the creek. Beauty started as they flapped their wings in front of her face, and she reared back with a cry. The branch to which she was tied bent. Lily was on her feet, her right hand on the big animal's neck, her left on the bridle. "Steady, girl. Steady." She made cooing noses and stroked the horse. Long languid strokes and reassuring murmurs. Beauty stamped her feet but began to settle down under Lily's loving touch. When the horse was still again, Lily unlooped the reins from the tree branch, put her foot into the stirrup. "Better be going," she said over her shoulder. "It's going to rain soon." She swung herself into the saddle.

I gathered up the picnic remains and stuffed them into Tigger's saddlebag and mounted with far less grace than had my niece. Lily led the way back to the farm, no longer chatting.

I didn't have much experience with children—in fact I had no experience with children—and I didn't know if Lily's preoccupation with a dead person's effects was normal. I suspected not. A thought crossed my mind. Something I should do? Something I should say?

Tigger lunged for a patch of grass and I had to pull his head back in line. Whatever I thought I'd had was gone as quickly as it had come.

The first drops of rain began to fall as we left the woods. The black clouds that earlier had been no more than a smudge on the horizon were moving fast in our direction.

Beauty found the path through the tomato fields. Barn in sight, she picked up her pace. The tomatoes were growing rapidly in their neat rows. Some of the plants were as tall as the horses' knees, sporting green and yellow orbs of varying sizes. I thought happily of the flavor of a fresh cherry tomato, still warm from the sun, on my tongue.

We were about a hundred yards from the barn, me dreaming of heirloom tomatoes cooked into pasta sauce, when Connor came out of the building, yelling.

"Help, help." He was heading for the house, running flat out. He saw us and changed direction. He waved his hands in the air. Lily dug her heels into Beauty's side, and the horse leapt forward. They covered the remaining distance at a gallop. I didn't have to urge Tigger to follow. Connor grabbed Beauty's bridle. "There's been an accident. Get to the house. Phone an ambulance. Now."

"My dad," Lily yelled, "where's my dad?"

"Don't argue with me, just go." He released the bridle and whacked the horse's glistening rump. She jumped forward, and Lily raced her to the house, bent low over the long neck. Beauty's mane streamed behind her. I slid off my own mount. "What's happened?"

"An accident. Jake. In the barn."

Leaving Tigger to his own devices, I ran into the barn. Connor followed.

Jake lay on the floor in a rapidly spreading pool of blood. His eyes were closed, and his face was white, and his breathing ragged. I dropped to my knees beside him. "Jake, can you hear me? It's Hannah. Help's coming."

His eyelids flickered, and he was looking at me. "Hannah," he gasped. "Hurts like hell. My leg. Dammit, Connor, couldn't you watch what you were doing?"

"We've called an ambulance," I repeated. I ran my eyes down his body. A tear in his right pant leg, at the thigh, the cloth soaked with blood. "Get me a blanket," I ordered Connor. "Quickly."

He tossed me a horse blanket, stiff with dust and horsehair. Taking care to keep it clear of the wounded leg, I laid the blanket over Jake's chest. He needed to be kept warm. I'm no medic, but I did have some basic first aid training to take into the world's dangerous places. "Another."

"I don't see one."

"A saddle then. Anything to raise his head."

Connor took an old saddle off the wall. I lifted Jake's head and Connor slid the make-shift pillow under. Jake gave me a grimace which I took to be an attempt to smile. Nothing was clean enough to use as a compress so I pressed the flat of my hand against the hole in his thigh. Jake gasped but his eyes stayed open. Bright red blood leaked between my fingers. My hand was dirty from the reins and the horse, but the doctors could worry about infection later. More important to try to control the bleeding.

"What happened?" Not that it mattered, but I wanted to keep him alert and talking.

"Fucking Connor stabbed me with the fork."

"A fork?"

"He means the pitchfork," Connor said. He was standing over me, throwing a long shadow across Jake's face. "It was an accident. I was in the loft, stacking the new hay and I turned around, not realizing he'd come up behind me, and tripped on something buried in the straw. I must have jabbed it into his leg. He fell."

I looked up. The barn had a second story, a loft about eight feet up, where hay and rarely used farm implements were kept. A conveyer belt delivered hay from the truck below.

"You mean he fell from up there?"

"Yes."

If Jake fell from that height, wounded and in pain and shock, he might have done some real damage to his back or neck. I thought, I hoped, the flow of blood was lessening. Under his deep farmer's tan, Jake's face was pasty white. His eyelids flickered and closed. "Connor, there should be first aid supplies somewhere on the farm. Do you know where they're kept?"

"Greenhouse."

"Get them. I need a clean compress. Everything in here is filthy, including me. "

He ran off.

"Oh, please. No." Joanne dropped to her knees beside me. Tears ran down her face. "Jake, Jake," she sobbed.

He blinked. "I'm okay, babe." His voice was low, each word an effort. "My leg. Hurts like hell."

"The ambulance is coming. Lily's waiting at the driveway to bring them down."

"My girl, Lily." He lifted his hand and touched his wife's cheek. She gripped it in her own. Her hands were encrusted with dirt, the nails torn and broken. Good dirt. Farm dirt. Scratches crisscrossed her palms and a band aid was wrapped around her thumb.

My own hand slipped on the wet, sticky skin as I kept the pressure on. "Don't move," I barked.

Liz arrived at a run, carrying a big metal box. "Here's the first aid kit." She put the box beside me. "Open it," I ordered. She did. I glanced in. Fully equipped. "Hand me that compress. Take the packaging off first, for Christ's sake."

Liz tore the wrapping away and held out the clean white square.

I lifted my hand from the wound; blood oozed but it definitely wasn't coming as fast as it had been. My right hand was wet and sticky and bright red with blood. I grabbed the compress and slapped it into place.

At that moment I heard the welcome sound of sirens coming our way. A few more minutes, then pounding boots and calm voices. I got to my feet and stood back to let a paramedic take my place. "He fell," I said, wiping my bloody hands onto my jeans. "From up there." I took a deep breath.

"I can't miss any work," Jake said as the second medic began unpacking a neck brace. "It's the busy season, you know, market day tomorrow. Wrap up my leg and take me into the house for a rest. I'll load the market stuff up later. "

"Shush," Joanne said, "You need to be checked out at the hospital."

"What about market?"

"There are more important things than going to the market."

Lily had followed the medics. She stood with her hand on her mother's back, her face a mask of fear. I took her by the arm and said, "We're only in the way. " We walked out of the barn. It was raining hard now, and a flash of lightening streaked out of the black clouds, followed a few seconds later by a clap of thunder. Tigger was standing in the lettuce beds, munching happily, heedless of the rain streaming down his flanks. "Where's Beauty?"

"I tied her to the deck railing."

"I'll get Tigger out of your mother's greens. You bring Beauty down and we'll put them in the paddock for now."

Lily looked at my hand, smeared red with her father's blood. "Is Dad going to be okay?"

"He cut his leg badly, but he's awake and talking. He'll be okay."

I went to the equipment shed where yesterday I'd watched Connor cooling himself off. I ran water over my hands. When the blood was gone, most of it, Lily and I gathered the horses and put them in the paddock. A police car pulled up, lights rotating and sirens screaming, followed by another. I ran across the yard to meet them.

"What's happening here?" the first cop asked. I didn't recognize him.

"An accident in the barn. My brother-in-law."

"What kind of an accident?"

The second officer, a woman, headed toward the barn.

"He fell and got a pitchfork in his thigh." Conscious of wide-eyed Lily behind me, I said quickly, "A bad cut, but nothing more. He's conscious and his wife is with him."

"Sounds good," he said. "We get a lot of calls to farms this time of year. Dangerous places, farms."

The paramedics wheeled a stretcher out of the barn. Rain fell. Joanne walked beside Jake, holding his hand and muttering comforting words. A couple of chickens, red heads bobbing, provided an escort. I heard Jake say, "Last week we ran out of potatoes early. Be sure you pack extra for us to take tomorrow."

"Yes, dear," Joanne said. When they reached Lily and me, standing beside the officer, Joanne stopped. "I'm going with Jake to the hospital. We might be a long time. Are you and Lily okay here?"

"I want to come with you." Lily began to cry.

"No, dear. There isn't room in the ambulance and there's nothing you can do. I'll call as soon as he's seen a doctor and we know more. Don't worry." Joanne bent over and gave her daughter a tight hug. "Your dad's a tough old guy. He's going to be fine. I need you to look after Aunt Hannah. Okay?"

Lily sniffed. I slipped my arm around her thin shoulders. "Call us when you can, eh?"

Joanne nodded and hurried to catch up. We watched as they lifted the stretcher into the back of the ambulance. A hand reached out to Joanne and my sister jumped in. The doors slammed, the second paramedic climbed into the front, and they drove away. Sirens broke the sound of falling rain, and red lights lit up the rain-soaked yard.

The two police officers joined us. The woman had her notebook in one hand and was trying to shield it from the rain with the other. "Can you tell me what happened?"

Water streamed down our faces and soaked through our clothes. The ponchos were still on the horses. "I wasn't there. Lily and I were coming back from a ride and we heard shouting. I went into the barn and Jake was on the floor. Bleeding badly from his leg. He said he stabbed himself with a pitchfork and fell from the loft. I did what I could to try to control the bleeding and keep him warm and then the ambulance arrived. That's all I know."

She made a note and tucked her notebook into her shirt pocket. "Are you going to be okay here alone, Ms. Manning?"

I wasn't surprised that they knew my name. "Lily and I are going to have hot baths and watch TV or a movie." I gave Lily what I hoped was a smile. "We might even order pizza for dinner."

"They don't deliver this far out," the cop said.

That punctured my cheerful balloon. "Oh."

"When will my dad be able to come home?" Lily asked.

"I'm sure your mom'll call soon as she knows. We'll be on our way then. Good night." The radio at her shoulder cackled and she turned away, fingers on the volume.

"Night," I said.

The police went to their vehicles. Red and blue lights reflected off puddles forming in the driveway and in depressions in the lawn. First one, and then the other, set of lights were turned off and the cars drove away. The wind whipped at my face.

"Come on, Lily. We're soaked. We need to get inside and change."

Liz and Allison stood in the shelter of the porch, watching.

"That's rough," Liz said, holding the door open for us. "But it didn't look too bad, right?"

"Right," I agreed. I kicked off the boots I'd worn riding.

"I hope Jake's okay," Allison said. "Time we're off, then. See you guys on Monday." She almost danced out of the house.

Liz gave me a grimace. "Right, a weekend of debauchery for some. What's going to happen tomorrow do you suppose? Who'll go to the market?"

"At a guess, no one. Jake certainly won't be and I don't think he'll want Connor going on his own. Where is Connor, anyway?"

She shrugged. "He comes, he goes. I'll be here tomorrow. I suppose I could take some of the stuff to the market, if they wanted me to." Allison leaned on the horn of her car. "Coming!" Liz shouted.

I glanced at the clock on the oven as I passed through the kitchen, following Lily upstairs. To my considerable surprise, it wasn't even six o'clock. With all that had happened, and the dark storm, I'd thought it much later.

Lily showered first and then it was my turn. I scrubbed my hands until I was sure I'd gotten every last speck of blood out and stood under the hot steaming water for a long time. I decided to put on my nightgown rather than get dressed again. I'd try my best to make the evening fun for Lily. Sort of like a sleep-over in her own house. Things would be tough around here for a while. With Jake laid up, Joanne's time and attention taken, the farm would struggle to get the crops harvested and customers satisfied. Liz, Allison, and Connor could do the work, some of it, but they couldn't run the business or make decisions and they needed constant supervision. I couldn't help either, not with the farming, but I could give Jake and Joanne everything I could. I'd hire a nurse, to take care of Jake if he needed it, and we could get a couple of extra farm hands to do Jake's share of the work. Maybe even a cook, to take some of the housekeeping chores off Joanne.

I combed out my wet hair, pleased with this line of thinking. Joanne would tell me that they'd manage, and Jake would say he wouldn't take charity, but who cared what they thought.

I studied myself in the mirror, seeking Omar lurking behind my eyes. No sign of him. As usual, whenever I'd gone a day without headaches, I began to hope I was on the mend. If Omar stayed away, I might be able to take over some of the management tasks. Perhaps soon I'd be able to follow a row of numbers on a computer screen and concentrate long enough to help with the bookkeeping and the banking.

I studied my face. Something was niggling at the back of my mind. Something I needed to remember.

I'd made a mistake. I'd said something wrong. I needed to make it right

But I couldn't' remember what that was.

It was so, so damned frustrating.

Thoughts dangled in front of my mind, remaining just out of reach. Like a child playing peek-a-boo, a flirt in a bar, teasing and then drawing away.

I tried to concentrate. I needed to remember. Something important.

It was gone, and I could not call it back.

I gave up trying and knocked on Lily's door.

"Come in."

She was sitting on her bed in a nest of fluffy pink and white stuffed toys and pillows. The book on the treasures of Afghanistan open on her lap.

"Hungry?"

"Yes."

"Let's see what's in the fridge. If we can't have pizza I'm sure we can rustle up something to see us through."

"Aunt Hannah?"

"Yes, dear."

"I need to tell you something."

I smiled. "Let's start dinner first, and then we can talk."

She jumped off the bed and wrapped me in a hug. I touched my lips to the top of her head. She smelled of citrus soap and lemon shampoo and clean water. Of good health and innocence and plenty of love. Her hair was wet, and she was dressed in her pajamas, yellow and white with short pants and smiling cartoon characters. "I love you, Aunt Hannah."

"I love you too, my dear."

"Dad's going to be fine, right?"

"He said so himself, didn't he? Don't worry. He has a bad cut on his leg, and they'll have to sew it up. Then he'll be able to come home."

I hoped I was right.

"It's a good thing Connor was there," she said. "So he could call for help."

I lifted my head. Connor. That was it. Something about Connor. Something I'd done wrong about Connor.

But what?

Nothing I could do tonight. I'd worry about all of that in the morning.

We went downstairs.

I hadn't bothered to lock the door after Liz and Allison. We never locked the doors in this house, except when it was time to go to bed.

Connor O'Leary sat at the kitchen table. He looked up as we came in. He did not smile. A gun rested on the table in front of him.

"Where is it, Hannah?" he said.

# Chapter Thirty-five

I remembered.

I'd told the police Jake had stabbed himself with the pitch-fork. But that wasn't right, was it? Connor had done it. He'd said it was an accident, and accidents happened around a farm all the time. Big animals, big equipment, hard physical work. Jake was fully conscious, although in pain, so Connor couldn't lie to me in front of him.

But I'd forgotten that, and when the cops asked me what had happened, my mind, which sometimes made things up to try to fit in facts it couldn't remember, told me Jake said he'd stabbed himself.

Did it matter?

Yes, it did. If I'd mentioned Connor, the police would have questioned him. Tried to find out exactly what had happened.

Where had Connor been since I went into the barn and found Jake, anyway? I'd sent him to the greenhouse for the first aid kit. Liz had brought it. I hadn't seen Connor since. He'd made himself scarce when the authorities were poking around. Unlike Liz and Allison and just about everyone else in the world who gathered at the sight of an ambulance and police cars and flashing blue and red lights, he'd slipped away.

Until now.

"Where is it?" He repeated. His fingers, still encrusted with farm dirt, caressed the gun. It wasn't a toy, but solid and substantial. Black and shiny and deadly. A Glock, if my memory could still be counted on.

Rain spattered on the French doors leading to the deck, the wind whipped tree branches against the house, the old wood shifted and groaned. Outside, the sky was as black as midnight, and inside the only light came from the clocks on the oven and microwave. The electric green glow was behind Connor and his eyes were black pools in an empty face.

I put my body between him and Lily.

Lightning flashed, a streak against the black sky, and a brilliant white flash filled the kitchen. Thunder followed immediately, the sound waves rolling inside the house. Lily and I jumped and the edges of Connor's mouth lifted.

The thunder was dying away and the light had gone when the office door opened. I almost shouted a warning, but Connor didn't move and his face reflected no fear of being discovered. He didn't even take his unblinking stare away from me.

A man came into the kitchen in a rolling swagger. He was tall and muscular, with thick wet lips, small eyes, shaved head, and a ragged goatee. Black jeans, black T-shirt, black Doc Martin boots that tracked mud and water across Joanne's clean floor. A thick belt was around his waist, a shiny silver and turquoise buckle in the front, an inlaid leather sheaf holding a knife at his side. It was the man I'd seen driving Connor to work. His cousin, supposedly.

"Who the hell are you?" I asked. No one answered. "Now look here, Connor, I have not the slightest idea what you think you're doing here, with that gun in this house. Nor what you're looking for."

Connor got to his feet. He picked up the Glock. "Step away from the kid, Hannah."

"No."

His friend crossed the room in three steps. He grabbed my arm and pulled me away from Lily. Omar moved.

*Not now, please, not now.* I needed my wits about me. I needed to be able to see. To think.

Lily cried out.

I forced myself to concentrate, to pay attention, to be aware. If my mind shut down, we were finished. Slowly, reluctantly, Omar stepped back.

"Sit down, Lily," Connor shouted.

She looked at me. I nodded, and she dropped into a chair, her eyes big and round in a pale face framed by long wet blond hair.

"That's a good girl. If your aunt will be just as good, we can finish this up and go."

"Why did you hurt Jake?" I said, "What's he ever done to you except give you a job?"

"Jake's of no consequence. I needed to get rid of him for a few hours, and if his wife left too, all the better."

"You couldn't wait until they went to a movie or something?"

"No, Hannah, I couldn't wait until they went to a movie or something. They never fuckin' went out, did they? I've been sitting in that damned trailer, hot as Hell, waiting for the house to be empty. But there's always someone around. Jake, your sister, you, those stupid giggling girls who think they want to be farmers. Marry farmers is what they really want. Besides, I'm sick and tired of working on this two-bit operation. Taking orders from a couple of fucking farmers? Selling vegetables in the market? I don't think so."

"Cops were getting too interested in this place," his pal said. "The longer we hung around, the more likely they'd take a bead on Riley here."

"Your name's Riley?"

"Never the fuck mind. And you," he threw the words at the big man, "can shut the fuck up."

"Who are you anyway?" I asked. As Omar retreated I felt myself moving with him. Away from my body. Standing to one side, watching these people. It hadn't occurred to me to be frightened. Maybe they'd shoot Omar and I could have my head back.

"Never mind," Connor said. "No more games, Hannah. I'm sick and tired of this business. I'm fed up with this fucking farm and that fucking small town. Give me what I want and we'll be out of here."

"Connor, or Riley, or whatever your name is. I really, really do not know what you're talking about."

"She gave it to you, Hannah. I should have realized that earlier. We've been wasting our time at Harrison place. I saw the book the other day and wondered. Then again this morning, and I knew."

"Book? What book? I can barely read these days. You mean Lily's books on the archeology of Afghanistan?" I sucked in air. "Oh, no. Hila? You think Hila gave me something? She didn't. You have to believe me." *Hila*. They'd killed Hila looking for… what? From where I stood, to one side, watching the proceedings, I saw anger boil up inside my body. After all that I'd seen, all that I'd experienced. All that Hila had lived though. To be hunted down in the one place she'd found safety. Killed. Murdered. For some object.

"You killed Hila, I assume," I asked. My voice stayed calm.

The man grunted. Connor glanced at him. "That wasn't supposed to happen. Jackson doesn't know his own strength sometimes. She didn't want to give it up, so we knocked her around a bit. Took off her pants, pulled her legs apart. Had a good long look and told her what would happen if she didn't tell. Like I'd want to get close to that mess of a face. They're terrified of rape, Afghan bitches, but I guess you know that."

"She didn't tell you. Maybe she didn't know what you were talking about. Just like I don't know."

"She knew. She was tougher than we expected, but she would have given it up. Unfortunately," Connor shrugged and gave an almost imperceptible glace toward his friend, "accidents happen."

"Yeah. When two guys are beating up a woman."

"How about we have no more accidents, and you hand it over and we'll be going. I don't mean you any harm, Hannah. I don't mind leaving you alive. I'll be long gone and Connor O'Leary will be sound asleep in his bed in Smiths Falls when the cops

break down his door. They can search for me all they want."
He smiled. Only half of his mouth lifted and I was reminded
of Hila's tortured twisted face. I'd happily hand over whatever
they wanted. But I didn't have anything.

Lily shifted in her chair.

My stomach rolled over. I returned to my body. I felt cold
sweat on my arms and sheer terror in my heart.

Lily. Lily had it. Hila had given it, whatever it was, to Lily
for safekeeping.

I couldn't stop myself from glancing at her.

Her head was up and her back straight.

Connor followed my eyes.

"Hey, Lily. Do you have something you want to tell us,
sweetpea?"

She looked at me through eyes as large as Black Beauty's. She
waited for me to tell her what to do.

"Hila gave you something, didn't she?" I said. At last, too
late, I knew why Lily had so many questions about inheritance,
about what would happen to Hila's property, the intense interest
in the book about the Afghanistan museum. My stupid, useless
damaged brain had been too sluggish to figure it out. "She asked
you to look after something that was precious to her."

Lily nodded. "She told me it was secret. I wasn't to tell anyone.
I didn't know what to do when she died. I wanted to give it to
the right person. But I didn't know who that was."

"What…" I began, but Connor cut through me.

"Now you can give it to me."

Lily hesitated. Jackson took a step toward her. He fingered
the hilt of the knife on his belt.

"Lily," I yelled. "Tell them."

She began to cry. Great racking sobs and streaming tears. I
went to her and put an arm around her shoulders. The two men
watched us, their faces as cold as the storm raging outside. "It's
all right, Lily. Hila wouldn't want you to…be hurt to protect
her secret."

"It's a box," she whispered. "Things from Afghanistan. They belong to the people of Afghanistan. They'd been stolen, and she wanted to give them back."

"That's a good girl," Connor said. A flash of lightning lit up his face. His eyes were pools of cruelty and his mouth twisted in contempt. How could I have ever thought him attractive? "Go and get me this box." He tossed his head to Jackson, who threw me aside as if I were a used tissue and grabbed Lily's arm. He hauled her to her feet.

"Get it."

"It's upstairs, in my room," she said.

"Go with her," Connor said. "Hannah and I'll wait here."

"No!"

Connor grinned. "No? Think you have a say in this, Hannah?"

"He is not going upstairs with Lily. Alone." I grabbed Lily's other arm and held on tight.

The man pulled. We were having a tug of war over my niece. He laughed. "I like to give it to the young ones. Make their first something they'll always remember." He looked down at Lily as if he were examining meat in a butcher's window. He put his hand under her chin and lifted her face. "Yeah, it'll be her first. What'd you think, Riley?"

"Get the damned box, and we can get out of here. The longer we hang around the more likely we'll be interrupted. We've no time for funny business."

Jackson grunted and jerked Lily's arm. I hung on. Connor's mocking laughter followed us out of the room. The man hauled Lily up the narrow stairs. She stumbled and fell to her knees and I pulled her back up. My mind was a blur of terror, but not, thankfully, of pain.

All I had to do was stay calm. Give them what they wanted and let them leave. I believed Connor when he said he wouldn't kill us. What would be the point? He had no reason to hang around here, and obviously no desire to. If he could disappear, the way he said he could, he might just as well leave Lily and me alive.

All I had to do was to keep everyone calm and try to ensure there were no further 'accidents.'

Jackson hesitated at the top of the stairs. He pulled Lily up the last step and shoved her ahead of him. "Where?" he said.

She led the way to her room. She dropped to her knees in front of the dresser and opened the bottom drawer. The stuffed animals on her bed, childish innocence personified, watched her. She moved aside her underwear, folded and stacked neatly, and took out a small wooden box. She cradled it in her hands for a moment. It was a rectangle about twelve by six inches, made with stripes of alternating types of wood. Brass hinges, dull with age, secured the lid. She pushed herself to her feet, cradling the box.

The man gave it a long look. He licked his lips, jerked Lily's arm so she cried out in pain, and said, "Let's go. You first, lady."

I returned to the stairs. I had my foot on the topmost step when he said, "Get downstairs. Tell Riley I'll be along in a minute."

I turned and looked up, into his face. His eyes were glassy and his lips wet and slack. "Back to your bedroom," he ordered Lily.

"No."

He grinned at me. "What, you want it first? That can be arranged." He shoved Lily aside as though she were a rag doll and reached for my arm. He pulled me up the step and swung me around so my back was to the landing.

I stood outside of myself, watching. Lily'd hit the far wall and fallen. She lay there, a bundle of yellow cartoon pajamas, crying. The man teetered at the edge of the steps. The knife hung loose at his side. This was an old house; the stairs were narrow and steep. A wooden bench, unused as no one ever came in the front door, was at the bottom. Under the window at the landing a set of sturdy iron candlesticks sat on a small table. They were kept there, with matches in the drawer, in case the power went out in the night.

His mind was on sex. No, not sex, on pain and terror and on being in control.

Not on protecting himself.

His gaze flicked toward Lily. I grabbed one of the candlesticks and lifted it high. He blinked, not quite understanding. Then, realizing too late he was in danger, his hand reached for his knife. I brought the candlestick down, hard, against the side of his head. He yelled. His eyes rolled back. I kicked out, slamming my bare foot into his right knee. He staggered, began to lose his balance. I kicked again, and he fell. Arms windmilling, he crashed onto the steps and rolled down in a mad jumble of legs and arms. He came to a stop at the bottom. I gripped the candlestick. He lay still. The back of his head had hit a corner of the bench. The occipital lobe. I let out a howl of triumph. I would be his Omar.

"Didn't think you had it in you, Hannah." Connor stood at the bottom of the steps, the Glock in both hands, pointing up at me. He glanced at his pal. He kicked the man's legs. "Not dead. But I don't have time, or the inclination, to carry him out to the truck. Mission creep. Always fatal. Do the job and get the hell out. Discipline, that's all that counts. Put that candlestick down and bring the box to me. And don't try any funny business. Easy enough for me to shoot you and then Lily and help myself."

I bent over Lily and gently took the box from her hands. It was heavy for its size. Inside nothing moved. She mumbled in fear, and I said, "He won't hurt you now." She struggled to her feet. We descended the stairs, me in front, clutching the box in both hands. I held it out to Connor like an offering. "Take it and get the fuck out of our lives."

"My pleasure. I thought you for a wimpy civilian," he said, with something approaching admiration. "So *traumatized*. So *sorry* for yourself. But you've got guts when you need them, Hannah. Sorry I can't hang around to get to know you better. Before I go, I need to make sure what I want's in the box. Turn it around so the hinges are toward you. Then open it."

I did so. Connor sucked in a breath. I couldn't avoid glancing down, and my heart almost stopped beating.

Gold. Gold and turquoise and pearls and lapis lazuli. Several pieces of jewelry, small, the work detailed and exquisite, were tucked around a bronze statue of a man. He was naked, well-muscled, heavily bearded, holding a spear in his right hand. The contents nestled in a bed of tissue. The box was crammed full: not only the statue and the jewels, but also what looked to be old coins.

Lily's book: the treasures of Afghanistan. Lost and then found.

Connor was welcome to it. Take the box and leave us alone.

I let the lid fall shut. Connor tore his eyes away. "I can't leave you two to phone the cops before I'm out of the driveway, so I'm going to have to shut you up for a while."

The box was heavy enough that I needed two hands to hold it. Should I throw it at Connor? If it fell, broke, scattered the contents, would he stoop to pick up his treasure and we could run for it?

Or would he shoot us first?

He laughed. "I was storing potatoes in the root cellar under the shop the other day. Thought it would be a nice place to hide something. Or someone." He misread the look of horror that crossed my face. "Don't worry. Your sister will be home sometime and she'll let you out. Let's go. Outside." He waved his gun hand, telling me to go ahead.

I went obediently. All I wanted was for Connor to take his box and be gone. A night in the root cellar would be cold and damp and miserable but it wouldn't kill us. We could eat carrots and raw potatoes if we got hungry.

But I knew something lived in the root cellar, be it a ghost or the product of my hallucinating, damaged brain, and I did not want any more contact with it.

*I can do this*, I said to myself. *For Lily, I can do this.*

◇◇◇

## May 13, 1788

Maggie placed the shawl and its contents on a tree stump by the front door and went to the root cellar. It had rained in the night and the earthen ramp was slippery with mud. She had not lit a fresh candle, and she left the door propped open with a stone to offer some weak light. She chose several sprouting potatoes, a few wrinkled carrots, and old turnips to take on the journey. Deep in thought, heart pounding with apprehension, she did not hear the snap of a branch or the squelch of mud, and she assumed that when the light faded a cloud had passed across the sun.

"Stealing from us, Maggie?" a voice said.

She whirled around, dropping the potatoes. The black bulk of a man was outlined in the doorway.

Nathanial stepped forward, his face in deep shadow. "I thought it odd for you to be so careless as to forget to lock up the chickens. I came back to check everything was in order. And what do I see outside my front door but your things, all packed to go."

"I thought it best this way," she said, keeping her head high. "So as not to upset Emily unduly. My brother has sent a message asking me to return to New York, and I am doing so."

"That I doubt," he said. "You've received no letters since we came to this godforsaken land."

She stepped forward. "Nevertheless, I am leaving."

"This is how you repay me for taking you in, giving you a home, feeding you, clothing you? Sneaking off like a thief in the night?"

Fear struggled with anger and Maggie struggled with both. She must not show fear, and she must not allow herself to waste time arguing with Nathanial. That would be nothing but an expenditure of energy she would soon need.

"Get out of my way," she said.

The earrings, hidden in a scrap of dress pocket, tucked behind a loose stone, filled her mind. She almost thought she could see them glowing, lighting up the dark recesses of the cellar. She dared not glance over her shoulder to check they were still in hiding. She would leave, set off down the road. Duck into the forest and circle back. Hide in the woods, if she had to, until she could be sure Nathanial had rejoined his family.

"I think not," he said.

"You cannot force me to stay here. I am...I am a free woman."

He laughed, the sound bitter and cruel. "We'll see how far your freedom gets you. How do you think you're going to live? Another word for a free woman is a whore. Very well, if that's what you want, time to start working." He began to unbutton his trousers.

"Do not be ridiculous," she said in a voice so haughty it would make her mother proud. "I do not intend to wrestle on the floor with you like a rutting beast. Stand aside."

"If I'd known you wanted to be a whore, I would have put you to work years ago."

Before she knew what was happening, he lunged toward her. He grabbed the front of her dress and she heard fabric rip and pearl buttons fly. He ground his hips against hers, his lust hard and urgent. He fastened his mouth onto hers and stuffed his tongue into her; he tore at her bonnet and wrapped his fingers in her hair. Maggie pulled back, freeing her mouth. She screamed and brought her hand up to rake her nails across his face and jabbed her knee into his crotch.

He released her with a cry of pain. He touched his hand to his cheek and his fingers came away dotted with red blood. "You bitch. I'll give you what you deserve."

She made to dodge around him but the space was confined, the ceiling low, the floor uneven. His face a mask of blood, rage, and hunger, Nathanial drew back his arm and punched her, full in the face. She fell to the ground with a cry and the back of her head struck the protruding corner of one of the rocks which made up the foundations of the house.

Her eyes flickered and she saw the small gap in the wall, close to her face. "Hamish," she said as her eyes drifted closed, the sound but a stirring of the air, heard by no one on this earth.

# Chapter Thirty-six

Connor hadn't bothered to turn on any lights, and the back of the house was wrapped in gloom. We walked into the kitchen, and he said, "Leave the box on the table. I'll come back for it when I'm done with you two."

I placed the box in the center of the table. It did not belong here, in a farmhouse, in North America. "You've been to Afghanistan. That's obvious; you know some of the words. But not with the army, I'd guess."

"Not with the army. Have to follow rules, regulations, march in straight lines, worry about things like human rights and protecting civilians. I want to kill ragheads and make money. Outside, now."

On the porch, I bent to pick up a shoe, but Connor growled at me to keep going.

We stepped into the night. Dressed only in my flimsy cotton nightgown, I was immediately soaked through. I tried to wrap myself around Lily, give her some shelter, but I couldn't accomplish much.

The door of the chicken coop was open although all the birds had wisely gone inside. Hopefully, the foxes were also tucked up for the night. The lights over the barn and greenhouse had switched on automatically, and I could see the horses swishing their tails in the paddock.

Gravel pricked at my bare feet, but I scarcely noticed.

Headlights came toward us. I held my breath. Police bringing Joanne home? Wouldn't that be lovely.

The car slowed and turned into the driveway, the beams lit up rain falling so hard it was as though a giant tap in the sky had been opened.

Connor stood behind me, the Glock pressed into my ribs. I cradled Lily.

The car stopped. The engine switched off although the headlights remained on. The door opened and the interior light came on.

Grant Harrison.

He approached us. I opened my mouth to say something, to warn him. But the look in his eyes stopped me.

"You found it then," he said.

"Yup," Connor replied. "The kid had it. It was in this house all along. Like I told you."

"You miserable slug." A cold knot of hatred settled in my chest. "You gave Hila sanctuary in your home and then you had her killed."

"She needn't have died," he said. "All she had to do was give it to me."

"She didn't like you, you know," Lily said in a small voice. "She gave it to me. Because she didn't trust you to look after it properly."

"Where's Jackson?"

"Inside. He's out cold. He'll live. Probably. Hannah here did a number on him."

"Not a problem." Grant studied me, and I knew the odds had changed considerably. Connor O'Leary, aka Riley, might be able to disappear, but Grant Harrison could not. He had a wife, property, a position in the community, a government pension.

Grant Harrison would have to see me—and Lily—dead.

I wrapped my arms tighter around my niece.

More headlights. Another car turned into the driveway.

How many people were involved in this anyway?

Harrison hissed, and Connor pulled me closer, the better to conceal the gun.

Rebecca Mansour's sporty little red convertible pulled up beside Harrison's car.

"Not a word, Lily," Connor said. "Or I'll shoot Hannah."

Rebecca switched off the engine, extinguished the headlights and got out of the car. She kept her head down and started to walk toward the house. Then she came up short. "What on earth are you people doing?"

We must have made a strange sight indeed. A woman and girl in their nightclothes, no umbrella. Two men, neither of whom had a reason to be here at this time of night. The rain teeming down, and Grant Harrison the only one wearing a raincoat.

"Evening, Doctor," Harrison said, sounding perfectly amiable. "Filthy night, isn't it? What brings you here?"

"I was at the hospital when they brought Jake in. Joanne asked me to pop by to check on Hannah and Lily." She looked at me. Then at Lily, wrapped in my arms. A question on her face. "Jake was going into surgery when I left. No damage other than to his leg, and they can stitch that up without difficulty. What are you doing out in the rain? Aren't you cold? Is something the matter? Hannah?"

"Nothing wrong. We're going to lock up the chickens for the night. That's all. Thanks for coming around, Doctor. Perhaps we'll see you tomorrow, at the hospital."

"I don't think…"

"You don't have to think, Doctor," Harrison said. He gestured to Connor. "Wrong time. Wrong place."

I felt the pressure of the gun against my spine relax and Connor step away.

Rebecca sucked in a breath.

"Go and stand with Hannah and Lily," Harrison said. "Quickly now. This is taking far too long."

Rebecca reached us. She touched my arm but kept her eyes on Grant Harrison. "The answer to all our questions, I suspect."

"You're a fool, Harrison," Connor said. "I told you when I called, I'd meet up with you later."

"Keeping an eye on my investment," Harrison replied, sounding as if he were in a board meeting.

"Enough talking. Doctor, you go first."

"Where?"

"Down there. Under the store. I'm locking you in for the night."

I dared a glance at Harrison. His right hand was buried in his navy blue raincoat pocket.

"No," Doctor Mansour said.

"What?"

"No. I am not going to be locked up like a barn animal the night before slaughter. Take your plunder and leave us alone."

Connor lifted the Glock. My heart stopped beating. Lily burrowed deeper into my side.

Rebecca turned to Grant Harrison. "You are a civilized man, for heaven's sake. Stop this, now. Can't you see how far this has gotten out of control? I have no idea what's going on here and what you people want, but I will not allow it to continue."

"You think you have a choice?" Connor said. "Typical raghead." He fired. I screamed and clutched Lily.

Rebecca Mansour crumpled to the driveway. Blood immediately began to spread out from her side. It mixed with rain water to form a pink, swift-moving stream running between pieces of gravel. She groaned, twitched, and then lay still.

"I can be a civilized man, when I want to be," Connor said. "I coulda taken off her fuckin' head. But I didn't. If help comes in time, she might live. I've done talking. Move, Hannah. Move."

Lily was shutting down. I half carried, half dragged her to the back of the shop. Our bare feet slipped in the mud, wet branches slapped our faces and legs. I fell, pulling Lily on top of me. I struggled to stand.

The smell. Meat left to rot. Decay. It was cold, standing in the teeming rain, but far colder down here. A wind carrying the chill of loss drifted around my bare feet and through the thin cotton of my nightgown. There should be no light down here, but I sensed, as much as saw, white trails of…what?

Lightning lit up the dark, and I dared a glance at the men above. Connor was at the top of the ramp, the gun in his hand. Grant Harrison stood behind him, watching.

"You don't think Grant's going to let you live, do you Connor?" I said. "You've got what he wants. I don't imagine he's prepared to share."

Connor grinned as thunder roared behind him. White teeth in a dark face. "A wooden box of old jewelry and an ugly statue. That's all he has. I have the contacts who'll pay for it. Keep going."

I pulled open the door. Inside, the root cellar was as black as hell. At least it was dry in here, although so dreadfully cold. We'd be okay, until Joanne came home or Liz arrived for work in the morning. But Rebecca? How long could Rebecca live without help? I shifted Lily in my arms and pushed her into the room.

A gun shot rang out. I froze, expecting searing pain. When it didn't come, my first thought was for Lily and sheer terror ran though me. But she was standing in front of me, staring over my shoulder, her mouth open in a round O of fear. Behind me, a heavy weight fell.

I turned.

Riley, the man I knew as Connor O'Leary, lay on his stomach in the mud at the bottom of the ramp. His right arm was outstretched, still clutching the Glock. The back of his head was missing. Grant Harrison held a gun in his hand. It was a lot smaller than the Glock, but from that distance it had all the power it needed.

"Wrong," he said to the still body. "I have my own contacts."

He lifted his head. White mist curled around his legs. The acrid scent of blood, Connor's lifeblood, mixed with the stench coming from the cellar. Grant Harrison took a step forward, the gun steady, his eyes focused on me.

Panic rose in my throat.

After all I'd been through. I was going to die, here in a root cellar in Prince Edward County, Ontario, among the fingerling potatoes and the carrots and my sister's canning.

Muscle memory. Soldier and cops have it. When their brain shuts down in panic the muscles are trained to simply carry on. To do what needs to be done. Soldiers and cops have it. I did not.

I wanted to roll into a ball and cover my eyes. Let Omar have what was left of me. Let it all end.

Lily whimpered.

Lily.

I shoved Lily as hard as I could and dove after her into the depths of the root cellar. She fell, and I dragged her across the floor until I touched the damp rubble walls. "Stay still," I whispered into her ear. I felt, rather than saw, her head nod. Her breath was coming in rapid spurts and I could feel the pounding of her precious heart.

The white mist provided me with some illumination. No one else could see it, I knew. No one else seemed to detect the rancid scent of death, feel the icy cold, or hear the soft well-educated voice of the black-haired woman. I scrambled along the wall, moving away from Lily.

I had absolutely no idea of what I could do to save us. I ran my hands across the mud-packed floor. Nothing I could use as a weapon came to hand.

Mud squelched and a black shape appeared in the doorway.

"My, it's dark in here. No matter, I'll wait for my eyes to become accustomed to the light."

I balanced my weight between my knees and dug my naked toes into the floor. I had nothing with which to fight an armed man but my body. It would have to do. To save Lily.

# Chapter Thirty-seven

"Hila's father, Wahid, wrote to tell me he'd come into possession of a fabulous collection of easily-transportable artifacts, probably from the unexcavated sixth and seventh tombs of Tillya Tepe. They would be worth a great deal of money to the right people. He couldn't sell them on the open market, unfortunately, not having a silly little thing like proof of provenance, and needed my help." Grant chatted happily. Waiting for a flash of lightning to illuminate the corners of the cellar. I stayed quiet, not wanting to provide him with a target. I could hear nothing from Lily, not even the sound of her breathing.

"He'd had enough of Afghanistan, the fighting, the ignorance, the corruption, and decided to get out. He needed money, of course, to settle his family comfortably in the West, and asked me to find a buyer for the treasures.

"When he was killed, along with most of his family, their possessions destroyed, I assumed the artifacts were lost. I didn't much care what happened to his daughter, but Maude wanted to help, and so Maude arranged to bring her to Canada. Lo and behold, I then discovered, through something Maude said, that Hila had saved her Koran and a jewelry box. I offered Hila money, sight unseen, for her box. She refused. She assumed her father was taking it out of the country for safe-keeping and she wanted to take it to the museum in Toronto to be cared for until it could be returned to the people of Afghanistan. Foolish,

foolish girl. She wasn't going to go to Toronto any time soon; she was terrified to be out on the streets of Picton, for goodness sake. I let it go, pretended not to care, bided my time. She never left the bloody house and her only friend was a little girl who liked Maude's stupid dog. Then she met you and went on your walks. So nice for her to have a friend. I searched her room, that took about two minutes, but couldn't find it. Realizing I had no further option but to force it out of her, I was compelled to find accomplices. I'd met Riley in Afghanistan. Not a nice man, but he did have his uses. I wanted him close. Maude certainly wouldn't have him in our home, but she happened to mention how hard it was to find farm workers these days. Riley and his pal kept an eye on Hila and snatched her when she was alone and out of my house. Sadly, they got a mite rough, and Hila died. Stupid, stupid girl, trading her useless life for a handful of trinkets. I assumed she'd hidden her treasure somewhere in my house. But where? Hard to do a proper search with Maude hovering over my shoulder every hour, night and day. You might be wondering why I'd allow those two goons to wreck my collection in search of the box." Grant laughed. "They didn't damage any of *my* possessions. As instructed, they broke some of Maude's cheap souvenirs, valueless trinkets, the ridiculous Royal Doulton tea set that was her mother's, but nothing of any real value."

Without warning, lightning flashed and the root cellar lit up. I could see Lily, cowering in a corner, Grant's face breaking into a grin, the gun firmly held in front of him, his elbows tucked into his chest. The gun swung toward me as I pushed myself to my feet. The lightning faded in a muffled roar of thunder, plunging us into darkness once again. Grant had me in his sights and the root cellar was too small to run. But I would try. To save Lily.

The drifting tendrils of white mist swirled together, gathered strength and substance, formed a thick fog. It trapped me in a field of white; cold so deep and so heavy it must be like being out among the stars enveloped me. All my bravado fled, and I dropped to my knees to cower in the dirt of the floor and cover my eyes. The scent of death and decay had gone and I could smell woodsmoke, human sweat, farm animals, homemade soap, tallow candles.

I heard a single word, a woman's soft voice, whispered on the mist. "No."

A man screamed. The gun fired. Once. Twice. Sound exploded through the room. Grant Harrison gasped, made a choking sound as if he were struggling to breathe. Something heavy fell to the ground. All went quiet. I buried my head deeper into my arms and closed my eyes as tightly as I could.

Cloth, rough and scratchy, brushed up against my naked legs. The fierce cold burned my skin. It passed over me, and I was frightened no longer. I uncurled and opened my eyes. I dared to look up. The mist gathered around Lily as it began to thin. A wisp reached out, caressed Lily's back. "Safe," a voice said from a great distance. "Safe."

The mist began to dissolve. It broke into long tendrils that petered away into nothing.

And then it was gone.

I crawled to the corner where I'd left Lily. I touched her, a terrified ball, and felt warm skin move. Then her arms were around my neck and she was sobbing. "Aunt Hannah. What happened? Where are we?"

"We're safe, my dearest. We're safe. Come on, up you get."

I helped her to her feet and then I reached up, feeling for the string that was tied to the light bulb. I pulled it, and electric light so strong it hurt our eyes filled the room.

Grant Harrison lay on the floor. Face down. He did not move.

I led Lily around him, keeping her head buried in my side.

Connor's body blocked the ramp. I lifted Lily over it and followed her without glancing down.

# Chapter Thirty-eight

Rebecca Mansour lay in the driveway, blood pooling around her. She was alive, her heart pumping. I had to get to a phone, but I dared not venture into the house in case Jackson had recovered. We'd have to run up the road. Make it to a neighbor or flag down a passing car.

Gravel dug into my bare feet. I didn't even dare go in search of shoes.

Lily pulled herself out of my arms. She headed toward Rebecca.

"We have to get help," I called. "Come on, we don't have much time." I couldn't leave her here alone.

She darted past Rebecca, going to Grant's car. I couldn't remember if I'd seen the keys in his hand. Had he put them in his pocket? I wasn't going to venture back down to the root cellar to look for them.

The door of the car was open, the interior light on. Lily leaned in and came up with a tight smile on her face.

And a cell phone in her hand.

# Chapter Thirty-nine

Rick Brecken and Gary Wolfe arrived, along with a steady stream of ambulances and patrol cars so numerous their lights banished the dark.

I told the first cops on the scene that Jackson was in the house. They went in, two of them, one at a time, moving slow, crouched low, guns drawn. Soon radios crackled to tell the paramedics it was okay to come in. When I saw movement at the doors, I pulled Lily into the shadows and held her against me, my head buried in the top of her hair. I did not want to look into Jackson's face as he was carried out on a stretcher, his hands handcuffed in front of him, the back of his head matted with blood.

Once the house was declared safe, I took Sergeant O'Neil inside, to show her the box, sitting peacefully in the center of the farmhouse kitchen table. Brecken and Wolfe watched her open it. Wolfe turned away, disgust all over his face, and left.

Disappointed, no doubt, to find that all this was about something as crass and common as money.

I was being bundled into an ambulance, against my protests, when Rick Brecken called my name. I hesitated, and then turned to see him crossing the lawn. The paramedic gave me a slight nod and jumped into the back of the ambulance. I waited for Brecken.

"Hannah," he said, "before you go." He hesitated, the words caught in his throat. "I want to say I'm sorry."

"Sorry?"

"I've known Wolfe for a few years. I knew he'd been in Afghanistan, figured he'd be able to give me some unofficial background on you. I contacted him, asked what he knew. I didn't realize there was something…personal between you two."

"Nothing personal about it. He hates me because he's a corrupt bastard and I'm good at my job. That's all."

"Yeah, I know that now. Anyway, I'm sorry. When he got my e-mail, he figured it was his chance to get back at you for whatever you did."

"I did my job, nothing more."

"I suspect he came here on his own, without telling his bosses what was up. They won't be happy to hear he's broken jurisdiction for a theft that got out of control.

"Good-bye, Hannah. I'll be leaving now." He held out his hand.

I looked at it, hesitating. Then I gripped it in my own.

The edges of his mouth turned up. "Take care of yourself."

He helped me into the back of the ambulance. The doors slammed shut, the vehicle started up, and I was taken to the hospital. Lily had been taken away earlier.

The police followed me, and I spent many hours going over the story again and again, while Joanne and an unfamiliar doctor sat close to me, daring the officers to upset me.

In the morning Joanne, accompanied by Jake in a wheelchair, came to tell me that Rebecca Mansour had gotten to the hospital in time, and although her wound was serious, she was expected to make a full recovery.

I insisted on seeing her, and a nurse wheeled me to her room.

Rebecca lay in bed, propped up, eyes closed. Wires and tubes ran into her body and machines beeped.

I sat by the bed and studied her. Long black lashes lay still against her brown cheek. "Thank you," I whispered.

The eyes opened. "For what? I did nothing but get shot." Her voice was a croaking whisper. I leaned closer to hear. "Not much of a hero. I'm sorry, Hannah." The sheet shifted and her hand appeared. Veins stood out and there were fresh puncture wounds in the skin. She wiggled her fingers and I touched them.

"My mother always said my stubbornness would get me into trouble one day. After all I've seen of cruelty and suffering the thought that those men had brought their violence and brutality here seemed more than I could bear. I simply was not going to do what they said. I guess my mother was right."

Her eyes drifted closed. I wheeled myself out.

As nothing was wrong with Lily or me we were released into Joanne's care before lunchtime. Jake would remain in hospital for another day or two, recovering from his surgery.

"He's not at all pleased," Joanne said in what I assumed was a considerable understatement. "He's going to be laid up for weeks. Connor's employment is, shall we say, terminated. And we have cops crawling all over the place."

She slowed down as we passed the long driveway to the Harrison home. Conscious of Lily in the back, neither of us said anything.

There were so many police cars in our driveway, Joanne had to park on the road. An assorted group of neighbors and tour-ists, and a couple of news vans, were standing on the verge or in the ditch watching the proceedings. Children ran in and out of the trees, but an officer was posted at the top of the driveway, keeping curiosity-seekers away. Last night's thunderstorm had not broken the heat wave, and a hot sun blazed out of a blue sky. Damp mud filled the bottom of some of the deeper depressions, but the ground was rapidly drying.

A van was parked close to the entrance to the root cellar. Men and women in white suits, looking much like space invaders, came and left.

"Can I go check on the horses, Mom?" Lily asked. "They'll be upset at having been left out in the rain all night with no food."

Joanne smiled and ruffled the top of her daughter's head. "Sure," she said.

Lily galloped off, her blond braid streaming behind her.

"She doesn't seem too traumatized by what happened," my sister said to me, folding my arm into hers. "I called Mom earlier. They're on their way. She's going to find a counselor for Lily, to make sure that if she does have any latent effects, she'll be cared for."

Sergeant McNeil saw us standing together. She broke away from the group of men she was with and approached us. She looked like she'd been up all night. As she probably had.

"Hannah. I'm pleased to see you back on your feet so quickly." McNeil studied my face.

"Right as rain."

"I thought you'd want to know that it looks as though Harrison was killed by a ricochet. He fired two or three shots. We're digging the bullets out of the wall now. The ricocheting bullet got him right between the eyes. If I may be so graphic. Foolish thing to do—fire blindly in the dark in such an enclosed space, with such solid walls."

"Very foolish," I agreed.

"All he had to do," she mused, "would have been to wait a minute or two for his eyes to become accustomed to the dark and then he would have been able to see you and Lily."

"Lucky us."

We turned at a shout. A woman was coming toward us, dressed in the white forensic suit with a hairnet on her head and booties on her feet. Her latex-gloved hand outstretched. "I found something interesting, Sergeant. Hi, Joanne. Look at this. Nothing to do with what happened here last night, but we found this in the walls, buried in a crack. Looks like it's been down there a long time. I guess it belongs to you people."

Joanne and I leaned closer. Sunlight broke through the patina of age and neglect and flashed off a diamond. No, not a diamond, many diamonds, brilliant diamonds, large and small, embedded in silver. Shreds of cloth were caught in some of the gems. We looked closer and made out the shape of two large earrings.

"Oh, my gosh," Joanne said. "Will you look at that? Jake will be so pleased. The legendary family treasure. Can I touch it?" she asked Sergeant McNeil.

"I don't see why not. We won't need it for any sort of evidence."

Joanne picked one of the earrings from the outstretched latex glove. She blew lightly on it, dust lifted into the air, and she held it up in front of her between her thumb and index finger. Sunlight seemed to be attracted to it. Sparks danced and tarnished old silver shimmered.

"An inheritance," I said. "For Lily."

"For Lily."

# Chapter Forty

I'd like to be able to say that Omar left me, permanently, that night.

But he isn't real and I've always known that. And whatever happened down in the root cellar was not able to heal my damaged brain.

But somehow that night did make a difference and from then on I steadily began to get better. It will be a long slow process, but at last I have hope that I might be normal again one day. I can keep a thought in my head, and I can add up a row of numbers, so I've taken over some of the account work from Joanne. I can read print and remember almost all of what I've read, which pleases me enormously. The pain is still there, still comes upon me unexpectedly, but I can manage it, most of the time, with my medication.

My family still fusses over me, and although I'm not ready to return to my condo in Toronto or go back to work, I've taken rental of a small vacation property in the county, not far from the farm, until Christmas. At the end of the year I will make some decisions.

And I'm writing this memoir, just to prove that I can. I don't plan to show it to anyone, except perhaps to Lily when she's older and can make sense of it.

As for the root cellar, it's now simply a dark damp place where the farm stores root vegetables and canning. No smell of death or of woodsmoke, no drifting mist, icy cold winds, whispering voices. Whether whatever was down there was tied to the earrings or simply waiting until the day when she would save Lily, I do not know. I hope she has found peace.

Marlene swooped in and would have snatched the earrings out of Joanne's hand had my mother, in full doctor-to-reticent-patient mode, not told her they didn't belong to her. So back off.

Marlene contented herself with spreading the story far and wide to everyone who was interested, and many who were not, about the discovery of the Stewart family treasure and how it proves that the Stewarts were the gentry back in the old day.

The police searched Jackson's room, where they found traces of Hila's blood as well as her Koran. She'd been killed there, Sergeant McNeil came to tell us, not long after she'd been reported missing. The body was dumped into the woods after the area had been searched. No doubt they'd stolen her Koran in case she'd placed a clue to the location of the box in it.

They couldn't ask Jackson, and he would never come to trial. He'd broken his neck in the fall, and lay in a coma for a month before he died.

McNeil took Hila's wooden box and its contents away that night. Evidence, she said. Experts from the Royal Ontario Museum were brought to study it and pronounced the pieces of exceptional value and quality.

On a cold blustery winter's day Maude Harrison, Rebecca Mansour, Jake, Joanne, Charlie, Lily, and I attended a ceremony in Ottawa where the treasure was formally returned to the people and government of Afghanistan. We were allowed a private viewing before the formalities. The pieces had been cleaned and laid on black velvet for best display. The statue, they told us, was Greek, probably second century B.C., the jewelry more modern, first century AD. The gold coins were Roman, of the Emperor Tiberius, the silver ones, the Parthian Mithridates II. As Lily shook the hand of the Afghan Ambassador, she told him she'd decided to become an archeologist.

I looked at them, the bronze god, the stunningly beautiful jewelry that would have adorned a nomadic princess, the ancient coins, one last time, full of awe at their beauty and their age, and feared that before long they'd once again disappear into the ravenous maw of war and destruction.

◇◇◇

**January 2, 1800. The diary of Mrs. Emily Stewart**
A new century, how wonderfully exciting. Richard says the new century doesn't really begin until next year, but I say pooh to that. Let us celebrate when we can.

It seems an appropriate day to begin writing again in my childhood book. I haven't looked at it for many years. I found it tucked amongst my bedding when we returned to the farm that day long ago, and I put it away. When I realized Maggie had left us, I was scarcely able to look at it without weeping.

I think about Maggie every day. I don't believe what Papa said, that she ran off with a travelling peddler. I was so angry at first, at her for leaving me. But then I remembered her telling me that I must keep up my reading and doing my letters and how I must always be strong and a true partner to my husband, never fearing to tell him if I thought he was wrong, and I believe she *was* telling me that she had to go. I hope she is happy, wherever she is. She was never happy here, although she tried hard to make me think she was.

I'm glad she took her earrings. She didn't know that I knew about them, but how could I not, when I would wake in the night and see her bent over them and the light from the dying fire throwing red sparks around her head.

The farm is doing well, I'm happy to say, now that Richard has taken it over. We're planning to begin building a new house as soon as spring arrives, so we don't have to live with his parents any longer. That horrid little shanty that was my family home can burn, as far as I'm concerned. We'll have to move Mother into the new house with us. It would scarcely suit to make her stay out there, although it would be nice to have her constant complaining far from earshot. Still, she has no one else, now that Father is dead, Jacob in prison, and Caleb run off to the city. I feel sorry for her sometimes, although she has no one to blame for her misfortune than herself.

Perhaps word will reach Maggie that I've married and am going to have a family of my own, and she will return.

I pray for that every day.